Eternal Solace

JEREMY GALLIMORE

/ ETERNAL SOLACE / 2

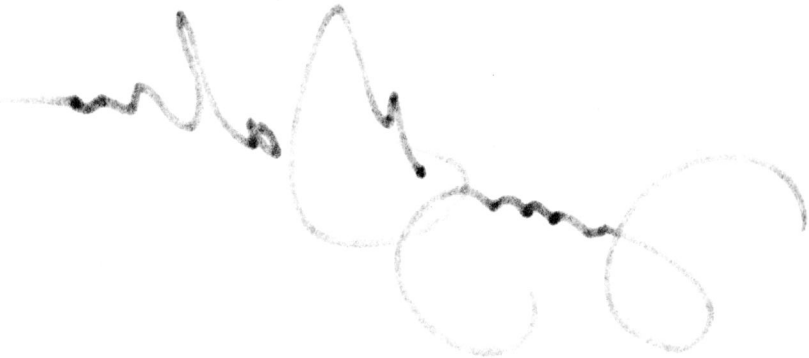

Dedication

Eternal Solace is dedicated to my brother Sebastien, who believed in me even when the odds were stacked against me. To Pouppe, for assisting in the creation of the vast world entailed in this story. To Kenny, for lighting the fuel I needed to charge forward and embrace the dream. And to Madalena, for truly understanding the vision and assisting in its growth.

For the countless words of encouragement given by my true supporters. For every entrepreneur dedicating their lives to their passion. For every aspiring author who never thought their words would ever touch a page. And for anyone striving to reach their fullest potential.

Copyright ©2017 by Jeremy Gallimore. Aside for the purposes of research or private study, or review as permitted under the Copyright, Designs and Patents Act of 1988. This publication may only be reproduced, stored and transmitted, in any form or by any means, with the prior permission in writing of the author. Inquiries concerning outside these terms should be sent to the author at the below email address.
partrizian@gmail.com

All rights reserved.

ISBN-978-1-9758-8284-6
ISBN-1-5323-4991-2

Published by Gallimorian Group
Edited by Apex Reviews
Editorial Consultant, & Proofreading by Therone Shellman for Therone Shellman Media

https://www.facebook.com/jeremy.gallimore.77?fref=ts

Prologue

The time to kill was now...

Focusing on the dark wooden board before me, I extended an anxious hand for my knight, then struck, killing a bishop and placing the king in...
"Check!"
I was in a dungeon-like stone chamber with a lit torch in the far corner and the shadowy image of a hooded man seated before me.
The man exhaled, then reaching a gauntleted hand out for his black queen, he killed my knight. He was silent and expressionless as I contemplated my next move. I stared at the board quizzically for a brief moment before realizing I would be trapped after his next move. My king hadn't yet moved, and my rook was in dangerous territory, although it was protected by a bishop and my queen had been taken a few moves back. This was bad; not horrible, but bad.
I advanced my pawn two spaces and blocked the queen's path. The queen attacked my

pawn, leaving her rear defenses open. I took advantage of the opening and moved my bishop diagonally, killing his pawn and putting him in...

"Check." Once again.

The hooded man smirked deceptively as he reached across the board for his bishop, which had been waiting on the outskirts, and killed my own bishop; I had been blindsided. Out of hopelessness, I advanced another pawn and the queen killed my now unprotected rook, it was...

"Checkmate!" the man said tonelessly.
I sighed and began removing the necessary pieces, placing them back in the original positions.

"You sacrifice too much, Casanova!" the hooded man advised calmly as he, too, began placing his pieces back in their original position.

"I thought this game was about sacrificing anything you must in order to trap the king," I said humbly.

"Sacrifice is needed...true indeed. Yet, that is far from what this game is about. You are the king, so it is necessary to think not only as a ruler, but also as a general. Each general you sacrifice weakens not only the power of the kingdom, but also the defense surrounding the king, which is you," he said, pointing at me intently.

I nodded silently while reforming my kingdom.

When the man finished, he held up a black wood carved piece.

"Do you know what this is?" he asked.

"The queen!" I answered confidently.

"And the most powerful general in the kingdom," he added passionately. "Yet, you sacrificed her to create a fortress for your king," he said with squinted eyes.

"I was...protecting my king at all costs," I retorted.

"You got your most powerful piece killed while creating your own death trap!" he blared emphatically, his words echoing off stone.

Silence permeated the darkness as what he said sank in. The man placed the queen back in her position and held his hand out without an expression on his dark, chiseled face. I reached for my coin purse and placed two coppers in his outstretched gauntlet, then glanced over at the dark stone walls and saw the place where a window should have been, had it not been covered with iron bars and a long black veil which blocked out the existence of sunlight.

"The time is drawing near?" I said after a long, dark moment.

Arkon nodded, with his eyes fixed on the wooden board before him.

"Three days..." he drawled dispassionately, "and I still don't regret my attempt to kill him. I only regret the long journey that lies ahead."

My look of confusion vanished as soon as his deadly black eyes flashed up to mine.

"I am ruined, Casanova...because I have sacrificed too much. I do not wish you the same fate as I have had."

Dark thoughts suddenly flashed through my mind as I revisited exactly what Arkon meant by his statement. I've heard his tale on countless occasions, just not from his own mouth. He stared down at the coins in his palm, as if he were examining their past. I stared at him in the same manner.

"What happened that night, master Arkon?" I inquired cautiously, hoping I wasn't chartering dangerous territory.
A few moments passed as he silently rotated one coin from the face of the phaux to the criss-

crossed daggers engraved on the back. He did this a few times, and by its fifth rotation I thought it appropriate to change my words, switch my attention back to the message he was trying to convey, but as the coin stopped and his lips parted, I stayed silent.

"Time was of the essence..." he began, his eyes transfixed on the wooden board."A moment too late would spell death for either of us, and I knew that." He inhaled, as if he were revisiting that horrible night, then exhaled. "There were sixteen hogs guarding the castle that night. Three of them were brothers from the Order and there in guard disguise to serve as my reinforcement. Two of us were sworn in together. Each of those men would have easily given his life for me..." he said, staring out into nothing in particular, then regaining focus.

"The king's bed chamber was in the highest tower in the east wing, but only a fool would think he would be in it that evening; he knew what was coming. He didn't know how or by whom, just that it would happen that night, and he was ready. The castle was quiet, save for the faint howling of the wind outside beating against stone. The spiraling narrow step well leading to the offering chamber was unoccupied. I stood watch as the three brothers quickly ascended the steps, and then I flanked closely behind. Midway up the steps, we heard faint whispers of a spell being conjured. I silently prayed we weren't too late. We quickened our pace as I reached for the blade in the side fold of my tunic. Three swords unsheathed ahead of me just as I found the counter spell. The disparate sounds of chants and moaning reverberated off the winding steps and got louder and more intense as we neared. We advanced to the chamber door swiftly, and two brothers flanked the sides as the third knelt down before it in a crouched position. Then the moaning suddenly stopped, then the chanting. The three brothers turned to me for the command...and I gave it." A flash of anger suddenly flared into his eyes.

"The four of us burst into the vast chamber, and hundreds of lit candles formed a circle around the huge, looming figure that was Zauber. As he stood on the high altar, before him on a lower platform were four wizards of the sixth degree, each of which can obliterate any mortal with a flick of the wrist. The brothers quickly surrounded the wizards and started to advance, completely unaware of the extent of their power, while I conjured up my book of runes and a black dagger."

He paused, took a breath in, and exhaled. I just stared at the man in awe, longing to hear his next words. In my yearning, though, I saw Arkon differently that day.

"He was a tall man of six-feet-five, lean and strong with long, matted hair pulled back into a tight cob-tail and the build of a former warrior. Yet, he was not known in the streets for his heroism in war; he was known as the last living mage to set foot in Partrizia, and most evidently for attempting to assassinate the king. His battle-scarred hands were each covered with rough leather gauntlets designed to expel any form of traditional magick, and his deep, sunken eyes were a maroon color that blended flawlessly with his dark, ebony skin. He was feared by all, loved by few, and hated by most — which is to be expected when you are great. My silent observance was halted abruptly by what sounded like the hilt of a sword crashing against wood."

"Play time is over in here! Let's go, peasant!" said a tall, burly hog standing just outside the doorway.

I sighed deeply, got to my feet, and locked eyes with Arkon for what could be the last time I would ever see him. As we stood eye-to-eye, a weak smile formed on his lips as he reached a gauntlet out towards me.

"Take care, kid!" he said as a warm rush suddenly formed between my eyes and slowly made its way down the bridge of my nose.

I took his hand firmly, and he pulled me into a tight embrace.

"Learn from my mistakes, Casanova..." he whispered, barely audible, "and do things the right way!" He slipped something heavy into my left tunic pocket; his eyes spoke of its importance.

I nodded as I felt heavy hands pulling me back out into the corridor and onto the hard stone floor.

"I will make you proud, Master!" I shouted just before the chamber door was slammed shut.

"Dead men have no pride!" the hog quipped, baring a rotten-toothed grin. "Now run along to the Chambers like a good peasant boy!"

"Go on, get!" ordered the second, much fiercer looking hog.

I quickly scrambled to my feet and down the dim corridor, not looking back once.

Approaching the entrance, I looked down and stared at the real reason Arkon wanted me to see him before his execution. I reached into my tunic pocket and removed a beautiful golden choker with a grand ruby as its medallion and wiped my tear-filled eyes.

"Do things the right way!" I repeated aloud the final words of my master, just before stepping out into the warm Partrizian sun.

CHAPTER ONE
Memorie I

"A king I shall never be...that is certain!"
Partrizia, 1869
Casanova Volkart

Flames danced between twin pillars as the torch between each rotten column lit a path down the narrow passage leading to my chamber. Heavy boots trudging over cracked stone echoed throughout the halls as I hastened toward my haven; I was not alone. Pulling out a rusted iron key, I stopped and glanced anxiously over my shoulder. Once I heard the footsteps recede, I drove a key into the latch and hurried in.

My chamber was arranged with the typical necessities of a peasant: a bureau and looking glass; a large pile of straw; a torch; a chamber pot; and a rusted metal washing bin. The only difference between my chamber and the dozens of others in this tower was the book lying patiently on the bureau longing to be given consideration, The Book of Runes. Finding a book in Partrizia was a rarity, as the king forbade the use of such defilement's, but this book was in memory of the greatest mage to ever grace this kingdom: my master.

    I walked somberly over to the window and peered out over the heart of the kingdom and the sanctum of evil, the Square, known as the pit of death by us common folk. The place where merchants passed through but never stayed after sundown, because at night the savages came out. Reaching into the fold of my tunic, I removed the hand of bread, two roasted sausages, and the skin of ale I had slipped from under the nose of three merchants. I tossed the bread and sausages down carelessly on the bureau, and standing in front of the looking glass, I took a strong guzzle of the bitter ale, drinking until my mind numbed, then slowly drifted.

    Plundering never appealed to me in the slightest. The most dishonorable thing one can do is wait until a man turns his back to steal his possessions, but living here within the walls of these four hideous towers we call the Chambers would drive out any bit of honor a man held within himself. The people dwelling here have nothing, or at least as close to nothing as you can get while still maintaining sanity - and even that was not often the case. So, I find it demeaning to see merchants traveling in and out of our Square with their jeweled beads, roasted hams and goats, and wines – flaunting the things found so prevalent in the North. Here, where a woman would be honored to receive a few lousy pieces of bread to feed her family. People are dying daily, from either starvation or murder. So, how could anyone say we dwell in one of the most luxurious kingdoms in the world when we are treated like we're less than humans? I refuse to let myself or any of my people starve while there is food at arm's reach, and that is why I steal. To see the look on a peasant's face after you've given them enough food to last a week with no worries, that is much more important to me than being labeled a Chamber rat.

    Staring out over the encampment, the last few hogs on patrol were guarding each merchant stand as if they were commissioned by the king himself. Shaking my head, I could think of nothing other than Arkon. What would he think of me now? Not even one year since his execution, and I already solidified myself as a Chamber rat. They only refer that name to people who are wanted for repeatedly thieving food from merchants. Fortunately for them, they smartened up since the rebellion and hid all the real food within tents guarded by hogs. Unfortunately for me, I was now a wanted man, which meant that not only was my face plastered on every poster from here to Deceptia, if a hog saw me and recognized my face, he had full reign to remove my head without warning.

    Back up in the North, there was no need for such measures. We always had plenty of food and water, wine and ale to spare as well. Many times, I would stare out the window of my chamber and look at the beautiful maidens as they traveled back and forth to town for either their husbands or secret lovers. I would imagine each woman as a queen, traveling from far off, just to be looked at and adored by me during their journey. The wondrous caves and waterfalls that beautified the coast of the upper region, I imagined would serve as their kingdom, and I would go through daring feats to claim her as my own.

    Here in the South, there was not much room for imagination. The daring feats I had envisioned from youth were now in finding a decent meal for myself each evening. The beautiful traveling queens were now toothless whores who would do anything you asked for a few coin...I mean anything. Staring out the window now, you could taste the bitterness in each Partrizian face, and if you listened closely, you could hear the screams of women being cornered and raped by men in black suits of mail each night. I turned away from the window and walked over to the pile of straw in the far corner. Lying down on the stiff pile, I attempted to get some much needed rest.

Boom Boom Boom!!!

The sudden thrashing at my chamber door startled me senseless as I missed contact with the pile and landed awkwardly on the stone floor.

"Who goes there?" I demanded, with more anger than interest.

"It's me!" a deep voice called from the other side of the arched doorway.

I winced slightly as I got to my feet, lifted the metal latch on the door, and pulled it back. A tall, burly figure burst through and slammed it shut behind him as long dreads swung wildly over his massive shoulders. He dwarfed the entire door as he leaned angrily back against it, panting and out of breath.

"What happened?" I said nervously.

"They killed him...they fuckin' killed him right in front of me, Cas!" Tiberius barked, slamming a hammered fist heavily against the chamber door. "For giving meat to a woman and child!"

"Who do you speak of?" I asked cautiously.
His deep brown eyes locked on mine, as if he were surprised I hadn't heard.

"They killed Cilas!" he muttered, deliberately slow.

I shrank back onto the stone wall of my chamber and stared out into nothingness.

"Cilas?" I whispered.

Hundreds of thoughts and images flashed through my mind at the sound of his name. First came the image of a tall, bearded merchant. The kind of man that would give up his own tunic if it meant you would stay warm during a cold winter night. The kind of man who would take food from his own stand to give to a hungry family, and the kind of man who would die for it.

I looked down as I felt a cool liquid sensation suddenly trickling through my fingers. I realized then I had been clenching the juices out of the sausage in my hand so tightly, it was now nearly indistinguishable. Wiping the grease on the leg of my britches, I remained silent, in disbelief, in dismay.

"How?" I asked after a moment's time.

"They cut his head off...in front of everyone in the Square," Tiberius said, with more hurt in his tone than anger.

My eyes snapped up to his. "They cut his head off?" I repeated angrily. "For giving his own food away?" I added.

The sudden malefic sound of swords unsheathing caused both of our horror-filled gazes to meet. In perfect succession, the two of us bolted toward the window and stared out into the dismal Square. Three hogs clad in black chain mail and the crimson cloaks of Partrizia slowly surrounded a young peasant boy of eleven, maybe twelve. Each hog wielded a Partrizian blacksword that blended entirely with the darkness of the Square. A half-eaten sausage was clenched tightly in the boy's raised hands as he slowly lowered himself down to his knees in surrender. Tiberius leaned forward, squinting.

"Is that...that's the boy Cilas gave his food to!" he said in disbelief, as the hogs advanced on the lad, a short sword unsheathed beside me.

"You stay here, and stay concealed!" Tiberius demanded just before bolting toward the chamber door and out into the darkness of the corridor.

"Tiberius!!!" I bellowed angrily out into the corridor behind him, but to no avail. Once his massive shoulders disappeared around the winding curve of the torchlit passage, I knew there was no stopping his wrath.

"Shit!" I said, slamming the door shut and rushing back over to the window.

I reached the ledge just in time to see the raised blacksword of a hog crashing down over the boy, then a tremendous cloud of dust flew up and filled the Square.

As the boy's deafening outcry echoed throughout the Chambers, my heart thudded anxiously as I squinted towards the dark cloud, hoping the dust would clear before Tiberius did something he would regret...The sound of a body crashing heavily through wooden planks sounded throughout the dark Square. Heavy scuffling transfixed with grunts and strains sounded as the moon shimmered soft light into a dark situation. As images slowly became visible, the boy was seen. Moaning painfully in a pool of red dirt with a woman beside him, he held a decrepit forearm with his left hand. Blood rushed and spurted out of his wrist, and his right hand was completely severed off. Two hogs became visible, both standing in a defensive stance, facing off. The third hog was lying face down in what used to be the wooden cart of a merchant, either unconscious or dead.

    Tiberius stood at the ready. Behind him, three figures emerged from the outskirts, then five, then ten. Within a matter of moments, the two hogs were completely outnumbered by nearly twenty savages, armed with short blades, cracked glass, swinging spikes - and they all wanted blood.

    One hog turned to the other, then back to Tiberius. For a moment there was a standoff, each figure behind Tiberius inching toward some type of weapon. Seconds passed, and I could not even imagine the kind of malice that was being exchanged between the two. One of the hogs sheathed his sword, then one of them turned back and walked toward the arched entrance of the Chambers. The other stood there for a moment, staring at Tiberius. As the hog inched toward his weapon, the figures behind Tiberius advanced closer. Turning back, it was as if Tiberius had just noticed the supporters rallying behind him. They were gaunt men, having missed a considerable amount of meals, but they were strong - and more importantly, they were loyal.

    The hog stood staring at Tiberius, then he spun on the heel of his boot and walked toward the entrance of the Chambers. Once the hog was clear of the Square, one of the peasants stepped out, lifted a blade to his heart, and mouthed a statement to Tiberius - something I could not hear because of the distance, but it must have been powerful, judging by the fist Tiberius raised to his heart and the nod of alliance he gave him. Glancing over to his right, Tiberius hurried over towards an old woman who was tending to the boy, the healer. He mouthed something to her, she paused, then she nodded reluctantly as a flaming torch was handed to her. I turned back into my chamber and dared not look back out.

    I subconsciously grabbed the satchel lying on the floor beside me and slowly walked towards the middle of my chamber. Closing my eyes, I braced my whole being for what I knew would come next. It was the horrifying scream of a boy...who had become a Phllame. A boy who just wanted a measly sausage. A merchant who sacrificed his life for the boy to have it.

Looking up, I was disgusted with the face I saw before me; the twisted life I have been diseased with. Staring into the looking glass, I saw the reflection of a man I had not been acquainted with in a long time. An angry man gazed back at me, a hurt man. Bitter tears moistened my cheeks, and I wiped them away roughly with the sleeve of my tunic. I had not felt this mix of emotions since they executed...no, since they slaughtered Arkon. Butchered him in the street like a fuckin' animal!

In a sudden burst of passion, I shattered the glass before me, thrashed the bureau over on its side until it broke into large wooden planks, and threw the pile of hay across the chamber in quick, grief-stricken succession. Standing there panting, out of breath, I looked across the chamber at what I had just done. Jagged edges of glass piled over sharp planks and ripped wood lay strewn across the stone floor. Wiping my face once more, I searched for the skin of ale that must have been hiding somewhere beneath the wreckage and found it. Lifting the skin to my lips, I took a long, rough chug and tossed the empty skin back into the wreck. Staggering, I stepped over glass and wood to get over to where the other sausage had flung from the bureau. Surveying the area, my eyes clung heavily to the image of a sheet of parchment lying halfway torn from the book of runes, beneath a sharp edge of glass and the stone floor. It was a mixture of lines and squares that formed no pattern, no words, no image. The only thing legible was a name scripted on the bottom of the parchment. Goto Hills, a strange name if you ask me, and certainly not Partrizian, yet the only sign of what message Arkon could have been trying to convey.

My chamber door swung open, and a shadowy figure stared back at me in the partially lit entryway.

"We have to go!" Tiberius demanded more than suggested.

I quickly turned to the window. In the distance was the formation of ten hogs marching towards the entrance of the Chambers, three of which were warlords clad in purple cloaks, the hunters. Shoving the half-torn parchment into my tunic, I quickly grabbed the satchel from beneath a wooden plank, along with the books that were strewn carelessly amidst the pile. I lifted the hood of my tunic over my head in an attempt to conceal my face and hurried out into the corridor.

There was only one way into the Chambers, and one way out. Hiding was not an option, because if either of us was caught, we would be killed. And if we tried to escape through the entrance, we would easily be spotted and killed by the cavalry heading this way.

"Hurry! This way!" said a hunchbacked figure ahead of us holding the torch in the corridor. As we neared the figure, I saw it was the same woman who had tended to Cornelius in the Square, the healer. She was an old woman, clad in black wool robes shabby from years of use, long, ragged grey hair wrapped tightly into a headdress, and beaming black eyes you would swear could see straight through your soul, judging by the way she stared at me.

"The parchment!" she said with an extended hand to me.

Confused, I looked to Tiberius, then past the woman to the scarcely armed men who flanked the walls behind her.

"The parchment?" I said nervously.

"Yes, give me the parchment in your tunic, do it with haste, lad," she said with her hand still extended towards me.

I reached a trembling hand up to my tunic, not out of fear, but because no one could have possibly known of the parchment except for the man who gave it to me, and myself. I slowly slipped the half-torn parchment out and reluctantly handed it to her. She examined it closely as I examined her face. Her brows furrowed as she scanned the parchment, as if she were a receiving a royal decree.

For over a year, I had been trying to decode the squares and jagged lines of the parchment, but the most I understood was that it was drawn by a man named Goto. After a while, I hadn't put any more thought to it. Now this woman I have seen three, maybe four times since I've lived here not only knew I had the parchment in my tunic, she was reading it like...well, like she understood what she was reading. Her eyes suddenly shot up to the low ceiling of the corridor, trailed her gaze further down the dark hall, and pointed into the darkness.

"To the plinth!" she said.

She walked forward, shouldering through the armed men flanking the walls. One of the men caught my eye as I followed behind the woman. The man was oddly familiar amongst the strangers, as if I had known him from long ago, yet when I passed him he only stared and uttered nothing. As Tiberius and I followed behind the old woman, the men formed a kind of shield around us. Reaching a dark, narrow passageway, she led us down a long stone stepwell. All the way to the base of the east tower, we charged as the armed men followed closely behind, blocking us from being seen. As we reached closer to the underground plinth beneath the tower, the heavy stench of mildew and rat feces filled our lungs as we reached a low ceiling passageway lit by only the one torch held by the woman leading us into what could be a death trap.

The dank smell of rotten wood and decay was becoming unbearable, but we pushed forward. My heart lurched and the sound of heavy boots and armor thundered from above our heads as we trudged through heavens knows what type of filthy, decayed underground passage this was.

Suddenly the woman stopped, causing me to run into the back of Tiberius.

"Wait!" she said, standing with her hand up. Seconds later, she turned back to the two of us.

"Does either of you have a sword?" she said, looking back and forth to the two of us.

I turned to Tiberius to see if he also found it to be an odd request, while in the middle of attempting to stay alive, but he did not return my gaze. He unsheathed a blacksword that gleamed even in the dark passageway. Handing it to her hilt first, she took it gently and handed him the torch as she slowly began prodding at the stone floor and walls with the tip of the blade.

"Where did you get the sword?" I asked, glancing away from the lady to Tiberius.

"I took it off the knight I knocked unconscious in the Square," he said, with his eyes fixed on the movements of the old lady. A slight smirk formed on the side of his lip. "I learned a few things from you about taking things when people are unaware," he quipped.

"I only take food, and you know it!" I retorted, reaching a shadowed hand into my satchel. "Besides, you have no problem eating whatever I've stolen, huh? I said, handing him the second sausage I had taken earlier.

He looked down at it as if I were handing him a gold coin and savagely snatched it from my hand. "You damn right!" he said, finishing it in two bites. He then shook his head dimly after a moment. "He became a phllame tonight, Cas...over a piece of sausage" he said sullenly. Glancing at the old woman, he gritted his teeth. "I should just take that blacksword back up to the Square and end it all right now!" he growled.

"Against ten hogs?! You will only end yourself...and I won't let you do that, 'cause of guilt." I said, raising a finger towards to the old woman. "This woman is helping us leave this place, getting us out. Tiberius, I am a wanted fuckin' man. You just knocked a hog unconscious - probably killed him - which now makes you a wanted fuckin' man. And now you want to go back?" I said.

The sudden impact of stone colliding heavily against stone thundered the passage around us, rattling the stone frame of the plinth as the old woman came crashing back into Tiberius' arms to get out of the way. Silence filled the corridor as I stood gaping stupidly at the stone rampart that suddenly sprang out from the side of the wall to block our path; it was a trap.

"I found it!" the old woman said quietly in the screaming silence.

A short moment of stillness filled the passageway, only to be disturbed by stone scraping slowly against stone as the rampart eased back into place. The faint clashing of swords sounded from just up the dark stoned step-well behind us.

"Val depose alacri!" a man cried out behind us in a foreign tongue.

It was one of ours! Those beaming black eyes were now flickering flames as they reflected off the torch in Tiberius' hand.

"They have us found," she nearly whispered

"We have to push forward!" Tiberius said commandingly.

I looked to him, then to the old woman. "Where did you place the sword to set off the trap?" I asked.

The woman pointed to a jagged stone set higher than the others as the clashing of swords ended, from just up the steps, too close to think.

"I'll hold them off. You two have to run!" said the old woman.

"And leave you behind? Not a chance," Tiberius said, and for once I agreed with the heroic act. This woman had possibly saved our lives. I couldn't go forward with her blood on our hands.

"This way!" I said, hurrying toward the rampart. Leaning down, I formed a foothold with my hands and kneeled against the wall. "Tiberius, you first! Put your foot here and jump over that lifted stone," I said in a rushed panic. He hesitated, then looked back towards the fighting, put his foot in my hands, and leaped over the raised stone.

"Get ready to catch!" I said to Tiberius, leaning over once more for the woman. She looked over her shoulder while putting a hand on mine. "No fears, no worries," I said softly to the woman. She nodded reluctantly and placed her foot onto my hands. "1,2...3" I said, throwing the woman as controlled as I could. She left my hands and landed heavily in Tiberius' hands.

"Behind you, Cas!" Tiberius bellowed.

Before I could turn fully, the sound of heavy boots and chain mail sprang from just paces behind me. In a giant leap of disbelief, I turned and jumped past the rampart, barely passing the jagged stone. Coming to a rolling finish, I landed heavily on my back and was only on my feet because Tiberius yanked me up to them. Laughter rang out in the passage behind us as the path was now illuminated by three hogs stalking towards us with torches, each with their faces as black as the night, and each wearing that twisted, evil grin of triumph, and they did not even know they were just strides from their death.

"Would you look at this...the little peasant boy thought he could just jump and take flight, did he?" the hog in the middle said, approaching slowly.

"Cas, this way. Don't turn back!" Tiberius bellowed from behind me. But a rage was building inside of me as I glared at the condescending faces of each hog and matched their grins.

Lifting a hand to my head, I slowly removed the hood of my tunic. Flashing an irrationally wide grin, I acquiesced with my hands raised.

"Yes, yes, I did! How foolish it was of me to have one of your hog brothers eating dirt up in the Square and actually think I could escape. I would say it was rather daring, don't you think?" I quipped with flashing condescension.

The grins faded, only to be replaced by dark faces. "You killed Percy?" said the indignant hog standing on the right.

"Oh, my apologies, did you know him?" I said, smiling ridiculously. "Yes, and after I introduced him to his maker, I had his two other hog lads running back, like little scared cunts!"

"Permission to remove his head, Commander?" said the hog to the left as he stepped forward, unsheathing a blacksword and pointing the tip toward me. Tiberius flashed beside me with his sword at the ready, but a raised hand brought the hog to a halt. His eyes touched the hand of his commander, and he recoiled.

"This man murdered Percy, and you delay in giving the order?" he barked out defiantly to his commander, voice echoing off flame shimmered granite.

"Step back into your position!" the commander ordered with a fiery blaze in his eyes.

The two men searched each other's eyes for a long moment as the commander waited for the slightest hint of insubordination; he received none.

"By orders of the Honorable King Zauber," the commander said through clenched teeth. "For the murder of Percy Mcglorian, third of his name, and 2nd lieutenant of the king's guard, I hereby sentence you to death!" he commanded, unsheathing his sword and pushing forward. Taking a step back, I put a hand on the sleeve of Tiberius' tunic and pulled him back just before the man reached the jagged stone, and then...faster than I remembered, the stone wall swallowed the men whole as they were wedged solidly between stone wall and rampart.

"Come on," Tiberius breathed as he turned to the old woman.

"No!" I said defiantly. "I want to see them dead."

The sound of stone scraping against stone sounded once again, and I was desperate to see the results of my ruthless deception. Blood painted the rampart with a luminous, almost eclectic form of artistry. Entwined through the various links of chain and mail were the soft entrails of men who once were. The soft, supple tissue of a man's head was clearly visible as red liquid welled and spurted from the crushed remains. Smashed so tightly together, the hogs looked freakishly abnormal, almost like hideous creatures. I pushed the thought aside as something flickered on the floor and caught my eye.

Kneeling down, I reached over and unsheathed a black-dagger from a scabbard. It was completely unfazed by neither the rampart nor the impact. I shoved the gleaming blade into my satchel. Still kneeling, I whispered softly into the ear of a dead man, "Tell your bitch, Percy, I said hello!"

"Cas! We have visitors!" Tiberius warned.

The sound of heavy boots and chain mail came from just up the stone step-well. Looking up, I saw the approaching glow of a torch, but I didn't stay long enough to see who approached. "How many traps are down here?" I said breathlessly as we hastened further down the passage with the forces of evil at our heels.

"Only one down here, that is why we chose this way." The old woman said panting and obviously unable to go much further. "The gates are just beyond that enclosure," she said, stopping and bracing her hand on the wall for support. "I...I can't make it that far..."

Tiberius stopped running and turned back. "What is the concern...we must go!" he said with adrenaline-filled vigor.

"She said she cannot go any further," I said, staring helplessly at the woman.

"Nonsense! I shall carry you the rest of the way!" he said, reaching a hand down to scoop the woman up.

"No, my child," the woman said, raising a hand to Tiberius, "this is as far as the vision has foretold! I am to die on this night, but I shall rest peacefully now that I have found the light."

She turned an awed gaze toward me. "For a grand destiny lies before him, and it shall be grand indeed," she said, touching my arm reverentially. "For the time shall come when you will return to this dark place, and you shall have with you the biggest army man has ever seen. With them you shall defeat the legions of darkness once and for all. You shall become a king, my child!"

I looked deep into the eyes of this woman, who had clearly gone mad in the passing moments, and said incredulously, "A king I shall never be, that is certain. Surely, your life has many years yet to have found another light." The faint pounding of boots against stone snapped me out of the trance. "Come with us, please, we will protect you!"

The woman smiled weakly and shook her head. Staring deep into my eyes, it was as if she saw something...something great.

"No, my child," she said, reaching her hand to my face. I slightly recoiled, then embraced her warm touch. "My future is no more, but yours is a future that shall illuminate a generation of kings and queens, gods and goddesses...a sacrifice must be made. Take this!" she said, pushing the half-torn parchment into my hand. "Go to the hills of Forbidden Truth, my child. Your destiny awaits you!" With that, the woman turned and walked back towards her death.

"Wait!" I cried out. The woman's footsteps stopped, but she was no longer seen within the darkness of the plinth. The sound of heavy boots and chains grew closer.

"What is your name?" I said.

"Val," she said softly.

I stared hopelessly into the darkness for a moment, then stood up straight.

"You saved our lives, Val...I thank you for that!" I never heard her response.

CHAPTER TWO

Memorie II

Casanova Volkart
"Keep this man alive, at all costs."
Oakwood Grove 1869

"Do you think they saw us?" I breathed, leaning my back against a heavy limbed oak tree, attempting to keep myself concealed within the shimmering fog of the wood.

"I reckon not!" Tiberius said, peering out from the womb of a plump shrub.

The Oakwood lay a few hundred strides from the gates, and it encompassed almost the entire of Partrizia. It was a vast graveyard of giant oak trees positioned as if they were each guardians of the wood, flanking the sides of a dirt path, each leading somewhere foreign and intriguing. The dried brush and shriveled leaves that cluttered the soft ground all gave the creatures of the wood caution of our arrival. A gust of warm air blew, and a pair of squirrels scurried past my leg, the birds above hooted and cawed at our approach, and the wood was suddenly full of life. A dark stench tickled my nose with a sudden dread that I was all too familiar with. And then it dawned on me: the Oakwood was not a wood at all; it was a burial ground. Some were killed in battle, others executed, but most have died for what we have just done: escape. I looked down at the dirt wedging through my boot with each stride and thought of my master.

    The wood was frightening enough for the common outsider. The cloud of fog that levitated past slowly, the guardians of the wood positioned for battle, and all the sounds that came with the night gave it a haunting feeling. The rustling of leaves could easily mean our death on this night, I pondered, staring off into the nearing twilight of the wood. We were now fugitives in peasant garb with no coin and no food, but luckily we were armed. The half moon stared down on us condescendingly, implying we would only have half a chance to make it through the night alive, but the distant sound of hoof beats and the heavy rattling of chain and mail in the distance suggested the opposite.

    "We have to keep moving," Tiberius said, rushing out across the dirt pathway to cover. I followed. Beneath the shield of a thickly oaked sentinel, we squatted uncomfortably, waiting for the patrol to clear. Within moments, the entire wood was swarming with vitality. The heavy clamoring of mail, the clanking of swords against plate, and the light trots of horses on their approach brought my unease to a frightening peak.

Focusing so intensely on the nearing cloaks, I had not become aware of the hooded man standing before me in the twilight, yet there he stood, nearly fifty strides from where we crouched. Staring out through the shadowy mist of the fog, his back to us, he faced west towards no man's land. He was a broad, fierce looking one. He was tall in stature and clad in a white hooded cloak that swayed gracefully in the wind and nearly enshrouded him within the whiteness of the fog. Has he been sent to capture us? I pondered warily. His head cocked slightly, as if he heard the thought. His size became more apparent as his heavy shoulder blades turned. Through the clearing fog, the hooded man slowly became more visible, and as the man stood to his full height, I gasped in terror. He was staring right at me.

"Shit! Get down!" I heard from distantly beside me. Mail clinked lightly and rattled, just strides from behind the oak we were shielded by, and the chargers halted. I found myself holding in my breath as the crunch of dried leaves neared. My face went lower to the earth as voices emerged.

"It came from this way!"

"Are you sure? I heard nothing."

"Might have been mistaken, but I could have sworn..."

My heart lurched as the swoosh of rustling leaves sprang from just overhead and the voices stopped. A sword was unsheathed, then the hoot of an owl sounded. Another gust of wind sent the bird to flight, and the silent night was penetrated by shrill laughter.

"Of all our years in gallant service to the realm, you are unmanned by the likes of a bird," he snickered. "The brethren should have a hearty laugh over biscuits and ale back at barracks." He laughed.

"We shall have no barracks!" an authoritative voice intoned. "Lest we find the likes of these scoundrels here in the wood and put a bloody smile on the necks of them both."

A sword slid angrily back into its scabbard, and the voices slowly faded into the night. As the hogs trailed away, I opened my eyes and gazed out to the path as the darkness prevailed. Dirt blurred my vision and found its way to my lips, nose, and somehow even the hair blanketed beneath by the hood of my tunic. I then became aware that I had been lying face down, heart pounding and sweating profusely. Scraping wads of dirt from my heavily knotted mane, I gazed anxiously toward the twilight for the man clad in white cloak, but he was not seen. My only vision was the dense fog that shielded us in a veil of smoky whiteness and the eerie cabin which stood well off in the distance, flanked by a host of oaks so tall that the treetops were likely to graze the moon with a heavy gust. It seemed to resemble an image I've seen before.

The wind whistled a soft haunting cry as it passed through fog and oak and wood. It was almost a cry of despair, a melody I knew all too well. Or maybe it was not despair. Maybe it was the lost souls crying out, composing a requiem for themselves, or perhaps it was Arkon. Getting to my feet, I glanced toward the west, and the only remnant of the man in white cloak was the fog levitating gracefully through the army of towering titans. I shall return with an army of shadows, huh? I thought guilefully. Or I'll return with my neck slit.

"She said I was to be king," I said, trudging through dried leaves and brush to keep stride with Tiberius.

"And yet you may!" he said, eyes darting to the left as a fox nosed its way fluidly through the hole of its lair. "Mages do not lie. They say what they see, and nothing further." I pondered his words thoughtfully. Arkon was a mage, I reflected while treading through the remnant smell of darkness and death, but now he was dead. He must have seen something in me as well during his last hours. He saw an aggressor that goes in blindly for the kill with no proper plan of action. Yet the look he had in his eye, the last look we shared, there was no hint of pity or grief. He smiled, as if it were not our final moment. As if this were just another test and he was waiting patiently for my next move.

Arkon believed in me. Although he had a...precarious way of conveying that to me, I just knew it. Master of enchantment is what they called him, and I was to be his student.

Just the thought of it grieved me. Of all the mental training I endured, all the sleepless nights, all the work I put forth to be the best apprentice I could be, it all ended in one night. Everything that was ever given me was taken by this kingdom. My beliefs, my allies, my life in the north, even my innocence. Now they give me the hope of becoming king. I will not be taken for a fool this time. It suddenly occurred to me that I had more friends here in this wood than I did in all of Partrizia. Stepping over the remains of a fallen log and twisted root, I pushed past the thoughts of souls lost and relished in the one I had beside me.

"You have always been true to me, Tiberius," I said after a long moment. "I thank you for that!"

"I have done nothing you would not do one in the same." The night grew darker as his words penetrated through fog. "We are brothers - if not by blood, then by honor - and I will release my final breath before I dishonor you."

"And I you, brother!" I intoned. Silence ensued, and the fog grew thicker with each stride. The truth is, I knew how highly Tiberius thought of me. Although he was older and wiser, he relied heavily on me for my...well, I honestly had no clue why he relied on me. Of all the qualities that would symbolize a good king, Tiberius exemplified them all. The man was fierce, loyal, and has sustained his honor since the first day he stepped into the Chambers.

    He spoke fondly of his days in the land of Noman; us peasants called it no man's land. It was named in honor of the late general Aventir Noman, whose sword was said to have cut through armor and mail alike with its flaming black blade. He died during the battle of the Black Sand just after lopping the head off of a hundred men, or so the tales say. These were treacherous grounds dividing Partrizia and Don Aldia. Many a battle have been fought there, and many men have soaked the dirt with their own blood. And yet, that is where he trained day in and day out, with the late, great Lucinius of the clan Blackwell - his grandfather and grandmaster of the dark arts.

    My heart suddenly froze solid in my chest. The two of us halted in the brush as panic painted my expression in one horrifying stroke. A voice sounded from near, a woman's voice. The most angelic voice I had ever heard, and she was singing. A melody of intrigue that even the gods would admire. Her voice rose in octaves from beneath the fog and sent ice through my veins. It was as if my senses were heightened and I was finally able to see, to feel for the first time. There were no words; only the humming chant of grace, of beauty, of love.

"The song of death!" Tiberius said, pressing forward down the path, eyes fixed on the approaching cabin. I turned to my brother, confused and in awe in the same moment.

"Is this what death sounds like?" I said as the woman's haunting moan enlivened my entire body, propelling me into a state of ecstasy.

"No, this is what it feels like...bliss," he said, looking down at his arms and body. "I'm not afraid to die, Cas." The sound of his voice was dark. "That is why I will never be defeated!" The moaning grew louder, more intense.

"I think she heard you!" I said, nervously observing the east with a wary eye.

"What?" He shrugged. "I have told no lie."

The leaves suddenly began rumbling amidst the brush beside my foot. Two squirrels raced fervently into their burrows just as a flock of birds broke out into sudden flight. The fog seemed to have died away, and the woman's song ceased abruptly, as her cries were complete. The cabin was now visible through the veil of darkness, but the dwellers of the wood were not. All signs of life had vanished from sight, only to be replaced with the night. Something was happening here, something dark.

"We have to go," I snapped.

"To the cabin!" Tiberius said with haste.

"No, we will be seen!" I said, gazing out through the clearing fog, but it was too late. He had already charged over toward the cabin and in through the vine covered door. Seconds later, I saw him clearly through the cracked glass of the window. The remote distinction of hoof beats sounded down the path and neared quickly. I crouched down beneath the shield of an oak and waited. Three horsemen emerged from the darkness, then four, and then five. Each clad in black robes of silk and a hood that covered the whole of their faces. They rode fierce and hard toward their unknown destination, the feeling of darkness only intensifying.

"Hold!" one of the hooded men ordered, and they slowed down to a trot. Panicking, I crouched further behind the oak, cold sweat beads trickling down the side of my head and nose. I could hear my heart pounding inside my chest, feel it thumping endlessly with its rhythmic assault. Of all places to rest...I thought as the men dismounted their chargers. For the first time that evening, the entire oakwood was filled with complete and utter silence. Neither a footstep, nor even the wind brushing against leaves could be heard. It was as if the five horsemen had slipped from their chargers and waited.

I slowly mustered the courage to breathe again. My heart tensed slightly, as I felt I was being watched, examined. But there was no one there. I gazed about for the man in white cloak, but he was not seen. I cocked my head to the side to look through the cracked window of the cabin for Tiberius, but he was not seen either. I snaked my head around the towering oak behind me and...five hooded men stood staring at me. They gazed upon me and yet somehow did not see; they were facing the north. Two grand rubies sat on the back of each hood, made to look like eyes. The men positioned themselves in a circle twenty strides from where I crouched. A torch was lit, and then another. A low murmuring was heard, and a horse whinnied in the distance behind the cabin.

Just get back on your horses and leave...I thought nervously, glancing over at the darkness of the cabin, only shadows staring back. Behind me, five torches were now lit. The flames made haunting figures in the dirt beside me as they swayed gracefully in time with the wind. The faint stench of mildew drifted pass my nose, and I leaned back against the oak for support. If I were to make a break for it, I would divert their attention long enough for Tiberius to escape, but then I would be caught. If I stayed here and they swayed into the cabin, Tiberius would be caught. I wheeled my head around the oak once more. Four of the torch bearing hoods encircled a fifth, who stood in the middle. Each torch was burning on short pikes, each driven into the dirt encircling flames around the man. I glanced toward the window once more, and the moment to make a decision was staring me in the face.

What would Arkon do? The thought seemed strange, yet appropriate for the situation. My answer came in the form of a hand grabbing my arm. Out of sheer panic, I would have let out the echoing shriek that would surely have had us caught, had Tiberius not clapped his hand over my mouth in a split second.

"Shhh!" he mouthed, pointing towards the hooded men.

"We need to move!" he whispered. "I saw where the horses were reined, just beside the cabin. We take two and kill the others!" I glanced over toward the cabin.

"Got it! But how did you get out of the cabin?" I intrigued.

"Back door." He winked.

"Good idea!" I nodded in approval.

He moved like a shadow. From the shield of one sentinel to the next, with flawless grace. It took sheer will to keep up with him, but fortunately we disappeared behind the cabin without being seen. The rancid smell of stale dung filled my nostrils, and the burning sensation made my eyes water.

Tiberius leaned his head casually around the corner of the cabin but flashed back with gaping eyes. "Oh shit!" he said, reaching a hand inside his tunic to the back of his britches. A dark knife was unsheathed and handed to me hilt first. "You might need this. Two of em' headin' this way!"

I took the rusted blade from his hand, and the weight of the thing became apparent when he released. How much blood has been shed at the mercy of this piece of iron? I thought as the shuffling of steps neared. I barely had enough time to panic. I clutched the hilt of the knife until my knuckles whitened, then waited.

Tiberius turned to me with murderous eyes, and just like that he was gone. Stepping around the corner of the cabin, I saw three horses reined, two hoods reaching for their waists, and one who did not reach it in time. In one blurring move, Tiberius slashed open the front of his hood, and blood sprayed and spurted out in a raging river of redness. The chargers stirred restlessly, and one reared back on its hind legs, whinnying his response to the sudden movement. The man dropped to his knees with a hand grasping his throat, but to no avail. The blood just kept pouring out and oozing through his fingers. Seconds later, he was dead.

In a rush, I turned to the charger who had just reared and swiftly cut through the rein. I grabbed for the rein, but the beast was too wild in him. The charger bucked and kicked roughly, missing my face by a hair's length. Clawing at the thought of freedom, he charged off, trampling another hood who came running toward the commotion. His chest and thigh bones cracked, and he lay moaning in his broken body. Two other black hoods emerged as I stepped up beside Tiberius, and then the moment of truth. Three men stared back at us through veiled hoods and red rubies attached to where the eyes should have been. I clenched my knife tighter, ready to die beside my brother.

One hood stepped forward, and Tiberius readied his fighting stance. A voice emerged from behind his hood, the smooth, unflustered voice of a trap. "It seems you have taken something that did not belong to you." His voice was deep and elegant. I stared at the hood confused but was too anxious to respond.

"We have taken nothing!" Tiberius said sharply.

"Ah, but you have!" he replied, red jewels directed down at the man moaning in a pool of blood and dirt. "You have taken a life!" he said calmly. "Is that nothing to you, warrior?" The rubies emblazoned on his hood seemed to glow slightly.

"I felt threatened, and I reacted. End of story!" Tiberius snapped, his patience growing thin as a string of silk.

The hood took another step forward. "I guess the real question is, how will you repay this debt, in deed or in coin?" he said with the calmness of a snail.

Tiberius lifted the point of his sword to the front fold of his hood and glowered. "Take one more step, and I will cut you to pieces."

The veiled man made no move, nor did he respond. In the interim, I glanced from the two hoods flanking his sides to the one moaning in the dirt. The front of his hood was down in the red dirt, and his right arm was dangling at a weird angle, his right hand was gauntleted. The veiled man with the tip of a sword piercing the apple of his neck also had gauntlets. The same rough-skinned black leather and spiked edges that Arkon wore.

"Pity!" the man said after a long moment of silence. The two men flanking his sides rushed forward so quickly, I barely had enough time to lift the knife in response. By the time the hoods reached Tiberius, the veiled man lifted a hand and they both stopped instantly. "I have the power to help you!" the man said calmly, unaware that he was negotiating with death.

"Really?" Tiberius spat. "It seems the only one in need of help is the man with a sword at his throat!"

"Ah, but on the contrary, warrior!" He laughed. "Tell me, how are you and your friend Casanova here planning on reaching your destination without a horse?" Even through the mask, I could sense the man had a menacing grin painted on his face.

"You know who I am?" I asked without thinking. Stepping forward, I examined the hooded man and tightened the grip on my knife, red rubies glittering towards me. I should have known I would be recognized; my face was on every wanted poster for as far as the eye can see.

"Why certainly, young lord!" he said with an awkward gesture of expression.

"Keep your fuckin' hands down!" Tiberius barked, his voice resounding through the darkness.

"And Tiberius of the clan Blackwell," the man continued, unfazed by the sudden outburst. "The journey for the two of you shall be long indeed. Please allow my associates to offer a token of friendship!"

"We are not friends!" Tiberius retorted harshly.

"No, we are not!" the man replied promptly, as if he already knew what would be said.

The two hoods rushed forward once more, but instead of attacking, they hastened past the two of us towards the two war horses that stood just strides away, Tiberius kept his sword at neck level. They slowly started releasing the steeds from their holds, one black and one white. The black steed was a fierce, angry looking destrier, hooting and bucking his defiance. The white horse was almost glowing in the night, as if he had been cleaned and polished just before the ride. The two were remarkable gifts indeed. "Do you take me for a fool?" Tiberius said as the two hoods handed each of us a rein.

"Not in the slightest, warrior!" he replied with a hint of aggression. "I take the two of you for the ones who will leave this place and return with an army powerful enough to release the people of Partrizia from oppression."

"You are Partrizian?" Tiberius said, incredulous. The man nodded in response. "Pull off your hood!"

The man hesitated, but after a moment he obeyed the command. "It would be of ease if you removed the sword from my neck!" he said coolly. This time Tiberius hesitated but then finally lowered his sword, keeping the hilt tight in his grip and his eyes fixed firmly on target. The veiled man reached a hand to the fold of his robe and peeled the silk slowly up over his head. Beneath the veil was the distinct face of a Partrizian man, dark and fierce. A scar ran across his face, as if it had been sliced open completely, the vile disfigurement made the man look about as grotesque as the creature I saw for the brief moment he was there. The expression on his face was one of assertion, and the distorted grin sculpted on the side of his lip was not one of humor.

"Hello, Tiberius!" he said.

Tiberius stared at the man with darkened eyes, silent as a cobra. I looked from Tiberius to the man, then back to Tiberius. Neither of the two exchanged words for a long while. The two men flanking my sides each stood firmly with a rein in hand, red rubies beaming down at me.

"We accept your gift!" I declared, breaking the silence, but no one moved; no one even flinched.

"I killed you!" Tiberius growled suddenly.

The scarred man nodded his acquiescence. "Yes, yes, you did. And yet, here I am with the power to help you help your people, our people. Our differences will never change, but our interests will always be the same."

"Is that what they taught you in hell, you fuckin' coward?" he barked, knocking the hilt of his sword into the man's shoulder and jolting him back two strides. "My only interest is keeping my brother and myself alive. That's it."

The scarred man brought together the bulbs of his fingers and nodded. "I can see you are fueled by your anger for me, Tiberius," he said firmly. "And this is good, yet our present dilemma is much bigger than you and I. This is much grander than even maintaining the glory of Partrizia. This is about advancement, and the only way to move forward is to destroy what is already built and begin anew. Now, I will not force your hand, but I will offer you these gifts, once again as a token, in the hopes that when the time comes...you will honor your duty as a warrior, you will protect."

Tiberius stared out into the moonlit darkness for a moment. His size was just as intimidating as his expression.

"Protection from whom?" Tiberius said darkly.

"The illuminaries have foretold of a war to come, six years hence. A battle the likes of which Partrizia has never seen or has of yet prepared for."

"So gather the clansmen and prepare for siege!" Tiberius said, undismayed.

"It should be that simple..." the man started, "if these were mere mortal men." Tiberius shot the man a dead stare, much longer than any man with sanity would feel comfortable with, before stalking towards him. "Enough of this foolishness. We have business to handle!" he snapped just before turning back toward myself and the two hoods that stood beside me.

"Rein!" he demanded, staring at the hood to my right with vicious eyes. The man hesitated, but then his rubies turned to the scarred man who gave a quick nod before the rein was handed over. Tiberius stepped up and swung his leg over the black charger, looking more regal than I had ever seen him before. The other hood handed me a rein as well.

"A deed must still be paid, Tiberius," the scarred man said, gazing down at the broken man moaning in the dirt.

"I will not fight beside a coward," he said, staring at the man with fiery eyes.

"As I said before, this is much bigger than you and I, Tiberius!" The man looked at Tiberius with a weird wrinkle on the side of his lip that resembled...a smile. The scarred warrior turned to Tiberius before continuing. His piercing brown eyes held a familiarity to them. "There is a woman you will meet that will show the ways of the true Shatoh warrior; however, she is not to be trusted. Tiberius, you are to compete in the Kamikhan for the name of our family," he said, "and return here not only when the two of you have reunited, but also when he has received his truth."

Tiberius gave a glare that was death and viciousness wrapped in swarthy fabric but uttered nothing. He turned the charger toward the west and urged the horse into a heavy trot. I did the same. The wind rushed through my face in an exhilarating charge of verve and freedom, we galloped toward the moon. Guardians whizzed past like shadows stampeding freely in the night. We rode hard, each crack of the reins and kick against the side of our chargers sending them jolting forward faster and faster until my hands were literally blistered and cracked from the friction.

Fearing my hands would give way, I pulled back slightly, slowing the steed down to a trot; it seemed about as relieved as I was. Tiberius slowed down as well, giving his new friend a brush down the thick hairs of his neck as he stared cautiously through the dark wood. The silence that followed denoted not anger, but a pensive reflection of what had just happened. The soft trots of our new companions left a hypnotizing impression in the otherwise silent wood.

A good ways ahead, torches were ablaze and voices started to carry throughout the darkness. Waves of murmurs and undertones livened the horizon. I suddenly became aware of how far we had ridden through the darkness. With growing apprehension, I pulled the hood of my tunic down further over my brows, concealed my face, and seized the reins as tight as I could with scarred hands. With the fading twilight overhead and the guardians of the wood now at a great distance behind us, no man going forward could possibly be a friend. We were entering ground we had never stepped on; the road untraveled.

"You look suspicious all the more with that hood covering your eyes," Tiberius said, breaking the silence. "We have to lose the tunics!" he said as he removed his own with one hand while holding his balance with the rein. The rough woolen vest he wore beneath exposed his broad arms, which looked much more defined than I had remembered.

"You are probably right," I said, reaching a damaged hand up for my hood. Unfastening my broche, I let the tunic fall back off my shoulders. I looked down at the gaunt frame that I had acquired through bouts of depression and one-meal days. Some future king I would be! I thought shamefully. Then my mind flashed back to what had just occurred.

Those terror-filled black hoods that surrounded us. Those threatening red rubies staring down at me. The man with the scarred face.

"Do you think they will follow us?" I said as we neared the edge of the wood.

"I doubt it." He shrugged. "They had us outnumbered and did not strike."

I pondered the thought for a moment, then decided it was a good assessment but a possibly fatal underestimation.

"I saw the way you looked at that man, brother," I drawled. "I have seen you upset many a time, even enraged, but never have I seen the look you gave to that man back there...how do you know him?"

He stared forward and was silent for a long while.

"He is my father..." he finally said, and the night went silent once again.

CHAPTER THREE
Memorie III

Casanova Gallimorian
"You don't need a motive, but I still think you have one!"
Village of Deceptia, 1869

As I'm staring over this once inhabited land before me, myriad emotions come to mind, the least of which was fear, as it lingered about as brazen as a foul odor. I was walking through a wasteland that was tinged entirely in crimson, possibly from the red moon hovering overhead, or possibly a glare from the flaming inferno I was heading toward. Bones crushed to bits beneath my war boots, and the smell of ash and fire suffused the air. Seared chunks of flesh muddled my path. The steaming remains of all that used to be Partrizia. The four age-old towers that made up the Chambers were well off in the distance, and even they seemed so ruined that they might come crashing down through the earth at the slightest gust of wind.

The thick, dank air was relentlessly unbearable. Heat speared in from all sides, as if a furnace were abroad. Somewhere in the distance, the light crackling of flames were heard. A few fluttering flakes almost gave the dreary wasteland the impression of a blissful winter night, until I realized that I had been sweating profusely and the flakes fluttering about were the last remaining memories of my people.

The air we once used for refreshment was now riddled with ash and small spurts of flames. But how? The stale, rancid smell of blood filled my nostrils until my eyes watered. An epic battle occurred here...I thought, but how could any army have caused this? As I walked amongst the ashes, blurry visions of children playing in the fields flashed through my mind, and nostalgia settled in. Roads that used to be full of people, merchants, priests, butchers, blacksmiths, were now a part of the very grime beneath my boots, wiped out of existence.

All memories were replaced with desolation and haunting imagery. Villages that used to make Partrizia a kingdom of beauty and astonishment were now cinders. Suddenly, as I rummaged through the clouds of ash, guarding my eyes with my hand, a figure appeared.

    The figure moved slowly toward me, consuming the short distance, and the size of this figure became more apparent as he neared. My heart shuddered intensely, his face the more indistinct as he approached. With each step we took towards each other, his face got blurrier and more distorted until I was close enough to touch his outstretched fingertips, and then...

    My eyelids snapped open, and I had to lift a hand to my face as a shield from the glaring sun. I sat up, and a small fire was blazing by a tall shrub nearby with long vines that coiled through each limb. On the near horizon, there were giant oaks with blackened lifeless leaves gazing maliciously towards me. The Oakwood looked haunting, even in the broad of day and at a well off distance.

    I suddenly lurched to attention, reaching for the blade slipped in through a fold in my britches. The sound of wood thrashing to pieces sprang from just paces behind me as I rushed toward the nearest cover. Looking down at my frame, I couldn't help wondering what I was doing. Even with a blade gripped tight in my palm and the desire to kill like Tiberius, there was no way a scrawny peasant of eighteen could strike fear in any grown man, unless he was frail or maybe too old to fend for himself either way.

Heavy breathing caught my ear, and then a snort as I leaned my back lightly against the vine covered shrub. With a surge of rage, I leaped from my concealment to see...the beautiful white destrier I had received as a gift the night before, reined just strides ahead. The black one was reined separately on the other side of a huge stack of logs. Gently grazing on the stalks of grass and brush before him, it was even more beautiful than I had remembered.

I lowered my blade and sheathed it back in through the fold of my britches. I approached the war horse with enough caution to be nonthreatening. Rubbing the hairs of its neck, I spoke gently to my new companion.

"You saved me from killing all those men last night." I smiled, stroking his back and feeling the warmth of his skin. He snorted again in response and nudged his head against my hand. It might have been to say we would be allies forever, or he might've just wanted to nudge me away so he could finish breaking fast.

"You are such a beauty!" I said in awe of my new friend.

"Is that what you say to all the ladies?" a deep voice said from behind me, too close for comfort. I spun around, reaching once more for the blade, but I was not coordinated enough. The blade fumbled dangerously through my fingers and landed tip first in the dirt just before I looked up to see Tiberius grinning stupidly with a pile of logs in his hands.

"Careful there, killer!" he quipped.

"I told you about sneaking up on me!" I shot back. "You were liable to lose a finger or an eye," I said, grinning from embarrassment.

"You know I'm too fast to lose both, Cas. Your best bet would be to go for the eye first!" he said, still beaming.

"You know..." I said with a sudden seriousness. "We should never go back! We can just go to the other side of the world to Cielo Placer, or even Cilan!

The smirk on Tiberius' face disappeared, and a dangerous undertone flashed in his dark eyes.

"And then what?" Tiberius said. "We leave all of Partrizia impoverished? Leave them to rot in the Chambers?" He sighed deeply before proceeding. "I know we should never return, brother...but that is what must happen for a change to occur! This journey is more than you becoming a king so you can wear a pretty crown on your head or walk around with your nose up. There are injustices that need to rectified, and we can only do that with a certain level of power," he counseled.

"Since when have you been interested in power, my brother?" I said with squinted eyes.

"Since they cut your master to pieces right in front of our faces," he barked so emphatically that a few logs fell from his hands to the dirt. "Since my mother was killed right in front of me because I was too fuckin' weak to stop her from getting beaten to death...since I..." He stopped and slowly shook the memories away.

I had never seen this side of Tiberius. All the reasons behind the madness and the viciousness suddenly came rushing up to the surface. The cause of his anger, his insane drive - it all made sense now. I was staring at a man with a purpose, a man with a mission. And here I was just trying to bury all my problems beneath the dirt and walk so far away from it that I've forgotten where it was buried. The silence that followed was resounding, but in that silence a conviction was made.

"Teach me to fight!" I said with a suddenness that was almost daunting. "If we are to go through with this mission and see it to its conclusion, I must know how to defend myself!" I continued with fiery eyes. Tiberius' stare locked on mine with the blank gaze of an unreadable man. I began to feel like maybe it was not such a good idea.

The logs dropped from Tiberius' hands and fell into a pile of disarrayed wood bits by his boots. He removed his new black blade fashioned from the hardest steel in the eastern part of the world, Partrizian gunthite. The polished black steel gleamed as it swayed from its scabbard.

"Pick up your blade!" he commanded with a blank stare.

I looked at the magnificence of the longsword clutched in his palm, and although the blade was of the same make, an experienced longsword against an amateur blade spelled suicide. In one blurring movement, Tiberius was in my face, sword at my neck and forearm pressed firmly against my collarbone.

"Hesitation will get you killed...and now you are dead," he said calmly.

"A longsword against a blade is hardly a fair fight!" I said breathlessly with my hands up in surrender. "Fair?" He laughed. "We are a peasants, Cas. Nothing about life is fair. Fighting is no different!" he said, releasing his forearm from my neck. "The only thing you think about when it is time to fight is to kill before you get killed. That's it!"

He drove his sword into the dirt and turned around to pick up the wood bits behind him.

"Lesson over!" he said, passing by, walking towards the fire pit.

I realized then that I was breathing heavily and my left hand was trembling uncontrollably under the weight of my blade. I truly was not ready for what just happened. I must have been mad to think I could handle a training session with the man I have watched kill at his own leisure. At first glance, you could see the man as a hero, the warrior that helped any person in need. But after knowing the man for eight years, I realized that the man just loved a reason to kill, which explains his "Kill before you get killed" mentality. The flames burned low over the pit as Tiberius kneeled down and fed a log to the fire. "We have to hunt!" he said, raising up from the flames.

"Hunt?" I said. Reaching for the hilt of his sword, he heaved the chunk of gunthite out of the earth and slid it roughly back into its sheath.

"You see that there?" Tiberius said, pointing toward the northeast as I walked up beside him. It was a hilled pasture, rich with sunlight, farmland, and the possible prospect of a civilization just beyond the hill.

"I sure do!" I said, staring out over the same prospect. "What do you think is past that hill?"

"Prey!" he said after a moment, then turned back toward the pit and stepped up onto his destrier. I followed suit. Racing through the pasture, we reached the end of the dirt lands and started to ascend the steep hill. Only heaven knew what lay before us on the other side.

Tension rose as we trotted toward the top of the hill. As we rode toward the peak, the sight was enthralling. Trees blanketed the grasslands before us, yet they were not the hideous, giant oaks we saw from the night before. They were dazzling sentinels that produced leaves of beautifully bright hues. Some reds and some pinks, some even held brilliant shades of purple and orange that were especially appealing. The birds overhead were in V-formation, gliding over a small village, judging by the winding dirt trail and smoke emitting from the fire pits. There we stood, at the top of the hill on our destriers, staring in awe at the beauty that lay before us.

"We hunt here?" I said skeptically.

Tiberius shook his head and pointed to his ear silently. Seconds later, I heard the distant sound of murmuring.

"This way!" he drawled, turning his reins toward the trail but stopping just before urging his charger forward. Down the dirt trail ahead of us was a marketplace swarming with people. Dozens of colorful tents and shacks lined beside each other, some serving fruits and meats, others served wines and spirits.

The sun glared beautifully through the leaves, splashing hues in every direction as we dismounted our chargers and reined up.

"We may not have to hunt after all," Tiberius said, staring at the overcrowded market. "You know what to do, right?" he said. I nodded sharply.

"But I may need to wear this," I said, snatching my tunic from the saddle.

"Listen..." Tiberius said roughly. "We go in, make our moves, and meet back here. No socializing. See me?!"

"I see you!" I said, eying the marketplace as a cobra would glare at its prey.

"Okay, let's go!" he said.

Approaching the market, the two of us split apart in opposite directions. I went straight toward the meat stand down the dirt trail, eying the merchant standing fifty or so strides away, and Tiberius went straight for the guard tent, as we always do. Thirty strides away, and I secured the blade concealed in my britches. Twenty strides, and I blended in flawlessly with the onrush of the crowd. Ten strides away, and I slowed pace as I caught eyes with a woman smiling toward me. She paused as she walked past, as if she wanted to say something, but then hurried off.

As a lady suddenly screamed in the distance, I knew it was time. With blinding speed, I brushed past the distracted commoners and merchants, slipped a handful of silvers from his purse, as well as two slabs of meat and a honeyed crab cake that looked too delicious to pass by. Hastening toward my next grab, I thrived off the tumultuous crowd. The blended mixture of voices and laughs, sighs and grunts all made my job much more convenient, but the faces...each face I passed had an awkward smile painted on it. I had never seen such a happy group. The women smiled amongst one another, the men spoke to each other with the same grin, even the lads were engaged in their own childish game of smirks.

    A lady merchant glanced my way as I approached. She must have been one, maybe two years older than dirt, but her smile gave her youth. Her head was covered with a silk tippet, and she wore a long black tunic beneath. "Welcome!" she said joyously; her accent was foreign.

    "Thank you, ma'am. May I ask, what is this village called?" I said, holding her gaze while I slipped a heavily jeweled medallion into the outside fold of my tunic.

    "Why certainly...you are in Deceptia," she drawled in a chopped, edgy dialect.

"I thank you, ma'am!" I said, walking back toward the dirt trail.

For some reason, I looked at the woman with disdain. In fact, I was disgusted at how easily I deceived the people around me. This was no longer for my survival, and there was no more justification for my actions. I was not feeding the less fortunate, nor was I bitter towards the merchants here; they were in fact a pleasant group. I was now convinced that...I relished this power. Breaking from the crowd, I walked down the trail with the confidence of a king toward our rendezvous. Tiberius was already there waiting.

"Any luck?" he said as I approached.

"Plenty" I said, walking past him to where the chargers were reined. "How many guards?"

"Six, fully armed and mailed," he said, stepping up onto his destrier. "I know they have at least 50 gold pieces in the hut. We need that!"

"First we eat, then we train...and then we take everything!" I said firmly and struck reins.

Dusk fell much later than I'd hoped. Blood dripped down the side of my head, and my entire jaw was numbed from pain. Training was much more brutal than I expected it would be. Regardless, we were on a mission that would mean our heads if we failed, so I pushed forward.

"One finger in the air if it's clear, see me?" Tiberius said, holding the lantern we found from a nearby cabin.

"I see you!" I said, pulling the brim of my hood down over my eyes. The market was clearing out, but there were still enough people to formulate my deceptions. Glancing to my left, I surveyed the guard tent; only three stood watch. They were clad in polished grey mail and blue cloak, fully armed, just as Tiberius said. Walking past their line of sight, I purposely tripped over a stone but grabbed hold of a man's cloak before I fell to one knee, slipping his coin purse right from his waist.

"My deepest apologies, sir!" I said, expecting a fight to break out, but it never did. Instead, the man turned back and helped me to my feet.

"Are you okay, lad?" he said with a warm grin.

"Yes. Again, my apologies!" I said, hurrying off.

Glancing to my left once again, the guards did not budge, which was just what I needed to see. I lifted one finger in the air and waited. "Fire!" a woman screamed moments later.

People from all directions started twisting and turning to protect themselves from the blaze that caught hold of a merchant booth and swayed dangerously close to the crowd. Women scooped up crying children, men held their wives close to them so as not to get trampled by the stampeding crowd, and I walked straight toward the guard tent.

Approaching the guards, they were just as chaotic as the women and children. Looking back and forth amongst each other and doing nothing.

"Get the water barrels!" I called out as I neared. Guards in Partrizia always kept water barrels inside the booth beside the valuables.

"They are sealed for the king's feast!" a young blue cloaked hog said in a panic.

"And what would the king say if you allowed the main market to burn to cinders?" I said impulsively. The hog turned to his commander, who then nodded.

"Do what the lad said!" he commanded as the blaze touched another booth, catching hold of the goods and smothering them.

Two hogs rushed into the tent, and the commander stood post outside, staring helplessly at the flames.

"This may need an extra set of hands. Here, let me grab a barrel for you," I said, lifting the flap to the tent. A hand landed firmly on my shoulder and halted my entry.

"No citizens allowed inside the tent!" the hog said forcefully as he entered behind his fellow hogs, closing the flap immediately. They could not be this stupid! I thought as each of them filed out of the tent carrying huge clay water jugs. When the commander passed, he looked me in my eyes.

"Ay lad, you want to tell me why your face is bleeding?"

"Yes, I do..." I said nervously. "And I shall upon your return."

"I remember your face, boy!" the hog grunted, and my heart froze inside my chest. "The next time we meet, you shall be rewarded for what you did today!" He nodded and then hurried off toward the blaze.

My heart slowed down to its normal tempo, and I readjusted myself. Fingering the air once more, I caught sight of the chaos we had just caused. A woman holding her baby close to her chest ran past the blaze, and it caught hold of her gown. She dropped to the ground to douse the flames and was trampled nearly to death. I turned my gaze away sharply and then lifted the flap to the tent. Tiberius had slashed his way through the back and filled his satchel nearly to its fill.

"Grab the wine!" he said, pointing to the ledge beside me. I snatched the flagon, and we vanished.

"Seventy-three, 74, 75 silvers," I slurred as I took the last gulp of wine with a grin fixed across my face. "We need more wine!"

"Show no face for at least a day or so...I believe those were your precise words," he reminded me.

"I figured one flagon would suffice," I urged.

"Your plan, your decision. But in my opinion, you need to lay off the wine and stay alert. We are fugitives now, remember?" Tiberius said.

"Ay, isn't that for true!" I sulked.

The abandoned cabin we discovered earlier that day during training was rubbish, to say to the least, but we made way. Its outer framework was entangled with weeds and vines, high grass covering the path toward the front entrance. It was surely uninhabitable, yet at this point it would just have to do; we were almost rich. Racing back from the marketplace, we were completely unseen. Staring out at the moonlit sky through the cracked glass edges of the window, I reached over for the lantern.

"There must be a tavern or something nearby. I am sure the folks at the market do not suspect either of us," I said.

"And the guards?" Tiberius urged. "The fucker wants to offer a reward for my help," I grinned

"Not after they count the earnings and realize they were swindled."

"Oh relax, brother! By that time, we shall be ghosts here, yet our legacies will remain" I said, using the wall as leverage to get to my feet. "Tonight we celebrate; tomorrow we become kings!"

Tiberius got to his feet wordlessly and walked toward the window.

"If you do not return by the time the moon reaches its zenith, I will come find you!" he said.

"Done!" I said.

Walking toward the village, I took the path of shadow and cobblestone, so as not to run into the same hogs from earlier. My head was spinning slightly, but I was able to hold my composure. Thankfully, this path seemed to be a direct route to where I needed to be. Torches were ablaze just through the trees ahead, and the drums were being played as shadowy silhouettes swayed back and forth throughout the night.

A bonfire was lit between two pillars, and before my eyes were...women, a dozen of them, half-naked and polished to a golden sheen. They were dancing in ritual. Women swayed gracefully back and forth through the cobblestone street, leading to paradise. The smell of sex and wine pervaded the air.

"Five silvers, and pick any one you like!" a voice charmed from beside me. I turned to see the grinning glare of a lad. He was a slim fellow, yet wiry and built for finesse. He was richly dressed, clad in a black doublet trimmed in gold edging, fashioned with a golden eagle broche, black breeches of the finest silk, and knee length combat boots. A longsword lay across his back, gold in the hilt, sitting in its sheath, and two daggers rested on either side of his waist. I couldn't help wondering on which side he kept his coin purse.

"I just want wine," I replied, staring ahead at the display of flesh.

"I was referring to the wine, outsider!" he quipped, pointing toward the overcrowded tavern. "I tell you what, first round on you, and the rest of the night free of charge!" he charmed.

"And why exactly would you do that for me?" I intoned.

"Why would I need a motive?" He grinned. "I come in peace".

"You don't need a motive, but I think you have one!" I edged suspiciously.

His smile dimmed, and the lad gazed toward a crowd of onlookers. My hand was gripped the handle of my blade.

"You see the man standing there next to the keg, with the green tunic and heavy beard?"

"I see him," I drawled, spotting the plump man with the empty mug in his hand.

"I am going to kill him tonight!" he said, eying the crowd. "But the first thing I am going to do is walk inside that tavern and drink myself blind. You can join me, or you can stand here gawking at women with no wine and no clue of why all these people have a smile on their face," the lad said with a wink, and he was off.

The music stopped playing, and the women followed behind this man in lavish garments. The thirsty crowd of onlookers were the only folks left in the street, and each wore a dissatisfied smile on their faces. It suddenly seemed so desolate on a street that had just been vibrant and full of life. I eased myself back into the shadows of the night. *Just get the wine, Cas...just get the wine,* I thought as I followed him straight through the swinging doors of hell.

Torches shone bright throughout the tavern, as the crowd was illuminated by perfectly placed flames. Dazzling flames glared throughout the room, hanging grapevines encircled the stone pillars flanking each side, and nearly hundreds of black glass bottles lined the wall before my eyes.

"You made the right decision," the lad said from beside me.

"I was intrigued," I charmed.

"Feast your eyes upon the elegance," he said, swaying his hand toward the black bottles lining the wall. "One shot, and you will want to marry your mom."

"Mr. Bines, would you like your bottle for the evening?" a beauty said, clad in silk and jewels. Her eyes spoke tales of elegant lies.

"No, my dear. I would like continuous shots until I forget my name this evening, thank you!" he quipped. "And the same for my friend...uh...I'm sorry, your name?"

"Casanova," I said mistakenly, completely forgetting that I was on the run.

"Casanova, it is a pleasure. The name is Raleigh, and my beautiful associate here is Elena, who was just off to get our shots, wasn't she?" he said, eying her vivaciously.

"Coming right up!" She smiled.

Elena trailed away, her hips swaying gently to the rhythm of the drums.

"You must come here a lot," I said.

"Yes, a business does call for attention," he said, staring out over the ambiance with pride.

"You own this tavern?" I said. "And the women." He nodded. "The whole bit". He glared intently through the dancing women, to the man in green tunic.

"You are not really going to kill a man in your own tavern, right?" I said in mock disbelief.

"I'm not?" he said and turned toward the crowd, mixing in with the beautiful women and rich nobles of Deceptia.

"Here is your shot, sir!" Elena said, eying my body and face like I was prey. "Enjoy the show, love." She winked, then flashed her eyes toward the crowd.

I took the glass, examined the black liquid for a moment, and spotted Raleigh edging toward his target. I threw the shot back just as he slipped behind the man and in one swift move slid a dagger across his throat and passed the blade to a woman, who then disappeared into the darkness.

As a smile formed slowly on my face and the man dropped completely out of sight, I realized that I had witnessed not only an extremely well-orchestrated display of deception, but also someone who could possibly be of use in the future.

Raleigh walked back with the grinning nonchalance of a jester.

"I see you tasted the house special!" he said.

"I did," I said, staring across the room as the group of commoners danced to the high tempo of the drums, each unaware that a man was dead beside their feet.

"Shall we?" Raleigh said, handing me a second shot. "A toast to new friendships and beautiful women!"

"Cheers," I said as we both took back the rich honey grape-filled taste of elegance. A woman suddenly screamed, and an entire group toppled over each other in the far corner as the drums stopped playing.

"He's dead!" the woman shouted. A tumultuous outrage sprang out, glass shattered against stone, and the crowd made its way toward the exit, only to be blocked by sentinels and thick burly men, ironclad and vicious to the eye, blocking the entrance with war hammers. Six of them spread throughout the crowd.

"I am afraid no one is leaving here tonight until the culprit is found!" said Raleigh, smileless walking toward the center of the crowd. "I want to see the man responsible for this."

He paced for a moment through the silent torch lit ambiance of deception, staring each man in the face. No smiles were exchanged, nor did the slightest hint of humor touch his words. At that moment, all was intense and alive in the room.

"No one is willing to confess to this savagery?" he bellowed angrily, staring down at the body soaking in a pool of redness.

Moments later, a charge approached. Not a formidable force; yet a force nonetheless. Three blue cloaks marched inside, each with an overbearing glare as they eyed the tavern suspiciously.

"Good evening gentlemen!" said Raleigh stepping forward into the torchlight.

"We heard a woman scream" the hog barked, disinterested in pointless banter.

"Whoa there soldier, I am here to help you find out what happened!" Raleigh said with his hands up peaceably. "A man was murdered here just a moment ago and we need to identify the culprit."

One hog stepped forward through the silent group eying each suspicious eye that would catch his.

"Is that so?" he said glaring intensely at Raleigh for a moment before continuing. "Because the irony is, any time a murder is discovered, we turn around and find you lurking somewhere in the shadows." he said eying the ceiling and walls of the tavern.

"Are you... accusing me of this murder?" Raleigh said through squinted eyes.

"And if I am?" the hog retorted viciously.

Raleigh exhaled and grinned nervously. "Well, then I would provide you with a witness who shall validate my innocence," he said. "And you think I am stupid enough to allow you to provide the witness? I will choose..."

"Done!" Raleigh said as my heart lurched violently in my chest. The man was mad, I thought leaning back as far into the shadows as possible. The hog's eyes glazed over a room full of nobles and mistresses, elites and warriors, blacksmiths and poachers. The only people who looked as if they did not belong were the man soaking in his own blood and me. The hog's eyes caught mine, and my heart sank down into the sleeve of my tunic.

"Hello there, young lad!" the hog said, uncharacteristically pleasant. He reached to his waist and slowly unclipped a coin purse. "I have here...25 gold coins if you can identify who killed this man," he said, pointing down at the body.

A moment passed as I eyed the body, then the purse, then caught eyes with Raleigh. An emotionless expression smoothed over his face as he maintained regal confidence. He looked me in the eyes and then turned his gaze. I turned to the hog. His intimidating gaze rested on my face for much longer than I felt comfortable with as he awaited my response.

"I-I don't know who killed that man! But I know that it was not him," I said vehemently, pointing at Raleigh. "We just walked inside and had one shot, then a woman screamed, saying a man was dead."

"Well, there you have it!" Raleigh smirked.

"What does he know? He's a fucking peasant," the hog said, staring down at me in disgust.

"You know, I think you have disrespected the patrons here enough for one evening. You may leave!" Raleigh said smileless, reaching a hand to the hilt of his blade.

"We all know you murder people, Raleigh, and by tomorrow night we also know that this decrepit cave you call a tavern will be property of the chieftain. So you can have your little laugh tonight, but all the laughing in the world will never bring your little girl back." The hog grinned viciously just before spinning on the heel of his boots. "Get this mess cleaned up by the morning, or be executed!" he laughed, stepping out of the swinging doors, followed by his two silent associates.

As the last of the hogs mounted their destriers and disappeared down the cobblestoned street, Raleigh turned to me.

"You impressed me, outsider,"." he said admirably.

"Why did you kill that man?" I drawled.

He turned to the silent crowd, fire blazing in his eyes.

"Get out!" he bellowed. "All of you useless cowards."

As the crowd dispersed, the only folks left inside were the three burly warriors hoisting the leaking body toward the back, two women fixing the decor of grape vineyards, Raleigh, and myself.

"The man betrayed me," he said grimly. "He had to die. But you, my friend, you deserve an honorable welcome to Deceptia." He fingered toward Elena, and she walked over with two flagons of wine. "You take these as a token of my gratitude for what you did tonight, outsider!"

Elena placed a tray down before holding two golden flagons.

"Is this wine?" I asked in disbelief.

"As you requested. And these," he said, pointing at the glimmering flagon, "solid gold, worth about as much as a small army."

"What is your story?" I said, staring in awe at the gold flagons before me. "Who are you, Raleigh?"

"I am just a businessman nova, with a very boring story behind me, nothing at all to be boastful of!" he said coolly.

"That hog said he knew you were a murderer. Healso said this tavern will be property of the king by tomorrow night. Sounds to me like you have a very exciting story behind you," I urged.

"Hog?" He laughed "Is that what they call them where you're from?"

"Uh, yeah, an old friend called them hogs. I guess it stuck with me," I said glumly.

"Grab a glass, friend. You want to hear something that might be of interest?" he said, lifting a flagon from the tray and helping himself to a drink. I reached for the glass and filled it nearly to overflow.

"Three days ago, my daughter was killed," he said with a painful grin. My heart sank. "The man I killed tonight was reporting my whereabouts to the chieftain. Reporting to him my dealings and the locations of my safe houses scattered throughout the village." He looked down at the empty glass and sighed. "They killed my little girl."

In a moment, the room darkened, silence came and passed.

"Tomorrow night..." he said fervently, "I have a job to do. In fact, I was thinking you might be of some assistance."

"Assistance in what way?" I squinted.

"Ever use a crossbow?" He smirked.

At that moment, a massive figure burst through the swinging doors, turning everyone's attention to the front of the tavern. His face was shadowed behind the flickering flames of the lit torches, and in his right hand was the long sword of darkness. In a blurring wave, Raleigh whizzed pass me toward the center of the tavern, sword drawn and ready for combat.

"Who goes there?" Raleigh blared.

"Death!" a familiar voice conveyed from within the shadows.

A burly warrior leaped out onto the shadowed man, only to get his arm yanked back so rough that it flung his face into the ground and shattered his front teeth.

"He wasn't important anyway." Raleigh shrugged "I am the important one in here, death. Come for me!" he taunted, tightening the grip on his longsword.

The man stepped quickly from out of the shadows and lifted his sword for the attack. Oh shit! I thought, leaping from the stool and rushing toward the action.

"Tiberius!!!" I bellowed, but it was too late. His black sword came crashing down over Raleigh's longsword. The impact was as if lightning struck inside the tavern.

"Tiberius!!!" I shouted and caught his attention in-between thrusts. He stopped and stared at Raleigh. Raleigh stared back, grinning stupidly in the face of death.

"Is this your friend, nova?" he said, eying Tiberius. "He seems upset!"

"Tiberius, let's have a drink and relax, brother. He is good!" I said, forcibly calm.

"Let us have a drink? Relax?" Tiberius said. "Oh, yes, let's! Because this fucker now knows both of our names!" he barked.

"This fucker was also offering your brother here some work, a three man job!" said Raleigh.

"Not interested!" Tiberius snapped, catching my eye and nodding toward the wine. "Grab two this time, and let's move!"

"I am sorry about that, Raleigh," I said. "My brother is very cautious with new people."

I took the golden flagons hesitantly into my hands and turned to hurry toward the swinging doors.

"The job is one hundred gold pieces...each!" Raleigh said distantly. Both Tiberius and I halted in mid-stride.

"One hundred gold pieces for each of us?" I said, turning back.

Raleigh nodded as a wide grin stretched his cheeks sideways and Tiberius emerged from beside me.

"And how do we know if we complete this job, you won't just stiff us on the coin?" Tiberius said sternly, but intrigued at the offer.

Raleigh pulled out an overflowing boiled leather coin purse and tossed it on the floor before our feet. "100 pieces now, 100 upon completion!" he said jovially.

"So what is this job, Raleigh?" I said "What are we going to do?"

"Well, gentlemen," he began with a devilish grin, "tomorrow night we are going to kill the chief..."

CHAPTER FOUR
Memorie IV

Casanova Gallimorian
"Change of plans, gentlemen!"
Village of Deceptia, 1869

"Bring it down lower and more to the left..." Raleigh instructed from beside me. "Precisely. Okay, pull the trigger." I clenched my finger back tight and released. The arrow went whizzing through the air and hit the target square in the center - only it was not the right target; it was red.

"Shit!" I snapped, lifting the lever on the crossbow and reaching for another arrow.

"It will take more than a few attempts to get it, nova, don't worry!" he assured. "Just remember, blue target is the chief" I nodded, slid the arrow in the groove, and adjusted its lever back.

We were looking down over an open pasture from the roof of Raleigh's massive estate. The pasture was teeming with dozens of targets, all of them red, except for one. The blue target was mine, but for some reason my aim was either falling much too short or well past its mark. It was nearly noon, I had been at this for hours, and the closest I got to hitting the blue was when I slipped on a patch of hay and triggered the arrow into the sky. I didn't see the purpose for doing this on a roof, and not on ground level, where I could actually aim straight and not at a weird downward angle - but for the amount of coin at stake, he could have told me to aim through a stone wall for the rest of the day, and I would do it.

"I shall return from town shortly. I have to scout the area for tonight," Raleigh said coolly. "Wine is in the cellar if you need it." He winked and was gone. The sun shone brilliantly overhead, its rays illuminating the beautiful scenery before me. I closed one eye over the crossbow and aimed downward toward the blue target. I slowed my breathing down until I could feel the heart beat in my fingertips. 1, 2, 3, pull! The arrow went whizzing boldly through the air once more and...red. I had enough of this, I thought, snapping to my feet in frustration. I steadied myself on the roof and slowly climbed back in through the window.

Inside the vast chamber was a massive bed lined with sheets and pillows of black silk. White laced curtains covered the windows, a mirror that stood from floor to ceiling, and a shelf was filled the entire wall with hundreds, maybe thousands of books. Stepping in through the chamber and out into the corridor, the luxury only continued. Golden fixtures laminated the red walled fortress as I touched everything I passed. How could a man so young have all of this to himself? I thought as I reached the top of a spiraling stairwell and descended.

White marble touched my boots as I meandered through decadence. Some of the most exquisite pieces of art lined the walls. Paintings of giants and barbarians fighting together in battle, a lavish dance party attended by only the finest of elite, and another showed the face of a woman. She was a very beautiful woman, with salt and pepper hair. She had the eyes of a seductress. In fact, her face was fashioned on half a dozen paintings lining the wall toward the cellar. Must be his mother, or maybe his wife, I thought as I reached the cellar and grabbed the first spirit I saw. ELEGANCE was engraved in bold letters on the side of the bottle, and the liquid inside was dark as tar.

    A heavy thud caught my attention, followed by another a moment later. I snatched a chalice from the ledge, walked back down the wide corridor, and turned into a warrior's dream. Weapons lined the walls of this immense chamber in perfect order by size and make. Longswords and short, half blades and full, all lined the left wall. Hammers, axes, crossbows and pikes lined the right. In the center, there were targets just as they were in the pasture, only these were dyed black. Just beyond the targets in the back was Tiberius swinging a mighty war hammer right through the body of a target, thrashing it out of its foundation. Hay burst through the dyed sack and scattered sloppily over the ground.

    "I see you found a new toy," I said, weaving slowly through targets toward the back.

    "My grandfather showed me how to use this!" he said, examining the war hammer with reverence. The hammer was iron and stone, wooden at the hilt, and strong, with illegible etchings going down the side. "He would be disgusted with me right now!"

"He taught you because he knew you would always make the right decision," I assured.

"And am I doing that now?" he snapped, "in the house of this grinning lunatic, preparing to risk my life to help him, all for the sake of a few coin? I did not become the soldier he trained me to be. I became a damn sell-sword."

"Your grandfather did not train you to become a soldier," I retorted, "a mindless minion following the orders of even bigger and more vicious lunatics who happen to be kings. For the same reason Arkon did not teach me to be a mage, to practice dark sorcery at the expense of my own people. These men taught us how to think, my brother!"

Tiberius stood silent for a while as memories sank in.

"Tonight shall either be the beginning of the rest of a very long prominent life, or it shall be the end of our misery. Either way, I am ready!" I said fervently.

"You are ready to die, at eighteen?" Tiberius edged. "Without a clue of what life has to offer?"

I looked down at my shabby tunic and baggy britches, my frayed boots and hands riddled with black smudge, and sighed.

"I have been dying my whole life, Tiberius. I think now I am finally ready to risk it all, even if I am wrong."

A silent moment passed as he just stared, his eyes stony and unreadable. I looked down at his outstretched hand and grasped it firmly. "Then you shall have my sword, brother," he said firmly.

An echoing crash sounded from down the main corridor, jolting us both to attention. Heavy boots came charging down the corridor as Tiberius readied his war hammer and I unhooked the hilt of my blade. Raleigh came bursting into the weapon room breathlessly carrying two heavy satchels.

"Change of plans, gentlemen," he said, "we have to do this now!"

Tiberius Blackwell
"Breathe, brother, just breathe!"
Village of Deceptia, 1896

"Do you have any idea how much thought needs to be put into this?" I entreated. "We cannot just walk into the barracks, kill the chief and escape without being seen. We don't even know the layout"

"Relax, big guy," Raleigh said, unrolling a scroll of parchment. "All your questions shall be answered with this."

He flattened the map out on a work bench beside the arsenal and pointed to the large mass in the center. "This here is the main barracks. In exactly one hour from now, the chieftain will exit the gates from the east, accompanied by a small militia, five, six soldiers tops. Nova, you will enter the blacksmith located at the northeast corner of the gate. You will walk inside and look at the blacksmith, but you will say nothing. He will then escort you to the back where you will have access to the roof. You will climb to the roof and position yourself in the far left corner, leaving you in perfect view and range of the front gates," he said in one long breath.

"Got it!" Cas said, nodding his approval.

"How do you know this blacksmith?" I said.

"He is a silent partner in my endeavors outside of the tavern, and he owes me a favor...a big favor," he said.

"OK, good. Big guy, you and me are on ground level here," he said, pointing to the lower east side of the barracks. "Our job is to wait for the kill, then divert attention from the blacksmith to here." He pointed to an area called Raging Valley.

"Divert them how?" I snapped.

"With a little thing I like to call, catch me if you can." He grinned.

"And once we reach this Raging Valley?" I asked.

"Well, then you will showcase that blacksword you got there and pray to the gods we come out alive. Destriers," Raleigh quipped.

"That's fuckin' suicide!" I blared angrily.

"Only if we're killed," he retorted.

"How about if I kill you right now and save us all the trouble!" I barked, stepping forward.

"I'm already dead," Raleigh said, unsheathing two short blades, "three days ago when I buried my daughter, and six years ago when I buried my grandmother."

My heart sank slightly, but I held the same demeanor. I knew what it felt like to lose someone so close to you; it ached. You start off attempting to be the brave knight, and then you become something else entirely. You become the one thing you train day and night to never become: a murderer. I glanced toward Cas, then back to this man before me.

"You didn't know," Raleigh said in disbelief, and then turned to Cas, "because you didn't tell him."

"I felt it was private," said Cas demurely.

"It is...you did right by me!" Raleigh said, nodding in approval. "Sheathe your blades," I said. "I should not have said that in your home."

"I've heard worse." Raleigh smirked, sheathing his blades. "But let's see what you do on the battlefield," he quipped.

I stared intently at the man for a brief moment. "You won't be able to see death when it comes for you." I smirked back.

"Nova, I'm starting to like your brother," he said while eying me. "Reminds me of myself."

"Are we going to stand here and banter or go kill the fucking chieftain?" Cas blared from beside the two of us.

"Right," Raleigh said, turning anxiously towards the sacks on the ground. "Nova, grab this satchel, and both of you change your clothes. I will meet you in the carriage. Oh, and big guy, you might want to lose the blacksword. It will draw us more attention than we need," he said and raced into the corridor.

"You didn't tell me his daughter died?" I said, lifting the heavy satchel and removing... a chain mail breastplate with the polished blue embroidery of a rood, a velvet blue cloak, a shining gray helm, chained leggings, and war boots.

"He wants you to dress like a hog?" Cas laughed, holding up a crisp black hooded tunic, boiled leather gauntlets, dinged grey britches, a crossbow, and one arrow.

"Son of a bitch!" I muttered and slipped into the rattling mail suit of armor.

We were racing down a congested road. Shepherds and herdsman cleared the street as our carriage sped noisily toward the high walled fortress in the distance.

"You have your crossbow, right Nova?" Raleigh said, holding his eyes on the road.

"Of course I do, but again, I don't think I'm equipped to handle..." Cas started but was quickly cut off.

"Good! Do you remember how you were aiming for the blue, but all morning you kept hitting the red targets?" Raleigh said.

"Yes," Cas breathed. "I remember."

"Well, change of plans, because the chieftain is the one wearing red." He grinned.

"You damn liar!" Cas smirked.

"I've been called worse," Raleigh quipped "Besides, if I told you to hit the red, that is when you would have hit the blue. Funny how the mind works, huh!" he winked.

"I'm sorry, I missed the humor in that," Cas said in jest.

"On a serious note, gentlemen, I want to thank you for helping me with this," Raleigh said, his eyes burning the road before him. "Any man who would risk their life for a murderer like me is a man of honor."

"We all have our flaws," Cas said, catching eyes with the man. "That does not mean you deserved what happened to your daughter."

"We both have lost ones we hold dear," I said, "and the only thing that can even partially heal that wound is vengeance!"

Raleigh pulled the carriage over to the side of the street and turned to the two of us.

"You guys remember the plan, and under absolutely no circumstances are you allowed to die on me," he said with fiery eyes. "There it is, Nova. Remember, not a word to the blacksmith, and only the man wearing the red cloak!"

"Make the kill and get out of there, see me?" I snapped.

Cas nodded, reaching down for his crossbow.

"Where are all the arrows?" he said, confused.

"You only have one chance, make it count!" Raleigh said. Cas sighed and leaped out of the carriage as Raleigh turned to me with flame-filled eyes.

"Now, about that vengeance you spoke of." His eyes darted toward the street, his grey helm gleaming in the sunlight. "In precisely ten seconds, a two man foot patrol will pass and service the blacksmith. They are on the inside, so your brother will be protected. As for you and I, we are on our own. Follow my lead, and the signal to engage are the words 'Well, there you have it!'" I nodded as two dark men carrying pikes approached the entrance to the blacksmith.

"Good, here we go!" said Raleigh as a brigade of seven men marched past the carriage, one of them wearing a fluttering red cloak, the rest clad in blue. Raleigh leaped from the carriage, his chain mail rattling wildly as he landed. I followed closely behind. Weaving through the thick crowd, we found a curved path to the brigade without being noticed. Approaching their left flank, Raleigh drew his sword, as did I, and all went silent in my head.

Fiery words were exchanged between Raleigh and the chieftain. The crowd slowly dispersed as my eyes searched each waist and blade hold; they were fully armed. Two scrawny, three medium build, and the last was heavily muscled. This should be interesting, I thought.

"But you sent the order!" Raleigh blared from beside me. "It was you, and I want to hear you say it!" He raised his sword as the six soldiers reached for their waists.

"And what?" The chieftain smirked in a voice much deeper than I had expected. "You will attempt to avenge her death here? With these odds, you shall be a martyr in moments," he quipped.

"That is where you are wrong, you blood sucking, disloyal, son of a bit..." Raleigh drawled but was cut short. The chieftain's head lurched back wildly as he fell sloppily to the ground. The soldiers drew their weapons as two knelt down to see the already dead chieftain lying in the dirt, with an arrow lodged through the front of his head.

"Well, there you fuckin' have it," Raleigh said back, stepping quickly as the soldiers lunged towards us. He turned, and ran as I kept close on his trail. Winding through herdsman and cattle, we turned right down into a deserted alley and cut across the market. Running along shadowed edges, we avoided a milk man's cart by a hair length. The soldiers behind us were heard but not seen. We ran and ran until I exhausted myself completely, and then ran further.

Approaching the last road before the grasslands leading to the valley, Raleigh slowed and rested his hand on a massive boulder as he panted breathlessly.

"Catch.. Your.. Breath, fast!" he said, barely understandable. I rested in the grass, armor clanking loudly as it hit dirt. Seconds later, a charge was heard and four destriers approached, then six, then nine. The brigade rattled the ground as it thundered towards us, and there was no time to run, nowhere to hide.

"Get to your feet, big guy, it's war time," Raleigh said, reaching a hand to help the lift. Standing solidly, we watched as the brigade encircled us entirely.

"Well, well..." the soldier started until I lunged forward and jabbed my blade in through his shoulder until it cut bone. He fell to the ground screaming. Weaving beneath the reach of the other horsemen, I hammered into one of the destriers, knocking myself nearly unconscious on the side of the beast. A heavy ringing sprang out on the side of my head, a warm rush spewed down the side of my neck down into my armor. I ducked beneath a blow and struck, catching a soldier in the stomach with the tip of the blade, but the puncture was caught by mail. I was swarmed, blue cloaks toppled over me, sending strikes down from overhead. I parried a blow, struck for the face of a soldier, and missed. I paid for it with a hilt to the face, but my helm secured my nose from being shattered.

    A soldier was yanked back violently, only to be replaced by two more. I lifted one by the knees and slammed him into the dirt. Unsheathing the blade concealed on my inner thigh, I jabbed it deep into the throat of another. I was finally able to catch a breath as I got to my feet, only to see Raleigh in a struggle with four soldiers carrying pikes and morning stars. I blindsided one with a slice to the throat from behind and ducked beneath the next blow heading for my helm. Then an agonizing scream demanded the attention from all those in battle; it was Raleigh. The tip of a pike was plunged into his shoulder, and he was falling to his knees.

    I thrust forward pas Raleigh and slashed viciously at the head of the soldier. The impact of the blade sparked his helm, he was dead before he hit the ground. Two young soldiers stood nervously before me, with both heart and lunacy. The one to my left lunged wildly toward me, only to be easily parried and tossed heavily to the ground. The other stood his ground and eased toward me with an unsteady stride. I leaned left, then spun wildly to the right and struck; the side of his neck ripped open.

I rushed over and knelt beside Raleigh.

"Breathe, brother, just breathe!" I said, lifting his head and keeping him conscious. The feeling of this was all too familiar. "Breathe, you with me?"

"Yeah, I'm with you," Raleigh smirked painfully. "Looks like you proved yourself on the field today." He winced.

"Likewise...I didn't know such a scrawny man could move like that," I quipped.

"Well, if I moved that well, I would've dodged this bloody thing!" He winced, staring at the metal edge gaping out of his shoulder. "Your gold is in the carriage...beneath the -" Raleigh said but was cut short.

"Worry about that later. For now, we have to get this thing out!" I said, elevating his back in my arms.

"Smooth tip pike, a strong tug, and I can bleed out in seconds," Raleigh said. "Take your cloak and keep it ready, jerk the pike out, and wrap the wound immediately."

I reached for the long hilt and readied the cloak. In one swift jolt, I pulled the pike out, blood burst and spewed through the surface instantly as Raleigh screamed bloody murder. I quickly wrapped the cloak under his arm and over his shoulder for as many times as it would take and tightened the end.

"Okay, get to your feet, we have to move!" I said, lifting him gently by his unimpaired arm.

"I have a safe house just down that road, that is where your brother will meet us," Raleigh said as I wrapped his arm around my neck and trudged toward the dirt road.

"Keep pressure on it!" a woman said from the corridor as she hastened to fetch a warm cloth and bandages.

"This looks bad," Cas said hopelessly. "How many hogs?"

"Nine," I said, pressing firmly on the wound as blood spewed heavily from beneath his arm, forming a pool of deep red.

"Nine?" she repeated. "Thank the gods you both are alive."

"No, thank the big guy," Raleigh said weakly. "Without him, I would have been done for." He coughed, exposing a red grin. "Good work today, Nova. Was that your first kill?"

Cas nodded despondently as the woman returned with a bowl of warm water and a white cloth.

"Elena, how bad does it look?" Cas said as she knelt down beside me, touched the hand I had been pressing the wound with, and stared deeply at Raleigh.

"You a very brave man, Mr. Bines," she said, unwrapping the cloak, "but a fool nonetheless!"

"I-I've been called worse," Raleigh coughed out as blood dribbled from his lip and rested on his chin.

The woman's eyes touched the wound for a moment and then quickly covered it. She turned her gaze to Cas' anxious stare, then mine, and shook her head.

"I am afraid," she started as tears welled in her eyes. "He will not make it past the night!"

"There must be a remedy or a potion to help him," Cas said quickly. "Even a spell, my master had a perfect spell for wounds such as this."

"I am no mage, honey, and magic is prohibited in this village," she retorted. "Candonia would be our best hope, but the travel there is no less than five days by ship."

"So we start now!" Cas urged. "I will not sit here and watch this man die in front of me, without at least attempting something!"

"Hey, Nova," Raleigh said weakly, squeezing my arm in anguish, "every man must face this moment in his life, and I've prayed every night that my last day would end just like this, bleeding out from battle, surrounded by a whore and two killers." He laughed. I had no choice but to laugh with the man; he was clearly mad.

"Elena," Raleigh said, "give them their coin, and then leave us."

"As you wish." She nodded obediently, handed each of us a sack of gold, then disappeared into the corridor.

"Dashing little fox, isn't she?" Raleigh smirked, staring at her body as she swayed out of sight.

"I do not see how sitting here will help you live," Cas said sternly.

"She lied, Nova... Candonia is only three days from here by ship." said Raleigh hopelessly, "but I will be dead by the morning, no way around it. Make a wrong move, and pay the price with your life. I know the game of swords."

"A very perilous game," I said without thinking.

"But we are all missing the key element that would make us invincible in that game," Cas said as Raleigh and I stared with intrigue. "...Immortality!"

"Immortality is a gift and a curse!" Raleigh said.

"True, a father may not want to outlive his child, but a warrior would surely want to outlive his opponent!" Cas said truthfully.

"True indeed," Raleigh said in defeat. A long silence prevailed before Raleigh spoke again.

"I once met a man who was said to be immortal," he began, "and he sure looked it, green scaly skin covered his whole body, tallest man I ever seen. He told me that true power lies not with the man in search of strength, but with the man in search of truth!"

"And what is truth?" I inquired derisively.

"Truth is, I had my whole life to search for it but never did. It's not until a person is lying on their death bed that they appreciate all that life has to offer," said Raleigh expressively.

"You should have been a poet," I quipped.

"I should have been many things," he grinned, "but the reality is, big guy, after all I have done, I deserved a beautiful death like this. Now all I want to do is die with a smile on my face. Look in the cupboard and hand me the tall black bottle."

Cas stood and did as the man said, handing each of us a goblet.

"Salute to the gods," Raleigh said, lifting his drink in the air and gulping the entire thing down. "By the morning," he started, "I shall pass into the spirit realm. But before I leave here, I want you two to make me a promise."

"And what promise is that?" Cas said eagerly.

"Promise me that you will find the immortal named Dimitrius and tell him... tell him I am sorry!" Raleigh said mournfully. "He will know what I mean."

"Where can we find this man?" Cas said quickly as Raleigh guzzled down the last of his wine.

"There is a cave." Raleigh winced achingly. Pausing slightly, he reached trembling fingers up to his shoulder in agony and removed a bloody hand.

"We have to reinforce the cloak," I said with haste, reaching for the wet cloth and dabbing away clumps of blood as it oozed relentlessly from the wound. Cas yanked down the silk curtains covering the window and handed them to me. I wrapped the wound as tight as he could bear and held it in place to knot it. His head was nodding painfully back and forth, and it soon became clearly evident. Raleigh was going to die, and the sad thing about it is that I actually was starting to respect the little fucker.

And just like that, he was gone. He might have been passed out from shock, or the pain, or even a combination of the two, but in my experience, he was already gone. I glanced at

Cas, who was staring down at Raleigh, sullen from grief. I rested Raleigh's head on the silk pillow and propped his back up onto the bed. His skin was dry and pasty, and his wound was reeking, beyond any ordinary healer's ability. Death was in the air, its stench so thick I could taste its darkness as it drifted. I lifted the satchel that was rested on the stand beside me as coins clanked and jingled inside of it.

"Where are you going?" Cas said distantly.

"For a walk" I snapped from the corridor. I couldn't take being in that chamber for another moment, and judging by the way this trek was going so far, it seemed death was very adamant on making its presence known, and feared.

The sun peeked anxiously over the mountainous region embodying the horizon. As far east as the eye would reach were trees and grassland, and wilderness. I was outside, lying beside a cabin in-between a bed of hay and a sickle. I must have fallen in my sleep, I thought lazily but then retracted. The side of my neck was throbbing. Pain shot down the right side of my back and up the side of my head as I attempted to reach my feet... and failed. My hands slipped, and I landed in some kind of oozing liquid, a red liquid; it was blood. Blood ran down the inside of my suit and formed a pool in the dirt

"Raleigh?" I said. The man stared blankly through the looking glass at a wound that was no longer visible. Blood stains covered his back and arms, decorated the ground with carnage, but he was alive.

"I saw her," he said, disoriented. "I watched her heal me."

"A woman? What is her name?" I asked.

"I don't know the woman. She had icy blue eyes, and she smelled like... like peaches," he said in awed astonishment, "the most beautiful woman I ever seen." He lifted the arm that had previously been scarred irreparably, but was now fully healed. It were as if I had not been a testament to a pike being jabbed through his shoulder just the day before.

"How did this woman heal you?" I said in disbelief.

"She held th-this blue flame to the wound, it gave off a cool, soothing sensation.

I was watching her work on me," Raleigh said with reverence.

I stared at the man quizzically, unsure how to take in what he was implying. The sheer notion of a healer appearing in the middle of the night and being able to bring him from death's door to complete restoration was absurd. And yet there I stood, speechless, staring stupidly at a man I had just pronounced dead the night before.

"This is impossible," I drawled reluctantly. But then I thought of the oakwood, the black hooded horsemen, my father. It seemed now that nothing was out of the norm.

"Raleigh?" a voice said from behind me it was Casanova. "H-how did you... why are you ali..." He was completely bewildered.

"I have to find her," Raleigh said distantly. "She healed me, and I have to find her."

"Find who?" Cas said.

"The woman with eyes of ice," Raleigh repeated, staring down at his bare chest.

"A woman... with eyes of ice?" Cas repeated with an incredulous eye towards me. Raleigh's eyes burned as he turned to face the two of us for the first time. Beside the blood and dirt stains that blotched over his face, neck, and almost his entire body, the man was fully healed. Not even the remnant of the scar was seen.

"Cilan!" he said.

"Cilan?" I said, anxious to find a method to his madness. "Who is that, the woman who healed you?"

"No," Raleigh said, snapping out of his trance. "Cilan is where you will find Dimitrius... and where I will find the woman who saved me!"

"And you are well enough to guide us there?" Cas referred to skeptically.

Raleigh stared blankly at Cas for a long moment before finally nodding his head. "I know the roads ahead like I know my last name," he said calmly. "So off we go, then!" Cas said excitingly.

"Wait," I snapped, "we have to find our way to the Hills of Forbidden Truth." I turned to Cas expressively. "We have business that needs to be done!"

"You expect to just stroll into the hills of Forbidden Truth, with no retinue?" Raleigh grinned. "You will be laughed at and escorted to the red lands."

"The red lands?" Cas said naively.

"And how will we attain this retinue?" I edged.

"Dimitrius is the answer, big guy," Raleigh said smileless. "And now that I have another chance at life, I want to do things the right way." He lifted his arm and rotated it once more, as if it were not attached to his own body.

"You have visited these hills before?" I asked, intrigued.

"I sure have." He nodded coolly. "And I was deemed unworthy."

"How do you become worthy of visiting the hills?" Cas said.

Raleigh stared intently at Cas for a moment before he sighed.

"He said that I was not teachable," Raleigh confessed. "That I was self-absorbed and only interested in vengeance, not justice."

"Dimitrius told you this?" I said, bemused.

"Not Dimitrius," Raleigh said reflectively, "the white haired bastard, Sinistro. He said that my life would get taken before its time because of my arrogance," he said, looking down at his right hand and testing its dexterity. "Guess I showed that fucker!"

"Well, if Dimitrius is the man we must impress to get into the hills, then that is what we shall do!" I said confidently. "How many days' ride?"

"Ride?" Raleigh sneered. "I'm afraid there is no wonderful carriage ride ahead for us for us this time. We must travel by ship!"

"By ship?" Cas grinned.

"Yeah, well... I hate to be bearer of poisoned soup, but there shall be nothing wondrous of this voyage ahead," Raleigh said sullenly. "Everything we encounter going forward is a test of will, a test of eligibility. And this time around, I will pass that test!" he said, eying the dark reflection staring back at him through the looking glass; only death stared back.

CHAPTER FIVE
Memorie V

Casanova Gallimorian
"A gift and a curse, huh?"
North Deceptia, 1869

"Careful... pull yourself up!" Raleigh shouted to me from down below. I was staring up at the lip of a massive ship, Joaquin S.S.R. was written on the side of it in bold blacks letters, and its anchor wedged deep down beneath the docks of Deceptia. The sounds of waves splashing and heavy footsteps sounded from beneath. Wooden crates were being carried up to the main deck of the ship and stacked one on top the other. And there I was, hanging from the side of the ship by my fingertips, with a bead of sweat trickling down my forehead onto my nose. I gathered up my strength and thrust myself up, caught hold of the barrel of a cannon, and wedged my way in through the narrow crevice leading to the womb of the vessel.

Inside the dark, dreary nook was a dozen or so cannonballs, a stack of wood, and two clay jugs filled with water. I turned back to see the sun shining brilliantly in through the crevice, yet the air was dark and chilled, giving off a dank, stale odor. Moments later, Raleigh climbed inside, followed by Tiberius, who had to force his massive frame in through the small opening.

"Those are mercenaries out there!" Tiberius cautioned breathlessly. "They aren't mercenaries, big guy..." Raleigh said dimly, peering out toward the sound of crates being stacked. "They are pirates!"

"Pirates?" I said surprisingly. "This far north?"

"It appears so," Raleigh said, shaking his head.

"We must get off the ship," Tiberius said quickly as the blast of a horn blared out from above us on the main deck, followed by heavy footsteps and cheers. "Unfortunately, that chance has already passed," Raleigh said ruefully. "We will be seen and transported to the bottom of the sea."

"So what shall we do?" Tiberius retorted. "Who is to say this ship won't be set out on a five-year voyage?"

"I am certainly not one to say," Raleigh confessed, "but at the moment my only plan is to survive until we reach the first island."

"And what of Cilan?" I said. "How are we to reach our journey's end if we are trapped in here?"

"We charge the door," Raleigh said confidently, "kill any man we see, and maybe have a few laughs while we're at it."

He reached down into the fold of his tunic and pulled out a black wooden brier. Sprinkling a bizarre smelling herb inside of it, he grabbed a handful of matches from beside the cannonballs.

"That does not sound like you're trying to survive; sounds like another suicide mission," Tiberius said coolly..

"You know, I think you should try this, big guy," Raleigh said, handing him the dark pipe. "It will take a bit of the edge off."

"I am not on edge, just cautious," Tiberius replied, staring out at the onrush.

"Then this shall be a very long, thoughtful voyage for you, my friend," Raleigh said as he took a match to his pipe and inhaled deep.

The sound of a horn blared three times as I walked toward the cannon, turtling my head through the narrow passageway. Down on the docks, ropes were being unwound and the ramp was no longer seen. Heavy boot steps thundered overhead as the pirates cheered harmoniously and broke out in song. We had set sail, and aside from being trapped inside the shadowy nook of a pirate ship, I felt for the first time in my life like I was truly free.

When I opened my eyes, the moon was the only form of light shimmering in through the dreary nook. In the corner beside the clay jugs is where Tiberius slept, his head lying back against a wooden plank mouth gaping savagely, and his right hand clutching the hilt of his sword. Raleigh was wedged awkwardly beside a bed of cannonballs and the barrier separating two wooden planks. Nostalgia settled in as the ship lurched over waves, and thoughts of immortality haunted my perception.

A gift and a curse, huh? I thought, glancing over at Raleigh. Perhaps at a time I would think so as well. To be alive for an eternity is a blessing bestowed only to the gods, and if Dimitrius were truly immortal, then he is a man I was destined to meet.

I pushed myself up to my feet, stepped over Raleigh, and shouldered my way to the front of the cannon. Staring out at the calmness of the water, my stomach churned and nausea settled in, but the brisk ocean air kept me at ease. I reached into the side fold of my doublet and pulled out the last of the dry tarts Raleigh gave us before the voyage. Biting into the crisp tart, a light rapping sounded from beneath the cannon. I stopped munching and listened once more, only to hear another light rapping and a scraping noise.

Bloody rats! I thought, finishing off the rest of my tart. Looking down, beside the cannon a broken plank stood atop rotten hinged bolts. I knelt down to secure the wood in place and...

"Anyone there?" a voice whispered from beneath the floor. "Hello?"

I reached down apprehensively, but then lifted the broken plank. The dark eyes of a pale lad showed through the opening, with light dirt smudged hair and a gleaming rotten toothed grin.

"Hi there, mate. A bit boring down here, isn't it?" the lad said.

"How did you get down there?" I asked, perplexed.

"I am traveling to Candonia," he said quickly, "in search of a cave in which I may find a treasure. Are you going to Candonia as well?"

"I'm afraid not, fellow," I said. "How old are you?"

"Fifteen..." he said, "but I must learn quickly if I am to sail across the seas in a pirate ship of my own one day."

"I have no doubt you will, young sir!" I said. "But truth be told, I am no pirate, just a man foolish enough to desire immortality."

"Really?" he said excitedly. "I want to live forever, too, that is not foolish!"

"I'm glad you don't think so." I grinned. "Tell me, what is your name?"

"Christian" the lad said happily. The innocence of his jovial nature made me think back not many years ago, to when I had not a worry in the world, and not a single obligation to my people.

"And what is your family name?" I inquired.

"It's just Christian," he said. "I do not know my family name, only what they call me."

"Well, that is certainly a good start for the captain of a pirate ship." I grinned. "Your anonymity shall prove to be a life saver in the years henceforth."

"And what is your name, friend?" said Christian.

"My name is Casanova," I said.

"Are you from Deceptia, Casanova?" he said with reverence.

"No, I am Partrizian!" I said confidently. "You are not from these parts here, are you?"

"No," he said sheepishly.

"Don't worry, your secret is safe with me." I winked.

The sudden sound of heavy strides and distant voices brought my attention to the entrance of the nook. I looked over to Tiberius, who was still fast asleep, as well as Raleigh. Panic rose in my chest as I attempted to stay as undetectable as I could. The boot steps stopped abruptly at the top of the corridor, and the sound of a door being flung open was heard, then slammed shut. Seconds later, another door was flung open and then slammed shut. Someone was checking for stowaways, I thought nervously, and that someone was approaching our hiding spot very quickly.

"Find a place to hide, Christian," I whispered fiercely. "I will come for you!"

As the lad nodded obediently, I couldn't help thinking of the kid as a little brother, probably how Tiberius viewed me. Of all the villainous characters I've met in my day, it would feel good to help a lad whose only crime was an undying thirst for adventure. As the footsteps neared, I nudged Tiberius' leg aggressively until we caught eyes. With a finger over my lips, I pointed to the entrance and he immediately unsheathed his short blade.

"We have to get out of here," I said in scarcely a whisper.

"No time," he muttered promptly. "Grab hold that plank and lift yourself over the entrance. When it opens, I will distract him while you execute."

The footsteps stopped right outside of our entrance, and I barely got my legs up and over the doorway before it flung open. At that moment, I realized that my dagger was lying on the floor next to Raleigh's leg, completely unreachable.

"Come out and show yourselves, you little bastards!" the man said in a rumbling voice. Silence filled the nook, and I wondered where Tiberius could have been for the man to not yet have seen him, or Raleigh.

A thick, stocky man walked slowly inside the nook as I turned my neck in a valiant effort to see his face. He was clad in a vest of boiled leather and padded sheepskin britches, a black handkerchief covered a head full of dingy unkempt hair, and the man was about as pale as a sheet of parchment.

"I told you the voices weren't from this galley!" an accented voice said from the corridor. "It was the one beneath this bay."

"I heard what you said, Caslon!" the man thundered from inside the nook. "But there is no room for error. The captain expects a thorough search, and that is what we shall do."

The distant accents of the two were almost indistinguishable as they receded down the corridor. I turned and swung down the wooden plank and landed lightly on the back of the cannon. Rushing past Tiberius, who was confused at my movement, I knelt down and removed the wooden piece.

"Christian..." I whispered loudly but heard nothing. "Christian!" A shuffling of garments sounded from behind me on the far side of the cannon just before three cannonballs crashed down and rolled thunderously across the wooden floor.

"That was a bad idea," Raleigh said distantly, struggling sleepily to his feet. "What are you two staring at?"

"Cas, who the hell is Christian?" Tiberius said. "No one is down there!"

"He is a young lad, I just met him!" I said, staring down through the gape in the floor. "We have to help him!"

"Help him?" Tiberius said. "You mean go out there and risk our lives to save a lad you just met through the floor?"

"Yes, risk our lives," I said, grabbing the fallen dagger from the floor, "as we have always done for those who could not fend for themselves."

"I don't know if you noticed," Tiberius said sternly, "but we are not in Partrizia anymore. Many lives shall be lost throughout the remainder of our travels, and it is my duty to ensure that those lives are not ours."

The quiet voice in my mind said that he was right, we should not risk our lives for a lad I had just met. But in my chest, I just knew that this was something I must do, even if I were to do it alone.

"For the record," Raleigh said, "I am in total agreeance with the big guy. But then again, I do owe you that favor, Nova, so you will have my sword if it is needed." I nodded and glanced up to Tiberius, who was staring back intently.

"And you, brother," I said. "Will I have your sword as well?" Tiberius stared blankly for a moment before he lifted the hilt of his sword to his chest.

"You will always have my sword, brother!" he said.

"Good, then," I said, sheathing the blade, "let's go save this lad!"

Charging down the moonlit corridor, we searched for a stairwell leading down to the under galley but found none. Only the steps before us, leading up to the main deck, guarded by three pirates. We stalked back silently as we made our way down the passageway. The sound of deep voices and laughter sounded from behind us as we stepped across the creaking, decayed wooden floor.

Down at the far end of the pathway was the stairwell we had been searching for. I hastened quickly down the wooden stairs, flanked by Raleigh and Tiberius, deep down into the womb of the ship. Reaching the bottom of the dank stairwell, I turned my head around the corner, and the same pirate from the upper level was standing in the middle of the corridor, still checking for stowaways.

"How many do you see?" Tiberius said from behind me.

"Just one!" I said.

"Well then, draw him out!" Tiberius said, sheathing his longsword and removing a dagger from his waist.

"Do not kill him, brother!" I said quickly. "We may need to question him."

"Well, that depends on if he wants to play nice," he retorted. "Now, draw him out before we lose the opportunity."

"Too late for that!" a stern voice said from the head of the stairwell behind us. The three pirates we saw a moment ago down the corridor were hastening toward us with rapiers and hammers. I turned and ran down the corridor, only to see three pirates approaching from down that way with, dark gleaming smiles; we were trapped.

"Lay down your weapons," the young pirate commanded, "and your lives shall be spared!" He was a dark youth of close to twenty, built to be a soldier and clad in a wolf-skinned cape, with leather britches and rough leather gauntlets.

"After you!" Raleigh quipped, uninfluenced by the threatening group.

"A stubborn bit we have here, aye?" the pirate said smileless. "We shall see how the captain feels about scoundrels who sneak abroad his ship. Capture them!"

"Not a good idea!" Tiberius said, twirling a dagger in his palm.

"We were commissioned by the king," Raleigh said quickly, averting the comment, "to escort Prince Nova here to the Isle of Cilan for commencement!"

"Commencement?" the pirate said, eying me with intrigue.

"The commencement of training to be king," Raleigh retorted confidently. "Which means riches and glory for all those aboard this ship!"

"Is that right!" the pirate said with greedy eyes. "And tell me, why would a king have an heir to his throne accompanied by two men, and not a proper escort?"

"I have learned never to question the command of a king," Raleigh said coolly. "I only follow his orders. He named this ship specifically and said the captain and his crew shall receive a grand reward!"

The pirate searched Raleigh's eyes for a long, dark moment, then he turned to me.

"Is all of this true... Prince Nova?" he said, his demeanor bland and unreadable.

"Yes, it is!" I said nervously, staring at the savages before me.

"Escort these two to the main deck, and make sure captain Joaquin is notified!" the young pirate commanded, nodding towards us. Before ascending the steps, I glanced back down the dark moonlit corridor for the slightest sign of Christian; there was none.

The creaking groan of the ship became more evident as we made way toward the captain's cabin. Three pirates lay sprawled across the floor from hard drinking. Another two stood silently staring out at the open sea before us, and the main deck was quiet and unoccupied. Nothing was heard but the sound of boots striding over wood and waves splashing from beneath.

The tall pirate with fair skin, dark, beady eyes, and the heavy build of a warrior knocked hard against the door of the cabin, and then waited. Moments later, the wooden door was flung open and we were all greeted with the edge of a rapier blade, wielded by a massive, portly man with a heavy black beard and the savage glare of a beast who had been searching for its next prey...and found it.

"M-my apologies, Captain Joaquin!" the pirate stuttered nervously. "I was told to notify you of..." The man was cut short by the fist that shattered his nose, sending him to the deck with a face and hand full of blood.

"Anyone else here to notify me of anything in the middle of my bloody night sleep?" Joaquin blared. The two pirates flanking our sides looked down and were silent.

"Good, then," Joaquin declared, glancing up at Tiberius. "I do not know you!"

"And I do not know you!" Tiberius responded scornfully. The two locked eyes for a long moment, neither man breaking his stare.

"Captain Joaquin!" a distant voice said urgently from behind us. "Captain Joaquin!" A thickly muscled pirate came running toward where we stood.

"Holy mother of Pious..." Joaquin's eyes gaped as he stared pass Tiberius' shoulder and into the shadowy darkness of the night. In the much too near distance was the likeness of a ship nearly three times the size of our own.

"Man the cannons!" Joaquin roared thunderously. Looking down at the bloody nosed pirate, he scowled. "Oh for fuck's sake, stop bloodying up my deck and man a damn cannon."

"Aye, Captain!" he muffled from behind the bloody hand covering his nose. The captain's eyes glared through the darkness toward the monstrous ship and unsheathed his rapier.

"Where is my damn quartermaster?" the captain mouthed to himself and then glanced up at Tiberius once again. "Neither of you belong on my ship. But if you will fight with us, I shall grant you a pardon and you may keep whatever you plunder."

Tiberius searched the captain's face, then turned to see the massive ship barreling toward us, its enormity becoming more evident with each passing moment.

"Your men are not disciplined!" Tiberius said sharply. "They will get us killed!"

"Not with you as quartermaster!" Joaquin said. "Now get that pretty sword you got there ready for battle." He ran off toward his gathering crew, fifteen men, possibly sixteen, and shouted orders as I turned to Tiberius.

"This is going to be bad" Raleigh said, staring up at the approaching ship dis-quietly. Elite blue banners fluttered gracefully through the night air just beside the rough leather shrouds. The hull was reinforced with crusade armor, and the ram was nearly double the size of our own.

"I must go back and find Christian before the assault," I said quickly as mortars were being filled and cannons were being loaded.

"You will find him and remain below deck until this is done, see me?" Tiberius instructed.

"I see you!" I concurred, glancing over at Raleigh, then back to Tiberius. "You two be careful, ya hear?"

"Likewise, my brother," Tiberius said as he embraced my outstretched forearm with his own.

"Raleigh, my friend," I said, "try not to get yo..." A loud explosion sounded from the front of the hull as the three of us were hurled across the deck. My head crashed into something hard as stone. In an agonizing daze, I staggered to my feet to see that the ship had rammed us.

"Brace yourselves for impact!" I heard distantly as the Elite ship directed its cannons toward us. In a swift motion, I leaped forward, grabbed hold of a metal rod clasping the deck cannon in place, just before the ship lurched wildly to the side. The impact of the cannons was enough to have three of Joaquin's men airborne, flying past my eyes. I staggered my way to the far end of the ship and descended the steps just as another round of cannons smashed through the left side of the ship.

Stalking down the corridor, I searched each cannon room and corridor, but nowhere was there any sign of the young lad. The dark moonlit corridor seemed much different as I searched every possible spot I would use to hide. I opened the next door and entered the nook.

"Christian," I whispered loudly. "Christian, it is Casanova." There was no sign of him anywhere. Thunderous blasts sounded from the main deck as the men roared with satisfaction. Heavy footsteps charged down the steps behind me just as I burst into the nearest nook, and I did not even turn to see who approached. The nook was identical to the cannon room we slept in, only there were no clay jugs full of water. The charge receded down the hall as I stood and listened for my chance to escape. That was when a shadow brushed against my arm, and I was suddenly wrapped into a firm grip, with my mouth covered tightly and something cold and sharp rested against my throat.

"One move, and I open your neck!" a voice edged intently. I raised my hands in mock surrender and elbowed his ribs with all my might. Reaching for the hand at my neck, I wrenched his wrist and turned it until his arm was extended behind him and his face was nearly touching the floor. That was when I noticed it was a tall, muscular lad, a lad who looked oddly familiar.

"Christian, is that you?" I said, incredulous. He turned his shadowy face toward my gaze, and his expression lightened.

"Casanova," he said with a gleaming smile, "you came back for me!"

"Of course I did" I said, loosening my grip on the young giant's leather vest and glancing toward the corridor. "We must find a more secure place to hide."

"I didn't think you would return once I heard the cannon fire," Christian said.

"I always keep my word," I said anxiously as a charge approached from down the corridor. "You know how to use that knife?"

"I have never used it before, only to scare people away!" Christian confessed.

"Well, it looks like tonight may be your lucky night, get down!" I said as two uniformed men rushed past the entrance. The two of us crouched back deeper into the shadows and waited for the next onrush of men to pass. This time there were four of them... and this time the footsteps stopped just as they reached our entrance. My heart lurched wildly as I glanced up into the dark, beaming eyes of one of the elites. He was tall and dark haired. His eyes, a shimmering sparkle in the moonlight. He was clad in the blue Velecian leathers and a strapping white cloak, typical of the Elites. I held my breath as I manned my position, the sound of battle held dominance in the night air.

"Do you see anything, sire?" a voice called from the corridor.

"I have eyes on the mark," he said coolly, my heart sinking deeper in my chest. We were found, I thought frantically as cold sweat formed beneath my doublet and trickled down my side. Something sudden and unexpected had to be done if I wanted to get the lad out of this safely, and there was no time for a plan. Without warning I lunged forward, blade drawn, and the distant sounds of troops and fighting and sword clashing all silenced. The only sound that remained was that of my heart pounding its way through my body and the sound of death as it lurked sullenly throughout the dark nook.

"Drop your weapon!" the Elite said with widened eyes of bewilderment. He reached a swift hand over to the hilt of his longsword and drew it fiercely. "Seize him!"

Three men from behind the Elite, clad in white cloaks, advanced pass his flank. I stood in front of Christian with the firmness of weathered stone and held my blade firmly.

"You will not get to him without going through me!" I blared confidently, although I was far from it. The Elite's face grew tight and stern, but then a smirk formed on his lips.

"Oh, we are not here for him, boy!" the Elite grinned devilishly.

Tiberius Blackwell
"We are not friends!"
Out at sea, 1869

"Fall back into formation!" I shouted as light rain trickled down the edge of my half helm. The cannons alone should have been enough to sabotage our crew, but luckily the pirates were a bit more resourceful than I had presumed. Their long, curved rapiers served as excellent tools against the boarding ropes, and with Joaquin at the wheel, our ship was flawlessly positioned to deflect heavy cannon fire. We were able to send a fraction of these Elite fuckers for a night swim, but now we were overwhelmed. Raleigh, who stood to my right flank, unsheathed two short blades and fixed his eyes on the massive ship attempting to board our own. Elites from every corner of the ship came swinging to deck by rope.

"They nearly double our numbers," Raleigh said promptly. I glanced up as the clouds opened up and gave way to heavier rain.

"Then we shall fight twice as hard!" I commanded. "Are you ready for battle?" Joaquin said savagely.

"Just make certain your men can follow orders!" I barked as six Elites swung down, landing heavily on the deck. The two pirates at the head of the ship recoiled and ran back towards our position, as planned.

"Ready your weapons!" Joaquin blared loudly as the pirates unsheathed rapiers and daggers, pikes and morning stars. The Elites advanced in swift, fierce strides, each clad in the indigo leathers of The elite brigade. In a blur, Raleigh lunged forward, his blades blurring down over the head of an Elite and blood sprayed heavily across the deck. In seconds, the entire deck was swarming with blue leathers.

"Men, advance through the middle!" I commanded quickly, turning to Joaquin. "You, follow me!"

I advanced along the left flank of the brigade and unsheathed my short sword, the rain intensifying with each stride. As Raleigh and Joaquin's men drew attention to the middle of the deck, I slipped behind the crowd and jabbed my short sword in through the soft part of an Elite's torso and pulled out a bloody blade. Joaquin followed closely behind, swinging his fearsome hammer through one Elite, knocking him to the deck, and then smashed his skull to pieces.

An arrow whizzed past and caught hold in a wooden plank beside my head. Cold air bit through the side of my neck as I reached up to it and removed two bloody fingers. In a rage, I seized the arrow from the plank and tore through the crowd, spotting the crossbowman as he positioned himself just beside the wheel. Without a thought, I rushed through the battle, weaved a blow to the head as the bowmen latched an arrow into its slot and closed one eye over the rim. I was too far to reach him, too many people in my path.

In a haste, I charged through the crowd and slipped, landing heavily on my back. I turned my head to see three Elites charging toward me. Blue leather swarmed all over as I fought to get back to my feet. The pirates were nowhere to be seen; not even Joaquin was nearby. Suddenly, a sword was shoved through the back of the Elite before my eyes, spraying blood over my face and tunic. In quick succession, Raleigh lunged two short blades through the temple of the remaining two Elites, their bodies dropped heavily to the deck.

"Good fuckin' deal!" I said thankfully, reaching out to his outstretched hand. Glancing out at the deck, nearly half of the Elite's brigade was wiped out, but more came in waves.

"I can't promise I can do that again," Raleigh said, his eyes fixed on the approaching soldiers. "We will never win this fight head on!"

"What do you say I get the swordsmen down on the main deck with Joaquin, while you take out those bowmen?" I said, sheathing my short sword.

"Already done" Raleigh said, just before he charged up toward the rear of the ship. I unsheathed my black sword and hastened down the steps leading to the main deck. Instantly I ducked down, avoided the morning star aimed for my forehead, and dashed a sword through the chest of an Elite. I didn't even look back to see him drop,; in a blazing madness I slashed the arm of a soldier clean off and wiped the edge of my blade across his blue leathers. Wetness poured from my helm down to the slick deck as the rain intensified. My vision blurred from beneath wet brows, but I pushed forward, backing two Elites into the captain's cabin.

"Retreat!" I heard distantly from behind. The two men before me were cornered, unable to reach the rest of the brigade. They raised their swords in surrender and placed them down at my feet. The Elite to my right removed his crossbow and placed it down to my feet.

"Please do not kill us, friend, we had no choice in the matter," the Elite said cravenly, but I was gone. I slashed my black sword fiercely through the air, and madness raged through the blade. Two headless bodies hit the floor in a heavy thud, and I stood there panting, possessed with a spirit of carelessness.

"We are not friends!" I said maliciously. Light footsteps from behind were heard as I shoved a sword up to the neck of... Raleigh.

"It's only me, big guy!" Raleigh said, staring at the darkness in my eyes, then glanced down at the bodies staining the floor of the cabin. "I see you were busy."

"Barely," I said coolly. "So what is the plan now?"

"Plan?" Raleigh entreated. "Those cowards went back running back to their homeland without a single coin!"

"They had us beat." I squinted in disbelief. "And they ran, just like that?"

"Just like that!" Raleigh grinned. "They knew what was coming, big guy, and trust me, it was coming!" he said smileless. My heart sank as I saw the results of battle lying before my eyes.

"Let's go show Nova how real warriors walk out of a battle," Raleigh quipped, "with bodies lying all around our feet!"

"Yeah," I said distantly. "I'm sure he will be thrilled."

Heavy coats of blood splattered over bodies sprawled across the deck, but something wasn't right. They outnumbered us by nearly double, and we still lived to talk about it? They ran! I thought repeatedly for a moment before the night went completely silent.

Three arrows whizzed past my head and hammered into the wooden plank beside me. As I turned back, nearly a dozen more took flight and formed a thick shadow across the moonlit sky. Before I could even react, heavy hands grasped the side of my head and pulled me down to the deck. In a heavy thud, Raleigh and I landed behind the cover of the ship's mast. Our eyes met momentarily... as he caught sight of my leg. I followed his eyes, and my body went cold. An arrow was wedged deep in my thigh, panic rushed through my pores like daggers of ice, and yet, I was numb to the pain.

"Can you feel your leg?" Raleigh said quickly from beside me. "Yeah." I nodded. "I can feel it."

"Okay, I need you to listen to me closely!" he asserted, but as his voice faded, my sight faded, until the only thing left was darkness.

CHAPTER SIX

Memorie VI

Reaching forward, I longed for the embrace of true meaning but received none. Only the spattering flames before me that formed the very end of the lifeless, fire consumed path I strode upon. It were as if I had been traversing through this wasteland for a lifetime, although I knew it could not have been nearly that. This was surely not what the afterlife held for the likes of a king. The path before me felt vast and never ending, but just as the thought emerged, it dissipated just as two massive pillars appeared a great distance away. Each possessed a towering inferno atop and controlled flames down along each black cylindrical frame. Sweat poured down my face, drenching my cloak as I neared. The blast of heat and dryness only intensified with each stride. I looked down at my hands, and they were completely unfamiliar to me, countless scars from battle ornamented each one. My skin looked tough as pig hide, and it was unusually dark and speckled almost entirely with even darker blotches, but I was huge.

Looking down at my immense size, I stopped in mid-stride to examine my body. I reached sweaty fingertips up to my cheeks; my face was hard as stone. Atop my head stood a ruby encrusted crown, the weight of which was light as a quill pen. I was fully armored in chest and body plate reinforced with iron mail, thick leather gauntlets with spiked edges, and steel vambraces covering my forearms and shins. Around me were bones, the bones of nearly a million corpses blackened from flame and weathered from years of idleness. This was the sleeping place of lost souls, something like the Oakwood, only this was no ordinary wood, and these were no ordinary bones.

Nearing the pillars, it slowly became clear that these were no pillars at all. They were huge towers giving way to a vast kingdom within. Attached to these towers were gates made entirely of onyx and decorated with the skulls of their enemies atop each onyx stake, which encompassed the entire kingdom within its protective embrace. I stepped forward cautiously, unaware of what I was seeing, and lifted my fingers to touch the wall. As they made contact, a sharp streaking pain shot through my arm, my chest, my legs, throughout my entire body. I stood there, paralyzed by fear, but with gaping eyes, for something approached. Judging from its immense size, I instantly thought of Dimitrius and eased my tension. But as it neared, a darkness I had never felt followed closely in stride. A blast of heat touched my face, and it took everything in me to stand firm and not wither from the intensity. It was as if my skin were melting into my bones.

"Keep moving forward," a dark voice urged, but no one was seen. "Keep moving, king!" I pressed forward, even through the murky smell of flesh melting and burnt coals, until I nearly reached the entryway between the vast towers.

"This way..." the voice called from just beyond the pillared entrance, "come unto me."

With each stride forward, the world around me got darker and darker until there stood only nothingness before me...

Memorie VI
Casanova Volkart

"Now that I have your attention!"
Cilan 1869

"Do you think he is dead?" a distant voice said, but nothing was seen. Only the darkness was visible, accompanied by the murmuring from just outside the dungeon door, pushing me swiftly toward the precipice of insanity.

"He better not be," a stern, rumbling voice retorted, "or Trocahl will have our heads!"

"Help," I whispered loudly, my throat sore almost to the point of voicelessness. "You have the wrong man!"

The chains confining my wrists and ankles clanked loudly against the stone floor as I thrashed for attention, only to be ignored or answered with silence. The air was frigid and lifeless. A sheer mesh was covering my face, obstructing a majority of my vision, but I was able to vaguely see shadowy images drifting past my eyes, neither of them distinct. The dungeon held a dim mildewy odor, as if it were deep down in the bowels of the earth. Wet, living things scurried pass my fingers and sent chills through my body, but the fear I held for those scurrying critters were nothing compared to the fear of what lay before me in my near future. It had been nearly two days since I had been captured, and with no form of light, I felt as Arkon must have felt as he passed his last moments in uncertainty.

My eyes started to feel heavy, my lips were parched, and nausea eventually settled in. My stomach contained nothing but the scraps of mead and water I was given nearly a day ago. My head swam as I nodded forward sleepily, but I promised myself I would not let this drowsiness get the best of me. I was not planning on getting eaten alive by parasites or whatever other critters that lurked there in the darkness.

Heavy boot heels approached from a distance, and the sudden presence was heard from down the corridor. The voices from outside the dungeon were now silenced. As the boot heels neared and stopped, a voice followed closely behind.

"Is the package intact?" a young sounding, wily man entreated.

"Yes sir, Trocahl!" the stern voice said. "Your package is awaiting attention!"

"Good!" the wily man said as a rattling purse full of coin was heard. "You will receive the rest when the job is complete!"

As the chamber door creaked open, my heart hammered intensely from beneath my doublet. Light shone in through the crevice of the open door as the torch illuminating the corridor sent shimmering rays through to the dark mesh covering my face. He was a tall, sinewy man with long, flowing hair that flailed gracefully behind him as he entered. My heart turned to ice as his shadowy presence loomed over me, watching me.

"If you only knew the lengths I had to go through to acquaint myself with you!" he chimed after a long moment.

"I have done you no wrong," I said weakly "Release me, and your life shall be spared, you have my word!" The laughter that followed sent a shivering chill down my spine as the sound echoed over stone.

"My life? Shall be spared?" he sneered. "Perhaps I have not properly introduced myself. My name is Sinnis Trocahl, the first of his name, chief lieutenant in the mystical order of Agishi and master mage of the twelfth degree!" said Sinnis confidently. "And you are the man I have captive in my dungeon, so there will be no more talk of life. We shall be speaking of death, if one of two things do not happen here tonight! First, you will release the names of the two scoundrels that accompanied you aboard that ship, and they shall be dealt with judiciously...or -"

"Or?" I said quickly, unaware if his next words would carry a threat or a more preferable option.

"Or second," Sinnis resumed calmly, "you will sign this parchment denouncing you of all dealings with sorcery of any form, all phases of mysticism, and the right of imperial sovereignty. You will then be released and escorted to any place of your desire."

"Done," I said quickly, "I will sign!"

The frankness of my answer silenced the man. Although I had not even the slightest concept of what mysticism was, or even what imperial sovereignty was for that matter, there was no doubt in my mind that I would never divulge the position of my friends to this man.

"Well, then!" the man said, clearing his throat, shuffling through his parchments. "You will sign right...here!"

"I cannot see anything from beneath this veil!" I urged

A cold chill suddenly permeated the dungeon. The hairs on my neck began to rise from beneath the collar of my doublet, and even with my sight being obstructed, I was able to sense fear washing over the face of Sinnis. He turned for the door and somehow slammed it shut, locking several iron latches into place. The hint of shimmering light from the corridor disappeared. Darkness consumed the dungeon just before a match was struck. The match was taken to a torch, and the dungeon shone bright once again.

"Look here, boy!" Sinnis said with sudden ice in his tone. "I will remove your covering when you have fulfilled your half of the bargain!"

"I will not sign unless I see what it is!" I said defiantly. Truthfully, I did not even know what to look for, but I did know that I wanted to see the face of this man holding me captive. In mid-thought, steel hands suddenly grasped the front of my neck, knocking my next words to the back of my throat. Breath was instantly drained from my lungs as I clawed and gasped desperately. My face tightened, I grew weak and lightheaded. Determined not to be broken, I held on until it felt as if my head would explode from the pressure, then held on further.

"Now that I have your attention," Sinnis said, releasing his iron grip from my throat. Gasping intensely, I drew in enough breath to fill my lungs to capacity and exhaled in short spurts until I slowly regained awareness, "this is not a request. You will do this, or you will be exterminated!"

"Unshackle my wrist, please... I will do it!" I said, leaning over to the side, panting from exhaustion. The man kneeled down slowly, and he was now so close I could feel his cold breath brushing against the mesh concealing my face.

"She told me you were smart," he said, removing a ring of keys and leaning into the lock. "But she did not tell me you would be so..."

Just as my hand was freed, I grabbed for the neck of the man but caught hold of a fist full of hair as he jerked his head wildly to the side. I yanked the man's head back and held it firmly. Stone fists smashed across my face and head as Sinnis tried to break my hold, but it was iron tight. Something that felt like a knee crashed into my nose, and pain exploded from my face. As the man's hair slipped out of my free hand, an endless barrage of blows came raining down from overhead. One after the other, I was being bludgeoned and beaten with no remorse; it was a wonder I was able to retain consciousness as long as I did, but it was now more than evident that I would soon be dead, alone, and without achieving anything I had set out to do.

"Sign it!" he blared, snapping me back to attention with a boot to the jaw.

Something heavy pummeled against the door, and the suddenness of the sound brought an eerie silence to the dungeon. Agonizing pain suddenly streaked down the side of my face. It were as if a dagger had been driven in through my temple and torn down my cheek, all went dark in one eye. I screamed bloody murder that night, my cries heard by the gods themselves. For it was in that moment that I slipped into delirium and witnessed the dungeon door nearly explode up out of its foundation. Shards of metal, stone and dampened particles came showering through the dungeon, hurling Sinnis violently into the stone pillar beside me.

Two figures in cloak appeared amidst the aftermath, and the temperature instantly dropped to a bitter frost. The figure to the left was a woman, her long, flowing hair was flailing behind her. Her cloak synched in at the waist, and the curvy silhouette beneath became more prominent as she advanced. The man beside her was so massive that he had to lean his head down to enter the dungeon. His huge frame blurred toward me as I reached my free hand up to block his strike, but it never came. When I opened my eyes, Sinnis was up against the wall being held up by his neck, but the massive warrior was silent. Pain shot through my entire body, my face heavy and numb from the beating.

Soft fingers grazed against my neck, and I nearly jumped out of my skin, but then there she was. The woman lifted her hand, removing the mesh covering my face, and fiery green eyes stared down at me, holding my gaze. Her flowing black mane was pulled back tightly in a ponytail that rested lightly over the shoulder of her white cloak and... she was breathtaking.

"We must go!" she said coolly, her voice the essence of purity. She touched my hand and peeled something slimy from off my skin. The shackles confining my wrists and ankles clanked heavily onto the stone floor as the locks were released. I flinched at the sudden sight of the black slime lining the walls, my hands, my doublet, everywhere. The woman lifted my arm over her neck, shifted my weight onto her shoulders and lifted me up.

"Solana, see him to the sanctum," a dark, raspy voice demanded, "then report to Brotus. I will handle Sinistro!"

My heart lay frozen solid in my chest, as I stared up into the eyes of a monster. Green scales lined the skin beneath his white cloak, covering his entire body. His face was hard and calloused from years of battle, and his massive frame dwarfed the small dungeon.

"As you will, my lord!" Solana replied obediently, shifting my shoulders toward the corridor. Blood was splattered over the walls and floor of the corridor. Two severed bodies lay sprawled across the stone floor just at the entrance of the dungeon, one missing an arm and leg, the other missing a head. Torches lit a path down the dreary passage as the woman hastened toward a distant stairwell.

"How did you know where to find me?" I asked, stepping over the bloody leg of a corpse.

"There are a great many things I know, but if I am to keep you safe, then first you are to tell me exactly what Sinistro has said to you," she said, ducking down beneath the lance of a stone warrior statue. "He is a very dangerous man and not to be taken lightly!"

"Sinistro?" I said. "He told me his name was Sinnis Trocahl"

"Is that so?" she snickered as we reached the bottom of a narrow stairwell. "And what else did he tell you during his visit?"

"He said something about signing a contract," I said dispassionately, "relinquishing me of sorcery and imperial sovereignty, something of that sort."

She stopped abruptly, removed my arm from her neck, and clutched both of my arms as she glared intensely into my eyes.

"Please tell me you did not sign anything!" she blared. "Please!"

"No, no, I didn't," I said quickly. "I could not see what I was signing!"

The woman examined my eyes and each of the cuts and scrapes on my bruised face. She released the firm grip she held on my arms, and her hard stare softened. Lifting a soft hand to my cheek, warmth suddenly rushed through my body. All pain and hints of nausea ceased. I was completely enthralled in the warmth of her touch.

"All shall be explained shortly," the woman said formally but then stared deep into my eyes, as if she were trying to read more than an expression. "I am so sorry this has happened to you!"

"This was not your fault," I reassured. "There was no way you could have prevented my misfortune!"

"Oh, if only that were true...get down!" she said, reaching for her blade. Two men clad in the blue leathers of the Elite suddenly appeared crossing the arched pathway ahead.

Kneeling down in the shadows of the stairwell, I watched as the two walked pass nonchalantly, completely unaware of the massacre just down the steps.

"When they pass, we will make a break for the door," she said, staring at the men in passing. "You will stop for nothing, do you understand?"

"I understand," I said warily, "but what is past that door?" Green eyes flashed toward mine, and darkness lurked from beneath her lids. Silence was answer enough.

As the guarding Elites reached the first bend in the corridor, the two of us bolted towards the arched doorway. Unhinging its large bolt locks, the woman lifted the plank and pulled back the heavy oak door. Hundreds of corpses cluttered the path leading to a distant forest as a bitter gust of wind sent ice through my veins. The vile stench of death filled my nose with each step. The sight brought me back to my dream of walking through the desolate wasteland, only this was no desolate land. Moonlight shimmered down against the edges of tree limbs, sending shadowy creatures dancing amongst hundreds of corpses sprawled about recklessly.

"By the gods," I whispered incredulously, "what has happened here?" The woman stared out silently over the vast land of death before her eyes finally touched mine.

"Retribution!" she snarled with a darkness I have only seen before in the eyes of one man.

Tiberius Blackwell
"We're going to find him... no matter what!"
Candonia, 1869

"Is this your idea of preparation?" Joaquin intoned from a distance. "Loosen the damn sails and ready the ship for docking!" The suddenness of his sharp voice snapped my eyes open, and the only image that came into focus was... failure.

Cold, frigid air bit through my flesh and formed a trail of goose pimples down my neck and arms. I got to my feet, took a stride toward the door and stopped abruptly. A throbbing pain streaked up the side of my leg. A red bandage was wrapped around my right thigh, and I couldn't bend my knee well enough to walk without the assistance of the wall. I was hurt badly, but the only thought going through my mind was... Casanova.

"Big guy," a familiar voice intoned from just outside of the small cabin. "Big guy, it's me, open up!"

I mustered up enough strength to guide myself toward the wooden door and opened it.

Raleigh's eyes met mine and then went down to the heavy bandage covering my thigh.

"We have to get you to a healer, you're losing too much blood!" he urged.

"No, we have to find my brother," I retorted, "my leg can wait!" I leaned back against the door and exhaled a long shallow breath; I was weak and lightheaded.

"And if he needs your help, you're going to lean against a wall while you fight to free him?" Raleigh said derisively. "You need to take it easy!"

"You need to take your hand off me," I growled. "It is your fault we are on this ship in the first place!"

"No," Raleigh spat angrily, "we are here because you were pursuing something, or have you forgotten already? No one could have anticipated that events would turn, but they did. Now we are outnumbered by these pirates, and frankly I don't even know what island we just arrived upon. As it stands, our mission of concern is getting you well enough to move." The throbbing was unbearable as I stared at the man defiantly. Somewhere deep in the back of my mind, I knew he was right. I knew this was a situation in which I would rely on the quick witted thinking of my brother, but now that was out of the question. He was gone... the one person I had sworn to protect.

"Those Elites are probably laughing at us right now," I said, looking past Raleigh's shoulder at the approaching footsteps.

"Never mind that now," he said, slowly turning his gaze toward the door. Seconds later, it eased open and Joaquin stepped in.

"How are you feeling?" he said roughly.

"Never better!" I snapped, his eyes met mine and then turned to Raleigh.

"Is that true?" Joaquin said incredulously. Raleigh inhaled.

"He is losing too much blood," Raleigh said "If he does not make it to a healer by nightfall, he will not make it at all."

"A healer?" Joaquin smirked. "Well, that may be a bit... implausible at this moment."

"And why is that?" Raleigh said, glaring toward the captain with a sudden disdain.

"Well," he started, "you may want to take a look for yourself. Here, let me help you get the big fella up to deck."

"No," I snapped. "I will move on my own!" I grabbed hold of the wooden plank and clutched until my fingers throbbed. I was leaning, with the weight of the world balanced on the heel of my left boot and the venom filled eyes glaring at my neck.

"There is no time for pride now, we must go!" Joaquin said, grasping my arm and wrapping it around his shoulder "If you want to fight me, do it when you're fully healed."

Staggering up the narrow step well, the sun glared down intensely from overhead. It was nearly midday, and the results of the night's battle were still prominent in my mind and before my eyes. We had been lulled into a false sense of safety... and we paid for it. Some paid with an arrow through the head, others were fortunate enough to pay with an arrow wedged through the thigh. But each and every one of us paid for this battle in some way or another.

"What happened to the rest of your crew?" Raleigh said, staring at the five remaining pirates that stood with rapiers at the ready.

"We lost many good men last night!" Joaquin said as Raleigh turned to him in disbelief.

"Five remain? From a sixteen man crew?" Raleigh asked hopelessly. Joaquin nodded as he stared hazily out at the horizon. Wild trees spread across almost the entire span of the coast. Heavy vines were suspended from tree limbs, and the smell of carcass lingered close by. The port was desolate, not a soldier in sight. The smell of burning wood touched my nose almost immediately.

"They would not have made it through the jungles either way!" Joaquin intoned.

"Captain," a voice from lower deck called out. He was a broad fellow, clad in boiled leather cloak and silver lined britches. "What are we to do with the lad?"

Joaquin stared off into the wilderness that lay before him, gritting his teeth angrily. There was an air around the man that seemed as if he had turned mad. Leaning against the ledge overlooking the water, he turned his head slowly toward the approaching pirate.

"Bring him along," he said, "we'll need all the hands we can get!"

"What lad is that?" Raleigh said as we locked eyes for a moment.

"Not the one you were describing," Joaquin said, "that's for sure!"

"Bring him here," I growled. The pirate glanced at Joaquin, who gave the nod of approval.

Moments passed, and a tall pale boy was escorted up to the main deck flanked by two pirates. He was a burly fellow, although his sunken cheeks looked as if he hadn't eaten in nearly a week and he was clad in a shabby gray vest and crushed leather britches.

"You know how to wield a sword, son?" Joaquin said roughly, unsheathing a short sword from its scabbard. The lad nodded, eying each man with a worried glare. "Then you shall accompany me and my crew. See him to the gear and supplies."

"Where are we off to?" the lad said.

"We are off to the gold, my boy!" Joaquin grinned savagely.

"What is your name, lad?" Raleigh interjected.

"My name is Christian!" Raleigh's eyes shot to mine and locked for a brief moment before I snapped.

"Where is my brother?" I inquired fiercely. Every eye was now locked on me from the outburst.

"Your brother? I am sorry, I do not know your brother, sir!" said Christian innocently.

"You knew him well enough for him to go back to find you," I edged, "and now he is nowhere to be found!"

"Casanova is your brother?" Christian said with gaping eyes. "They took him, those men in blue leather. He came back for me, and we were attacked."

"Did you see them take him?" Raleigh said.

"Yes, I saw it all," Christian said nervously. "I tried to stop them, I really did!"

"Did you hear them say where they were going?" I added. "Or why they wanted him and not anyone else?"

"No, I am sorry!" Christian said, glancing down at my bloody leg and the awkward position I stood in leaning against the mast. "But I will help you find him. He kept his word and came back for me, so it is only right."

"He will do nothing of the sort!" Joaquin snapped, his eyes fixed intently upon me. "Now I spared your life, as well as your friend here, because you two helped me during battle, but this lad is still a castaway on my ship. That means he shall work for me, or he shall work for no one." Our eyes locked for a long, hard moment. Fire rose from within me, and it seared through my pores as I contemplated my next move.

"Fine," Raleigh said, stepping between us. "Fine, keep the lad, we need to push forward and find help for this wound." Joaquin nodded and turned back to me.

"Then forward we push." He winked, and it was in that very moment that it became noticeably clear... I was going to kill him.

My fingers clutched tightly across the shoulder of Raleigh's doublet as he eased me down against the fallen stump of a tree that stood just before a stream. The stream stood out of place for the tumultuous jungle we were in but gave it an oddly calm veneer. It had been nearly three hours since we left the ship, and aside from the chattering of birds and the occasional quarrels between Joaquin and his men, there was no sign of life in this wilderness.

"You not looking so good, man," Raleigh observed as he sat down in the dirt beside me, gnawing on the finishing remains of his tart. "You need to wrap it again!"

The air around me was unnaturally cool for this time of season, and I was quickly losing the feel in my leg. I couldn't even imagine how I looked at that moment. I glanced up at the sky and shielded my eyes from the oncoming sun. It was just about four hours until sundown, but I didn't have it in me to take four steps further.

"We have to push forward!" I urged, digging my palms into the dirt in an effort to push myself up onto the stump, but I failed miserably. Cold sweat enmeshed the inner fabric of my doublet. I stared across the small stream, and there was Joaquin working a few of his men along with the boy Christian to the bone. The lad had two rapiers chopping down shrubs nearly as tall as he was to form a path. He was a strong lad, I must say, and determined. Shame he was now warded apprentice to a fool.

"Rest up, big guy, you will need to preserve your strength for the night," Raleigh said, staring ponderously out across the stream, "or for that captain you want to kill!"

Our eyes touched but were quickly broken by the snap of a twig just strides behind us. Each of us turned with blades drawn and saw the tall shrubs swaying back and forth vigorously. Something was stuck in that shrub and was desperately trying to release itself. Raleigh advanced, holding his blade at the ready. Moments later something squealed, the shrub split apart, and a warthog came bursting out, scurrying in all directions. It was a fast little fucker, took Raleigh a long while to corner him. But in the end when he returned with the hog, skinned and bare, it was time well spent.

"We leave in five, soldiers!" Joaquin shouted from upstream. Apparently, Christian had cleared quite a few shrubs with those vicious looking rapiers of his, enough so that now a path was clearly visible for us to move forward. Raleigh pushed the remains of the hog deep into his satchel and swung it over his shoulder. Lifting my arm over his head, he raised me from the ground in one swift upheave.

"We're going to find him..." he said in scarcely a whisper, "no matter what it takes!"

I nodded. I honestly wanted to believe that it could happen, that we would find Casanova and everything would go back to how it was. But I knew things would never be the same again.

"We proceed north," Joaquin instructed as we approached the group. Each stare was as disgruntled as the next, even the air seemed dissatisfied, judging by the heavy gust that followed his words. "Ready destriers, your supplies, and be quick about it."

"We need more rest," one of the pirates pointed out. He was a heavily built man, possibly of Partrizian descent, judging by the dark skin and faint accent.

"You need to do as I say!" Joaquin snapped. "Elsewise you may find your way alone through these jungles at night with a destrier - that is, if the wolves don't find you first and eat you alive."

"The only wolf I see in this jungle is the one that presumes himself a leader!" the pirate returned irately. The two exchanged fierce stares, each man seconds away from drawing unnecessary attention our way.

"Enough!" I blared, louder than expected. Half a dozen ponderous eyes searched my face, but I ignored them, all except one. "What is it you wish to accomplish here? Besides all out mutiny?"

"I am here for one reason," Joaquin said disconcertingly, "and one reason only, Gold! No one asked you to jump aboard my ship, but you did, and here we are. And if you ever undermine me in front of my men again... I will kill you!"

Raleigh lifted my arm from over his neck so quickly, I only felt myself falling before I caught hold of a tall shrub. He unsheathed his longsword and pressed forward. The air turned hazy around me as I reached over for the hilt of my sword. In a blink, Raleigh slammed his forearm into the collarbone of the captain and drove his back to the dirt from the force. Flustered, Joaquin struggled within his grip, but the hold was iron tight.

"Threaten him again, and I will cut you to pieces and feed you to the wolves myself," Raleigh said savagely. The men of his crew gazed down at their vulnerable captain with disdain, but neither of them made a move. Raleigh sheathed his blade and released his hold on the collar of Joaquin's cloak.

"Now, enough of this banter. Let us move forward!" Raleigh suggested.

Shimmering rays of pinks and purples splashed vividly throughout the wilderness as the sun eased down behind the distant mountain clear. The group moved in silence now, after the captain was knocked down to size, but the trouble was no longer Joaquin and his antics. Trouble was, it was nearly sun fall, and it seemed as if we had not gained crucial ground. The wild trees surrounding us only became more treacherous the further we traversed. The shrubs were now heavily thorned and almost impossible to cut through with much progress. The hanging vines were so thick that even an ax was no longer able to clear a path, and my leg, the pain had numbed it entirely; that was what scared me.

"This may help a bit," a friendly voice said from behind me. It was Christian, holding out a small bowl of shredded leaves. "It's poppy herb, my father said it can help with open wounds."

"Yes, I know of the poppy herb, thank you!" I expressed kindly. "My brother spoke very highly of you."

"I should have been stronger," he said with his eyes touching the dirt. "My father always told me that."

"And I should have been faster!" I said, staring down at my leg. He grinned. I found myself genuinely smiling for the first time in a long time, although more so from delirium than anything else. The lad walked back toward Joaquin with his eyes down in submission. Raleigh emerged from a nearby bush, hoisting his trousers up coolly.

"Snakes out here in this wild; might want to protect yourself when it's time to take a piss," he grinned, glancing down at the bowl in my hands. "Poppy herb, huh. Where'd you get that?"

"The lad, Christian," I intoned, unwrapping the drenched bandage from my thigh, exposing a bloody massacre. Sprinkling the herbs over the wound, a rush of ice streaked through my leg. The cool sensation brought feeling back into my leg, and I hoisted my heel onto a boulder as I re-wrapped the wound.

"You know," Raleigh started, gazing up at the dusk filled sky with contempt, "I might have been wrong to pin the man down like that."

"He deserved every bit of it," I shot back, pulling my bloody trouser leg back over my thigh.

"True indeed, yet he is the only man who knows piss about this bloody island," he pointed out. "Soon we will be surrounded by night, and who knows what lurks in the night out here."

"Wolves, I presume." I grinned painlessly, but my head swam. My lips were parched and cracked from the journey. Nausea rushed through me like an angry sea during a raging storm. I turned to the side and gagged, but nothing came out. Only the heavy drool spilling from the side of my lips and the sudden heaviness I felt in my head. In the distance, I heard Raleigh.

"Wait," he said vehemently, gazing at nothing in particular, "you cannot leave!" His words received no response. Raleigh hoisted me up and shouldered through the heavy shrubs before us, but Joaquin and his men pushed forward at a distance where it was nearly impossible to catch. Dizzy with drowsiness, I leaned my body forward. Christian turned back with despair in his eyes, but after a moment he too turned and hurried toward Joaquin. There we stood, the sun concealed almost entirely behind the hilled horizon.

"They left us?" Raleigh said.

"Can you blame them?" I said drowsily. "I am in no shape to serve a purpose for them now."

"We have to keep moving!" Raleigh urged, pushing through the shrubs with his bare hands and getting a gash in return for his troubles. The thorn caught flesh and split the side of his hand. As blood dripped slowly from the wound, Raleigh ripped the other sleeve of his doublet and quickly wrapped his hand.

"Leave me be," I said. "No sense in both of us being wolf prey. You can still catch up to them and have numbers against whatever is out there. You don't owe me anything!"

"I am not doing this for you," Raleigh expressed. "Each of us started this journey for our own reason. Since then, we have all lost something. But that does not mean we lose sight of our purpose for being here, which is getting you strong enough to find your brother."

"You're right," I said after a long moment. "You're right, we will push forward no matter the cost."

"That's the spirit!" Raleigh said, stepping forward with me. "Now if we can just find higher ground, we can possibly..."

Something growled from within the thick shrubs ahead of us.

"What in the name of bloody hell?" Raleigh removed my arm from his neck and lowered me down. Quickly unsheathing a dagger, he lowered himself as low as he could without drawing attention this way.

"Was that a tiger?" I whispered, my heart pounding uncontrollably in my chest.

"No," Raleigh whispered roughly, clutching his dagger until his fist turned white. "Sounded like something faster!"

The shrubs before us rustled as something heavy brushed against it. Twigs snapped and broke beneath thick paws, as the beast moved flawlessly through the thorn bedded shrubs. There was nowhere to run, and I couldn't even move if there was. My wound had not been tightly wrapped, and the covering was undoing itself. To the east, the sun receded behind wild trees that gave the horizon a hint of richness, higher ground would come from that way or none. I unsheathed my blade as a precaution and eased down further, my leg throbbing from the awkward angle.

From between thick, thorn filled vines I saw a blur of blackness that I could have swore was big as an ox. It stalked slowly toward us, probably crouched low just as we were, and it was hunting. Golden iridescent eyes flickered from up ahead as I caught sight of the black beast from enough distance to run, but not far, and in my condition I would be caught before I even got to my feet.

"A panther!" I edged, crouching down lower. Raleigh's eyes widened as if it made a difference between lion, tiger, or wolf. Either way, we would be devoured here in this jungle. "Whats the plan?"

"Not to die!" Raleigh returned softly, leaning his head back against the dirt with his dagger transfixed across his chest at the ready. He closed his eyes to slow his breathing and waited. A brushing movement was heard from behind us, and my stomach instantly turned to water. Either it was Joaquin and his crew here to apologize for leaving us to fend for ourselves, or there was another panther lurking in our midst. The beast from behind moved so swiftly, it barely stirred heavy vines as it approached. I glanced at Raleigh; his eyes were gaping as he stared up at nothing in particular.

"Hey," I said in scarcely a whisper, "get ready!" I braced myself as the beasts approached from either side.

A shadowy figure emerged from behind, and hazel eyes stared viciously back at me from behind the slanted lids of a woman's face. She knelt down beside Raleigh and glared through the thick vines at her approaching game. Fox fur draped around her neck and down throughout her deerskin over cloth and trousers. She carried a longbow on her back, and a thick rope was wrapped around her arms from wrist to elbow with a blade affixed at each end, and her face had three black stripes of paint under her left eye.

A black figure leaped from overhead toward the woman snapping at her legs, but she weaved just out of harm's way. Raleigh pushed himself to his feet frantically, swinging his blade viciously but only caught vine. The beast halted, spotting the new mark and raced toward Raleigh, its thick black coat glistening under the pale moonlight. In a panic, he froze, flailing his blade out before him wildly. With a swift suddenness, the animal lunged through the air straight for Raleigh but was jerked back violently. The woman held the thick unwound rope loosely in her palms, and the panther crashed to the dirt with a blade through its back. Panting, the woman stared down at the creature savagely, as if she were repentant. She knelt down and whispered words of a foreign tongue, a prayer of some sort. When she was done, her eyes turned to mine and her face was blurry, although she was just before me. The wilderness started to spin uncontrollably around me. Raleigh stood just strides away, and even he was now indistinct. I tried to say something, anything, but as I stared up at the moonlight, the darkness slowly consumed my every thought.

CHAPTER SEVEN

Memorie VII

Casanova Volkart
"Petty antics? Not my thing."
Cilan, 1869

The air was raw and icy as it bit through the thick fabric of my doublet and straight through to the bone. The rock filled gritty trail leading up and through the heart of Cilan was now upon us, and my only cause for still being with this strangely attractive woman was the hope that I could find the nearest coastline. We had advanced nearly half the night without any disturbance, but now a strange silence whispered in the wood. Heavy stones crunched beneath my high leather boots as I raced to keep up with this mysterious woman, but with no good fortune. She was too fast, too agile to be caught as she maneuvered swiftly through the trees, her white cloak billowing softly behind her.

"This," I said breathlessly into the night, leaning against the nearest tree, "is as far I will go. I told you I have to find my brother."

"Your brother is strong, Casanova," she said, turning, "as are you. It is imperative that you continue your mission."

"He is my brother!" I blared defiantly, my words echoing throughout the silent forest. "I will not continue this journey if you do not tell me what is at hand. Where are you taking me?"

"But he is not your brother," she intoned, "he is your closest ally that you call a brother."

"How could you know that?" I stared, incredulous.

"I know much about you, Casanova, but there is no time," she said quickly, her gaze extended through the trees ahead. "They are coming!"

My chest tightened as she stared out over the vast expanse of nothingness before us. Listening to the screaming silence of the night, it seemed as if a presence was approaching, but nothing was seen. "Who are... they?" I said just before the shadowy image of a man appeared from within the looming darkness of the wood.

"Are you well?" the man said, staring at Solana. He was tall and thickly built, with heavy arms bulging from within the sleeves of his hooded white cloak and a gleaming great sword sheathed at his side. His eyes were shadowed beneath the brim of his hood, but they were a rusted bronze, and the leery aggression within them showed hints of a dark past. A woman appeared walking beside him, her sharp, stony gaze fixed upon me as one would regard a rare and beautiful gem... sitting within the mouth of a serpent. A jeweled broche was fastened at her neck, holding together a black cloak with the image of a red dragon emblazoned on the back, and she was fully armored in mail and plate. Daggers at the waist, two short swords sheathed at her back, throwing blades sheathed in leg holsters, and a double edged chain blade dangled from her palm.

"Yes, I am well," Solana said, turning. "Casanova, this is my brother Brotus and my sister Isis."

"If my sister is right about you," Isis said, studying me warily, "then it is our highest honor that we escort you to your destiny Casanova."

"I thank you," I said demurely, "but as I told Solana, if my destiny does not involve finding my brother in the near future, then I am afraid I shall have to postpone my fate until I do."

"Loyalty," Brotus intoned, "an impressive virtue for such a young mortal, one that shall serve you well as king!"

The silence of the wood intensified as I stood motionless, in a mixture of fear and disbelief. Who were these people? I pondered as a light mist drizzled down from overhead. Thick clouds formed and drifted toward the moonlight, giving life to an approaching storm.

"We have to move!"Brotus said with his gaze fixed on the dark clouds forming the horizon.

"Casanova, you do not know this yet" Isis said, turning to me, "but there is a woman out there that..."

"Isis!" Solana blared.

"What?" Isis returned coldly.

"It is not your place, and you know that!" Solana exclaimed.

"So it is okay to lead him into a life he knows nothing of?" Isis said, her nostrils flaring with fury.

"Regardless of circumstance, you took an oath!" Solana pointed out.

"I am fully aware of that, Solana," she said with disdain. "Brotus, say something! You of all people know the significance of what lies ahead."

"Petty antics?" Brotus quipped. "Not my thing! If the two of you wish to bicker on, then so be it, but leave me out of it while we have a mission to complete."

"Casanova, I know you are confused, and of good reason apprehensive, but if your brother is in any grave danger, then I will personally take you to him," Brotus said, staring off into the approaching clouds, his rusted bronze eyes sparkling against the moonlit sky.

"And you are to know of my brother's wellness? How is that?" I returned, incredulous.

"I have a way..." he started. "I just need you to trust me!" Brotus reached a broad calloused hand out toward me, and we locked eyes.

I studied the man's bronze gaze down to the light stubble across his broad face. He showed no signs of a threat, although a trained killer rarely does. His demeanor was stern, and he was disciplined, judging from the way he handled this situation. Green eyes stared at me from my left, dark blue eyes from my right. Bronze eyes glared toward me from just ahead as the distant sound of thunder emerged. With no ally, no one around me with a familiar face, no one who truly cared for my best interest, any decision felt wrong. When I took his hand, it was more so out of compulsion than fear, although you would never tell by the way my heart pounded in my chest.

"Hurry, this way!" Brotus called from just paces ahead, but the rain was so thick that the forest looked like a swamp with trees scattered throughout it. Deep puddles of mud and grime soaked my boots deeper down into the earth with each stride. We were heading for the immense summit that rested just across the field. Heavy rain showers blurred my vision, and my doublet was so drenched that I could scarcely find a place to wipe my eyes as I struggled to keep stride with the brawny man in the white hooded cloak. As we neared the towering haven, what originally seemed a short journey turned out to be a cold, wet, and vastly tiring trek through the cold, muddy marshland.

Stepping in through the gaping mouth, we nearly collapsed beneath the high ceiling entryway of the massive cave. I was wet, exhausted, and just strides from three people of whom I knew nothing more than a name. A cold gust rushed in through the opening of the cave and left goose pimples racing up and down my back. I sat motionless for a long moment as I steadied my breath, my eyes darting in every direction.

The ceiling of the cave was so steep, there stood only blackness when I looked up. It was as if I were staring into the sky on a night when the moon abandoned its post, but there were stars, hundreds of little beams of light shone down, neither of them enough to illuminate the darkness. A stream of moonlight shone in through the opening, enough to see that this was no ordinary earth forged cave.

Intricate etchings were carved into the stone wall beside my head. Vivid inscriptions of men and women kneeling before two crowned men, each vastly different from the next. One held the symbol of life emblazoned atop the front of a ruby encrusted crown, with fire surrounding his great crimson cloak. The other held the symbol of truth atop an onyx encrusted crown surrounding in ash. The silence that lurked in through the lip of the cave was so sudden, it was eerie. The heavy tumultuous rain that turned the forest wood into a marshy swampland had ceased so abruptly, it was as if it never even happened. The shuffling of garments brought my gaze to Solana as she unhooked the back of her white cloak and let the silk descend softly into a pool around her feet.

Her shapely body was sculpted like that of a goddess. Long black hair cascaded down to her thighs, and those curves... she was indeed a sight to behold. My lips were open, but not a word was uttered from them; only the choppy gurgling sounds that I had just realized were coming from my own mouth. Isis emerged from the darkness with three dry tunics, and she handed one to Brotus and one to Solana before she turned to me.

"I think he likes your sister..." She smirked, handing me the tunic. "At least someone does!"

Emerald eyes searched my face curiously for a moment before her gaze broke at the sound of a distant howling. Howling? In a cave? I thought as I got to my feet and shrugged off my heavy doublet.

I felt unusually embarrassed, lifting the drenched under cloth over my head, exposing a bare, gaunt chest and unimpressive sized arms. The dark blotch on my side had started off as a small speck but grew over the years, until it nearly covered my entire rib. And now as six eyes stared my way with equally disparaging looks, I felt insecure for the first time in a long while. Isis squinted intensely at my ribs as she approached.

"Is that...?" she started but stopped abruptly. "Brotus, is that?" Brotus nodded knowingly.

"Dimitrius will know what to do," he said indifferently. He removed a torch from the wall and unexplainably set it ablaze, my heart growing solid in my chest.

"Dimitrius?" I repeated. "The immortal?"

"The immortal!" Isis mocked. "How adorable is he?"

"Yes!" Solana interrupted, her words both icy and abrupt. "Dimitrius the immortal!"

"So he does really exist?" I intrigued.

"Why don't you ask him when you see him?" Isis winked, her black cloak brushing against my face as she swayed past.

"He is expecting us!" Brotus said, holding the lit torch up toward the ceiling. The sudden movement brought a beautiful long, winding path into view before us. The curved trail ascended around the heart of the cave, a vast cylindrical ice form that went up and through the cave ceiling.

Brotus doused the blaze and set the torch down at the foot of the winding step well. Touching the ice form, it instantly came alive, a low humming sound was emitted from the structure as it began to spin, illuminating the cave with colorful splendor. Long, jagged spikes of ice decorated the walls and ceilings, and hundreds of ice warriors stood sentinel up the trail just strides apart from each other. Carved etchings decorated the walls as if to tell a beautiful tale... a very long, winding tale that somehow seemed never ending.

"As you shall come to see..." Brotus said, his eyes fixed on the vast expanse of stone steps before him. "The road to immortality is a very long and treacherous journey, but you only notice it when you start counting each step." As he began his ascension up the steps of ice and stone, the hood of his cloak shrouded him further within mystery, Isis turned.

"He is such a showoff." She winked and followed her brother.

896, 897, 898... My palm was numb and rigid when it touched the ice form to keep myself balanced upright. My body was numb and trembling. The air was ice, and so dry my breath blew out in a cloudy haze just before my eyes, I was panting from exhaustion. To my right the spinning ice form rotated so vigorously it appeared to be standing still, to my left was clear and open space with no rail to support myself against.

899,900,901... each step pushed me further and further past my breaking point, but I pressed forward. Cold sweat trickled down my sides as the tunic clung tightly to my skin, Solana turned.

"Just a short while further, Casanova," she said, her eyes a sparkling reflection of the ice form beside me.

"Why is it so cold here?" I said through chattering teeth, my lips completely numb.

"It is the purest way of cleansing oneself of impurities," she retorted coolly

"Is that what I am to do here, cleanse myself of impurity?"

"No, my child." She stopped in mid-stride, as well as the others. "You are here to restore balance!"

The cylindrical ice form beside me began rotating slowly at first, then faster and faster until it became a blurring solid form that flashed brilliantly throughout the cave. Dashing hues came alive, purples, greens and blues made the entire cave sparkle richly. The ice sentinel hovering over me was clad in a thick grey fur coated in a layer of frost and ice, along with the massive halberd he held in his right hand. His face was that of a skeleton, bony and sharp, with wrinkles across his cheeks, giving hint of skin that had once been present but was now so dry and brittle that it could shatter at a touch. The gaping holes in his face, signs of where the warrior's eyes had once been, but as I stared deep into the empty sockets, I could swear the warrior was looking straight through to my soul.

"Casanova..." a distant voice called out. Bringing my gaze up slowly, I was staring at the blurry image of a woman who held an outstretched hand toward me. "Take my hand!" the woman mouthed, barely audible, but my vision was waning and it felt as if I were suddenly plunging into oblivion. Colors that were just moments ago flashing radiantly, faded into the darkness. Air whooshed pass my face as my body dropped into an endless abyss... an abyss that descended to the very soul of the earth. My heart lurched as I felt the rush of blood race to my head. I lifted my hands up to brace for the coming impact, but then...

"Casanova," the voice called once more. When I opened my eyes, I was staring into the gaping holes in the face of the sentinel. Solana stood just beside me with a hand extended. "Take my hand!" I stared at her stupidly for a moment as Isis turned back, followed by Brotus.

"Is there something wrong?" Brotus said, squinting, his dark gaze hard and stony but concerned.

"N-no," I stuttered in confusion, reaching for Solana's hand. "Everything is well, I just... feel light headed!"

"That is natural," Solana said, "when standing amidst such power. It shall soon pass."

"We are here!" Brotus intoned, just before the entire cave was immersed in darkness. When the flame was lit, we were no longer on the winding step well and the cylindrical ice form was no longer seen. The vivid sparkling colors that previously illuminated the entire cave were now replaced with gloom. A long stone corridor appeared before us, shrouded in shadow. Warm currents brushed against my skin as we advanced down the hall in silent stride.

Sentinels flanked the dark walls here as well, but these warriors were different. Much taller and more fierce looking than the others, these sentinels were fully armored in black ring mail, with black helms emblazoned with the same sparkling rubies found on Tiberius' father and his men. The trio stopped abruptly and turned to the chamber they stood beside.

"He is awaiting your presence," Brotus said, nodding toward the door. The three of them held their gazes to the ground as if they were leading me into the fiery pits of hell.

"Try not to seem so jovial," I quipped but received no response. Smirking to myself, I turned and reached a trembling hand toward the chamber door. Truth was, I was terrified of what lay beyond it. In a cave like this, it seems you either find something amazingly beautiful or... A soft hand clutched the sleeve of my tunic, and I turned.

"Be careful... Casanova," Solana said softly. Her eyes touched mine and then fixed firmly on the ground. I nodded silently and lifted the latch to the chamber.

As the chamber door creaked open, a stream of blue light streaked out into the dim corridor. It was not the immense size of the chamber that impressed me; in fact, the room was quite the same dimensions as my chamber back in Partrizia. The difference here was that the entire wall in the far end was a blue flame that set an ominous tone to the chamber. The massive hooded man facing the flames stood motionless as I entered. I wheeled around when the heavy door slammed shut behind me, but the sound barely made the man flinch as he continued to stare through the flame with his back towards me. A long moment of silence followed until the man inhaled, as if to begin.

"Do not be afraid of me!" a deep, raspy voice intoned with a slow, deliberate tone that made him seem larger than life itself. He wore a long hooded white cloak that covered him entirely, his dark presence in sharp contrast with the blazing inferno before him.

"I... I am not certain we have met before," I said to his back. "Dimitrius?" His shoulders were powerful looking, wide as an ox. He stood nearly two heads over me, and one of his arms looked to be the width of my entire body.

"Oh, but we have..." the hooded man urged, "right here in this very chamber. You were a lad just shy of seven years with nothing to offer the world, but hints of what you will become in the future."

"A king?" I said as nearly a half-dozen have uttered before me.

"Is that what you have decided to become?" he asked calmly, although the raspiness of his voice gave a malicious edge to his tone. "Or is that what you have been told?"

"It..." I started, but then paused. I honestly had not put any previous thought to the query. Is my decision based on personal desire, or public obligation? the question floated around in my mind before I gave my remark. "It is what I have been told."

"So what is it you have decided to become?" His words alone were very simple, yet became the most complex arrangement of syllables once put together. I took longer to respond to this query as the man stood silently amidst the flames, just watching, waiting.

"I have decided to become immortal, as my master had strived to before me," I said after a long silence, completely satisfied with my response. "As many before him have strived, and also failed," he drawled slowly. "Tell me, what is it that intrigues you so about immortality?"

"It was my master's last mission... I would do anything to continue his legacy."

"Would you be willing to die to continue it?" he said. Again with these damned riddles. Had I not known this were a test, I would have failed before I started.

"That would be counterproductive!" I said.

"Well, that is about as truthful as one can get!" he quipped.

"You said we have met before," I said matter of factly, "and yet you greet me with your back."

"Because your heart is heavy," he said calmly, "you must be of purest mind and of purest heart to look upon my face."

"I have many tasks left unfinished," I stated truthfully, "many people I have to help. My brother and I were separated, and I am intent on finding him."

"Be of ease, my child," Dimitrius said, and it was in that very moment that I felt the heat of the flames touching my skin. The sudden rush sent thoughts of tranquility racing throughout my body. I felt light, no longer aware of the cave, nor even the world around me. Flashing images of my dark past that once haunted me came and passed. Thoughts of Arkon with his rigid exercises of the mind and unorthodox methods of teaching appeared and faded. All thoughts, hopes, dreams, aspirations, goals... were no longer in existence. Only the pure, blissful feeling of certainty and knowingness lingered on within me.

When I opened my eyes, I was peering at the huge silhouette of a shadowed man approaching, his heavy steps nearly inaudible as he neared. His hood rested low over his eyes, but not enough to conceal the darkness glaring back at me from beneath. His face was rough and battle scarred. Thick scales ornamented his features with a grotesque tinge of green and gray. Looking up, his immense size made me take two steps back before I even noticed I was moving. I could never have imagined a sight so horrid.

"My deepest apolo..." I immediately stopped speaking as his hand was raised.

"No apology is necessary," he said respectfully. "I know what I have become, but what is more important is that I know who I have become. Knowledge of self is the ultimate form of immortality, living forever is just the side effect of that knowledge. As for your brother, I shall ease your mind, my child."

He glared down at me, and his dark eyes slowly began changing. It was as if his very pupils were dissipating right before me, until they were mere bulbs of white energy shimmering from beneath his hooded brim. Images began to form from within them. Wild trees and heavy shrubs came into view. Within the trees, dozens of natives clad in furs and feathers were leaping from branch to branch, leaves rustling wildly around them as they moved. Arrows rained past their heads as they passed; they were warring. It was unclear to me why I was seeing this as black smoke rose from the distant horizon. Nor even as the images drew in closer to the heart of the battle and twelve lady archers stood sentry, waiting for the approaching natives to pass. It was the one single scream that brought my mind to a seizing halt.

Tiberius Blackwell
"Ready your sword... and do not get in my way."
Candonia, 1869

"This is not going to work!" Raleigh blared with huge, gaping eyes. Cold sweat streamed from my forehead and drenched the shreds that were left of my shabby tunic. Feverish flares of hot and cold flashes raced through me in a simultaneous clashing of the polar opposites. We were outside but beneath the raw hide that stood erected and kept in the heat of the flaming torch.

"It will work, because it must!" the old man returned. He wore heavy furs around his neck and wrists. His boots were made of the same material, only they were interlaced with a thick inner lining that made it possible for him to move quickly and stealthily through the trees and shrubs. White and red war paint covered his face, and his smoke grey hair was fashioned in a long interlocking braid that was nearly long as the spear he wielded. "But another outcry like that, and he will disclose our position." "You hear that, big guy?" Raleigh said. "Here, sink your teeth into this and scream bloody murder if you want."

He lifted the cloth to my dry, cracked lips, and I bit down on it with all my might. Turning to the old man, Raleigh nodded. Just then, the flaming torch neared my leg once again and I braced myself for the touch. When it made contact, I wailed like a virgin of twelve years. The old man waited for the pain to peak before pouring a cool solvent on the wound, and the dryness of the liquid formed a white pasty gook around the wound. A chilling sensation rushed through me. The gaping hole in my thigh began to whither and whiten as skin does after staying under water for too long, and then it warmed. Purple and blue bruises formed on the front of my thigh as the solvent seeped in through the wound and tingled, like a thousand tiny spiders were crawling just beneath my skin. A flap of the hide was lifted, and shimmering rays of sun cascaded in through the opening.

"Chieftain..." said a thin, sinewy lad upon his approach, "the village is compromised!" He was garbed in thick wool, and distress rested behind his heavy stare. When the old man lifted his eyes to survey the lad, it was with a calm revere.

"Deploy the warriors!" the chieftain said, his eyes glazed and distant.

"The warriors were engaged, Chieftain!" the lad urged. "Only three remain for service."

"Then send for my daughter, she will know what to do," the chieftain dismissed the lad and handed the torch to Raleigh.

"Yes, sire," the lad said, vanishing from sight.

"The infection is receding, but there are still fragments beneath your skin," the chieftain said. "I am afraid there shall be no time to remove them."

"What does that mean, Chief?" Raleigh turned to the sound of heavy footsteps approaching.

"It means he indeed may never enter battle again."

"I am fine!" I snapped. "Just pour on some of that pasty shit on it again, and I will be on my way, old man." The flap was lifted once again, and the sun brightened the small area. Four warriors entered the tent, two lady archers and two native barbarians stopped just before the chieftain.

"Father," the lady archer said with her eyes on the progress of my wound.

"My dear Caliah," the old man said, "how fare things in the clan?"

"Seven deaths have plagued our land," Caliah intoned "our clan brothers to the north have deserted their posts and left the gates open for attack. We must leave if we are to preserve the woman and children."

"How many men?" Raleigh said, a notable savagery in his tone.

"A clan of thirty strong were seen breaking through the first layer of gates," one of the barbarians said.

"They have set fire to our crops and started burning down the woodlands," said the other.

"And how many men do you have left?" Raleigh pressed.

"Twelve archers, ten warriors," Caliah said, already defeated.

"I will lead your men to the gates," Raleigh said, with fiery eyes. "You and your archers reinforce the rear!" Caliah looked upon Raleigh with uncertainty.

"You are an outsider," she said, not unkindly, "this is not your battle!"

"Did you forget that you saved our lives?" Raleigh replied. "Or is that not reason enough for me to do what I love?"

"I did not do it for you!" Caliah snapped. "I did it because your friend would never have survived the night with that much blood loss. Your love is of swords and blades, not the way of the bow," she pointed out firmly. "This is not your fight, outsider!" The two exchanged long, heated stares before the chieftain finally intervened.

"Seven of ours have fallen," the old man said in scarcely a whisper, "and many more shall perish on this day!" He turned to me and dabbed my sweaty forehead with the cloth. "Many more deaths shall follow unless you unify. Steady your heart, my daughter!" The woman stared at me as if I had disrespected the very ground she walked upon.

"Ready your sword..." she finally said after a stare of death, "and do not get in my way!" She turned, lifted a fist to her chest and bowed at the neck to her father, and then she was gone. Raleigh checked his blades and adjusted his sash with a rough jerk of his fist before he turned to me, wearing a smirk that was only fitting for the death crazed mad man.

"Wipe off that grin, fool," I said, my head resting weakly on the rough cushion, "or it's likely an arrowhead'll wipe it off for you!"

"This one is for you, brother!" he said, with an edge to his tone that hinted of death, with just the slightest touch of murder. His smile was no longer visible when we clasped forearms as true warriors would, where there had previously been doubt and uncertainty, it was now clear. This man was not only a fearless warrior, he also proved himself a loyal ally.

"Be of good fate, brother," I intoned, just before he nodded and blurred from the tent. The chieftain turned to me and sighed deeply.

"May the gods be with us!"

CHAPTER EIGHT

Memorie VIII

Raleigh Bines
"After this... I shall owe you nothing more!"
Candonia, 1869

My heart raced as the distant sound of battle and drums of war filled the humid air with thoughts of death. As we lay in wait, I turned to the warrior kneeling down beside the womb of the nearest shrub, his fist wrapped tightly around a heavy spiked club.

"How many battles have you fought, warrior?" I asked.

"Three," he returned coolly, his eyes darting left and right, although the threat was nowhere in sight. Setting a trap for your kill requires extreme skill, a flawless strategy and manpower. A lack in either of these things would get sloppy, and in war, sloppy means death. Snaking my neck around the tree I was leaned against, I quickly spotted the seven variously positioned sentries rustling noisily through the shrubs. This will never work, I thought, double checking my blades once more.

"I still remember my first battle. I was so young... and uncoordinated!" I reflected with a smirk. "It ended so fast that before I could reach for the hilt of my blade, I was flung from the saddle and thrown into the front lines." As the sound of native horsemen resounded heavily in the distance, the warrior stood expressionless, staring blankly between the trees ahead. Perhaps my words have not yet hit home... I thought as I stared at the muscle-bound brute, whose only idea of battle is this primal, jungle lay in the bushes shit. Waiting amongst the trees instead of using our speed and home advantage. Maybe this might help the situation... I thought as the horsemen drew close.

"You know," I began, "after your brothers over there are slaughtered piece by piece and tied to the back of a horse, only to be dragged to a very slow, painful, agonizing death... then maybe you will allow me to take a leadership role in this battle, like a true warrior!"

"My orders are to wait for the ambush!" he barked staring through the vines ahead "Not to go on some reckless frontal assault that is sure to get us all killed. Like it nearly did your friend back there huh?"

My face tightened, and blood rushed through my head. I fought back an urge to draw my sword and remove the head from his sinewy neck, but the screams that followed brought the attention of anyone within a hundred strides. What sounded like nearly twenty horses neighed uncontrollably, and it gradually became clear what the commotion was: they were burning their horses alive. It was in that moment that I unsheathed my sword and began pressing forward. Turning, the warriors and archers stood scared, motionless, each staring through the vines with fear in each of their beady eyes.

"Ladies..." I said. "Warriors! All those who wish to sit here like cowards while these horsemen invade your homeland, burn down your villages, rape your women, kill your chief!" My eyes shot to Caliah, and fiery hazels stared back at me. "Then I shall meet you all at the bloody gates of hell. But for those who want to stand and fight for your village, fight for the women and children, fight for honor, then join me. And I promise you all, this will be a battle for the ages, my friends. Who is with me?"

Twelve archers and ten warriors stared back at me, not one stepped forward. They all stood staring stupidly over my shoulder. I turned as black smoke rose from the distant horizon. With it came the rotting stench of burning flesh. Even Caliah now stepped forward in horror.

"What... is happening?" she drawled skeptically, her eyes a smoky reflection of the death that approached, her tone growing ever more fierce.

"You," she said, holding a condemned finger pointed out towards me, "you drew them here!" The eyes of every native standing before me grew wide with disbelief and anger. A few walked over and stood behind Caliah as reinforcements.

"You don't..." I said, "really believe that, right? What purpose would it serve for me to lead these savages into a jungle?" Neither of them spoke nor made a move to advance. I turned my back to the savages, sheathed my longsword and unclipped the latch holding my two twin blades.

"Fine!" I said in scarcely a whisper, staring at an almost certain death before me. "I'll do it myself!"

Three man approached from a great distance, their faces covered entirely in black paint as they emerged from the wild trees. They were thin, sinewy men, each clad in heavy furs and golden chokers around their neck and wrists. Six others rose from the high grass to my left, twelve more appeared through the grass to the right. My heart lurched, and my blood went cold. They just outwitted us with the oldest trick in the book.

"What do you mean retreat?" Caliah snarled. "You are the one just a moment ago so adamant on running face first into battle, and now you turn into a suckling babe?"

"I am no suckling babe!" I blared louder than expected. "I am a seasoned warrior of more then five battles, I can read a trap from a hundred strides off. If you do not turn back with me, then I shall return only to escort the remains of your dead back to your father." I felt hazel eyes burning through the side of my face, but I did not return the stare. I glanced anxiously over my shoulder at the small group of natives approaching; it was now or never.

Inside, I was adamant on following through with one plan: run back to the village get Tiberius and get the fuck out of here. Although the formation of these savage natives were scattered, they had numbers, and I knew that I would only be leading these people to an early burial. Sighing with annoyance, I nearly ripped the blades out of my sash and glared at Caliah with flame filled eyes.

"After this," I spat, "I shall owe you nothing more!"

When I turned, ten natives armed with long spears emerged from the distant shrubs. The men moved with such speed and grace, they appeared to have blurred through the wild trees. Before I could blink, a heavy spear thrashed through the vines en route to the side of my head before I ducked and weaved under it just in time. The vines were ripped to shreds from the attack, and behind the heavy shrubs stood three of the fuckers exposed, each staring angrily toward me. The twisted smirk on my face must have angered the men, because when they advanced, the barrage of attacks were savage and with ill intent. Quickly unsheathing my longsword, I slashed viciously through the crowd, nearly filleting the first two that appeared, but my attack was only able to disarm them momentarily before they advanced again. Spears came from all directions, and each parry brought me at least a second to think before another spearhead was thrust toward me. I was a sitting duck here, just as I knew I would be, but at least I knew how to maneuver in these situations.

    I ducked down beneath a low spear thrust and rolled swiftly beneath another. When I looked up, I was on the left flank of one of the savages, and I made sure my presence was felt. Bringing my sword down heavily, I removed the man's ear. Blood spewed and spurted from the side of his head before I took it off with a heavy slash. Blood sprayed a mist of red across the shrubs. I let go of the sword and quickly reached for my twin blades. In dramatic fashion, I lunged forward, driving the blades in through the native's chest and yanking them quickly back out. When I turned, I was almost eye to eye with the tip of a spear, but my blade reached it just in time to parry with a dangerous spark of steel against steel. The force of the blow broke through the parry and grazed the side of my head. Pain streaked through my face, and my head swam, either from the impact or the anticipation of the pain to come.

When I looked up, nothing stared back at me but the sun glaring down and the two birds soaring just overhead, as if they were revealing a story. I felt my mind slipping from my grasp. Hidden thoughts that were previously suppressed now came to the forefront.

"Get up, my child..." a soft angelic voice said, but when I looked, there were only the two birds and the distant sound of fighting. "Get up and do what you were born to do, my beloved!"

Beloved? I thought ponderously but quickly dismissed the thought. Although it had been nearly ten years past, I could never forget that voice. My heart turned with excitement, hoping the face on the other side of my lids would be hers...

"Raleigh..." a distant voice called out. "Raleigh!!!"

When I opened my eyes, a stale, hazy odor touched my nose. Smoke drifted past my nostrils, and my heart went from yearning to an instant dread... I pushed my palms into the dirt and got to my feet. I felt for my twin blades, but they were gone, as well as my sword. The vision in my right eye was fogged, almost entirely blurred out. My hands were drenched in a deep red liquid, as if I had cleansed my hands in blood... All around me were bodies dismembered, shrubs with blood splattered recklessly across them. Some bodies covered in black war paint, others with war stripes just under their eyes, Caliah's men. At my feet, a man's torso was torn from its upper half, and entrails lay in a wet, slimy pile. I took a step back in disgust and nearly lost my footing over a body. Two blades stood lodged in its chest as it lay motionless in the dirt.

"Raleigh... where are you?" a familiar voice called as I leaned over and jerked the blades from the chest of my kill, leaving dark red smears on each.

"Over here," I returned, looking quickly down at my hands once more and dreading the fact that I could not remember anything. The shrubs rustled heavily from up ahead, and it was Caliah who burst through them first. There were bruises on her neck and face, a slash going down her arm, and her deerskin over cloth was cut almost entirely to shreds so bad that it now resembled that of a ragged vest with blotches of red scattered among its fabric. The next face to emerge from the bushes was the warrior I wanted to behead earlier. The man's face was filled with dirt and blood, but his eyes held a look of admiration.

"You are such a fool..." said Caliah grimly with a glare that could make even the most vicious warrior cringe. She wrapped her arms around my neck and pulled me to her, entirely unexpected. She held me firmly for a long moment, but when she released, her eyes were filled.

"I am so sorry!" she said as tears welled from within her lids and fell endlessly. She dropped to her knees, her bow landing sloppily in the dirt. Her outcry was so intense that a flock of birds took flight from the sudden shrill.

"Hey... hey!!" I said, softly placing a hand on her back but quickly removed the blood-stained palm. "It is all over now, we can go back, rest, regroup, and fight another day."

When she lifted her head, her hazel eyes were completely bloodshot. It was as if she had lost a mother, or her child, or... Two figures appeared from just beyond the bushes. Ripping my blades out, I lunged past Caliah and grabbed hold of...

"Tiberius?" I said, bemused. "How did you...? Why are you here?"

One of Caliah's barbarians was holding Tiberius upright, but the cloth wrapping his leg was the work of an amateur at best. Tiberius looked down at my hand, and I quickly released my grip, leaving a red smear on the collar of his doublet.

"Sorry 'bout that, big guy," I said, patting down his collar, "but why is the chief not with you?" Silence filled the dusk air with a tangy unease. I turned to the barbarian holding Tiberius up on his feet, and his eyes touched the ground. Caliah was shaking uncontrollably, her knees wedged into the dirt, sobbing with her hands covering her face. I turned back to Tiberius and shook my head, dismayed.

"No!" I said, my heart sinking to the pit of my stomach. "They killed the chief?" The glare in his eyes spoke of horrors far worse.

"He was held down," Tiberius said. Caliah's cries grew louder and more intense. "Forced to watch the women being raped, beaten and set afire. They wanted him to surrender the location of something, but I could not think much past the screams, the smell. There were so many of their men within the village, we had no other choice..."

"No other choice?" I squinted, confused.

"We had to play dead," he sighed. "We trashed the tent to make it look as if it had already been ravaged, and we waited."

"Shit!" I thundered viciously. "Shit, it was my fault." "There is no way you could have seen this coming. You did what you felt..."

"He did..." a soft, unfamiliar voice said; it was Caliah's. "He saw it all coming. It was I that did not see!"

"What is her meaning?" Tiberius said, with narrowed eyes. "And what in the name of the gods happened here?" His eyes went down to the severed bodies scattered amongst the wild trees, the splattered red mist sprayed across the leaves, my blood-soaked hands.

"He saved our lives!" a rough voice returned. The warrior standing beside Caliah was approaching with an expression of gratitude within his beady black eyes. "He told us to turn back because it was a trap."

"A trap?" Tiberius echoed. "This does not resemble the outcome of a trap, unless it was set by you!"

"He killed them all..." the warrior blurted. "We were instructed not to assist in his aide, but when he was surrounded, Caliah gave the word and we pressed close to battle. Our brothers..." He stood staring at the fresh blood soaking into the dirt, tears welling in the corner of his eyes. Bodies were sprawled about in disarray, too many to count, too grotesque to view for longer than a moment. "Our brothers will not soon be forgotten!"

"Hey, warrior!" I said coolly. "About what I said earlier about your brothers, I only wished to gauge the loyalty of the men I fought beside!"

"And what did you assess?" he replied. I looked around at each face beside me, each scar and bruise, each terrified face disguised with courage.

"I have assessed..." I started, "that I would not want to be stuck on a godforsaken island like this, without either of you by my side!" I said, but the funny thing about that statement was that I actually meant it.

"So what are we to do now?" Tiberius said. A dark moment passed by, and silence filled the night. All eyes drifted toward Caliah, awaiting her next command. Caliah's eyes went from her burning village to the mountainous hilly terrain that formed the horizon.

"We will bury our dead..." she said glumly but with authority, "set fire to our enemies' corpses, and then we shall have to set out in search of a new home." The two warriors turned immediately and began lifting the bodies of their loved ones.

"In search of a new home?" Tiberius said, glancing up at the approaching night and then down to his leg. "You are forgetting one minor detail..."

"You are right," Caliah said, defeated.

"Big guy, didn't you have somewhere you needed to be?" Raleigh urged suggestively. "A place with hills and truth, possibly the whereabouts of your brother!"

"I did not forget my mission, Raleigh," Tiberius said with nonchalance, "but it seems you forgot we are stranded... on an island!"

"And it seems you forgot..." he returned sharply, "that there is something waiting just for us at the coast." My eyes suddenly lit up with remembrance. How could I have not thought of this myself? I stared back at the grinning man with slight fondness before he turned to Caliah.

"You ever been on a pirate ship?"

CHAPTER NINE
Memorie IX

    Shadowy images slowly began to emerge within the darkness of the land. People I did not know, places I had never been all flashed before me in a smoky mirage-like reflection and then faded back into darkness. The burden of each step was now unbearable; I was exhausted. The weight of my armor and sword and crown was more than any typical man had to endure, yet I was no longer a typical man. I was king, and as king my purpose was to take on the burdens of an entire nation. I stalked forward, toward the direction of the voice, but as my boots sank down further into the wet dirt, only silence accompanied me within the darkness. To be honest, it may have been hours since I last heard the voice, might have even been days.

    Maybe this is what happens to unrighteous kings...I thought, trudging forward. They travel aimlessly through whatever oblivion I was in, until they either die of starvation or the silence eats them alive and they turn completely mad. But it wouldn't explain what I could have done to be here, alone. There must have been thousands of kings who have ruled worst than I could have, millions of dark sorcerers and evil mages who should be here instead of me. I should be in the physical realm, helping my people, finding my brother.

"Agishi..." a voice whispered so suddenly, I stopped in mid stride to be sure I heard it.

"Who's there?" I cried out to the darkness, turning in all directions. "Reveal yourself!"

"The seerum." The voice was slow and drawn out, but nothing was seen. "The serum, Agishi"

Agishi? I thought.

"Dark seruuuum!" the voice returned, barely audible, as if they were struggling to speak.

"Please get me out of here!" I blared but only received the faint howling of the wind and the distant crackling of flames.

"Ooopen..." the voice said after a long moment. "Ooopen... eyes!" My eyes are open, but I cannot see!" I blared back.

I slowly lifted my hands up before my face and saw nothing. I lifted my boot from the dirt; wet, sticky slime was wedged onto the bottom of it as I felt around for something, anything to grab hold of, but there was nothing. A chamber door squeaked open from just strides away. The distant sound of swords clashing was heard for a brief moment. The sound of a body colliding with stone was also heard just before a heavy grunt sounded and then faded. Footsteps neared and stopped just beside me.

"He is still weak," an indistinct voice said from so close, my heart lurched.

"Will he survive is the question!" an angered woman said from beside me; without a doubt it was Solana.

"Yes!" the indistinct voice answered. "But his condition will require..."

"What is it, Razuhl? What does he need..."

Memorie IX

Casanova Volkart

"Who are you, Solana?"

Southern coast of Cilan, 1869

The setting sun gave hints of distant pleasures well off in the horizon. The promise of higher ground eased my former suspicions of starvation as the mountainous regions neared, but the lingering ache in my chest proved unbearable the further we pressed. Tiberius was yet alive and breathing, yet he was hurt, incapacitated for battle. He was now solely reliant on Raleigh, which would have eased tension had this not been Tiberius I spoke of.

"We must hurry," a dark, raspy voice said from the head of the group, "darkness approaches!" Dimitrius was not a man of many words; hell, it would be a bewilderment if he were indeed an actual man. His massive shoulders out sized any I have ever seen, yet he moved with such grace, such elegance, that you could not look upon him without acknowledging his divine power, the very presence of a god.

"As you wish, my lord!" Brotus nodded, becoming suddenly authoritative. "You heard the command, let us save words 'till our destination is reached." Isis greeted Brotus' remark with a look of scorn, as she had been the only voice heard within the silence of the cobble stoned pathway.

"I merely wish to set the lad's mind at ease," she remarked. "Silence within grave situations can sometimes prove to have the opposite effect of that which is desired."

"As too shall traversing this road absent the company of sun!" Brotus said, staring ahead toward the darkening horizon. "Solana, see that the mind of Casanova is at ease."

"This way!" Solana said, veering slightly to the left. "Let us not interrupt ceaseless quarrels and discuss your destiny." Solana shot her sister a look of authority, judging by her cutting stare.

"You know..." I said, staring ahead, "you never told me what Sinnis Trocahl planned to do with me once I signed that contract. Nor have you revealed your connection with the man, nor even your true intent for me. I shall not continue to walk down a path of shadows when I know now where my brother is."

"There are many things I must tell you, Casanova," she said, her eyes moistened, "many things I must show you! But under oath, I am unable to reveal these things until you have proven yourself ready."

"Well, surely your oath does not refrain you from revealing one query that I am intrigued by..." I said, gazing upon her eyes. "Who are you, Solana? Where do you come from?" She paused a moment, as if collecting her thoughts. Her eyes revealing a troubled past, and yet an even more troublesome future. Her hands were concealed within the folds of her tunic, but somehow I knew they were clammy and trembling, for reasons unknown.

"Casanova..." she said softly, slowing her stride. The trees in the near distance began trembling around us, and the heavy gust that followed froze my blood solid within my veins, the look in Solana's face turning to dread.

"I want you to take this!" she said sharply through gritted teeth. I looked down at the shimmering steel in her hands. Dried blood stained the hilt and almost halfway up the blade. Along the hilt were small etchings which transcribed the word Sacrifice on one side, and the word Courage on the other. The look in her eyes held the same carnage it held that night, back at the dungeon. It were as if the kind, affectionate woman that stood before me just a moment ago had vanished, only to be replaced with a dark effigy. When I touched the hilt, a rushing jolt surged through my arms, my chest, throughout my entire body.

"What is happening?" I said, confused by the trembling surroundings.

"This is how you shall prove you are ready!" she said, staring out into oblivion. My eyes surveyed the darkness for a moment before Brotus stepped up to my flank, baring his teeth viciously. A great sword gold of hilt was clutched in his hard fist. Dimitrius and Isis appeared so quickly before me; it were as if they had materialized from thin air. A huge war hammer that appeared to be the cause of a considerable amount of murder was gripped firmly in his palm. Isis wielded two chains with spiked edges and a blade tip, a truly queer weapon from the sight of it.

"What is taking Celeste so long?" Dimitrius barked as the trembling intensified.

"She was summoned, my lord..." Solana said, unclipping the blades from her tunic sash. "shall I request her presence at once?" Dimitrius turned to me, his black eyes glaring intensely against the shimmer of moonlight.

"No!" he said, holding my gaze. "If all goes as planned, then her presence shall not be needed... Isis!"

"Yes, my lord!" she said at once.

"Take control of the battle here," Dimitrius ordered. "I mustn't leave the cave unattended"

"Yes, my lord." Her eyes touched mine, and when she smirked, I saw almost a splitting image of the look Raleigh took when he was anxious for battle.

"Brotus, see it done!" Dimitrius ordered.

"Aye, my lord!" Brotus returned.

"Casanova," Dimitrius said, "see yourself through this alive, and we shall bring fire down upon the ones responsible for your grief!"

Six shadows suddenly presented themselves on horseback from a distance, wielding morning stars and halberds. At the head of the unit, atop his war axe a black banner with a broken skull transfixed on it was billowing in the dusk air. They were clad entirely in black, each face covered to the top of the nose so that only their eyes were exposed. When the leader dismounted, he jabbed the banner down into the dirt. As each dismounted at a far enough distance, the tension grew with each passing moment. But everything unraveled with deliberately steady suspense like a ceremonial ritual.

"A ploy," Isis intoned unabashed. "Brotus, get ready!"

"Born ready, sister!" he returned, stepping forward to stand beside her. Two of the horsemen stepped forward. Isis and Brotus followed the signs and slowly approached the masked men as I stepped up behind them, only to look down and see Solana's hand gripping my forearm.

"Not yet!" she mouthed softly, her eyes fixed heavily on the approaching danger. I looked up just as Brotus and Isis stopped before two masked men. One was huge, heavily built and approached brandishing an enormous war hammer in his right hand. The other was slim and walked with such a grace that he appeared almost too confident. Two long swords were sheathed on his back, exposed over each shoulder. I gripped tightly on the short sword and silently prayed to whatever gods would listen. Words were exchanged, but by the look of it nothing yet to worry ab... "If that is what you wish," Isis' voice thundered intensely through the thin air, "then it shall be resolved with blood!"

"Ready your sword..." Solana breathed, slowly reaching for her twin blades. "On my mark, we rush their flank and bring death down upon them."

"Understood!" I nodded with complete confidence, even as cold sweat trickled down the pits of my arms beneath my tunic. I looked down, and my hand was shaking just as much as the trees were just a moment ago, the short sword trembled in my palm before I mustered up the strength to grab firm hold of the hilt. I looked up, and Isis was everywhere. There were six clones of her standing next to Brotus, each prepared for attack. To the far right side stood Brotus, angling in for an attack that should have been clearly seen, judging by how slow it was. But as he lifted his great sword overhead and brought it down heavily over the enormous masked man, it was as if his head exploded on impact. Blood burst out the top of the man's skull so fast, it splashed back into Brotus' face, giving him the blood splattered face of a savage murderer.

"Now!" Solana drawled loudly. I charged forward, and before I could blink twice, I was in the middle of the action.

"Casanova, your flank!" a voice called with urgency. I turned to see Brotus' eyes gaping toward my blind side. Kneeling down just in time, I looked up to see a sword slicing over my head. Everything moved at a slow, almost unreal pace. My instincts flared, and I reached up with my free hand in time to grab the masked man's hand, twist his weapon from his grasp and dash my sword into the soft part of his belly, all in one motion. Staring the man in his eyes, mostly out of disbelief, I saw nothing but a hazy grey mist where his eyes should have been. There was no color, no pupil, no life behind that mask. Two arrows whizzed past my face, and I slipped one just as the second one grazed my cheek. Blood sprayed from my mouth, and my head jerked to the side, nearly a dozen masked men approached from my flank. Behind me, another dozen or so masked men emerged from the trees... we were surrounded.

With no time to think of my next move, I did the only thing Arkon had taught me to do in a hopeless situation such as this. I held my ground until the last possible moment, breathed in as much air as my lungs would hold, and let out a terrifying war cry as I charged through the middle of the oncoming brigade. The battle went by the pace of the rhythmic thumping of my heart in my chest, slow and measured.

    My mind was suddenly clear and full of purpose. Lifting my sword, everything felt natural. I parried an underhanded blow from one and ducked beneath his fist right before I drove my sword straight through his right eye. Blood spurted from his face. As I jerked the blade out, the smell of blood and death energized me. I turned to my left just as Solana's blades punched through the chest of her mark. From just ahead, Isis ran towards me and flung her arm out. A heavy chain blade came swooshing over my right shoulder and sliced straight through shoulder of the masked man behind me. When I turned, a fist caught the side of my cheek and I hit the ground with a heavy thud, my sword slipping from my grasp. Dirt flew up when I hit the ground, and before I could push myself to my feet, a fierce kick to the stomach had me curled in fetal position. A kick to the jaw sent blood splooshing from my mouth as I was swarmed by these soulless creatures, with no hope of escape. An energy arose from within my chest, a feeling queer and unfamiliar to me. The moon shimmered brilliantly overhead in the heart of a star filled sky. A pressure built up inside of me, it was almost as if my body were about to erupt. The kicks and punches raining down over me were no longer felt. Only the unbearable stretching of my body being pulled in all directions from the inside out. My chest burned as if a torch were set to the front of my tunic, and it only intensified as I held my body from tearing to shreds. The burning stretched from my chest to my neck, from my back to my legs, and as the feeling became unbearable, I was no longer able to hold back the inevitable.

Suddenly, the burning was no more. The pain streaking throughout my body from various wounds faded just as sudden. Darkness consumed the cool night. The stars and moon vanished, the men, the trees everything, was no longer in sight. My body was numb almost entirely aside from the tips of my fingers. Heavy footsteps approached, and I clasped my fingers through the dirt, reaching for my sword but found nothing but mud and insects. I lay there hopelessly in wait, for my approaching death to arrive.

"Casanova..." a distant voice called out, It was Solana. "Get him back to the cave, Celeste will revive him!"

"Did you see what he just did sister?" Isis said gravely. "This is well pass her expertise." I tried to say everything was fine with me, but my lips were no longer felt. I clasped my fingers through the dirt once more.

"Dimitrius will know what to do!" Brotus said with certainty. "For now, we have to clear these bodies from the road before her next legion identifies our location." My fingers clawed endlessly at the dirt, but no one noticed. Inside I was screaming bloody murder, but to my own ears not a sound was emitted.

"And what of Casanova?" Solana said sharply. Something touched my hand, and I instantly grabbed it. Solana's hand jerked back as if she were startled at first, but then she touched my hand once more and felt the grip of my fingers against hers. Soft whimpers sounded from just before my face.

"Brotus...look!" Solana said softly, lifting my hand with hers still clasped within it. Warm drops fell upon my fingers, too warm to be rain and too soft to be blood. Lifting my hand to her face, she rested a warm tear filled cheek against the back of my hand. Soft whimpers were heard, followed by the sound of bodies being dragged across cobblestone a short distance away.

"I will always be here for you!" she whispered in my ear. Soft lips touched the back of my hand, and I felt her warmth, her tenderness. Without sight and without a voice, it was hard to express the feeling transferred between us at that moment, but it was a joy I never had the pleasure of knowing. It was a feeling of comfort and serenity, a warmth that could only be produced by that of a goddess. My thoughts weighed lightly down upon me. If I were to perish at this very moment, I would sing praises of rejoice in the spirit realm. For not only did I die fighting for what I believed in, but I died in the arms of a woman who cared deeply for me. And that, there would be the best death a man could ever ask for.

Tiberius Blackwell
"This is only going to end two ways."
Candonia 1869

"The coast is just beyond those shrubs..." Caliah said as the smell of water and sand filled the air. I turned to my right, and when I caught eyes with Raleigh, it was only for a brief moment before the clamoring of axes against wood sounded from just ahead. My hand instinctively went for my waist and gripped the hilt of my sword.

"Get down," Caliah mouthed towards us as she knelt beneath the cover of the wild trees. She cocked her head to the side, held up two fingers, and flicked them toward the east. Raleigh and I positioned ourselves to her far flank, shielded by a tall shrub. Through the shrub, natives could be seen, but without verbal communication with Caliah, I could not tell if these were friends or foe.

"What do you see, big guy?" Raleigh whispered from an awkward kneeling position.

"I am not sure," I said, squinting. "It looks as if they are examining the ship!"

"Examining our ship?" Raleigh said sharply. As he reached a hand up to the shrub, dried leaves crunched from a short distance behind us as the two of us whirled around simultaneously. We were both staring into the eyes of a lad maybe ten years. His face was painted white with a blue stripe beneath each eye, a spear nearly twice his height and a handful of arrows, but no bow. The lad's eyes gaped open upon seeing us, but before he could open his mouth to scream, Raleigh blurred towards him and clamped his hand over his mouth just as sound emitted.

"Now why would you want to do that?" Raleigh taunted in the boy's ear. The boy twisted and squirmed but was held by the iron grip of Raleigh's grasp. Raleigh jerked the boy's head back, unsheathed one of his blades and held the shining steel under the soft part of his jaw.

"I am going to take my hand off your mouth now..." Raleigh said fiercely, "and if you scream, I will push this blade up through your mouth and into your brain, we clear?" The boy nodded nervously as a wide grin formed on Raleigh's face. "Test me, kid!" His twisted grin slowly disappeared as he eased his hand away from the boy's mouth. Luckily, the boy was smart and decided against his first inclination.

"Good lad," Raleigh said sarcastically. "Very good lad, is he not, big guy?"

"How many men do you have with you, boy?" I said with my hand still on the hilt of my sword.

"My family," the boy said, heavily accented. "My family."

"We will bring you back to your family," Raleigh said coolly. "We just need to know how many men are out here with you, then you may go!"

"I go?" the boy said, taken aback.

"Yes, you go!" Raleigh said with a mock kindness. "I go!" the boy said vehemently. Raleigh clamped his hand over the boy's mouth once again.

"Quiet, boy," Raleigh said. "Or you will get this!" He held his blade up to the boy's neck once more, and the boy suddenly looked confused. Shaking his head, he pointed through the shrubs.

"Yes, I know," Raleigh said, lifting his hand slightly. "Your family is there, and we will bring you there. But how many men are with you?" Caliah suddenly emerged from my flank.

"Jetha!" she exclaimed just before running to the boy and throwing her arms around him. "Jetha, how did you get here?"

"Who is this, Caliah?" Raleigh said, confused, as the two warriors accompanying Caliah approached from behind.

"We are spotted!" one of them said with gaping eyes. I lifted my foot and put it back down to test its strength. It was still throbbing, but a bearable throb, one that could be ignored once my adrenaline was engaged. "Three are on the approach!"

"Are you strong enough?" Raleigh said, staring down at my leg.

"Stronger than you!" I shot back.

"Good," he said, staring through the shrubs, "you can prove that in about... ten counts."

I leaned my back against the tree and waited for movement. Caliah held the boy in her arms, shielding him from the oncoming danger. Her two warriors shielded her from the same danger. Raleigh pointed from me to his chest, then over to where we would strike. I held my ground as he got into position. Seconds later, whispers sounded from just beyond the shrubs, followed by crushed leaves beneath bare feet and twig snaps.

"Ready?" Raleigh mouthed towards me. When I nodded, Raleigh stepped out of hiding.

"Gentlemen..." he blared loudly, drawing the attention of three natives in black war paint, "it seems you have found my ship for me!"

The men drew axes and spears and charged forward, one of them right into the hilt of my sword as I turned from concealment and delivered a death blow to his forehead. Before me were the same two black painted faces of the natives that took the life of Caliah's father. I stared angrily toward them as Raleigh approached from my side. Caliah and the two warriors emerged with bows drawn and spears at the ready. In an instant, the two were surrounded.

"Lay down your weapons!" I commanded. The two held their ground, turning in each direction to see who would strike first. "Do it now!" I blared, approaching them with the tip of my sword. The two stared stupidly at me until I lifted my sword for a deadly over handed strike.

"Wait!" Raleigh shouted at the last possible moment.

"Wait for what?" I returned angrily. "These are the men that killed her father!"

"And that is why they should fall by her hands brother, it is only right!"

My eyes went from the native and to Caliah.

"Is this your wish?" I said, holding the native's gaze.

"Vengeance is something my father despised..." she said and paused for a moment. "We shall take them as prisoners!"

"Prisoners?" Raleigh and I both said in unison.

"Caliah, this is not the treatment you would receive had the sword been in the other hand," Raleigh said truthfully.

"This I know," she returned, "but it is what my father would have done!"

"Then so be it!" I said just before I snatched the spear from the trembling hand of the native. The other willingly offered his spear to Raleigh in gratitude. Raleigh's nostrils flared, and he punched the native in the nose. Blood gushed from his face as he brought his hand up to cup the blood in his palm. Before Caliah could say anything, Raleigh was already through the wild trees and halfway toward the ship. Caliah turned to me and sighed as the warriors gathered rope to bind the captives.

"He shall not last long with such hostility within him," she said, staring at Raleigh's back as he stalked away.

"True indeed," I said, nodding, "but with what we've been through since last full moon, I could not see him lasting this long without it. Give him time, he will grow on you!" I turned, just as the warriors stood the captives to their feet. The one with the broken nose looked at me with hate filled eyes before he was pushed forward through the wild trees.

"These two may pose future trouble!" I said as they passed.

"Then we shall keep a watchful eye over them!" she said, swinging her bow and quiver over one shoulder and grabbing Jetha by the hand.

Approaching the ship, it appeared much bigger than I remembered although the banners flying were of the same auburn and gold with the name Joaquin displayed on the side of the hull in carved wood and steel.

"It is massive!" Caliah said, staring up at the vastness of the ship.

"Big guy..." Raleigh called from the upper deck. "You might want to see this!"

Climbing up the side of the ship, a stale odor met my nose and lingered all around. The smell was both vile and sweet both at the same time. A dull pain streaked through my leg, but I ignored the pain and lunged up barely catching the brim of the ship with my fingers. Raleigh grabbed my hand and pulled me up and on deck, where the smell only intensified.

"What is that wretched smell?" I said, my nostrils flaring with disgust. Raleigh pointed just ahead at the deck where there stood a piece of cracked wood. Pulling me to my feet, Raleigh and I both stared down through the deck. Half a dozen eyes stared up at us, frightened nearly to death and covering each other for protection. They were pale of skin, dirty and clearly frightened.

"Who are they?" I said, incredulous.

"Beats me!" Raleigh shrugged.

"Did those men hurt you?" I said. A woman nodded and pointed to her mouth. "They hurt you in your mouth?" She nodded vehemently as the child she held in her arms stared with gaping eyes. Caliah approached slowly from behind, but it was Jetha who shot past first.

"Mama!" he cried out. "Mama"

"Jetha do!" the woman exclaimed. "Jetha do!"

"Do?" Caliah said, pressing forward, speaking in her native tongue. "Do aca porte?"

"Aca porte mai, kalambe at a quis!" the woman said as tears fell effortlessly down her face. "At a quis, hemaldo!"

"Hemaldo?" Caliah raised a hand and covered her mouth in shock, and she stood there in disbelief.

"What did she say?" I said softly in the passing silence. A moment later, she collected her words and finally spoke.

"She said." She took a deep breath and sighed. "She said they have been eating their captives."

"Eating their captives?" Raleigh repeated angrily. "And you wish to spare these fucking savages?"

"I wish to do things as my father would have!" she shot back.

"Then you shall perish in the same manner he did!" Raleigh blared.

Before I was able to stop her, Caliah lunged forward, grabbed for Raleigh's neck and pinned him to the hull. Lifting his hands in surrender, he stood there within the mercy of her fury.

"I should have chosen proper words for the occasion, my lady," Raleigh said. "I am sorry!"

Her eyes were flames, and her grip did not loosen, even as I placed a hand of caution on her forearm. In a blur, two spears were pushed into my face and neck as a familiar feeling began to consume my every pore.

"This is only going to end two ways," I growled with my hands raised in mock surrender. "One, you drop your spears and my friend and I will forget this ever happened."

"Lay down your weapons!" Caliah commanded, releasing her hold on Raleigh's neck. The warrior to my left immediately laid down his spear and stood at attention. The warrior with the feathered mane stood defiantly with the tip of his spear against my neck, so close I could feel the blood trickling down into my tunic.

"Tell me..." the warrior said, gritting his teeth defiantly, "what is the second way this will end?" In one swift move, I clenched the spear in an iron grip and wrenched the warrior forward straight into a hard knee. The sound of ribs cracking sounded on impact. The warrior reached a trembling hand up to his chest, a look of terror written across his face as he sank down to his knees. I looked down in disgust as I reached over to my waist.

"Tiberius!" was heard from a distance well off, I ignored it. The pain in my leg was numbed by the rushing flames streaking through my body. I drew my sword up and down heavily over the warrior's head. Blood leapt from the strike and sprayed in all directions. With a savage tug, my blade broke through the remaining bits of skull as his lifeless body hit the deck with a heavy thud. When I looked up, Caliah's terrified hazels, along with her one remaining warrior, were fixed on me as if I had committed the ultimate travesty. Raleigh stood firm, his eyes darting back and forth between the two. The captives looked down at the corpse and shifted nervously within the confines of their chains.

"When we were back there..." I blared savagely, pointing back at the distant jungle behind us, eyes fixed firmly on Caliah, "you were commander, and that was acceptable because it was your land. Going forward, I am taking command of this ship, if this is something anyone has an issue with, now is the time to remove yourself or be removed!"

Silence ensued... only the sounds of beating hearts and blood oozing through cracked wood were heard for a long moment. Caliah turned to the warrior and spoke words in her native tongue. When she finished, the warrior nodded and spoke passionately in indistinct words.

"Sounds like an issue to me," Raleigh said, unsheathing his twin blades.

"No," Caliah said "Choompa did not follow my command, and he was dealt with accordingly. Azla here has voiced his allegiance, with one condition!"

"Condition being what?" I asked placidly.

"That you will protect us in this foreign land!" she said, suddenly vulnerable. "We are a simple people, and we are not equipped for dwelling amongst outsiders!"

"That is without question," I said firmly, "you will not be harmed so long as you remain loyal, but I am on a mission, and you must follow my every order if it is to be accomplished!"

"Uh, big guy, we have to move now!" Raleigh said, staring out across the coast with wide eyes. Hundreds of black painted faces suddenly emerged from the wild trees, wielding axes and black spears.

"Ready the masts for full sail!" I commanded, eying Raleigh before I turned. "You two, bows in hand." I unsheathed my longsword as a precaution, although I would not be needing it for this battle. I took my position behind the captain's wheel and turned it as far west as it would turn. When I looked back, Caliah released the string of her bow setting her arrow at full launch. It was enough to drop one, but there was no need. As the ship began picking up speed, a smirk formed on my cheeks as I stared out at the open sea before me.

"Just sit tight, Cas..." I said quietly. "I'm coming for you, brother!"

CHAPTER TEN
Memorie X

Casanova Volkart
"And... what part did you say I was to play in that?"
South Cilan 1869

I awoke to the sound of soft humming and the melody of a harp being played masterfully just paces away. The smell of roasted and honeyed cakes filled my nose with richness as I turned my head toward the sensation, but when I opened my eyes everything was blurry and the images were in vast distortion. Lifting my head from the pillow, my entire body throbbed so much, it left me nearly incapacitated. I arched my neck up to look down at my body, and I could barely see anything aside from the deep blotches on my chest, my arms, my legs. I opened my mouth to call out, but when the music stopped playing I fell silent as I felt the presence of someone in the room approaching. Soft footsteps swayed toward me as the something soft and silky brushed against the stone floor, approaching.

"Fear not, my lord," a voice said, the same voice from my dream, "it shall not be much longer!" I opened my eyes and stared deep into the blurry image before me, but to no avail.

"Solana?" I asked apprehensively.

"No, my lord!" the woman said, shifting slightly. "Solana is my sister, and she told me to tell you how very proud of you she is. My name is Celeste!"

"Celeste?" I said as a sudden nausea emerged. "Y-you, I know you!"

"Do you?" the woman said, amused.

"Y-yes, you were there..." I started but then recoiled with remembrance. "You saved Raleigh's life!"

"Yes, I did!" she returned, nodding humbly.

"Are you going to help me as well?" I asked quickly. "Can you cure me?" "The answer to your queries are yes and no," she said, her presence fading slightly as she disappeared into a far corner.

"Yes and no?" I repeated bitterly "Are you going to play a mind game with me as well?"

"No, my lord!" she said distantly. "My instructions are to prepare you for the journey ahead. You asked if I would help you see, and the answer is yes, I will. You then asked if I can cure you, to that the answer is no!"

"Well, why not?" I returned sharply. "I have gold." I patted down my coin purse and although it was lighter than expected, it would still serve its purpose.

"It is not gold I seek, nor anything else material, my lord," she said.

"Why do you keep calling me that?" I edged. "I am no lord, I am not even able to rule my own life and if you seek nothing material then what is it you seek?" A long silent moment passed as the blurred woman stared down at me. Did I offend her? I thought as she just sat there staring at a blurred room. A moment later she lifted a hand over my face and just as my entire life flashed before my eyes, a cool icy sensation traveled throughout my face, down my neck, and into my chest. The feeling was almost identical to the one I felt when Solana healed my face after Sinistro got a hold of me, only this time it felt more potent. A rush of purified energy surged through my body and as the numbing pain began to subside, images started gaining clarity before me. Celeste removed her hand and brilliant rays of sunlight burst through the slightly open curtain illuminating the whole of a vast circular chamber. In front of the curtains stood a table with a parchment and quill rested on it beside a candle. Beside me, a blond haired woman stared down at me. A small glass of water was in her hand and the tips of her fingers were moist.

"There we are..." she said smiling. "What can you see now?" I looked at the woman with incredulous intrigue. Her eyes were like two golden coins and in perfect harmony with her long blonde locks.

"Let us focus on your cleansing before we speak of me."

"My cleansing?" I squinted and looked down at my body. Dozens of black blotches covered my frail body.

"Yes, please drink this and we shall see the extent of your needs," she said reaching the small glass out toward me. When I put the glass to my lips, I almost expected to be magically rejuvenated. To have beams of energy explode through my skin as it healed me back to perfection, but none of this happened. In fact on the contrary, the cold clear liquid was so thick I nearly choked trying to get it all down and once I finally swallowed the last bit of it, I dry heaved for a while before I vomited it all up and onto the stone floor by Celeste's sandals. My head swam in all directions and the walls began to spin uncontrollably. Celeste pulled my coarse hair back over my ears and gently stroked my back as I coughed up the rest of the vile liquid.

"Wh... what did y-you give me?" I stuttered nauseously, gagging in between each purge.

"I must find Dimitrius!" she said quickly, just before she stood and broke for the corridor. Before I could blink for a second time Dimitrius came charging into the stoned corridor, followed closely by Solana and Brotus. The three stopped just by the bedside and stared silently for a long while, as if they were examining the beauty of a rare tiger, but still cautious of its ferocity.

"Razuhl!" Dimitrius growled after a long, awkward moment of examination.

"Razuhl?" Brotus said seemingly antagonized.

"He must see Razuhl before nightfall tomorrow," Dimitrius continued.

"Or what?" a voice said approaching from behind, it was Isis.

"Or..." Dimitrius sighed grievously, "or he will not live to meet the woman he must kill!" Isis' eyes widened and she disappeared into the corridor followed by Dimitrius.

"Have him prepared to leave within the hour!" Brotus ordered not unkindly and then vanished into the corridor as well.

"The woman I must kill?" I repeated, just as he stepped out.

"I will explain everything to you on the way, but I need you to know that at this very moment your brother is on a ship in route for where we are going," she said in scarcely a whisper. My eyes brightened and a spark of energy rejuvenated my mood.

"Are you certain of this?" I said cheerfully. "How soon can I see him?" A grim look shadowed her face as we caught eyes.

"Casanova the extent of your injuries are far more..." she paused as if trying to find the proper words to use, "sensitive than we had anticipated. By the end of this journey you will not even remember your own name, let alone the name of your brother and friend."

"Raleigh?" I said incredulous. "Is Raleigh alive as well?"

"Yes he is," she replied confidently.

"Well then, as long as they're safe I suppose we can proceed." I sighed. "But I need you to tell me of this woman I keep hearing of!"

"Her name is Bambola..." she said reluctantly after a long pondering moment. "And prophecy says that during the war to come, she will raise a force numbering in the millions to reclaim her glory in the realm."

"Reclaim her glory?" I said. "And what glory did she have in this realm?"

"Well with the help of Sinistro and his order of assassins, she was nearly successful in completely destroying the Solace, leaving the realm vulnerable to her dark forces."

"I'm sorry, the Solace?" I asked.

"The elixir you just spewed all over the sheets" she smirked.

"Well I don't blame her," I said as another wave of nausea swayed over me.

"Problem with that is, without the Solace the realm would be overrun with her legion of shadows. Blood thirsty soulless creatures so powerful that even the mystics would not be able to protect mankind from her path. She would ultimately bring an end to mankind and create a world of darkness with which she would reign over for eternity."

"And... what part did you say I was to play in that?" I asked.

"Casanova you are going to kill that woman and restore order to the realm," she said demurely as I eyed her blandly.

"Do you realize I am a lad of scarcely twenty years and I am no warrior?" I said. "My brother is the one you should put your trust in. I can barely hold a sword with proper technique."

"Neither age nor technique is the reason you are here today Casanova," she said warmly, "it is the strength of your heart and most of all your will that has awarded you this grand opportunity. However..." The suddenness of her mood change brought my heart to a freezing halt, "it is of utmost importance that we find out why your body has rejected the Solace."

At that moment, images of my past streaked through my mind in a blur. Faces I had long forgotten, places I had visited, things I have done all came to the forefront. That stone chamber with the dim torch in the far corner, that dark chiseled face staring back at me from across the wooden board, that bloody dagger gripped in my palm, that look of fear in her eyes, the flames. As each image emerged and faded from my mind, a single figure stood at the forefront.

"Casanova, tell me what you know about your father?" Solana said eyeing the blotch on my chest. If her awareness was on point she would've noticed the heart palpitations thundered upon hearing those words.

"I have no father!" I blared louder than expected. "I mean, I never knew him. Some say he was executed at the stake for dabbling in witchcraft, others say he was killed during an initiation into some kind of order. But regardless of who he was or why he died, I grew up without a father so that is all I know."

"I want you to think back Casanova. Think back to your earliest memories, memories of your childhood, anything!" she said with a sudden sense of urgency. Her emerald eyes sparkled toward me with a sense of despair I had yet to see on the woman. It were as if she knew so much more about my past than I did and that scared me. For in my mind it felt like my entire past before the chambers, before Arkon, before Tiberius had been erased, utterly burned from my mind with only bits and pieces of what molded me into who I am today.

"I-I am sorry I can think of nothing," I said, staring back into the eyes of who at that moment had to be the most beautiful woman I ever laid eyes upon. The room slowly went from warm and soothing to now cold and distant. The sun shimmering in from the window no longer filled the room with its warm embrace, it was now cold and bitter. My head was spinning in all directions and as if I were plunging down to the very pits of hell, shadows rushed over and through me until I was completely shrouded in darkness.

Brotus Satyre
"We shall see when the time comes."
South Cilan, 1869

"But why?" Celeste said, her eyes a shimmering reflection of doubt. "Why would he reject the Solace?"

"He did not reject it," I said distantly. "I mean, I don't know! But after this mission we shall have all the answers we need." She glared back at me with that familiar look.

"After this mission?" she repeated. "Are you meaning to disregard the warnings I've presented to you?"

"It was a command!" I said mechanically.

"One that shall start the war we are not yet prepared to fight!" she returned. I nodded, eying the etchings on the wall before me.

"I know," I said in agreement, "but just as I know, Dimitrius also knows."

"And let me guess, you would put your life at risk to accomplish a greater good but you would not preserve your life for the woman you love?"

"This is not about our love, Celeste," I said firmly. "It is about my oath to this order, the one I do not take as lightly as others may!" One look in her eyes, and I knew I had traveled far across the line of no turning back. Her eyes swelled and filled, but she turned so quickly I was not able to see a single tear drop.

"Celeste wait, I didn't mean you!" I called out from behind but she was gone, out of touch with anything having to do with the likes of me. I ran through the wide corridor passing the life sized statute of Pious and the banners of war, but before I reached her chamber the door slammed shut in my face. I closed my eyes and reached out to her with my mind but she already had a spell conjured up to block my thoughts from entering hers, typical Celeste. I placed my palm on the door and thought silently to myself, "Until I return, my love."

    I used to love this life... I thought as I turned back toward my chamber to prepare for the journey. True indeed, in the beginning it was rough just as in any new way of life. But the benefits of being a mystic well outweigh the pressures of being mortal. But then again it is not every day you see a mortal strong enough to perform the death ritual and live to speak of it. With some training, this may well indeed be the man to lead us to victory in the war to come.

    "I wouldn't count on that, brother!" a voice said from so close behind me, I felt the warmth on the back of my neck. I whirled around and was staring at the dark shadowy image of...

    "Isis! What did I tell you about reading my thoughts?"

"Never read my thoughts Isis, never speak to me in that way Isis. Never do this and never do that! That about right?" she said grinning.

"Why don't you ever listen when I speak?" I said firmly.

"Because that would be no fun." She winked. "Besides, you have bigger dragons to slay at the moment."

"Bigger dragons to...? What foolishness are you speaking of now?"

"This foolishness," she said, stepping to the side just as heavy footsteps sounded from around the bend of the shadowy corridor. Flames danced in hurried succession against the stone wall of the corridor as the steps neared.

"Who goes there?" I said authoritatively.

"'Tis Solana my brother!" the voice returned before she finally emerged from down the shadowy hall. "Casanova is non responsive," she said in a rushed panic.

"Non responsive?" I reaffirmed incredulously.

"Yes brother we must hurry!" Solana said.

"Isis, ready your armor and report to the carriage!" I commanded.

"Yes brother," she said surprisingly with a sense of seriousness and then disappeared into the shadows.

"Solana, what happened?" I urged.

"I do not know brother," she returned, "his eyes just faded out in the middle of discussion."

"Faded out? Did you tell Dimitrius?" I asked. "No, he was meditating I did not want to disturb him," Solana said. "We need your guidance Brotus, this cannot be done without you."

"Then my guidance you shall have sister," I assured, "meet me by the carriage, I have something to do before our departure." Her eyes narrowed as they went down to the exposed part of my chest before I could cover up.

"Brotus?" she said. "What happened to your che..."

"Nothing!" I shot back quickly as I turned back toward my chamber. "Armor up and be waiting by the carriage, I shall arrive shortly."

I hurried off down the corridor and left her standing alone, although I still felt the heat of her eyes searing through my back. I let out a breath of relief as I reached the first bend toward the stairwell leading to the hall of bliss. Turning to my right, I pushed into my chamber and slammed the door shut behind me, binding the locks with my mind. My skin was losing color and my hands were shaking uncontrollably. I rested a hand on the window ledge to steady myself and forced my way to the bureau. Beads of cold sweat formed on my forehead as I staggered across the chamber. Lifting the small vial of myst from the inner pouch of my tunic, I looked up and saw the withering reflection of what I would soon become entirely, a monster. The black blotch forming on my chest was prominent through the opening of my tunic and it was a wonder why Celeste hadn't noticed it before Solana did.

    My lips were dry and pasty and my tongue was watered down as if I would vomit at any moment but I closed my eyes and lifted the vial to my lips. A burst of energy ran through me with such an intensity that I staggered back into stone before I could collect my bearings. As I finished the last bit of the black liquid, the blotch on my chest went from black to red all the way to brown until it was no longer distinct. The strength in my legs returned first, followed by my acute sensory. The color of my skin returned to its normal bronze and the scars on my face and neck and hands, all faded until they were no longer visible. A small flicker of light caught my eye and when I turned, there she was. Golathine, my most prized possession staring back at me with a shimmering gleam. It was hard to imagine that the great sword I have used during many a battle still had such a youthful vigor. No dents no scratches, it was truly a gift from the gods when Dimitrius handed it down to me, even though I felt myself unworthy of the honor. Little did I know, the responsibility of wielding such a sword would come at great lengths.

  I lifted the golden vambraces lying just before Golathine and placed them on my forearms binding them together tightly around my wrists and elbows. My body was already reinforced with armor but where we were going, I needed much more than protection from swords and blades. I grabbed the necklace Celeste forged for me from the bureau and tied it around my neck. I just could not wrap my head around why we would be bringing Casanova to see Razuhl, of all people. The man was a complete lunatic in my humble opinion-him and his psychotic brother Zamul.

After tightening the greaves around the back of my shins, I slid on my black boiled leather gauntlets with the spiked edges and gave myself one more good look. I looked primal and war ready, but deep inside not having Celeste's blessing before I go into battle left a void in my chest. One that I struggled to ignore, but to no avail. I grabbed Golathine with a fierce intensity and charged out into the corridor with only the thoughts of death and carnage in my mind.

"I personally would like to commend you," Isis said from beside me. I struck the reins fiercely and sent the stallions into a spur before I responded.

"Commend me for what?" I said, keeping my eyes on the dirt path before us.

"For finally growing a firm pair of balls and telling her how you truly feel!" she returned coolly. "I mean that is my sister too, but ever since you and her have been..."

"Keep your voice down!" I barked, turning slightly to the side to see if Solana overheard.

"Calm down brother, trust me it is not Solana you should worry about knowing your weakness," Isis assured with a smirk.

"She is not my weakness, she is my heart and right now my heart is currently opposed to this mission," I said distantly, with thoughts of Celeste's warnings weighing heavily on my chest.

"Opposed to the mission?" Isis said incredulous, as she grazed a whetstone over her blade. "Give me a break Brotus! Celeste could never do what we do and you know it. What about when you assume the throne? Do you think she will agree with even half of the decisions you will be forced to make?"

"We shall see when the time comes!" I returned.

"No you will see when the time comes!" she answered fiercely. "I already see where this is going and it is only going to end either with you hurt, or her hurt and I will not let that happen with this much at stake."

"Who will be hurt?" Solana said from close behind.

"Nobody!" Isis and I both said in unison.

"Oh good, because time is of the essence here, he is not doing well at all," Solana said despondently.

"We shall reach the hills by nightfall," I assured. "The temple is only a few hours from there."

"We are staying with him until he is healed right?" she said, but received no answer. "Right!" she persisted.

"He is not coming back with us Solana!" I confessed.

"Excuse me!" she said uncharacteristically calm, as everything around us suddenly stopped. The steeds, the trees we passed, even Isis was just frozen in idle space. I looked behind to see if Casanova was conscious before I started, he wasn't.

"I know what you're going to say but..." I attempted before she lifted her palm.

"Brotus, don't fuck with me," she said in the calm, seductive manner that made her Solana. "You know what happens when your little sister gets mad, don't you?"

"It was not my decision!" I said, holding my composure.

"Then who's was it?" she blared. I eyed her disconcertingly, waiting for her to know. She had to know, we all knew.

"Dimitrius gave the command" I drawled, the words fell loosely from my tongue.

"For him to go live amongst those wolves, those heathens?" she retorted.

"Those heathens are the only ones with the myst!" I said, finally understanding this mission.

"And why would we have need of the dark serum?" she said.

"Well, we know he is one of us but he rejected the Solace," I pointed out, "which leads me to believe he must live amongst these wolves to become the wolf we need him to be when the time has come!"

"Now that is some quick thinking." She winked turning to the frozen embodiment of Isis, she shook her head. "Unlike this one, she used her ability before the first sword was unsheathed!" We laughed like we never have before. When all was quiet again I stared deeply into my sister's eyes.

"He will be protected Solana," I said, with a sudden seriousness, "of that you can be certain!"

"Then I shall rest this in your hands brother!" she nodded, as time resumed and life was restored to the scene all around me. Solana continued eying me before turning to our sister. "I will attempt to rest and assume night watch. Isis, keep an eye on Casanova. If he wakes then wake me."

"Yes my sister!" Isis said, her eyes burning the side of my face but I refused to meet her gaze.

"Tell me this sister..." I said in a authoritative whisper. "During our last battle when the shadows approached us, why did you use your special ability?"

"I thought I saw her!" she answered distantly, as if she were picturing her face before her at that very moment.

"Bambola would never risk being overtaken by exposing her location before it is time. The next time we see her, she will have an army numbering in the millions."

"The next time we see her, she will swallow this sword from tip to hilt!" she said gritting her teeth.

"Now you know that is not how it will happen sister. She is a hundred times more powerful than when you trained her and a thousand times more powerful since she joined forces with Sinistro."

"Do you still doubt my ferocity after all these years brother?" she said eying the side of my face.

"I do not doubt you in the least my sister, but just as you cannot allow me to be hurt, is the same way I will not allow you to proceed blindly when you and I both know Bambola's ability. I know how she thinks and I also know how Sinistro thinks. Neither of them will stop until Casanova is dead."

Silence consumed the eve, the only thing heard was the sound of hoofs colliding with dirt. Isis turned around and saw Casanova on the verge of fading to the spiritual realm. Solana rested softly beside him with her arm clutched beneath his.

"They look so peaceful" she said, I nodded knowingly.

"Cherish this moment my sister," I said, "for it shall be the last few moments of peace either of us shall experience before the time comes."

Tiberius Blackwell

"My name is Tiberius Blackwell!"
North Cilan, 1869

"I don't know about this big guy!" Raleigh said clenching the age old map which served to be a life saver for the journey. As the ship slowly approached the harbor and prepared for docking, there was an eerie feeling in the air. The coast was filled with rotten corpses scattered about recklessly, each with a black tinge covering their chests as if they each attacked at the same time and with equal force. In the distance, a tremendous wooden stake with word Agishi written on it stood boldly for all to see.

"Give me the map!" I said, staring despondently toward the horizon. I smoothed my hand out along the edges until it was completely flat and traced a finger from Partrizia to Deceptia, then from Deceptia to Candonia, then from Candonia to... Cilan! This couldn't be right, I thought to myself as I gathered my bearings to lead the group through a battlefield that was so fresh, the corpses were still smoking.

"Are you sure this is the place?" Caliah said stepping up beside me.

"Yes!" I said with an uncertain validity. "You and the boy gather all the supplies you can, we set out on foot within the hour."

"And what of Azla?" she returned glancing at the barbarian beside her.

"He will come with us!" I said. "We need as many hands as we can get if we are to scour this land for anything that might want us dead."

"He is not well spoken in your tongue!" she pointed out, kneeling down to clean the boy's face with a damp cloth.

"Good," I returned, "because we have nothing to discuss. Raleigh, ready your sword!"

"Already done!" Raleigh said wielding a freshly whetted longsword and the hilts of his twin blades visible through the front fold of his ragged tunic. A slight look of madness was written on his face.

"You aren't going to be a problem, right?" I said to Azla who stared back at me stupidly.

"Don't worry, I'll keep an eye on him big guy..." Raleigh said staring out across the harbor, "but on a more serious note, who do you think caused all of this?"

"Don't know but it doesn't matter," I said calmly. "My brother is here, so this is where we will begin our search."

"I don't know big guy, it looks an army with a lot of manpower did this!" he said despondently. "My guess is we need a lot more hands than we have on deck."

"And my guess is, if you want to run back to Deceptia where it's safe, then feel free! But I'm on a mission, and nothing will stop it's completion."

"You know what your problem is..." Raleigh returned just out of earshot to the others on deck.

"No what is my problem?" I said tightening the grip on my blade. "Your problem is you are so fixated on a straight path, that you can't even fathom the hundreds of other paths leading the same place." My eyes narrowed as I tried to find the meaning of his words. Although I was seconds from just ending this dialogue with a devastating blow to the windpipe, those words seemingly resonated with me.

"Look..." he continued. "I chose to follow you, not because I need you. Nor because I was intimidated by you. I chose to follow you because I trust your confidence and me, I am all fucked in the head." He pointed a double jointed finger to his temple, with an unstable grin that spoke of madness. "I didn't even get a chance to bury my daughter, mourn her death, in fact I was nearly killed in avenging her. You said you're on a mission aye, but I am on a few missions of my own not the least of which, to meet the woman who healed me and to stay alive long enough to see your brother as king."

    I loosened the grip of my blade and stared at the man. The truth was I needed Raleigh, although I would never admit that to a soul. His swordsmanship is unlike any other I've fought beside, but at what point does a warrior turn his aggression toward the hand that leads him? My grandfather used to always ask me, right before hours of intense training. "At no point," I would always answer. Till this day I would never know the true significance of the query. I stared back at Raleigh and truly saw him for the first time. His deep brown skin glistening against the sun's rays. His close shaven hair making him look much older than he was. His calloused hands which was undoubtedly the result of years and years of weapon training. It would seem the man and I were more alike than I would care to admit.

"My problem is not that I am fixated on one path..." I started slowly, "my problem is, I no longer have my brother's advice. He always knew what to do in situations like this and..." I paused as I searched to find the right words. "I was never as good with strategy as he was."

"I don't know if you noticed," Raleigh said, "but we have fought together, killed together and as of now I am prepared to fight to the end with you by my side. In my book you didn't lose a brother back on that ship, you gained one. And on my honor we will find Cas together, or die trying. But we have to be smart big guy!"

"Then what is your suggestion?" I returned.

"I'm glad you asked," he grinned unfolding the map, "we advance through here in triangle formation. One of us, possibly the boy, will scout the area while the two of us follow behind at a distance so as not be seen. We have Caliah and the barbarian over there in the trees for aerial support. The boy's mother and father will hold up position here on the ship and at the first sign of danger they let loose the oil barrels and rain fire down from the deck. With a small bit of luck we can push right through to the hills, which is all the way here!" he said, pointing to the other end of the vey long isle that made Cilan the most beautiful, yet dangerous island in the east.

"Sounds like a good plan" I said coolly, "but now that we are thinking clearly, there is no way the boy's parent will agree for us to use their son as bait out there. Especially if we don't even know what we are up against."

"And that is why we won't tell them," Raleigh said just as Caliah emerged from the lower deck. "All set?" he grinned changing his demeanor entirely.

"Yes I am ready, Jetha will be here shortly," she said glancing out to the coast.

"Are you okay?" Raleigh asked surprisingly unsmiling, as if he were actually concerned.

"I am... as well as one could be that just lost everything they have lived for!" she confessed sullenly.

"Caliah you saved our lives and we will never forget that kindness," I said turning to meet her gaze, "but that is the only reason why you are here with us!"

"What he means to say is..." Raleigh said shooting me an incredulous look, "we are grateful for you helping us and we will protect you and your people from here on out. But we need to know that you are with us, no question." She looked back and forth between us and her people before she nodded.

"Yes I am with you..." she said, "but without question? I would at least want to know the plan before I blindly subject myself to it."

"The plan is simple," I said glancing at Raleigh. "I will set out on foot and draw out any threat. You and your barbarian friend..."

"Azla..." she injected, "his name is Azla!"

"Okay you and Azla" I said through gritted teeth, "will take position in the trees once we have reached pass the coast. Jetha and his parents will hold the boat while Raleigh covers me on ground support. We push through until I send word that it is safe to proceed." A soft shuffling sound caught all of our attention as we each spun around in ready position. It was Jetha staring back at us with a disheveled tunic draped recklessly over his head. Caliah turned to us and smirked at the way Raleigh and I were positioned. Our hands were each placed on the hilt of our sword but each of our bodies were twisted awkwardly. So awkward that if it had indeed been an enemy, we might have bashed foreheads and knocked each other unconscious before the fight even started.

"I will go help him with that tunic," Caliah said still smirking.

"She's with us big guy" Raleigh assured.

"I hope she is... for the sake of her and her people," I said eying Caliah suspiciously, "let's move!"

Always stay loose, always be ready... My grandfather would engrave those words into my head constantly, during each lashing and after each training session. But this was not training, this was the real thing. There was now an actual threat lurking out here, just waiting to uncover the mistakes my grandfather seemed to always reveal in my fighting style. Keep your hands loose, stop gripping the hilt so tight, if I were your opponent you would already be dead. Those pestering nights were never-ending, the days yielded the same effect. I hated my grandfather for his vicious ways. I hated my father for killing my mother, I even hated my mother for being too weak to stand up to him. Hatred and combat was all my young, naive mind ever knew and now I have become the man set in his vicious ways.

I looked down at the blade in my left palm and twirled it once, twice, three times. Partially out of habit, but mostly from nervous anticipation. Never turn back... I thought to myself as I stepped over the arm of the many corpses ornamenting the sand. His body was not to be found amongst the hundreds of bodies that lay dormant, as if they were waiting for something, someone. My eyes darted back and forth through the trees in the near distance ahead. There was no sign of an army, nor even a battle. Death was the only thing lingering in the thick dusk air. I lifted my hand and closed my fist tightly, the signal to follow at a distance. Soft movements were heard from behind as I stepped forward toward the vast wooden post, Kamikhan it read in bold letters.

"What does it mean?" a voice said from behind. As I turned, Raleigh was staring at the large wooden post as well, twin blades in each palm at the ready.

"Our final test!" I said knowingly. The word was of single most importance to my grandfather, for it was the ultimate test of strength and skill, two components he always said were to embody the Shatoh warrior. The Shatoh warrior being one who has formally defeated the great Agishi in the Kamikhan tournament.

"How appropriate?" Raleigh quipped, staring through the eerie forest that lay ahead. "Our real test is going to be surviving a night in there with these people."

"Our people!" I reinforced. "You said she is with us, that means all that she cares for is now in our care."

"If you say so big guy!" Raleigh stopped before the wooden post. "Just remember the mission is your brother, not the safety of these people."

"We will get my brother back..." I urged. "Just stay loose, stay ready. We have a long journey to go and on this journey, the only people dying are the people that stand in our way, got it!"

"Understood captain!" he smirked but quickly lost all expression when the sound of hoofs approached from the west. Two whistles came from the trees where Caliah and Azla stood watch. I turned back to see Caliah pointing to the east and Azla to the west. I turned to Raleigh and briefly locked eyes with a killer.

"You know what we have to do!" I said unsheathing my longsword and holding ground.

"Right!" Raleigh said blurring toward the nearest cover.

"Hey..." I called out behind him. "No vigilante shit!" "What do you mean?" he said, incredulous. "You are going to wait for them to approach?"

Turning toward the upcoming hoof beats, a group of black cloaks approached with haste. Their numbers grew immense as I stood watch, until nearly fifty horsemen were in sight and quickly advancing. In a matter of seconds I was surrounded by masked horsemen bearing black banners with a red serpent.

"Yes, protect the others!" I said, slamming the tip of my sword into the dirt beneath my feet. Raleigh's voice was heard distantly but then faded, until the only thing heard was the sound of my heart beating and the voice of my grandfather.

Always stay loose, always be ready... I exhaled in jagged, irregular breaths and watched as the horsemen formed a vast circle around me. One of the horsemen stood out from the others. The one holding the black banner with the serpent, the only symbol that shown clearly for all eyes to see, the one with two longswords crisscrossed on his back, the only one that stared me in my eyes as they circled. As they slowed to a halt, the thought of never fulfilling my mission crossed my mind. Never finding my brother, never telling him how much I admired his guidance, how much I needed that guidance. The sun concealed itself behind the mountaintops before me. Pinks, reds, and purples all meshed together into a beautiful portrait of sunset, but the only thing I could focus on was the bloody carcasses lying all around me. The killers around me as well and the amount of blood I was going to shed before I woke up in the spiritual realm. The horseman bearing the banner stepped down first and punched the stake in through the dirt.

"You are not of this land, are you warrior?" It was the heavy accent of a woman. She approached with such a confidence, it well surpassed any other I have met. Long flowing hair was pulled back into one ridiculously long braid. Her eyes were the only thing visible through her mask, those dark, heinous, soul sucking eyes.

"Is that why you bring an army here?" I said calmly. "For conversation?"

"No darling." She smirked, her honey colored iridescent eyes shown through the slit of a mask. "I bring an army here to kill. I present you with the query because it is customary for one to kneel down before a queen."

"I have no queen!" I retorted sharply. "Nor do I kneel before everyone who proclaims themselves to be one." Three horsemen dismounted and halted just as the woman raised her hand in the air. Two of them held a palm by their waist, ready for the command. The other one held the hilt of a morning star and slowly began spinning it as I caught eyes with him.

"You know, many years ago," she said staring down at the blood-filled sand, walking toward me with her hands clasped behind her back, "when I was but a mere girl my father commanded the same gesture of respect from me. He said the deed was required from all those inferior to him. He also said, the world is governed by two and only two components... fear and control!"

"Your father sounds like a power crazed prick!" A deranged look formed in her eyes before she continued.

"I know..." she said, still smirking, "and that is why I killed him! May his soul burn eternally in the pits of misery. But I did not bring up my father to damn his soul any further than I have already. My point is, we all have to do what we must do, before we can do what we want warrior, it is the way of this world. Soon you will understand that!"

"I might," I said unflustered. "I might not... I am here for one thing and one thing only. If you are not here to help, then you are merely a deterrent!"

"My my, such passion for such a young man." Even behind her mask, I can tell she was smirking. "My men are lacking that kind of passion, uhm, sorry I didn't get your name!"

"I didn't give it to you!" I said coolly.

"I think I like this one," the woman said turning back to the three masked soldiers dismounted behind her. "I'll tell you what, maybe we can help each other. Why don't you tell me your purpose for being on my island and if it is feasible, then I will help you myself!"

"In exchange for what?" I pressed.

"In exchange for what?" she repeated mockingly, her grin hidden beneath the black veil concealing everything but her eyes, those dark, malicious honey eyes. "Why, in exchange for your allegiance of course. Your expertise with that sword you got there and possibly a position in the most powerful army in the world."

Allegiance? This woman was either mad, or she just didn't understand exactly who she was standing in front of. But as thoughts of lashing out on these people crossed my mind, a touch of rationality sank in. I was not alone, no longer could I make decisions based on my own safety. What if the others are discovered because of my actions? What if they are executed as I have witnessed on countless occasions? What if they are imprisoned? "The Kamikhan..." I said, staring once more at the large wooden post, "is the tournament held here in Cilan?"

"It was born here," the woman said stepping up beside me to stare at the post as well. "Only the most skilled warriors are even eligible to be invited!"

"I cannot promise, you will have my allegiance," I said. "But I can promise you this, get me in that tournament and when I win you will help me in my purpose for being here, deal?"

"Well I cannot promise your eligibility, so it would seem we are both at a stalemate," she said, her eyes fixed on the wooden post, "but I am somewhat intrigued by your offer. Tell me, have you ever fought in this magnitude before?"

"No," I confessed, "but my grandfather was the first and last sword master to have spilled the blood of an Agishi, I only wish to finish what he started." Her eyes narrowed as she searched my face for the slightest hint of sarcasm, she found none.

"Impossible!" she said after a moment. "For that to be true then your grandfather would have been..."

"Marcellus Blackwell, first of his name, third son of Peron Blackwell, master swordsman of the twelfth degree and head general of Aventir Noman's army and leader of the clan Blackwell," I said mechanically. The words spilled effortlessly from my lips and in doing so, caught the attention of the nearly fifty horsemen before me... and a woman.

"What is your name young man?" the woman asked seemingly unfazed.

"My name is Tiberius Blackwell!"

"Well Tiberius, it appears you and I have much to speak about," she edged. Even through the black veil, I could tell she had an evil smirk engraved on her face.

CHAPTER ELEVEN

Memorie XI

Casanova Volkart
"You shouldn't have done that!"
Unknown location, 1870

When I opened my eyes I was alone, in a chamber barely big enough for a grown man to dwell in comfortably. A small table was wedged in the corner just beside the cot I was lying on. Looking down my body was in its normal state, no sign of the trauma I had just put it through. But whatever it was that I did, I hope to never do it again. I could still feel the currents rippling through me.

I wiggled my toes, the feeling was restored. I moved my legs and shifted on my side. The door creaked open and an old woman appeared in the doorway. She was a short hunchbacked woman with a long curved nose and dark beady eyes. She wore a black hooded cloak and under tunic with laced britches and a golden medallion dangling from the woven black thong upon her neck.

"Hello ma'am!" I said politely, I received no response. She merely entered the room, knelt down and picked up a rusted metal bin. She shook it once, twice, three times and then set it down. She walked over toward the table, pulled out a white handkerchief, placed it gently on the table, then turned on her heel mechanically and walked toward the door.

"Pardon me, but can you tell me where I am?" I called out, but again received no response. "Lady!" I blared louder than I had meant to, but to no avail. Before she opened the door, a parchment slipped from her tunic and fell to the floor. Unaware of it, the woman opened the door and disappeared into the darkness of the corridor. I sat there speechless, unaware that there were still people of such a low caliber in the world. Perhaps she hadn't heard my query, but who was I kidding. The woman had walked into the room just beside me. I quickly came to the logical conclusion that the woman could only have been ignoring me because she was jealous. Jealous that I was here to become king and she was probably here for one thousand years and did not accomplish anything.

The small piece of parchment stared back at me from the dark stone floor. I lifted my legs and swung them over the edge of the bed until my feet made contact with cold stone. Pushing myself up, I slowly staggered toward the parchment.

It was a thin, flat piece ripped from the bottom of an old scroll. Only three words were written on the parchment, but those words were solid and bold as if they were a message. You are him I said aloud ponderously. You are him? What could that mean? Could this be a message for me? No, I wasn't even supposed to read that parchment.

Soft footsteps and indistinct mumbling brought my attention to the door. The sound came and passed, but no one entered the chamber. It happened again three times within the span of what felt like hours but after the fourth time, a knock was heard. Walking toward the heavy wooden door before me, I almost expected to see Tiberius on the other side. Maybe even Solana and her beautiful green eyes, here to rescue me once again. Even the thought of Raleigh flashed through my head for the quick stride toward the entryway. The heavy oak door eased back and revealed an unfamiliar face on the other side, I shuttered at the sudden thought of where I was, who these people were, who I was...

He was a tall man with dark fearsome features. He was richly dressed, clad in a long black velvet robe, and a polished silk under tunic. The tunic was decorated with medals of some sort and his dark glaring eyes were looking down at me completely unreadable, I could do nothing but stare. "Solana has informed me..." the man finally said after a long intense moment of awkwardness, "of your interest in my teachings."

"Your teachings?" I said, unclear of anything further than my name at the moment. "I, I am sorry but I have not been informed of your teachings!"

"Oh, but you have!" the man returned knowingly. "In fact, not only have you been informed of my teachings, but recently you performed a ritual that has been in my family for over three thousand years. A ritual that has been taught to over six thousand elite mages, but was only successfully completed by two." The man's narrowed eyes looked down on me accusingly.

"Where did you learn it?" the man queried.

"I learned it from nowhere," I stated. "I do not even know what I did, nor why I am here. I have been trying to find my brother ever since I arrived on this island and somehow I keep meeting new people, none of which are able to help me find him!"

"What happened to your brother?" the man asked.

"Well, nothing happened to him," I retorted, "it was me that was taken and held prisoner on a ship in route for this island."

"By whom?" the man asked quickly.

"His name was Sin... Sinnis something I can't remember!"

"Sinnis Trocahl!" the man growled.

"Yes that is it!" I said. "How do you know him?"

"Everyone in Cilan knows him!" the man said. "He is the richest man on the island and the most powerful. The question is, what did he want with you?"

"He was trying to get me to sign something, a contract I believe" I confessed.

"A contract stating what?" the man pressed.

"I am not sure, I was masked and couldn't read it. So I would not sign it!"

"And that is when Dimitrius and Solana came for you?"

"Yes it is." The man nodded, turned on his heel toward the door but stopped just before it.

"Dinner will be served in the feast room shortly," he said, then disappeared into the corridor.

"Wait," I called out, "are you going to help me find my brother?" I received no answer.

The knock at the door was startling at first, but relief quickly followed. The man's mention of a feast had my stomach twisting and churning. At that moment I realized I hadn't eaten anything possibly in days and my weakness was the result. I got to my feet and staggered toward the door. When I opened it, I was surprised to see a lad maybe two years my junior.

"Hello, I was instructed by Rahzul to escort you to tonights festivities." the lad said mechanically.

"Razuhl?" I squinted before I remembered, the man never told me his name. "Oh yes, the man in the velvet tunic, I presume." "Y-yes, yes that is him," the lad stuttered joyously, "and I, I am, they call me. Mmy name is is Albert Pecconius the thhhh third of his name."

"How do you do Albert Pecconius the third of his name?" I returned smiling. "I am Casanova!"

"I-I am well, thank you," the lad smiled, clutching the scroll in his hands nervously, "ppplease this way Casanova, they are awwaiting our arrival!"

"They?" I said, but the lad was already halfway down the corridor.

The corridor was none like I've ever seen before. Its tall regal walls were covered with crimson banners and staffs, swords and halberds. Torches lined the grand hallway, a plush crimson carpet lined the floor and each oak door I passed was barred and reinforced with steel shafts. The hall seemed never-ending, as the end of it was shrouded in shadow. My stomach folded into a tight knot.

"Hhhere we are Casanova!" said Albert from within the shadows. His arm was extended toward a door left slightly ajar. As he pushed his way inside, nearly two dozen quiet onlookers sat staring back at me. There were four tables all aligned to form a square in the middle of the grand feast room. Which seemed proper being that the large table standing in the middle held the biggest feast I had ever seen. There were mountainous plates of broiled pig with onion, honey custards, bean pies and sweet peas, roasted venison and many more dishes I never heard of or saw before.

My mouth was watering, stomach was churning. It took everything in me not to run over to the table and stuff my face. But then I realized, the entire room was silent. Every eye in the room was fixed on me, each with a different expression. Some were eyeing me with gaping eyes as if I were returning back from the dead. Some stared longingly, as if they were excited that I had arrived. The anger filled eyes all came from the one side of the room, that one table on the left, and it felt as if their eyes were burning a hole right through me.

"Don't be shy, we are all friends here!" said Albert from beside me, making his way toward the table on the far side of the room. I followed Albert toward his table as the eyes of nearly everyone in the room followed me.

At a quick glance, I counted nearly twenty cloaks. Most of them wore grey and black, very few of them were clad in a deep purple, but only three of them wore red cloaks. Maybe that is why everyone was staring... I thought, as I looked down at my dirt filled tunic that was once a gleaming black, but now a grey, dinged and shabby pile of rags.

"Finally!" I overheard a woman say from within the crowd, I kept walking.

"Let the feast begin!" Razuhl announced from the far corner of the room. I had not even noticed the man standing there, watching me from a distance. In a blink, the quiet room of staring eyes came alive. The long grim faces all transformed into happy, jovial expressions.

I looked around and could barely find Albert amidst all the noise and chaos. There were many people from different facets of life in this place. Some were dark as the night others were pale as milk but what stood out the most of all, were those three men in red cloaks. They were still sitting down, still holding a grim expression on their faces, still staring at me.

"Casanova, over here!" Albert called from somewhere unknown. I looked around for the familiar face amongst the different faces around me, found him. He was sitting down alongside a girl with red hair flowing out over one shoulder of her grey cloak. Sitting beside her was a fat lad in black cloak. His face was round and pudgy. His cheeks bulged from the massive amount of food he had stuffed in it and each of his massive legs were nearly the size of a keg of ale.

"Is this for me?" I asked sitting down beside Albert in front of a humungous plate of everything imaginable.

"Sssuu shuuur surr..."

"Yes it is, he means to say!" the red haired girl said smirking, Albert nodded in agreement

"Thank you for this!" I said politely, glancing once again at the red cloaks. They were still staring at me.

"No need for thanks. You will return the favor sooner than you think!" the girl said, lifting a bowl of lentil soup to her lips.

"Youuur welcome friend!" said Albert. "Shee me-means to sssay!"

"No I didn't!" she returned. "We didn't even meet yet, how are we friends already?"

"My name is Casanova!" I said reaching out my hand.

"No!" the giant lad barked from beside the girl. His eyes were suddenly fixed on me, not unkindly but with a hint of desperation behind them. "I would not touch her if I were you!"

"Oh," I quickly pulled my hand back, "my apologies, is this your lady?"

Albert shook his head nervously but stayed silent, the giant lad did the same. The girl was staring back at me, I did not understand what was happening but my hunger was overwhelming. I lifted a leg of lamb from the plate and stuffed it in my mouth to avoid further tension.

"You have never met a mage before, have you Casanova?" the girl smirked coolly, shoving a boiled potato in her mouth and gulping down a swig from her mug.

"I have..." I returned. "I trained under a master mage for three years!"

"A master mage?" the girl and the giant lad said in unison.

"You do not look like a mage," the girl said, "nor a fighter! How is it you have come across a master mage?"

"I-I don't remember how we met but Arkon was the strongest mage west of the pits, and the last known mage in Partrizia!" I said boastfully, taking a deep gulp from my mug and continuing on my plate.

"Well then, in that case," the girl said sliding on a sharp edged gauntlet and reaching her hand out towards me, "my name is Scarlet. You already know little Albert here!" she said smirking as we clasped palms.

"Stop calling me that!" Albert ordered, scowling. He was holding two scrolls of some drawings.

"Oh posh Pecconius, you know I'm just jesting," she winked, "you can show him drawings later on!" He blushed, nervously adjusting his parchments.

"And my name is Tomin" added the giant lad, reaching out a fat, grease filled palm toward me.

"Can I ask you lads a question?" I said, discreetly wiping the grease from my hand left from Tomin on the side of my britches. "Who are the red cloaks over in that corner?"

"They are the sixth degree sorcerers," Scarlet said calmly, "the one with the flagon in his hand is Zerolin, little Albert's older brother." Albert scowled again but continued on his honey custard instead of countering back.

"The one that just stood up is Shinn, and the other one staring at you like he wants to shove his fork into your throat is Rahsorz, our leader and the son of Razuhl."

"Leader?" I squinted. "What is this, some kind of cult?"

"This is the temple of the Agishi," Tomin said with a mouthful.

"The Agishi?" I said, thinking out loud. That voice from the wasteland called me the Agishi... I thought as I surveyed the room for the red cloaks, but they were no longer seen.

"Aren't you going to tell him what the Agishi is?" Scarlet said nudging Tomin's arm.

"Oh right," Tomin said, sucking the last bit of grease from his fat, pudgy fingers. "The Agishi is the top fighter in all of Cilan. The Agishi tournament is held each time an Agishi dies and the winner will become the new Agishi."

"Understood," I said nodding, "so Rahzuhl is the Agishi?"

"No!" Albert said from the other side of me. "The former was just killed three days aaggogo!"

"You were so quiet over there little Albert, I almost forgot you were still here!" Scarlet said, smiling.

"Killed?" I said. "By whom?"

"By the masked queen and her Imperials assassins!" Tomin said sullenly. "We have been at war for over a century."

"The masked queen!" I smirked, thinking of Raleigh and my brother. If only Tiberius heard the madness going on here, I thought smiling in remembrance.

A heavy hand suddenly slammed down on the table, making all the plates and mugs jump. Albert's plate fell and shattered on the stone floor, his scrolls fell but he quickly snatched them before harm was done. My mug of ale almost poured right in my lap before I caught it at the last moment. A wave of anger passed over me and I saw the reason for the disturbance. One of those red cloak bastards was standing at the far end of the table grinning stupidly at Albert. He was broad of shoulder and his face had features so sharp it could cut through a loaf of bread. His eyes were a light olive and his brown locks fell perfectly over one eye.

"Sorry there Pecconius," he quipped, the others at the tables grew silent and stared down at their empty plates. I looked over to the far corner where Rahzuhl had been standing, he was no longer there. "Didn't mean to startle you!"

"Piss off Shinn!" Scarlet said with flaring nostrils. "Here, let me help you Albert!" she said kneeling down to help pick up the pieces of cracked porcelain.

"Piss off?" he repeated in jest. "Now, why would I want to piss off, when pissing on is so much more fun?" I turned to Tomin and the giant lad was sitting there, eyes down in his empty plate, grease all over his pudgy face, silent. I turned to the other unfamiliar faces at the table, everyone was silent. It were as if they were all terrified of this man in red cloak, but I wasn't. I tightened the grip on the handle of my mug and smirked, just as Raleigh would have in this situation.

"You find something funny there, outsider?" Shinn said, slowly making his way to my side of the table.

"Some sense of humor you have there," I said nodding, "I just find it strange how a man can have his face drenched in ale and still find a way to jest about it." I felt the eyes of the others at the table burning the side of my face, I ignored them. The red cloak strolled toward me squinting.

"My face is not drenched in a..." In a swift movement I leapt to my feet and slammed the mug of ale into the side of his head. The liquid splashed in all directions, down onto his cloak and under tunic. My smile vanished and the entire room had gone utterly still. Shinn reached up and slowly wiped the warm liquid from his face and now disheveled hair.

"You shouldn't have done that!" he said calmly. The plates and mugs all began vibrating around us as he stretched his palms out to his sides. A low humming sound was emitting from them and his eyes began altering, until they went from brown to a complete black. My entire body went limp and I couldn't move, not even breathe. I gasped and clawed at my neck for air but some invisible force was clenching tight to my throat and the sweat forming on my forehead suggested I would lose consciousness at any moment.

"That is enough!" a deep accented voice ordered from the other side of the room. The other red cloak, the one they call Rahsorz had been the one to give the command. He glanced at me with dagger filled eyes, then turned and left toward the doorway. Zerolin, Albert's older brother followed closely behind him. I eyed the man before me and after his red cloak allies left the room, greeted his drenched face with a grin.

"It was nice to meet you, Shinn!" I smirked. "Oh trust," Shinn said, wiping his face on the back of his hand. When his face reemerged, his glare was now in an equally twisted smirk. "We have not met just yet outsider!"

Raleigh Bines
"I told you he would return..."
North Cilan, 1870

"He left us!" Caliah said, as the last of the horsemen trotted out of sight along with Tiberius.

"No," I said, shaking my head, "he will return for us."

"Is this why he was so adamant about being the one to greet those masked men?" she pressed. "Because at first chance he would continue on without us?"

"That was never the plan," I assured, although only through his words could one truly give explanation to such actions. "He is the one that told me watch you all until his return. Maybe he is making sure it is not a trap before he calls us out. We will just wait here until we receive signal."

"Receive signal?" Caliah returned, unkindly. "And if we do not receive one?"

"Then we will dust off our fuckin britches and move forward," I shot back. "One thing we will not do, is wallow in sorrow because of something we do not know for sure."

Caliah was silent, although I knew at any second she would have another query that I would have to answer...

"Well then what do you suppose we do for shelter?" she said. "Nightfall is soon approaching!" I looked out at the dusk filled horizon, the air was fogged, gray and dismal. There was a winding trail of gravel and rock ahead, leading into a forest well off in the distance. I turned around and saw the barbarian, Jetha, his mother, father and Caliah. They all stared back longingly, waiting for an answer, my answer.

"We seek refuge in that forest for the night," I said, sounding confident, "there we should find some game, hopefully an abandoned cottage and at the least a good night's rest."

"We will never make it there by nightfall if we travel at this speed!" the barbarian pointed out. I looked up, the sun was well beyond the highest mountain in the west and only the threat of darkness loomed within the gathering twilight. Turned out the brute was right, the forest was indeed well off in the distance. A greater distance than I cared to travel when I knew not of what lay within this forest. My lips were dry and pasty, possibly from the lack of ale, lack of food was also a possibility.

"How well can you use that thing?" I asked, glancing down at the barbarian's hand where a longbow was clutched tightly.

"Well enough," he said humbly.

"Yeah?" I edged. "Prove it!"

"There is no time for games Raleigh," Caliah entreated, "we must hurry!"

"This is not a game but we mustn't do anything in haste," I said turning back to the barbarian, "we are going to lead the way. We will continue forward with the original plan!"

"The original plan?" Caliah squinted angrily. "You mean the plan where our leader did not desert us for another leader?"

"Yes," I said flatly, "that plan. But first, we will see if he is up to the task!" I turned back toward the forest and then back to the barbarian.

"How are you on arrows?" I said as the brute slid one from his quiver.

"Three more left" he edged, turning back to check his rear.

"And you?" I said, eyeing Caliah.

"Sixteen," she stated, staring with dispassion. I glanced over toward Jetha and then his parents.

"If we are to survive going forward we will need unity, we will need trust. Now, the reality of it is some of us will not make it to the other side. My mission, is to have as many of us alive as I can before Tiberius returns."

"You are a fool if you think he will return!" Caliah said, adjusting her blade clutched in the folds of her sheepskin over tunic.

"Then a fool I shall be," I shot back, "but this fool would have left you all behind to fend for yourselves if it wasn't for Tiberius!"

Five sets of eyes stared back at me, and I realized I once again had put my boot in my mouth. Although only two of them understood my words, the sudden feeling of being a careless leader came over me. Tiberius would've had the right words to say to rectify this. Casanova would know exactly how to maneuver his way out of this, but me? I was standing there, staring at the dark narrowed eyes of those who I promised I would protect.

"Listen..." I squinted, staring off into the distant forest ahead. "Did you hear that?"

"We heard everything you just said!" Caliah blared angrily.

"No, shhh!" I said, placing a finger over my lips. My eyes darted in all directions. Somewhere in the distance the gallop of horses was heard. The air turned dim and foggy around us slightly. A slight smirk formed on my lips.

"I told you he would return..." I said confidently, staring out at the approaching black cloaks, there were of three of them. "That must be him there, in the front carrying the longbow!"

As the words left my lips, the one leading the pack reached behind him for an arrow. From out of nowhere, the tip was lit until all that was seen from the distance was a ball of flame.

"Head for cover!" I cried out, as the arrow slipped from the bow and went straight up in the air heading toward us. Caliah turned and snatched Jetha, the barbarian shielded her back with his.

The arrow landed at a well off distance, indicating the act was a sign. We were trespassing on a land we were not supposed to be on. The three horsemen stood motionless upon their destriers awaiting the next move.

"Tiberius... brother!" I squinted, holding my hands up to show it was me but to no avail. Another arrow was slipped out and lit aflame. Heavy footsteps sounded from behind. When I turned, the barbarian was by one side, Caliah on the other.

"I'm sorry," I said, staring out at the black cloaks with a rage I had not felt in a long time, "again!"

"You won't get rid of us that easily warrior!" Caliah said, fierce hazel eyes glared toward the darkening horizon. I unsheathed my longsword, unclipped a dagger and stood at the ready. Two bows raised up on either side of me.

"We fight with you until end!" the barbarian said edging forward, I nodded.

"Ok then," I smirked, "on my mark!"

"My name is Bambola!"

North Cilan, 1870

Tiberius Blackwell

The road was rough and gravelly, skewed and unfamiliar. Clouds of fog formed all around, shrouding us within the cover of smog but my mind was clear and focused. I vowed to myself, never to trust a soul after we left the gates of Partrizia. But that was before I got an arrow plunged through my leg. Raleigh did not have to help me one bit, but he did. And Caliah, had she not saved Raleigh and I back in that jungle I would not be here surrounded by horsemen, contemplating my next move.

"Lucinius Blackwell" a commanding voice said from beside me, it was the masked woman. My attention was drawn by the familiar name. "Your grandfather was Lucinius Blackwell, correct?"

"That is correct" I said, nodding.

"You know," she began, "I have never met a more ruthless warrior than Lucinius, he served the Order faithfully until his very last breath."

"The Order?" My head suddenly became enflamed, my eyes full of fury. "He was a

Blackwell, he never served any Order. That is the very reason he was murdered."

"Your grandfather was not murdered Tiberius, he was executed!" the woman shot back. "Your grandfather reached out to the Order when it became known of what your father did."

"My father?" I said incredulous. "How is it you have come to know my father? He never traveled this far east!"

"And yet, his betrayal has touched much further than just Cilan," she said. "Tell me, what do you remember of your father?"

"I remember killing him!" I snapped. The image of my father in that black hooded cloak back in the oakwood lingered in my head for a moment. His betrayal? I thought and then, images of that night swirled through my memory.

It was a dark night, under the shadow of towering sentinels and a sky that showed no hint of the moon's presence. The dagger in my palm was so heavy that it flung from my grasp the moment I unsheathed it. Kneeling down, I brushed my hand through the dirt to find it and when I lifted my hand, the hilt of the dagger was warm and sticky like it had been submerged in sap, or maybe even blood.

Always stay loose, always be ready... My grandfather's words echoed through my head, my eyes darted in all directions.

The smoke issuing from the lodge ahead made it look both dark and uninviting but I was prepared to do what I must for the woman I held closest to my heart. I gathered up the sleeve of my baggy tunic and ripped the seam from my arm. Covering my nose and mouth with the torn remains, I charged in through the door of the smoke filled cabin. The two figures I saw first were each bearing swords, the third held a torch. My mother was on the floor, bound with shackles on her wrists, ankles and roped at the mouth. Two of them spun to meet my gaze as I held my blade up in a ready position.

"Step back slowly!" I ordered from the doorway. The only movement now was the man with the torch. He turned slowly, until his familiarity became more evident.

"Father?" I squinted in dismay. "Wh-what are you doing?"

There I stood, staring face to face with a man I held nothing but the highest admiration for. A man that if he gave me the word, I would slaughter a whole nation for. A man that I loved what I presumed to be unconditionally, until that very moment.

"A sacrifice must be made, my son!" His eyes were distant and unreadable almost enchanted. The crackling of flames brought my attention to the nook beneath the stairwell. Smoke was issuing from beneath the heavy oak door that was now filling the entire cabin with such an intensity, I could feel the brush of heat breathing against my face.

"A sacrifice?" I trembled. As he turned back, the soldiers flanking his sides advanced toward me. I dove forward, just as the torch dropped from his hand and the floor became a river of flames.

"Nooo!" I cried out, as the two soldiers caught hold of my arms and held me back from the inferno. I pushed them back and flailed my dagger about like a man mad. The edge clipped two fingers off one of the soldiers as I readied for his response, none came. He only dropped to his knees wailing and held out a bloody hand before I ended his misery. My dagger punched through the side of his neck and his body fell to the ground with a heavy thud. Agonizing screams came from within the gathering inferno, my mother's scream. Smoke and flame filled my lungs and my father was no longer seen. The place where my mother was lying just a moment prior, was now engulfed in flames. I stood there staring at the blaze, unable to move, unable to think, not even able to cry. It was not until two heavy hands dragged me out of that cabin and flung me to safety, that I realized I had just witnessed my first execution.

"And it is for that precise reason, you will make an extraordinary general one day!" the masked woman explained. "You are fearless and you know how to get the job done no matter the circumstance."

"And you gathered all this from one conversation?" I contended.

"Of course not my child," she snickered. "I gathered this from your energy. You are emitting powerful waves of anger. Why is that, Tiberius?"

"I told you, I am in search of my brother!" I barked, much more severe than intended. Behind me six swords unsheathed simultaneously, the seventh was mine. I spun around and was staring at six masked men, each waiting for the command. Which made it much easier for me, because I had no commander. Lunging forward, I palmed the face of the closest soldier and shoved him back viciously as I positioned myself to ward off the first approaching sword. With a quick thrust I parried a heavy blow to the head but the impact was enough to push me back into something heavy and solid. The edge of my sword had drops of fresh blood trickling down the blade and into the hilt. I reached up to my neck and removed two red fingers. Rage filled my veins and spewed from my pores as the formation of six surrounded me and prepared to advance. In a wild display of erratic movement, I dropped down to one knee and gathered a handful of dirt and gravely rock. My eyes felt as if they were burning from fury and everything went silent, save for the drumming of my heart.

  Standing up at my full height, I tossed the dirt and rock up into the air. As their gazes went up to what was thrown, I slashed through the throats of the first two. I charged into the chest of another but he was a stone and would not budge. Reaching his arms around my head, he squeezed until my face felt so tight it could burst. My sword was no longer in my palm, it was lying in the dirt too far for my arm to reach. I felt life leaving my body as the blood filled my head. The throbbing in my leg emerged from the awkward position I was held in but with much effort I grabbed hold of the dagger in my leg holster and stabbed the iron edge through the soldier's knee. Bones cracked and shattered beneath his breeches as the impact sent his body jerked forward wildly, not one scream was emitted. In one deadly motion, I lifted and drove the blade deep in through his skull. Blood sprayed and spattered all over my face, head and into my dreads. Fragments of brains and bone was oozing out the top of his head as I jerked the blade out fiercely, his body fell lifeless to the dirt. My eyes swung back and forth wildly as if I were possessed but as my gaze touched the last three soldiers, they were lying face down. A sword was sheathed aside from me and when I turned the masked woman met my eyes.

"It seems..." she edged, clouds of breath forming through her concealed face, "you shall be much more than just another sword in my army."

"Your men drew on me!" I barked fiercely.

"Under no order of mine!" she returned calmly, taking a black cloth to the edge of her sword.

"And you propose that to ease tension?" I shot back. Her left eye twitched as if she were going to respond thunderously, but then a soft chuckle emerged from behind her mask. She turned, knelt down beside the bloody corpse beside her and placed a hand on his. Then turning to meet my gaze, she sighed.

"No Tiberius," she started, "but maybe this might put you at ease."

Reaching a hand to the back fold of her war breeches, she removed a dagger with the head of a dragon at the hilt. She lifted her hand and started chanting softly at first then more fierce. Lifting her hand over the face of the bloodied body, she pulled his mask off and held her sliced hand over his mouth until blood started oozing down her gloved palm. His skin was dry, almost grey looking and his eyes were entirely black, glassy, lifeless which was strange being that he was only killed just a short moment ago. But when her blood touched his lips, the color began to return to him. He eased from pale and pasty, to a light bronze and his sunken cheeks began to expand and fill out.

"What are you doing?" I quavered nervously, but received no response. Instead the man's chest slowly began to rise and fall. His fingers started moving in the dirt and when the blood completely saturated into his flesh, he rose.

My lips trembled uncontrollably and the blood rushed from my face. Breaking out in a cold sweat, I maintained my full height and composure although inside, the only thought running through my mind was my father. Is this how he was brought back to life? With blood magick?

I looked up at the other masked soldiers that surrounded us and I noticed they too had black, glassy eyes revealed through the slit in their masks. Each set was staring placidly back at me. Mixed emotions ran through my body as goose pimples formed up and down my arms and neck. A cold chill brought my eyes back to the woman who was staring at me with an icy gaze. I attempted to speak, to show my unwavering bravery and a demeanor that did not reveal timidity nor fear.

"Who are you?" the words were distant, as if they were not from my own tongue, my lips quivered like a frightened child. Her eyes did not meet mine for a long while. It were as if the magick took slight effect to her physically but then, she turned. Her eyes were now entirely black and fierce, flaming. Even her own soldiers surrounding her shuddered in fear as she rose to her feet. My heart pounded my chest so intensely it felt as if it would burst through my ribs at any moment, but I stood my ground and eyed the woman before me as if she were not the embodiment of all I have come to know as evil. She swayed toward me slowly enveloping me in her dark aura before her lips finally parted and she uttered four words that would change the entire paragon of my existence.

"My name is Bambola!"

CHAPTER TWELVE

Memorie XII

"I know what you did, Partrizian!"

Agishi Temple, 1870

Casanova Gallimorian

The night was long and silent save for the soft flickering sound of a torch in the far corner of the small chamber, barely down to its last ember, yet my eyes were the only things en-flamed as I lay open eyed staring at the ceiling.

Truth was, I may have overstepped my welcome by what I did earlier that evening. What was I thinking? You are not Tiberius! I told myself as I stared a hole through the stone ceiling until my eyes ached. I expected the retaliation would come soon but when a fist pounded emphatically at the chamber door, my heart stopped. Couldn't have been this soon?

I quickly surveyed the room for anything I could use as a weapon, a blade, even a rusted sword would do. But as I approached the door gripping the burnt out torch with a trembling hand, I felt as if I were walking a very short road to my untimely death.

"Who goes there?" I called out formally.

"Ghost!" A strong commanding voice answered from behind a heavy layer of reinforced steel and wood.

Ghost? I whispered lowly, shuttering in my tunic and slowly started back stepping to the furthest corner of the chamber. My heart lurched in my chest and cold sweat ran down my neck.

"I was sent by Razuhl!" the voice urged, before I realized my back was pressed firmly against stone. Was he sent here to kill me? With a name like Ghost, he could not be at my door for idle conversation. The knocking resumed, this time a slower, lighter tone sounded and I forced myself the courage to press forward toward the door once again.

"My apologies, I had a restless sleep" I confessed pulling back the heavy wooden door, staring up at the looming figure standing before me. His eyes were shadowed beneath a shimmering crimson cloak but he was not one of the three from the feast room the night before and he looked much older than the one they declared their leader. His face was rough with a long scar along the side of his face from temple to chin. He held a wooden box in his left hand, a lit torch in the other. He shouldered his way into the chamber and placed the box down on the small table.

"As did I," Ghost offered, turning to meet my gaze. His eyes were a soft jade yet within them spoke of a vast world from which I knew nothing of, "it seems you have also had a restless journey here. All the way from Partrizia?" I nodded, revisiting the place I once called home. Each face from the chamber flashed to memorie before me vividly, each set of impoverished eyes glaring back at me, each silently pleading for my help.

"Yes it was indeed a restless journey thus far," I admitted, "yet this is not the end for me. I am here on this island looking for my brother."

"Whatever you are looking for in this realm, is also looking for you," Ghost advised. "Always remember that Partrizian!"

I nodded acquiescently, although I was not entirely sure what he meant. He turned his back to me, unhinged the wooden box on the table and opened it. His movement was slow and controlled, as if he were paying precise attention to detail. His shoulders were so broad, I could not see what he was doing.

"I know what you did, Partrizian," Ghost intoned after a long, thoughtful moment, my stomach turned to water. With his back still facing me, I could not tell what the man was implying, what exactly did he know? Did he know I was a thief, and wanted in Partrizia? Did he know I killed the chief and was now a fugitive on two regions? "Shinn has been a fuckin' thorn in my leg from the moment he put on that cloak, he deserved what he got!"

"Oh," I sighed with relief. "I thought you were sent here to punish me for my actions!"

"I am!" he returned, turning to meet my gaze. "This is your first punishment and you are to treat this with as much importance as you have in finding your brother!"

Ghost held out a small wood carved, pointed needle in his palm. I took the carving in my hand and examined it closely. Its edges were perfectly aligned and sculpted into an impressive little weapon.

"It's beautiful," I expressed, examining its grooves and contortions.

"I am glad you think so," Ghost offered, "because you will carve and deliver 1000 of these to me before the week has passed"

"One thousand?" I repeated.

"You do this for me," he said, eying me intently, "and in return I will teach you how to survive what is coming for you!"

"Coming for me?" I edged nervously.

"Surely you didn't think you would just walk in here and humiliate the grand regent, the same grand regent who's father is now seated upon the imperial throne of the gods, and get off without a scratch... did you?" Ghost asked, evaluating me closely. "Shinn wants to challenge you to a Diamake!"

Diamake? I mouthed silently. My heart suddenly dropped to my stomach and liquefied. The word couldn't mean anything less than death by some queer form of excruciating pain.

"I know you do not know what that means but trust me, it is better that way," he entreated. "For now..."

He turned, lifted the open wooden box from the table and placed it down on the bed beside me. Inside were over a dozen small wooden rectangular blocks, each the same size. He reached the gnawed tip of his finger into the box and removed a block. There was nothing particularly special about the slab of wood, only for me to transform the block into the perfectly carved needle he presented me seemed utterly impossible.

Reaching into the folds of his cloak, he removed a small metal tool with a sharp, curved edge at the tip. It was the kind of utensil that looked like you should clean your teeth with, but as I took it in my hand it was much weightier than I had expected.

"It is called a sheik. This will be your only friend here. You will love it, cherish and adore it because one day, it will save your life!" I nodded thoughtlessly, thinking of Arkon and all of his unusual teachings. Of all the tests I had to endure, of all the will-bending missions I had to go through, how was my life going to be saved by a tool almost small enough to disappear in the palm of my hand.

"Your example is there," Ghost said pointing toward the finished dart on the table. "Now get to work!" Ghost ordered.

"But you didn't show me how to use th..." I stopped short as I looked up, the chamber was empty.

Raleigh Bines
"I think they approve of us!"
Catia, Eastern coast of Cilan 1870

The frigid wind cut through my skin like a fresh blade, so sharp that you don't even feel the damage until its already done. Each cut and open wound was numbed from coldness but I could feel life leaving my body just like the dying fire before me, nearly down to an ember.
"You have to drink this!" a calming voice said from beside me as the brim of a steaming bowl eased toward my mouth but it throbbed even to lift my neck. I opened my mouth and my lips were nearly stuck together from drying blood. My sight waned as the night deepened but those black war stripes and hazel eyes before me were sharp and distinct. Other than some minor cuts on the side of her face, she was seemingly unaffected by the battle we had just endured. Never have I seen such power in all my years, from just three men.
"Thank you," I offered, just before swallowing the warm herb filled liquid. The steam warmed my body but the lingering pain

from the scars still remained. Her eyes searched my chest for a moment but then she regained focus.

"You are truly impressive with those blades" Caliah mentioned as she slid her hand under my neck and lifted me to a seated position against a sentinel tree.

"I can't even remember what happened fully," I said wincing painfully, eying the dark shadowy surroundings that made up the forest. "Where is the boy?"

"Jetha's father is... old," she entreated. "He is convinced this land is cursed and refuses for them to leave the coast. I have Azla watching over them until morning, that way we can figure out the next move"

"It is cursed..." I admitted.

"It is?" she repeated, eying me savagely. "You gave us your word we would be protected, and you bring us to a cursed land?"

"I think the bodies lining the coast was a clear indication that this would not be a merry ol' land of paradise,"I said, smearing dirt on the open wounds lining my arms.

"Well then, why did you bring us here?" she returned angrily.

"OK, first off, I did not bring you anywhere!" I answered coolly. "You came of your own accord after a small, insignificant incident happened like... your village being attacked. Look, I do not want nor do I have the energy to fight with you. If we are going to stick together then great, but if you want to leave and handle this island on your own, even better. I have someone I need to meet here on this island and I will not continue to let everyone else's feelings get in the way."

"You are not used to having people who follow you," Caliah said, standing to her full height, "who believe in you, right?"

She was a fierce one, I must admit. The look in her eyes spoke of hidden terrors that have not touched the surface in a long time, and in that hazel reflection I saw a flashing image of myself.

The years have passed by so quickly, it was as if just yesterday I was looking up into my grandmother's eyes for the first time. Those beautiful, majestic gray eyes that held the highest regard for me alone, her Raleigh. I used to cherish the beauty of everything, the sun, a nice green pasture, even the words decorating the page of a book. For it was not until the twelfth year of my life that I was gifted with sight. Unable to see the beauty of a sunset or the magnificence of an exquisite painting was the loneliest feeling of my life. I can still remember the darkness, the deafening silence that consumed my mind for all those years, the loneliness. I do not know how, but it was my grandmother who repaired my sight. My grandmother who opened my eyes to the wondrous world that surrounded me every day of my life.

My beloved... she would say to me every night before I slept. She was the first woman I laid eyes on, and at that age I thought she would surely be the last. Her beauty I have yet to see reflected in another, that is until my Elise was born. She had the same breathtaking eyes, the same nose, the same laugh.

"No," I finally answered, just as a warm drop fell from my left eye. "I am not used to it. You want to know what I am used to? I'm used to seeing everyone who follows me either dead or gone and never coming back."

The tears that followed the first drop now fell freely and effortlessly down my face as I let it all go for the first time in...

ever. I saw my daughter's face before me, my grandmother, everything I held dearest to my heart slowly vanishing until the only thing seen was the hazy reflection of the woman now knelt down before me. A warm hand touched my arm, and the hairs on the back of my neck rose. Her forehead touched mine, and I could have been wrong, but it seemed as if the entire world around us disappeared for just that moment.

"I will not ask who you have lost, Raleigh," Caliah whispered from so close, I could feel the brush of sweet breath against my lips. "Nor will I ask you to feel any differently than you do. I only need you to know that we are here to stay. You are the only strength we have right now, and whatever your mission is, as I told you before, we will fight with you until the end. But I need to know you will do the same for us!" She brushed my tears away with her thumb and rested a soft palm against my cheek as I leaned my head into the embrace. Staring into her eyes, I was lost for words. Deep down beneath that rough, edgy exterior was a scared little girl just dying to be wanted, protected. A girl that just lost her entire life as she knew it. A girl who only asked for the same loyalty she has given me to be returned.

I touched the hand warming my face and held it there as I held her eyes. I pulled her hand slowly toward my lips, she didn't pull it back. I planted a soft kiss on her palm before her hand stiffened. Looking up, her eyes were gaped, looking over my shoulder as if a sudden death were approaching. A twig snapped in the distance, beneath the weight of something heavy. My eyes widened as I blinked tears away and shifted my back slightly upright.

"What is it?" I asked, unclipping one of my blades.

"Wolves!" Caliah mouthed, with my hand still clasped in hers against my face. Leaves rustled from too many directions to distinguish as the fog rose slowly from the twilight.

The vicious snarl that sounded froze my entire body solid, but my arms and legs were like jelly. I glanced up at Caliah, and we locked eyes for a moment that lasted an eternity. This was not exactly how I imagined it all would end... eaten alive by carnivorous beasts in a land I knew nothing of. I could only think back to lying down within the wild trees of Candonia, almost in this same position, fearing the threat of my life against a panther. However, tonight was much different. Gold iridescent eyes stared back from within the veil of darkness. Then another set of green eyes opened beside those and another, until everywhere I looked, a pair of beastly eyes was staring back at me.

"There are seven of them," Caliah whispered, her lips barely moving, "show them no sign of fear, and they will move on." I nodded, but my lips were quivering uncontrollably, my tunic was almost entirely saturated in sweat, and my eyes were fully dilated. Caliah clutched my hand tighter as the beasts neared. Stepping through the shimmering twilight, I finally caught sight of the leader of the pack. The beast was much too solid to leave it in the hands of fate, but my body was too weak even to lift my blade for an attack; I was done for.

I looked up at Caliah, and her eyes were closed, as if she were calling upon the gods, I closed mine and did the same only I knew nothing of who I would pray to. Our hands clasped together so tight, our palms whitened. With my eyes closed the forest suddenly came alive with sound. From the low snarling sounds that neared, to the brush of leaves against paws, to the erratic thumping of my heartbeat and Caliah's fused as one within our palms. So this is what death sounded like, felt like... I thought as my eyes trembled beneath its lids, dying to open. But what would I see once they were open? And when I saw it, what would I do?

Ironically in that last moment of truth, behind clenched lids I saw Casanova's face, a hazy reflection of it at least. His Partrizian features, those dark eyes that spoke of an even darker past, his mysterious way. Maybe if I were more like him, I would not be here... or maybe if it were not for him, I would not be here. Either way, the fear running through my veins stopped short when I opened my eyes.

The shadowy figure before me was black furred and massive with bared razor edged teeth, his growl low and deep as he approached. Caliah's grip tightened against my palm as I stared death in the face. Those golden eyes... something about them seemed familiar. They spoke of divinity, of elegance, almost with a human like emotion behind them.

The wolf stared back at me as if it were longing to speak, to tell me not to be afraid. The pack closed in slowly, as the nose of the leader touched my boot. It sniffed my foot and then up my leg as the others closed in until they were surrounding us. My heart thumped heavily as an eerie feeling of serenity filled the air. The pack of killers stopped and sat calmly around us as the leader was now so close, close enough for me to slash him to pieces but I didn't move. I couldn't, the feeling I was enveloped in was one of clarity and peace, a calming sensation. The wolf's eyes went to Caliah and searched her face, sniffing its way toward our clasped hands. Its wet nose touched my hand, and I felt goose pimples rising up my arms as I waited for the attack. But the wolf just licked the hand I held Caliah's with and then hers as the pack just stared silently.

    The tension grew as she caught sight of the wolf. But as she eyed the beast suspiciously for a long while, what resembled a smile formed on her lips and she met my eyes with hers. I looked down at our clasped hands, then back to her.

    "I think they approve of us!" I said, stroking the back of her hand with my thumb until the wolf saliva was gone. Her cheeks were flushed, but she did not turn away. Instead she embraced my touch and stroked the back of my hand as well. The wolf made a slight squealing sound just before sitting down and resting its head on my leg. The rest of the pack followed suit and lay down as well. My heart was stampeding in my chest when I lifted a trembling hand up and rested it lightly on the wolf's neck. Gently stroking its soft fur in one hand and holding Caliah's in the other, it all felt like a dream. Some form of twisted enigma that would only make sense if... hell, it would never make sense that a nice pack of wolves came and relaxed with us for a night and saw us safely through our journey. Imagine Tiberius' reaction to that... I laughed inside as I eyed the anomaly before my eyes. Caliah rested her head on my shoulder and I could have been wrong, but the feeling I held in that moment was compared to none I have ever felt before.

I woke up to the sound of distant laughter. The tree I was lying beneath shaded me from the glaring sun but pain lingered from the night before. Wiping my eyes with the back of my sleeve, I turned to the left and snapped to my feet in a rushed panic. So it wasn't a dream... I thought to myself, staring at the massive black wolf seated before me. Its golden eyes almost sparkling as the sunlight hit it. The laughter continued from nearby as I stared at the creature.

"You scared me!" I told the wolf, almost expecting a response. It squealed and stared back at me stupidly before his attention suddenly drew to the fields and he darted off. The fields were green and rich, full of game and opportunity. I turned toward where the laughter was... it was Jetha.

Caliah and Azla were walking towards me, Azla sweating profusely with both arms filled with firewood, and Caliah holding a heavy satchel in her hand looking like my future everything. The pack of wolves were all different shades of grey, black, brown, and each with its own distinct features but none were as big as the leader. I never imagined being this close to a pack of wolves would be such a calming experience, but it was.

I turned back toward the fields as the sound of something heavy scampered toward me. It was the black wolf with what looked like a rabbit between its teeth. He scurried over towards me and dropped the rabbit at my feet as I kneeled down to brush the back of his neck with my hand. Its fur was black and shimmering as it circled around me excitedly.

"Good job." I smirked, lifting the fresh rabbit from the dirt and eying it closely. "Is this for me?"

"In here!" Caliah said approaching from beside me, holding out an open satchel. I pushed the hare into the satchel just as a pile of wood was placed down in the dirt before me. Azla stood to his full height with a longbow and quiver secured around his blood stained chest.

"Morning warriors!" I said, standing.

"You saved my life!" Azla said, disregarding the greeting.

"Did I?" I squinted, turning to Caliah whose eyes were touching the dirt with not even the slightest hint of emotion, and then back to Azla.

"You did!" Azla said smileless, reaching his hand into the satchel by his waist. "This is for you!" When he removed his hand, I shrank back slightly. It was the head of a man that had clearly met the bad end of a spear, a dozen or so times. Dried blood rested along the side of his face and neck, the results of the open gash on the side of his head. I smirked, eying the two equally.

"Seems like you had an exciting night!" I quipped but quickly lost my humor as Caliah's eyes touched mine. They were red and puffed with deep, dark lines beneath them. I looked back and forth between the two of them as they just stood silent before me.

"Did I miss something?" I said slowly. Tears swelled in Caliah's beautiful hazel eyes and her lips quivered as she tried to speak, nothing but whimpering sounded from her lips.

"Jetha's parents were killed!" Azla said quietly, but the tension in his voice showed his calmness was forced.

"What!" I exclaimed "By whom?" I reached for my waist and unhooked my blades. Azla pointed to the head lying in the dirt beside my boot.

"There is one of them, the other got away!" Azla revealed.

"Well... at least you got this fucker!" I sighed, looking over toward the field. Jetha was running and laughing with wolves and doing all that a lad of eleven should be doing. "You didn't tell him yet, I gather?" Azla shook his head.

"Good!" I snarled, adrenaline suddenly running through me like wildfire. I ripped a blade from my waist and cut the sleeve of my filthy doublet completely off, then did the same for the other. "Now tell me everything that happened!"

Tiberius Blackwell
"As you wish!"
Depitz, Eastern coast of Cilan 1870

"Why is it you all wear masks?" I asked after reining my horse to the tallest sentinel I ever laid eyes on. The road was rough at first but as we neared the gathering horizon the road was much smoother, but narrow. So much so that the fifty men that followed nearly had to walk in two single files. Around us weren't the trees you ordinarily find in a forest. The leaves were iridescent, almost glowing in the sunlight. The air here was much warmer than that on the coast, which was a relief. Then I thought of Raleigh, of Caliah. Without a doubt they would feel I abandoned them, as they should. I made no mention of them for their safety of course, but this was not Raleigh's mission, it was mine. I could never live with myself if this journey that I caused the death of innocent lives, they have already been through too much. My attention was drawn to the approaching steed, it was the woman.

We arrived at the heart of Cilan by the rise of sun and were now in a town called Depitz, she announced earlier but I was incoherent at the time. It wasn't every day that you saw a man brought back after his body already went cold, I thought turning to my left. The burly man in mask beside me turned and eyed me, the corners of his eyes crinkled as if he were either smirking or glaring at me murderously. Either way, after I removed his head a facial expression would be the least of my concerns.

"Do you want to answer him Gringus, or shall I?" Bambola said, dismounting her steed and swaying towards us with the grace of royalty.

"I have no words for this outsider, my queen!" he intoned eying me, his voice much deeper than humanly possible.

"You don't have value over your life either, do you?" I returned gripping the hilt of the blade on my leg as I turned toward the man I had just killed hours ago.

"We have the rest of the day to release tensions, Lieutenant. For now, we are on a mission that I intend to complete before the sun reaches its peak," Bambola said, smirking with an eye toward the horizon.

"On a mission?" I squinted. "What mission is that?"

"Well, consider this your official initiation to our legion." Bambola smirked, her eyes fixed on the soundless horizon.

"Initiation?" I said but was quickly silenced. The dust particles and rocks began trembling beneath my boots. The leaves and trees closely followed suit as a tremendous cloud of dirt rose in the distance. It was as if a sandstorm were forming, but we were not in a desert. An open pasture such as this one could not have produced this much of a disturbance unless...

When the dust finally settled and cleared it was as if my eyes were playing jests on me. The entire scenery, the trees, the pasture, even the sun had vanished from sight. Before me was a stone stairwell leading up and through a vast mountainous peak. Atop the mountaintop was a temple with tall iron gates enclosing it within the darkness of the moonlit sky.

"Where are we?" I asked, disbelieving, "and why is it night here?"

"We are still in the same place, Tiberius," Bambola edged amusingly. "It is your eyes that have been blinded, your thoughts that have been warped, your reality that has been altered. This is the true reality, the very world as seen through the eyes of the divinity. As for the reason it is night...it is always night here my child, for it is through the darkness that everything has been created."

Looking up at the distorted sky, the moon was shrouded by the cover of clouds yet it was no ordinary moon. This moon was red and gave off a crimson tinge to the tremendous mass of land before me. The ground was unusually smooth beneath my boots, but the air was thick, almost alarmingly so.

"Everyone armor up!" Bambola commanded suddenly, unsheathing a longsword. "Today, we are here to take the first step in fixing the wrongs that have been done to us. Today, we take back what is rightfully ours in the realm. Today, we make our enemies bleed!"

"You heard the queen!" Gringus shouted. "Fall into position and ready your weapons...that includes you, outsider!"

Before I could return a smart remark a distant screech sounded, followed by war horns. I turned to see three soldiers in black mask with trumpets to their lips. Bambola lifted her sword toward the mountaintop and the entire cavalry charged forward leaving the air filled with dust until it was only me and her left standing. I clenched my sword tight in my palm as I prepared to follow whatever command I had to in order to stay alive.

"Come, Tiberius," she said stalking off to the side. "I want to show you something." I thought to sheath my sword but quickly dismissed the notion and followed the masked woman. She walked and walked until it felt as if she were abandoning her own people... seems we had one thing in common so far, but then she stopped. She held her arms out before her and images began forming at will. Images of people, but not ordinary people. A group of dark hooded men stared back with glaring eyes. Some of the faces I recognized from a time long ago, faces

I had hoped to forget. My father stared back at me, his dark aura radiating powerfully amidst the group of hooded men. He just stood there, his mouth moving as if he were speaking but no words came out. My grandfather was there as well, his sharp stare made me stand up straight for a moment. His mouth was moving as well and although I could not hear his words either, I knew what he was saying.

"Always stay loose...always stay ready!"

"That is sound advice," Bambola said before I realized I was speaking aloud. "But sound advice from the wrong person could spell death!"

The group of men before me faded into the darkness and a hideous figure now appeared from within the smoke. A huge, green, scaly creature stood before me with a broad chest and large powerful arms. His eyes were completely white and he was surrounded by a group of women and one man. Each of them looked war ready, armored up in golden shield and helm. A bloodied blade was in the creatures palm and it appeared they were having a ritual for some kind of dark order.

"I do not understand what I'm seeing!" I said squinting, confused.

"Ah, but you will my child," Bambola urged, lifting her palms higher creating the very image of smoke with her hands. When the images faded and reemerged, my heart dropped to my stomach. My sword slipped from my hold and I let it. I fell to my knees and palms, my dreads shielded my face from the tears as they fell down one by one until they formed a puddle in the dirt beneath me. My hands trembled uncontrollably, closely followed by my legs. The sight of it, brought me back to the night when my mother was taken from the realm. I never had a chance to mourn her like a son should have, never had a chance to show her how strong I was, how much I truly loved her. After this night, there would be no more mourning, no more regrets, no more love. I wiped the last bit of tears on the back of my sleeve and let out an awful war cry.

A hand touched my shoulder and attempted consolation, but there would be none of that. There would be no more of the man that held empathy for a single soul.

"Tiberius, I am so sorry!" Bambola said as I slowly rose to my feet a new man. I pulled my hair back and tied it down. I reached down into the dirt and lifted my black sword, gripping the hilt with a new-found evil residing within me. Taking one last look at the image, I stared until my eyes burned. My brother lying in the dirt, the knife plunged into his heart, the blood trickling from his lips. I stared until the image was burned into my mind for all time. To remind me of the last piece of innocence being completely wiped away into oblivion. I lifted the hilt of the sword to my chest and did the only thing that I felt was appropriate in that moment, I got down and took a knee.

"I, Tiberius Blackwell," I said through gritted teeth, "first son of Marcellus Blackwell first of his name, third son of Lucinius Blackwell, master swordsman of the twelfth degree, do hereby vow my allegiance to you. You shall have my sword... until my last day!"

"Ah, rise my child!" Bambola said, invigorated. "Rise as one who shall do and see many wondrous things in the future. Now off to Roma we go, let us join your new brothers and make our plans to rain fire down upon those responsible for your brother's death!"

"As you wish!" I snarled and charged forward.

CHAPTER THIRTEEN
Memorie XIII

The night grew dark and eerie across the deepening twilight. Red tinged dirt and fragmented rock littered the wasteland before me, but the bones were no more. I was nearly on the verge of collapse but my mind was still firing in all directions. Each of my senses were acute and ready, although I could not remember the last time I saw the presence of any mortal nor even the last time I had any sustenance. This punishment would bring anyone to the brink of insanity, but not me. I turned back quickly to assess the distance I've traveled from those immense flaming towers but they were no longer seen. I was now in the heart of this dreary land of solitude, of hopelessness.

I stopped in the middle of the vast expanse of nothingness. I unclipped my vambraces and let them fall, the steel clanking loudly as they fell to the hard dirt. I dropped down to a knee and removed the greaves covering my shins one at a time and then stood at my full height. A huge load was released, but when I reached to my side and removed the chest plate and chain mail, I almost didn't feel my body at all it was so light. There I stood in the middle of the wasteland completely naked, yet in my advanced form. The black blotches on my skin were now so prominent, so deep that they hardened and scaled up across my chest and hands. Hard, scaled muscle coiled around my arms, legs and belly. The thick staff of flesh between my legs dangled and rested heavily against my inner thigh. My shoulders and chest were massive, pulsating with raw energy. I felt power and wisdom amalgamating within me, an energy I had not felt in all my years, but in that moment I understood it all.

    Being away from all the people, the deceptions, the bloodshed... was a blessing disguised as a wilderness and I was now coming to terms with that. Maybe what was meant to be a punishment initially was actually no punishment at all, but yet a way to reveal the true essence of what it meant to be immortal. The silence, the stress, the loneliness... it was all to see if I was ready to advance to a higher level of consciousness, I understood that now.

A soft, sizzling sound brought my attention down to the dirt. My armor had completely fused into the very grime beneath my feet and was now only ashes remaining by my boots. My boots? I looked down at my bare feet and the black char that outlined them, they too were reduced to ashes. What was happening to me? I thought as my body slowly began levitating off the ground and stood suspended in mid air. My heart palpitated violently, pounded against my chest so intensely that I could not mask the beating. A surge of energy was rushing through my veins and I was almost certain it was flames, judging by how intense the heat grew in just moments. Something was happening to me internally and I didn't know what it was, but worst of all, I didn't know how to stop it...

Memorie XIII
Casanova Volkart
"Trust your power, Agishi..."
Agishi Temple, 1870

My eyes snapped open, my body drenched in cold sweat once again. Around me were hundreds of small intricately designed wooden needless and the scraps left behind from endless carving.

"He must not be in here!" a female's voice said from the other side of my chamber door.

"He has to be!" a male voice replied. "Ghost said he would be in here until his punishment is complete."

"Well let's go, or we will miss the evening meal."

"No!" the male said. "We have to make sure... we don't want the wrong person looking for him."

I swung my legs off the bed, knocking down a dozen or so needles before I reached the door.

"You found me!" I said staring back at Scarlet and Tomin with a grin. Truth was, I was happy to see the pair. It must have been days since the incident and ever since, I have been cramped in this small chamber without the presence of anyone but the old lady bringing my food and removing my garbage.

"You're alive?" Scarlet said, squinting in disbelief. "I mean uh, you're okay!"

"Don't I look okay?" I smirked, knowing I must of looked like I hadn't bathed in ages.

"No, you actually look like shit," Scarlet returned, eyeing the wood scraps all over my tunic.

"Needle tips?" Tomin asked, staring at the floor. "Casanova, it must have taken you the entire time you have been here to complete this."

"Three days to be exact and I still have about 600 to complete before the week is over," I said matter of factly.

"Six hundred?" the two said in unison.

"You didn't even apply poison to the edges yet," Scarlet warned.

"Poison?" I squinted. "I was not told to apply poison!"

"Not yet you weren't" Scarlet said, shouldering her way into the small chamber. "Ghost must have not fully explained what these are. My advice, you will never finish this in two days without help!" I looked up at Tomin, who stood nearly an arm's length taller than everyone.

"I don't say this often," he said, "but she is right!" Scarlet punched Tomin in the arm and he folded like a huge bear.

"I was only kidding" he sulked, rubbing the back of his arm.

"So was I..." she returned with a grin. "Now Casanova, whispers in the temple say you are to battle Shinn in the Diamake."

"Yes, I was told," I shrugged, "but I am more concerned with finishing this task before I even ask what a Diamake is!" Scarlet's eyes widened as she turned to Tomin and then back to me.

"Ghost didn't tell you?" Tomin asked, an anxious look was written on his face.

"Of course Ghost didn't tell him!" I spun around and was staring at the grinning face of Shinn. He was standing in the corridor shrouded in shadow, his crimson cloak making his deadly aura seem just a bit more dangerous "Then again, I wouldn't know how to tell the poor boy either, the details are much too honorable to be spoken of by a traitor."

"A traitor?" I found myself repeating aloud.

"Oh, I guess he didn't mention that one either!" Shinn's deep olive eyes touched mine, a condescending grin painted on his face. I held my ground and said nothing. "Well I wish I had the time to explain, but I have training to do for the Diamake...happy carvings!" he said, glancing down at my tunic and then the floor, grinning. Just as his shadow trailed off down the flaming corridor, I turned to the pair.

"Okay..." I said, turning, "what the fuck is the Diamake and how do I win it?"

"This will never work!" I said to no one in particular. I was standing in the weapon room, thirty-two steps from the entrance and presumably thirty-two steps to the far wall, directly in the middle of the room. A wooden stick was in my left palm and I was clad in one of those ugly grey tunics every initiate wore upon arrival... oh, and I was blindfolded as well.

"Stop counting your steps..." Scarlet's voice said from somewhere to my left. A sharp pain streaked through the right side of my face and I dropped heavily to one knee. "That will get you killed!"

I pushed myself up to my feet angrily. The wooden stick was no longer in my palm, it flew away just as I was struck. I palmed the area around me and found nothing. My back was struck by something hard as stone and when I spun around the same object thrashed into my knee so hard, I heard the bones nearly crack beneath the skin.

"This is not my idea of training!" I blared angrily.

"I know," a voice said from an unknown location. It turned out Scarlet not only knew how to throw her voice off of solid objects, but she could also alter it to sound distant or far, man or woman... Great! "This is how you get yourself killed! Training will not begin until you allow your body to do what it was designed to do."

"Designed?" I said into darkness.

"The people who brought you sure have kept a lot of secrets from you, which is only going to hurt you in the long run but enough time has been wasted now. I am going to tell you why you are here."

"Scarlet, I don't think that is a good idea!" Tomin said from behind me.

"No..." Scarlet roared in return. "Enough is enough, Tomin! This code of honor crock of shit here is going to send him to an early grave along with the whole lot of us. A grave we won't even see coming until the hole is already dug. Now, he will never win the Diamake without our support and that means our full support. No lies, no truths withheld."

"Go ahead!" I told her. "I need to know Scarlet, please!"

"Fair enough," Tomin said, turning back toward the entrance. "I will watch the door just in case we have visitors."

"Casanova promise me you will never repeat these words to a single soul, as it is punishable by death!"

"I promise Scarlet," I pleaded. "I will never betray you!"

"Casanova you were created by the order of mystics as a weapon!" she said. "A weapon to save mankind from the final war, but a mistake was made by the woman that created you."

"The woman that created me?" I said. "You mean my mother?"

"Not quite..." she said, "but there is no time for explanations, just listen," she returned, I stayed silent. "This woman attempted to reproduce an ancient ritual that would transform a mortal into a god. However when she attempted this spell, the rubies she had dipped into the Solace were switched by rubies dipped in dark serum. In doing this, an imbalance was created within the entire realm not the least of which created another being. A woman more powerful than the gods themselves emerged from the ashes and out of fear and uncertainty the mystical order immediately banished her to the realm of thought for a century."

"So if she is banished," I began as she stopped, "then why would we have to worry about her in the final war?"

"Casanova, the woman was banished one hundred years ago" she advised, "she is now here, in hiding until the final war."

"War!" a voice whispered from so close, it seemed to come from inside of my head. I spun around so fast, I nearly lost my footing as I reached up to remove the blindfold. The room was dim and candlelit. Four imperial altars lined the far wall with only one door separating them. Scarlet and Tomin both stood with blindfolds, glaring toward that door.

My hand was trembling, and somehow I slowly came to realize we weren't alone in here. Something dark was lingering within these walls, and somehow I felt the power undulating through me. A deep humming sound came from the far left side of the training room, almost like a growl.

"What was that?" Scarlet said, snatching her blindfold off, her eyes a flaming reflection of the hundreds of candles lining the walls.

"You two heard that?" I said, staring at the door. Tomin nodded, reaching a hand behind his back, and when it reemerged there was a small book in his palm. Flipping through the thing incessantly, he mouthed a few lines from each page before he flipped to the next. The growling sounded once again, and this time it was distinct and with more intensity than the first time.

"Tomin, what is the issue?" Scarlet barked as she held her wooden rod out before her as if it were a magick wand.

"I'm looking, I'm looking..." he said, flipping almost to the end of the book and stopping. He mouthed a few lines to himself before his eyes grew three times their normal size. "We have to get out of here, now!"

"What is in there Tomin?" I asked, my eyes locked on the wooden door. Tomin slowly started back stepping, stuttering something indistinct.

"Death!" he called out just before he disappeared into the shadows. Within seconds, it was only Scarlet and I standing in the middle of the vast room nearly touching shoulders. Her wooden rod was trembling, but she still held it as a warrior would hold out a sword.

"I can never rely on him!" Scarlet snarled in scarcely a whisper. I looked at her gauntleted hand, and it was shaking uncontrollably.

"Take off your gauntlet!" I said instinctively.

"I am fine!" she barked.

"For now," I shot back, "that thing sounded big enough to break through this wall, and if it does, you are the only one that can stop it!"

"Stop it how?" she said, dropping the tough act and showing her vulnerability. "I don't even know how to use this thing!" She slipped off her gauntlet and held her hand out before her as if it were a foreign object she was told to decrypt. Black markings lined her hand and arm in a tribal scheme and a deep red aura was shimmering softly around it.

"You're about to find out!" I said, edging toward the wooden door.

"Agishi!" the whisper came from just behind me.

"What did you say?" I said, turning.

"I didn't say anything," she said nodding toward the door. "Let's do this!" I shook it off and pressed forward toward the arching oak door. My heart suddenly lurched violently and I quickly reached a hand to my chest.

"Casanova, what is it?" Scarlet asked with concerning red eyes

"I don't know," my eyes were gaping as I tried to understand what was happening. "My chest feels like it's... burning!"

"Burning?" Scarlet repeated. Soft footsteps sounded from just outside the entrance. Scarlet and I both ducked down, scurried off into opposite sides of the dim training room, and I disappeared behind a velvet curtain just as the doors eased open and then shut. Two figures were standing just in front of the archway marking the entry to the training room. Both of them were hooded, one in red, one in black.

"This serum is not to be revealed until after the Diamake. He is much too powerful to be faced even in his original form," the man said from beneath a black hood with gold etchings down along the hood, with his hand fixed firmly inside the inner fold of his cloak. "Yes, master," the red cloak answered, my eyes widened at the familiar voice.

"Kneel before me!" The man in red cloak knelt down before the black hooded man and bowed his head until his forehead nearly touched the ground before the chanting began. Words of a foreign dialect filled the training room in the form of reverberating hums and a long drawn out incantation.

Whatever was happening over there needed to be stopped, but there was no way I could do it myself. I pulled the curtain back slightly to get Scarlet's attention, but she was engrossed in the ritual happening in the center of the room. My heart was pounding at my chest as my mind went in all directions in search of a fast plan. The black hooded man removed his hand from the fold of his cloak and revealed a small vial with a black liquid in it. He slowly unscrewed the top and eased toward the red cloak before him. It was now or never...

I slipped from behind the curtain, consciously aware of staying within the shadows, reached for the handle of the heavy oak door I heaved it open with one strong tug. The sudden movement sent the red cloak leaping to his feet.

Shinn! I confirmed silently from within shadow and Razuhl!? The two stared at the open door as if they were looking in the very face of death itself.

"Who goes there?" the black hood called out, quickly placing the vial back into his cloak. Shinn stood there with palms facing upwards, humming something indistinct. His eyes were entirely white, just like Dimitrius' were back in that cave.

"That won't work!" Razuhl warned. "You are not nearly as powerful as what lies behind that door."

"Give me the serum!" Shinn barked, eyeing the open door, but strangely there was none of the vicious growling we heard earlier. "Then I will have enough power to defeat it... and Casanova! Is that not what you wish?"

"My wish is irrelevant when we have..." All the candles in the room suddenly blew out and were replaced by darkness. I could no longer see Shinn or Razuhl, even Scarlet was no longer in sight. I stood so still, I could feel the beat of my heart against the front of my tunic. Once again I had the strong feeling something was in the room with us, a spirit of some kind or maybe something else entirely.

"Casanova, it's me!" a voice whispered. I spun around, startled, about to scream murder just before a soft hand clamped my face. Her palm was boiling hot and her eyes were flaming almost inconceivably so. "I don't know how, but I think I doused all the candles"

"Scarlet... your eyes?" I said.

"Yes, I know," she started, wincing in pain, "we have to make a break for the entrance, I don't think I can hold the flames back much longer."

"Scarlet, we will be seen!" I pointed out. "They are still in here, I can feel them!"

"So we must run fast!" she said, eyeing me with a vicious intent.

Give her the serum... the whisper came from inside my head, from within darkness but this time I knew it was not Scarlet. It was the same whisper I have been hearing since I entered this temple, the same one that haunted my dreams. The serum, Agishi.

Two vague shadows formed the silhouettes of Razuhl and Shinn before me. Neither hooded apparition saw us approaching. My heart was pounding endlessly but my dark instincts drove me forward straight past where the two stood silently awaiting the presence to emerge from the open door. My body was now moving of its own accord as I felt a rush of pure energy flowing through my veins, empowering me. I slipped the vial straight from out of Razuhl's cloak just as I blurred past. The two of us reached the entrance, saw the light cascading in from the corridor.

    Scarlet nudged at my arm to keep going, but when I looked back she was reaching out to stop from falling.

    "Help... me!" she pleaded through jagged breaths. I grabbed her just before she hit stone. Her eyes were en-flamed and rolling into the back of her head, her whole body was boiling with heat but I held her close as she started shaking uncontrollably. I pulled off her hood and swiped strands of sweat filled red hair behind her ear. Dabbing the sleeve of my tunic against her face, I cleared the sweat forming on her forehead and cheeks.

    "It's okay, Scarlet..." I said softly in her ear, "Just let it all out, it's okay!" Her body shook and shook until it was to a point where I thought she would literally explode, but then it stopped.

    "It's them!" Razuhl blared as the candles reignited. There was no time to think, no time to run. I uncapped the small vial of black liquid, held it over Scarlet's lips and glared back at Razuhl.

"This is the serum, isn't it?" I heard myself saying. He was frozen in place. He slowly reached into the fold of his cloak and realized he was fucked. "What happens if she gets it?"

"She dies..." he replied almost too quickly, "and then you die shortly thereafter!" His heart was racing, somehow I felt it. Something about his tone was forced, along with his calm demeanor. I looked down at Scarlet and she was fading in and out of consciousness. Staring back up at the pair who had just moments ago planned on using this serum to sabotage me, I could only grin back at his response. I poured a drop of the serum onto her lips and watched it seep into her mouth. Razuhl lunged forward but it was too late, the liquid had already dissolved on her tongue. Scarlet's hand lifted toward him just before he leaped to the side. A bright burst of flame exploded from her palm so wildly that before I knew it, we were thrust back into the corridor. My head crashed into something that felt like stone and I was dazed for a moment, but still conscious.

Dirt filled the corridor so thick, I had to cover my eyes with my sleeve.

To my right Scarlet was staring open eyed at her palm, her body lying amidst a cloud of dust and a trail of blistering stone. Steam was issuing from her hand as well as the stone beneath her. Inside the weapon room, Razuhl and Shinn were staring back at the open door but... it was no longer there. The jagged edges of stone before me were sizzling, fragmented and broken rock was shown in place of where there had just been a wall moments ago. The candles lining the floor all alongside the walls were now lit brilliantly. I turned and exchanged gazes with Scarlet.

"That was unreal!" she mouthed, glancing from her palm down to the vial in my hand. Out of touch with her, the world or any thought other than the power I held in my palm, I too stared down at the vial in awe. Is this what I have been in search for this whole journey?

"Do you know what we just did, Casanova?" I heard Scarlet say from beside me. I shook my head, still eying the vial.

"You have just condemned yourselves to death?" Razuhl said, emerging from the shadows with Shinn closely behind. Shinn's eyes were dark and glaring as he approached. All along the side of his face were dark markings, some kind of design that faded just as it was seen. His palms were both facing me, extended out to his sides. Scarlet leapt to her feet and held a glaring palm to his face.

"Don't even try it!" she snarled, her right palm radiating with energy. I looked back and forth between the two, and before I could react Shinn lunged forward and pinned me to the wall. I closed my hand over the vial so tight, I thought the small glass would break in pieces.

"You better be what they say you are..." he snapped, clenching his hand over my throat, "or you will die, of that I will be sure!" His eyes were dark and glaring, but there was something different about the man before me.

Behind him, in the weapon room it sounded as if an immense stone was heaved across the room. Dust flew out into the corridor as the three mages before me halted to a stop. Scarlet and Shinn were standing face to face in mid motion, but their attention was now fixed to what made the sound. Shinn's hand was still gripping my neck, but he had turned to an awkward position to see inside the training room. The candles were shining brilliantly, but there was nothing seen inside the room. Some living presence that I couldn't see, only feel, as it glared at us from within the shadows.

"Get your hand off me!" I barked, shoving Shinn back into the stone wall. When I looked at him, it was as if he hadn't even noticed. Razuhl was staring into the room with gaping eyes as well, not even aware that I could have killed him that very moment. I just stared at him clutching the small sheik that ghost gave me in one hand, the vial of black liquid in the other.

"The golinth!" Razuhl said in scarcely a whisper, almost in fear.

"We have to clear the temple," Shinn said quickly, "all the women, children and students must be gathered to the gates."   "No," Razuhl commanded, "no one must know of this. It will cause an uproar that will surely draw it out. We need to get in there and banish it before it goes on a warpath."

"Banish it?" Scarlet interjected. "I don't know if you realized, but that requires more than just two advanced mages." Razuhl's gaze touched mine for a moment before he turned. The ground quivered and stopped once and then again beneath my boots and as I brought my gaze up, Razuhl quickly flared into motion.

"It's on the move," he barked, "we have to do this now!" Razuhl charged into the corridor followed by Shinn, I looked down at the hand clutching my sleeve.

"Don't leave me!" she said, her eyes a flaming panic. "I don't think I am strong enough to handle whatever this thing is," she said, her lips shaking from the trembling stone beneath us. "Take the serum, Casanova!" her voice echoed in my head for a long while as I stared at the liquid with a dark intent. "As long as I am here, you won't ever have to fight alone," I said as a bright light caught my attention from inside the weapon room. Razuhl was holding a long staff in his palm and the white bulb on the end was glowing brilliantly, the ground trembled violently as the thing approached. In a rushed panic, I unscrewed the top of the vial and put it to my lips. Powerful shock waves jolted my body upright as I ingested the thick black liquid and I dropped to my knees. It wasn't painful, but it also wasn't painless. It was raw energy rushing through me in powerful waves indescribably euphoric. My body was roaring with heat, as I felt a complete and utter change come over me.

A loud, crashing explosion sounded from the weapon room. Shards of rock and metal and glass came bursting from out into the corridor. I shielded my face with my sleeve from the thick clouds of dust. Loud orders were being made somewhere in the distance, but I only heard muffles, my ears were ringing. To my left, Scarlet was staring open eyed into the room. A beam of green light flew across, searing stone in its path and disappeared, then another followed by a massive roar that shook the entire temple. Stepping into the room beside Scarlet, I saw a huge, looming creature almost as tall as the ceiling. Its skin was hard and brittle, like stone, and its eyes were two glaring beams of green staring back at us... at me.

"Focus your energy, Scarlet!" I said, staring at the monster in front of me. Arkon used to tell me all the time, focus your energy, Casanova. Somehow, that advice seemed appropriate for the moment.

"You absorbed the energy from the candles and held it within. I want you to do that again but instead of focusing on the candles, focus on the golinth!" The creature lifted a massive stone foot and stepped forward to charge, the ground trembling wildly as it approached.

"Casanova, I'm not powerful enough!" she said, cringing at the approaching monster.

"Scarlet, do it now!" I commanded, just as Razuhl deflected a heavy blow. Sparks flared out from his staff in all directions as he crashed into Shinn and the pair toppled into the darkness. The monster turned its gaze towards his next target, us. He lifted his foot once again. but this time I read its moves and leaped out of harm's way. I turned to see Scarlet's gaping eyes lost in the moment. There was no way she could gather enough of its energy to slow it down. I tried to think on my feet, but as the creature spotted me and started charging, it was inevitable... I would die in the most painful way imaginable. Everything around me went silent as the image of my final moment in the physical realm was burned into my mind.

A hazy apparition of Solana appeared before me in all of her marvelous splendor. That long flowing black hair, those green eyes, those lips... everything I needed in my life in one woman. I should have told her how I felt about her. How she made my insides cringe whenever she touched me or how my heart skipped a beat whenever I was with her.

"Trust your power, Agishi..." a voice whispered from within, "embrace your true self!"

The whisper brought my attention to what was happening inside of my body. A dark energy was streaking through me, sparks of raw power trickled all through my arms and legs. My chest expanded slowly and contracted, expanded slowly and contracted. I opened my eyes to my approaching demise with an odd confidence that exuded from my very pores. It felt as if the entire world slowed down for just that moment. The golinth was charging wildly, but it was as if it were not moving at all. I turned to Scarlet and she was lifting her hands up to cover her face from the attack. I grabbed her and shoved her out to the corridor. The golinth charged at me, but I stood my ground. Warm currents shot through my hands and when the thing got close enough, I lifted my palm. The creature was a tremendous stone being that could only be created through some powerful form of dark magic... but when I lifted my palm, its eyes grew bright as powerful beams of light and energy shot out in directions. Its mouth opened and the thing let out an agonizing roar that I could feel streaking through my very bones as if it were... in pain. When I closed my fist, everything around me went dark. As dark as the dungeon Sinnis Trochal locked me in. As cold as my heart felt in that very moment.

All sound ceased to exist, save for the slow, hypnotic beating of my heart against my chest. The soft crackling of fire singed stone sounded in the near distance. The candles adorning the imperial altars shone brilliantly from all four corners of the room. My head was fogged, but I was still able to distinguish the queer feeling from the reality of what I just did. The three bodies before me were shielding their eyes and coughing violently, and I was in a fog. I felt myself slowly falling back, into a deep abyss. The pleasant parts of my soul felt as if it were slipping free of my grasp, the part I needed. The effects of the serum were now in full effect and I could feel its darkness slowly start to pull me under.

"I got you!" a deep voice said as I landed in the heavy hands of...

"Ghost?" I said looking up weakly, as I still felt my body sinking backward even as he held me upright.

"Yeah... it's me!" the hooded man snarled, glaring at Razuhl. "Scarlet, see Casanova safely to his chamber, I will send for you!" I felt my arm lift and rest on small shoulders, but she felt strong as she hoisted me upright. I felt my body gliding effortlessly toward the corridor.

"I was right about you wasn't I?" she said, staring straight ahead. Her face was charred and full of dirt.

"About me?" I squinted, my head drifting back and forth from the nausea.

"You really don't remember who you are, do you, Casanova?" she said, turning me into the corridor toward my chamber.

"He has returned!" a woman from the shadows said pointing. The woman in magenta cloak dropped to her knees and kissed my feet. Behind her stood a group of maybe ten masked faces each shadowed beneath deep magenta hoods with mailed armor beneath, one by one each of them bowed their heads as Scarlet and I passed.

"He has returned!" the woman chanted, her forehead touching the floor.

"Who are these people?" I asked, staring at the long line of warriors we were approaching.

"They are called the guardians..." Scarlet whispered, I nodded acquiescently. "They are the ones who maintain natural order in the realm."

"Well, natural order has definitely been disrupted" I pointed out, glancing down at my palm. It was shaking uncontrollably and a dull, lingering pain was pulsating throughout my entire body. The warriors stood at attention as Scarlet and I passed, each placing a fist over their heart. I winced painfully as Scarlet leaned forward, reached her palm up toward my chamber door and without touching it somehow unlatched the metal on the inside. The door creaked open and as it shut behind us, she turned.

"You just obliterated a golinth with your bare hands!" she said, narrowing her crimson eyes. "Reduced the thing to dust!"

"I know!" I said staring down at my trembling hands in disbelief as she stared at her own in the same manner.

"Casanova, it screamed when you lifted your hand!" she said marveling at the power lying dormant within me.

"I just wanted to protect you," I said thoughtlessly as the chamber door creaked open and a hooded figure appeared in the archway.

My heart instantly sank in my chest as the haunting figure eased into my chamber. I had no weapon, save for the iron sheik from Ghost, but it was much too small for the man that approached.

"Rahsorz... what are you doing here?" Scarlet said from behind trembling lips, as she eyed the dark presence stepping in towards us. His deep crimson cloak shimmered lightly in the temple draft. His demeanor was calm yet menacing all the same. He eyed me intently, with fierce eyes even though they betrayed a slight melancholic air. For some reason the man before me was more fearsome than the golinth I had just reduced to dust. The man just stared... a dark, penetrating glare that was not nearly as threatening as the power I felt emanating from within him. His smoky grey eyes were piercing and cryptic under thick brows, holding no expression at all even as they bore into the very pit of my soul.

"You two have made a grave mistake..." he finally said, his voice despondent as his eyes touched us both. My heart sank into my chest as I awaited his next words, the judgment, but that never came. He reached up and removed the hood of his cloak. Beneath the soft crimson hood, his skin was dark and hard. Calloused wounds ran across the side of his head and neck in blotches not much different from my own. The air of sadness deepened now as I looked back at the man. Staring at the similarities of his imperfections and mine.

"Mistake?" Scarlet returned, as Rahsorz slowly pulled his hood back over his head.

"The serum is in you now, use it wisely. There is no turning back from here!" he said before he turned back to the corridor, and just like that, the man was gone. Scarlet and I exchanged glances for what felt like the first time I actually saw her, she looked at me in the same manner. An undeniable wave of understanding washed over me as I looked into the eyes of the woman, Scarlet - and not the young girl actually standing before me. Her eyes were gaping and a fiery blaze was lit within them. She was scared and so was I, but I carefully searched her eyes for meaning, and found it. Her lips trembled, for her next words would change the course of fate for a millennia to come.

"Casanova...your eyes are bleeding!"

Raleigh Bines
"You should not be here!"
Catia, Eastern coast of Cilan 1870

The morning sky was a dismal grey, with no hint of the sun's presence. Brisk winds howled and cut through tunic and flesh as heavy clouds receded over the distant horizon. It was always cold on this side of the world, but the night we just endured had been a dreadful one indeed. My breath came out in soft clouds as I unclipped my twin blades. Fresh flakes of snow fell and landed all across the land resting lightly on scattered leaves and the blades of grass all around me. I cocked my head to the left and locked eyes with a cold blooded killer. His rich, massive coat was speckled with snow and his teeth were bared, snarling as he turned his head to meet my gaze. I lifted a finger to my lips to hold the silence as the black wolf licked its chops and fell quiet. Knight is what I finally named him after long pondering. Azla was leaning his back against a towering oak forty strides from where I was crouched, with a finger pointing toward the stable in the distance. I pointed to my chest then out to the stable. The barbarian nodded just before disappearing behind the shield of the oak sentinel. The ground was soft and uneven in certain places, but not the path we chose to initiate our attack.

"You sure he is in there?" I snarled, my voice coming out raspy and hoarse, but firm.

"No..." Caliah said, eyeing the irregular smudges in the hilly path. "But it is the first sign of civilization. We will need to proceed with caution!"

"Yes." I nodded in acquiescence. "If you can keep up!" I winked before charging down the dirt path as a madman would.

Heavy paws scampered through the snow specked grassland behind me as Azla kept watch from a distance. Thirty strides up the dirt hill, the stable became more distinct. Black smoke issued from the rear of it and there was not an animal in sight. Twenty strides up the hill and I veered off the dirt path. The stale scent of burning flesh made my nose cringe but I pushed forward, vengeance drove my warpath. Ten strides and everything in my body was screaming for blood.

    Blood rushed to my head as I lowered my shoulder and charged in through the heavy doors of the stable. Close to twenty sets of terror filled eyes stared back as Knight came rushing in to stand at my flank.

    They were all commoners, each clad in shabby cloths that would not be adequate for a cool breeze let alone an entire winter here. They were surrounding a tremendous fire pit holding their hands over it to keep warm. A young child was crying uncontrollably in the back. Three women were huddled together near the fire, one was sweating profusely, her lips trembling as the other two held her close. In the far east corner, three bodies lay lifeless, stacked one atop the other wrapped in rope and cowhide in the far corner of the stable, they were burnt black. For a split second, I did not know how to approach this situation. Knight growled and nudged his head against my leg. We caught eyes as he awaited my command, those sparkling yellow eyes spoke of a deep ferocity just waiting to be released.

"Who are these people?" a soft voice said from closely behind. Caliah searched the room in the same manner I did, with an anxious uncertainty. Her long sleeves of rabbit fur concealed her chained blades as she came to stand by my left flank. She searched each pale face in the stable, examining the place as one would regard a museum of wild reptiles, with heed rather than excitement. Nothing revealed the hint of a killer.

"I do not know..." I drawled, eyeing the man on the floor shaking. His skin was pale and pasty. Sweat covered the whole of his face and neck, giving it a rich, luminous gleam. Knight snarled and stood at attention as a woman in ripped, grey tunic approached from the rear end of the stable.

"You must not be here," she said, again and again until it appeared they were the only words she knew. Thin mangled grey hair rested over the face and neck of the frail woman. Her face was sheened with sweat and her lips were cracked from the bitter cold, but she continued to repeat her words endlessly.

"You must not be here," the frail woman drawled airily as she gently dabbed a cloth on the forehead of the man lying in her arms, in complete trance. Azla was a thick, heavily muscled warrior who had without a doubt killed many men. He too was clad in rabbit furs lined with cords of horse hide. Around his ankles and wrists were sharp dagger like tusks of bamboo and around his neck was a leather thong adorned with the tooth of some wild beast, maybe an alligator, or even a wild boar. Caliah wore the same one around her neck.

"Are they the ones responsible?" he said, stepping in the stable from behind. His longbow was clutched tight in his palm and you could tell from his tone he did not come here to help the sick or inquire for their well being, he came for blood.

"No, they aren't!" I intoned, more disappointed than anything else. I sheathed my twin blades and turned back toward the door I had knocked entirely off its hinge. "We must continue further. Let's go, Knight!" The wolf let out a disappointed whimper and went charging out the door into the snow glazed pasture.

"Right!" the warrior said, placing his arrow back in its quiver he followed behind.

"Continue further?" Caliah said to our backs. "And what of these people? What of this plague?" I turned slowly, thinking of a nice way to say what was on the edge of my tongue, but failed.

"Yes, continue further!" I snapped. "What would you suppose we do? Help them and infect ourselves while we're at it?

"We have to do something," she retorted firmly. "We can't just leave them here to die!"

"They were here dying before we got here!" I said, much louder than intended. I turned slowly, only to see the eyes of every man, woman and child in the stable fixed on me. "I'm starting to get this foot in the mouth thing pretty down pact huh?"

I was grinning until Caliah shot me the look of death. She ripped the fur from her sleeves and covered her nose and mouth with it. Tying wisps of fur and cloth together behind her neck, she made a mask for herself. Kneeling down beside the grey haired woman, she handed her the other fur and helped her wrap her nose and mouth with it.

"Is this your husband?" Caliah asked, staring down at the dying man in her arms, the woman nodded.

"You should not be here!" she said, wiping the man's face with a pale hand full of cracks and age spots.

"You have done more than your share here," Caliah pointed out, "let us help you!"

The wind howled and cried outside as Knight charged back into the stable. He was usually energetic and playful, but when the black wolf rushed in and stopped silently in the far corner of the stable, I knew something was wrong.

"What did you see out there, boy?" I said, walking over to him. "What did you see, Knight?"

The wolf wagged his tail fervently as he whimpered in the corner. He was staring out the window facing the north. It appeared everyone was watching this window as well, waiting for something or someone to suddenly emerge from the unsettling horizon.

"You should not be here!" the woman's voice was suddenly strong and forceful. When I turned, her eyes betrayed a darkness that would unnerve even the fiercest of warriors.

She reached for the water jug beside her with haste and doused the flame in the fire pit. The difference was instantly felt, the sickly men and women began huddling against each other for warmth. We now lay in wait, cold and within the heavy gloom of winter. I swayed toward the far corner of the stable, blade in hand and with my back against the wall. I turned my head to the window and my heart lurched.

"Who are they?" Caliah said icily. Azla stepped up staring open eyed out the same window, Knight whimpered softly nudging his wet nose against my boot.

"The Nephilim!" said the unexpected voice of a man from the corner. He was sweating profusely, but in his eyes I saw coherency. For as far as the eye could reach there were hundreds, maybe thousands of... grey men. It seemed the only accurate name to call these tremendous creatures walking around. They were tall as the treetops and their skin had a dry and pasty grey tinge. Their hands and feet were much longer than a regular man's and they only had two fingers and two toes on each. They must have been drawn to the warmth of the fire pit before the lady doused the flame. The ground was now trembling as they approached the stable.

"The Nephilim?" Caliah said, turning to Azla and then to me. "Are they not a myth?"

"I suppose not!" Azla said, staring toward the approaching herd.

"You should not be here," the grey haired woman drawled distantly.

"How do we kill them?" I asked no one in particular. The man who had spoke stepped out of the shadows, accompanied by a walking stick and he looked more weak and frail than anyone else in the stable. He was a pale man, short and hunchbacked with a wide nose and bushy mustache. He was clad in a drab, grey tunic that was damp and travel stained, he slowly limped his way toward where I stood.

"You must be quick on your feet..." the man started, as he too looked out the window at the approaching horrors. "And you must have no fear!" Almost instantly, I felt the workings of a vicious grin forming on my face. The man and I stared eye to eye for all of two blinks before I glanced at Caliah. The look in her eyes told me everything I needed to know. That I was crazy, insane, a madman... everything I needed to see in that moment. Before she could object to what I was about to do next, I stepped forward to the old hunchbacked man and stared into his deep, hollow brown eyes.

"Tell me what I need to do!"

CHAPTER FOURTEEN
Memorie XIV

Filann Gunther

"I want the ruby!"

Mincia, East Cilan 1875

The dreary inn was unusually crowded the first time I saw the masked knight. A tremendous fellow indeed, the biggest I've ever seen. The locals say he visited this inn for the past two nights, and each time he ordered the same thing, Stalin, the darkest most bitter ale sold in these parts. He was armored in iron face plate and the black cloak and mail typical of the imperial assassins. His hair was long, thick and dreaded beneath a lion half helm and his hands were covered with heavy iron gauntlets. Some say that if you looked directly in his eyes it would curse your very soul, but I believe the legends were much too lenient for the group that sat in the shadowy part of the inn. For on this night, I gazed upon his eyes and did not lose my soul, I only lost everything I had to fight for in a single moment.

    Mystic's lair was a small, drab inn on the outer edge of the town Mincia. Thinking back, I had no idea why it would be called Mystic's lair, the mages and mystics of Cilan were a myth along with the hundreds of other lies parents would tell their children to frighten them to obedience, but something was to happen this night. For it was the night after the Agishi has passed to the spirit realm it was prophesied, and not only that I could feel the tension hovering that night. The inn was frequented by the common folk of Mincia and avoided by most other royals, which made the presence of the masked knight and his six guard retinue abit queer to most, but not I. This was to be a fortnight of transition, the period where the fiercest warriors gather to prepare for the Agishi tournament. By the looks of it, my wish for a worthy opponent has finally been granted.

    "Keep staring and you will give us away!" said Kara holding a tray and handing me a drink before moving to the next table. She was right...hell, I hadn't even realized how obvious I was staring on that side of the room.

I lifted the mug of ale to my lips and drained it before I turned to my brother.

"Keep your eyes open," I warned him, although his eyes betrayed no sign of unawareness. Eliann was always ready for battle, the problem was he was almost never ready for diplomacy.

"I say we end this all tonight..." he said through gritted teeth, his eyes betraying intent just as mine had just moments ago, "right now!"

"Easy, brother," I said drawing his attention to the poster beside us. THE LEGENDARY AGISHI TOURNAMENT it read in bold letters. "Father taught us better than to dishonor ourselves outside of the arena."

"Yes, but now father is dead and I believe it is by the hand of that fuckin' heathen!"

"We do not know that for certain!" I shot back intensely, "Now, father is dead, but that does not mean his teachings have died with him. We will leave fate to the gods and fight him in the arena, not as wild beasts in the field."

"Wild beasts in the field resolve their matters with blood, not countless hours of training and strategizing, just fighting."

"And that is the difference between us, brother!" I said calmly. I could see in his eyes that he did not know if I meant the difference between wild beasts and man or the difference between him and I. "Let us go, we have much to prepare for!"

Staggering to my feet, I felt the wrath of my brother's eyes against my neck, but I pushed forward through the sea of bodies filling the inn. Countless heads turned to look as I swayed past, doubtlessly recognizing royalty among them. I closed the front of my robe, concealing the grand ruby pendant hanging from the golden choker upon my neck, before stepping out into the chill of the night. The moon was at its fullest and the air was much dryer than it had been the night before. Winter was soon approaching... I thought as I made my way to the side of the inn where our horses were reined. Turning the corner, my blood suddenly went cold in my veins. The huge figure looming in the darkness held a torch before him, the whole of his face was seen from behind the flames. His hair hung loose and wild beneath his helm and the iron plate concealing his face was streaked with blood. His imperial black cloak fluttered softly behind him and a heavy two handed black sword stood erected in the dirt before him. The weapon made his presence seem that much more frightening, but nothing terrified the Gunther clan, not even the thought of confronting this situation much earlier than I had planned to. I extended my hand out behind me to block my brother from advancing; this could be resolved with subtlety, I thought.

"I expected you!" I heard myself saying aloud.

"If you expected me you would have never stepped foot out of that inn," he said, his voice rough and hoarse behind iron face plate. I felt the presence forming behind me. I turned back and three imperial assassins with pikes and blades drew closer. Behind the masked knight, another three assassins emerged from the shadows.

"What is it you want?" I said side-stepping into defensive position, hand on hilt.

"I think it is clear what they want, brother!" said Eliann, unsheathing his longsword. "They want blood!"

"Sheath your sword," said the masked knight. "I have not come to shed blood, lad!"

"Then why have you come?" I said through gritted teeth, for I already had an idea of what this was about. His eyes touched mine with a fierce knowingness, I pulled my robe together tighter.

"You know why I have come, Filann," he said, the torch a flaming inferno before him. "I want the ruby!"

"It is an heirloom, for the name of my family," I said firmly. "You can attempt to take it in the arena!"

"Is that your answer?" the masked knight asked, his eyes betraying no emotion. My heart pounded in my chest, cold sweat streamed beneath the pits of my arms, my palm was sweating as it gripped the hilt, but I stood firm.

"Yes, it is!" I declared.

"Gringus!" the masked knight called out just before a big burly soldier stepped forward, the biggest of all his assassins, and grabbed Eliann by the neck. He yanked his head back and slipped a dagger to the front of his throat. I unsheathed my sword fiercely and stood my ground.

"So you will save your ruby for the sake of your family, but you would let your brother die?"

"Don't do it, brother!" Eliann blared defiantly. Gringus yanked his head back once more, this time he was not able to wrench free. The dagger pressed against his neck until a line of blood fell from the edge, flames surged through my veins as I prepared myself.

"Before you do something you will regret," he said from behind iron face plate, "three imperials were sent to your royal apartments with orders to kill everyone if you return with that ruby. Do you also want to lose your brother for an heirloom that you don't even really know how to use, Filann?"

The monster spoke, but the only thing I could think of was my wife, my daughter, my mother, waiting to be slaughtered, and it was all my fault. How had I not seen this coming from well off, as my father would have? The very name of Gunther was soon to be wiped out of existence because of my stupidity, and the only thing I had to show for it was a senseless honor that I would soon die with. A sudden aggression came over me, an indescribable anger. Memories of my father flashed in and out of my mind, battles we've fought together, the lessons he taught. My eyes blurred and I blinked away the wetness.

    I clenched the hilt of my longsword until the bones cracked in my hands and lunged forward. The first one I went for was the one at my brother's neck. The swiftness of my blade startled the big brute and he released his hold on Eliann just enough for him to break free and palm his sword. The blade that sprang out was long and richly made, its hilt was made with raw ivory and dragon bone. Eliann struck the brute with the force of a god, the blade made contact with mail but did not pierce it. The big soldier was knocked back two steps before lunging forward again. A pike was shoved in my face just before I slipped the blow and countered with a low knee slash. The masked soldier staggered forward and I shoved my blade up into the soft part of his neck. The masked knight stood motionless, watching.

    An iron fist slammed into the side of my head and lifted me in the air from the force, it turned out to be the hilt of a short sword. When I landed, I was staring at the edge of a boot just before it crashed into my mouth. My head hit the dirt hard and I saw my brother for a brief moment before I was overwhelmed with boots and pikes. I felt hands groping for my robe trying to get to my choker, but the dagger in my thigh rig proved vital for such close quarters. I stabbed a hand through flesh and bone, the assassin dropped to the dirt beside me screaming. I quickly got to my feet and charged forward into the crowd of imperials surrounding Eliann. I rolled in the dirt toward one of the imperials and slashed for groin but caught mail. I got to my feet and my brother now stood behind me, five imperial assassins before us. The two of us stood back to back both of us enraged with vengeance, before we realized the masked knight was no longer there... neither was his sword.

 The five assassins before us suddenly stopped fighting. They held their pikes and blades down by their sides and were all staring toward the shadowy presence behind us. When I turned, my heart dropped into my palm and my blood turned icy in my veins.

 "Kara?" I heard my brother say in scarcely a whisper.

 "Help me please, Filann!" she gagged, beneath the firm grip of the masked knight, her eyes were streaming. He held her by the back of the neck like a butcher would hold the chicken he was intent on decapitating.

"Filaan," the masked knight roared, "cares nothing for you or for his family...and it is a shame!" He turned her around and grabbed her throat, lifted her with one arm and held her suspended in the air. His eyes touched mine with a burning madness, and in that very brief moment all was lost. He slowly gripped and squeezed the life out of her until her body went completely limp as she dangled in his outstretched palm. It was a long moment before she was released and fell to the dirt like an animal, a wild beast if you will.

I turned to my brother and we locked eyes for an eternity that flashed in a second. His long brown locks were flat, matted, and damp with sweat. The expression he held in his grey tinged eyes was of a dull sadness, a look I have never seen on my brother.

"My brother!" he mouthed to me as the burly imperial behind him made his move. I quickly grabbed for my blade and drove forward, but I was too far away, not fast enough. The masked soldier he called Gringus drove a pike through my brother's back and I watched in horror as the bloodied iron tip punched through his chest.

    The night suddenly grew colder as I watched my brother slowly drop to his knees. The look of sadness lingered in his eyes before they rolled back into his head and he fell hard to the dirt. It took everything in me not to cry out, not to curse the gods for allowing this savage to take everything from me. I thought of what my father would do had this been him. How he would react to this situation, how his honor would have directed him down the right path in a moment just like this. But the only thing that screamed at me from the inside... was vengeance.

    "See you in the arena..." the masked knight said, turning his back to me.

    "You will pay for this with your life!" I cried out, my words echoed from within the alley, I heard no response. Only the wind whistling softly and the distant sound of drums and laughter. The imperial assassins faded into the night and the only things remaining in the dark alley were two people I lived, breathed, and would have easily died for in a moment's notice. My last glimpse of all that I knew as family, I was alone now, forced to fight a battle I didn't know if I was ready for. I wiped a face full of blood and tears on the back of my sleeve and prepared myself for the long journey ahead. I pulled my robe in tighter around me, reached up to my neck and my ruby was gone.

Brotus Satyre
"Come unto me, my child!"
Hall of Judgment, Cilan 1875

"And who is to blame for that?" said the immense being of light before me from his throne.

"It is my fault, lord," I said bowing my head apologetically. "In no way am I trying to shift the blame nor create any justifications. I only ask that you consider the options we had at the time. The world was literally resting on the shoulders of only five mystics, my lord, we now numbers in the hundreds of thousands. The mistake is not to be taken lightly in the least but if you would just show mercy in your judgment, I will make sure she is disciplined!"

My head was still bowed, eyes burning the ground before me. The six beings that sat before me were undoubtedly burning a hole in the top of my head, Dimitrius being one of them. The audience of nearly two score of mystics behind me stood silent, still and edgy. This answer would not only make or break the true essence of what mysticism is today, but if this goes wrong, we would have no chance in the war to come. A bead of sweat formed on my forehead and fell. I watched silently as the drop hit stone and dried, until it was no longer there, then I received my answer.

"Mercy shall be shown..." the being said. My head rose and I looked into the eyes of the most powerful god in all the omniverse and beyond. Pious, father of all mysticism dark and light, was the head and founding father of the light council. He was clad in purple velvet cloak, a silky white under tunic and his jeweled fingers held rings of all different colored jewels. His hair was pulled back into a sleek ponytail that was so tight that it fixed his eyebrows into a perfect arch and he held a tremendous scepter in his broad hand, a flaming sapphire was sitting atop of it. Any member who has risen above the sixth degree of mysticism is required to kneel before him and receive the grand ruby and sapphire of the mystics, one of the highest honors in all the different orders. There are many frauds, many mortals that claim to have knowledge of its true powers, but no mortal can withstand its power once the seal is broken, that privilege is for the gods alone.

"Mercy shall be shown?" a harsh almost beast like voice said approaching from the dark shadowy corner of the council chamber. As the massive being emerged from the shadows, the air in the chamber suddenly went cold. My heart was thundering in my chest, screaming to get out. The council was silent, the onlookers staring from the backcloth fidgeted in their seats nervously. All but Pious and Dimitrius who stood calm and unfazed, for they were the only ones who truly knew the being that stepped forward, more than knew, the three of them together were legend. I've seen the viciousness of the man that approached, those dark villainous eyes that could make the very depths of your soul cringe, those tremendous shoulders that spoke of unfathomable strength. He was clad in black silks and cloak, a grand ruby pendant hung from his neck and rested just above his big chest, nearly glowing with energy. He had the same face as his brother Razuhl, only his was stone hard and scarred from battle. The aura in the chamber had gotten so dark that black smoke issued softly from his cloak as he swayed past and stood before the empty throne between Pious and Zauron, the chief lieutenant of the council.

"I was not finished, Zamuhl!" Pious said with the authority of a god, when his eyes touched mine, my heart turned to ice in my chest. "However, balance cannot be maintained without a sacrifice. Tell me, what have you to offer the gods for this mercy you seek?"

"Sacrifice?" I said, incredulous. "I, I have nothing to sacrifice, only..." I thought of the most important thing in my life, the very thing I breathe and sleep for. The very thing that I would give up the life of mysticism to protect was now the only thing of value I had to offer the gods as a sacrifice. I thought of her warning all those years ago. This is precisely the decision she was trying to help me avoid making, and now it will be the biggest regret I will ever have to make.

"Only what, warrior?" Pious pressed. In the passing moments of silence, I could not think of anything I would rather do than to turn around and say fuck them all, but I needed them. We all needed them, even Dimitrius, who was now in the crosshairs of his own dignity and respect as a god and the mistake of his daughter Solana, one that slowly transitioned into the biggest miscalculation in the history of mysticism.

"I sacrifice to you and every god present in the council..." The tone of the chamber was so quiet that I could hear jagged irregular breaths coming from three rows behind me, without a doubt it was Isis.

You better not, Brotus! Her thoughts floated through the ether and enmeshed with my own.

"I offer you..." I began but halted as the outstretched palm of Dimitrius that was extended out toward me from his throne.

"A sacrifice is required." His voice thundered emphatically throughout the vast chamber. Not even Zamuhl dared interrupt him when he spoke. "Then a sacrifice shall be made. I hereby relinquish my position as the ruler of the physical realm and appoint Brotus as the new leader of the mystical order of Agishi."

The uproar that rose from behind was like none I have ever heard. The hundreds of mystics, mages and dark sorcerers that filled the hall behind me voiced their disapproval vehemently, some even left the chamber in disgust with the decision of one of the most loved gods sitting up there in the light council. Even I looked at the man completely lost for words, but Solana's outcry was the loudest, most distinct of them all.

"Father!" she cried out, her voice shrill and full of emotion. She pushed through the rush but was quickly apprehended by the white cloak swordsmen that guarded the sanctum. Heavy tears adorned her face like morning dewdrops on an open pasture. When her red, bloodshot eyes touched mine I saw the hurt, I felt the pain of my sister and of the hundreds of magie flooding the chamber behind me. Each painful memorie, the hurtful past of each one in the chamber suddenly was dropped heavily on my shoulders. In that moment I finally understood the burden Dimitrius had on his back for the past seven centuries of rulership. I understood that being the leader was not glamorous as one would think. The internal suffering one would have to endure, the secrets one would have to hold inside, the disappointing choices one would have to make was enough to crumble the average man.

"Silence!" The voice that sounded was one of authority. The noisy rush of disapproving voices came to a halt, the entire chamber fell silent as they waited on the word of Pious. "The god Dimitrius has spoken and if it is the wish of Brotus of the mystic order of Agishi, then the entire physical realm will be in his control, effective immediately. Brotus, what say you?"

I felt the wrath of 500 faces awaiting my answer. One thousand beady eyes staring at my back wishing they could slam a sword through it at that very moment. But then the council of Isis came to the forefront of my mind from five years ago. "What about when you assume the throne? Do you think she will agree with even half of the decisions you will be forced to make...?" Her words echoed for an eternity. I looked into the eyes of the man that I know for certain did all of this so that he could pave the way for me to become what I was destined to be. I looked down at my side, Golathine stared up at me with all her golden magnificence. I grabbed the hilt and unsheathed the heavy sword from my waist. I stood up to my full height and stared the god Pious in the eyes, those deep blue terrifying eyes, and I gave my response.

"I, Brotus, son of Darien the warlock, hereby accept the position as ruler of the physical realm and all responsibilities that come with the position."

"Come unto me, my child!" Pious said rising to his full height. A grand ruby was placed in his palm from a servant. I held my hands out before me with Golathine shining brilliantly from my palms as I ascended the steps leading to the council of light. The eyes of each god were laid upon me watching my every movement toward the ruler of the omniverse. I now stood before the council in a kneeled position waiting for the next words of the god.

Soft footsteps neared almost indistinct, I only felt the presence of power standing before me. Golathine was lifted from my palms, and when I looked up the god Zamuhl held a mighty hammer in one palm, Golathine in the other. His features and that of Razuhl' were so distinct that I could barely tell the difference in the twins only that Zamuhl was much bigger than his brother and he had a viciousness to him like none other. In one devastating strike the god slammed the ruby in place on the hilt of Golathine and handed the golden sword back to me. A rush of energy flowed through my body as I have never felt before, power I could only dream of shot through my hands and arms so intensely that I was engulfed in what seemed like an energy shield of flames. There was no doubt in my mind that this newfound ability could possibly be the beginning of the end. But the fact of the matter was, I had been ready for this moment for centuries, and now that it has finally come I will show my worth to the gods, especially Dimitrius.

"Much praises to you, warrior, you deserved this privilege," said the god Zamuhl, "but now a lot rests in your hands, more than it has ever been in the past, remember that!"

"Yes, my lord," I said kneeling before him. "I thank you all for the opportunity to prove myself." I spoke to the entire council, but my eyes rested on Dimitrius who stood with the most confidence in his decision.

I will not fail you... my lord! I spoke to him through thought, the nod he responded with was all I needed to see. When I turned around, I searched the vast chamber for the two faces I desperately needed to be there and found them. Both Isis and Solana stepped forward and took a knee just before the foot of the steps and touched their foreheads to the ground.

"I accept you as my leader from now until my last breath," the two of them said in unison. I expected Isis to be there for me, but Solana? Her support brought me to endless tears until the reality of my position was instantly brought to my attention. "Your first mission as ruler," said Zamuhl upon reaching his throne, his demeanor was all seriousness, "is to use that sword, protect my son at all costs!"

Casanova Volkart
"You are not yet ready to fight me!"
Agishi Temple, 1875

Five years have come to pass and there was no sign of the peasant I once was. Holding my rough calloused hands out before me, I examined the lines of blood and rough edges in my palms. The look in my eyes was one of rage although I knew this would be over in an instant. Glancing to my right, I felt a presence lurking behind me. I grabbed the hidden dagger from my back sheath and spun fast and low. Green slime splattered across my face as the blade slashed deep through the goblin's stomach. End trails spilled from his front, but I had no time to watch him fall, I wiped my face on the back of my sleeve and kept moving. I trudged up the murky steps and didn't stop until I reached the bell tower. When I reached it, I grabbed the hammer beside it and rang it for all to hear.

    As the bell sounded for the seventh time, I felt the sudden urge to fall to my knees. I touched my forehead to the ground and cried as I have never cried before. Tears fell endlessly from my face as I embraced what just happened. Descending the winding steps of the bell tower, I looked at my palms once again. I would have never believed I could, until I did. Stepping out into the arena, cheers sounded from both sides. I lifted my hands in celebration as I embraced the energy surrounding me.

    "Casanova, you did it!" said Scarlet from a distance. Albert and Tomin were beside her both cheering as well. Razuhl was approaching, holding the reward for my hard work all these years. Beside him were Ghost and Rahsorz, each holding a golden scepter of the ruby and sapphire. The crowd became more thunderous as the three of them now stood before me.

"I proudly present to you the sixth degree of mysticism and the honorable red cloak for your successful defeat of 100 goblins in the tower of Pesh. Do you swear to take this and use it to teach others," said Razuhl emphatically. I tried to catch eyes with my master, to get his approval, but he held his eyes forward as Razuhl continued his passage, "and to never cause harm on those who share your gifts?"

"Yes, I swear!" I announced, taking the red cloak and the golden broche indicating the highest degree in mysticism. The soft velvet cloak was soothing to the touch, but I knew exactly what this cloak really meant. It was my informal invitation to compete in the Agishi torunament, with the same deadly arts I have been training to suppress since I arrived at the temple. The same tournament that would have me enslaved to this place, this world. I have established the most invaluable friendships in that darkness, friendships I would never betray. A warm tear traveled down my cheek and rested heavily in my thick goatee. Friends that would never stop fighting, that would never leave me to fend for myself in a world I knew nothing of... I thought maliciously.

It was his duty to protect me, to make sure his little brother was safe until the end, five years and he never even came looking for me. If it were up to me I would have scoured this whole island until I found him. I looked down at the broche in my hand once again and did all I could to hold back the tears, luckily anger camouflaged my sadness. I caught eyes with Rahsorz and motioned toward the temple, he nodded.

Stepping into the shadowy portal leading back into the temple, I stopped and pulled off my blue cloak and replaced it with the red. I lifted the hood over my head, pulled the brim down to my eyelids and embraced my newfound glory. Rahsorz stepped up beside me and the two of us were silent for a long moment. Staring at the rough jagged edges of rock and mortar before us, I couldn't help marveling at how far I have come since I was that lost little peasant boy, practically begging to be protected.

"You know," Rahsorz said walking slowly in stride, "Ghost is not pleased with your request. And if I am going to be frank, neither am I!" His eyes glared toward me and although we were now officially of equal rank, those dark poisonous eyes still terrified the shit out of me.

"I wish you would stop being frank... and start being Rahsorz!" I snarled, but then focused my anger. "Rahs, eventually we will have to use all this power we've acquired to save our own lives, you know that, right?"

"Of course I know that," he said uncharacteristically somber, "but you belong here, fighting with your true family. Not going back to the savage way of life you lived through previously, the ones you love will never understand the life you lead now and have led for all these years. They will never understand what you are now!"

My senses suddenly flared in all directions. My lead foot grew numb and the pain that shot through the side of my head brought me down to a knee. I reached out and Rahsorz grabbed my hand, pulling me to my feet. He was screaming out to me, but I heard nothing, only the heavy pounding of my heart. I wiped my face and looked down at a hand full of blood. I closed my eyes, and when I opened them Rahsorz was staring at me, waiting.

"Did you hear what I said? No one will understand!"

"Just tell me this, brother," I asked, brushing off the vision, "are you with me or not?"

"Cas?" he started but stopped, sensing the seriousness in my tone. "I am with you, brother!"

"Good, because someone is here that does not belong," I said unsheathing my longsword. "I can feel them!"

"I don't feel anything!" he said, but I was already halfway back to the entryway.

Stepping out into the sun, I glanced up at the hills and saw the man clad in white silks and long flowing hair as black as the darkest night. It was too far a distance to see his face, I only saw that he stood looking down over the arena from the highest cliff and his aura was so prominent that the hairs on my arms stood at attention.

"Look," I said walking toward the man on the cliff, "he is the man I have spoken about!" Rahsorz stepped forward staring up at the cliff.

"Wait, Cas!" he called out, I stopped but did not turn. "Does this mean you will fight in the tournament? With your family?" his words trailed off in the distance and I continued walking. I did not turn back even as I reached the foot of the hill and started my ascent.

    I climbed the vast mountainous hill until the tips of my fingers bled. My hand slipped on the next grab and instantly I saw my life flash before my eyes. There I stood, dangling from one hand and nothing but the setting sun and sky there to greet me on the other side. I was so high in the air at this point, I stared down at the distant treetops. Something slipped from my inner sleeve, but my reflexes were at their peak and I snatched it straight out of the air before it flew out. I looked down at my palm and held the small vial of dark serum, as if it were the very essence of life itself. The truth was, I felt the change coming a very long time ago. It is just now, it was becoming noticeable. The recurring dreams that have been haunting my sleep for years have now returned and each night I saw further and further into the nothingness of my existence. I was empty inside, hollow to my feelings, austere in my demeanor.

    Arkon told me that sacrifice was needed, true indeed, but that was far from what this game was about. In my young mind I thought I understood that jewel, but as each day passed and I emptied another vial of this darkness into my body, I feel as if my very reason of being here was lost in translation. I came here to learn, to grow, and although I have indeed grown into one of the most complete fighters in the realm, my sanity has and continues to be my sacrifice.

    I lifted the small vial to my lips and drained the liquid. My body roared with energy and power. A power to be relished by any mortal walking the physical realm, but it was a dark power and I knew it. I somehow knew the consumption of this poison would one day turn me into a monster, into what Dimitrius has become.

    I lifted myself up and barely caught the next hold but I was back in position to finish my ascent. Pulling myself up and over the edge of the cliff, I was instantly immersed in a sensation I knew nothing of. Powerful rays of energy surged through me, very much unlike the power of the dark serum. This energy was pure, almost absolute. Standing at my full height, I felt my body tightening as blood surged through my muscular arms and thick body. Although the armor wore me down, I wore mail under my cloak and britches at all times even when I slept. The metal clinked softly as I pushed forward, no one was in sight. Two long daggers sat crisscrossed on my back beneath the cloak. Poisoned needle tips lined the inner fold of my cloak at the ready and my longsword rested discreetly at the waist. I was battle ready and nobody could have told me anything otherwise.

"Show yourself!" I cried out turning in all directions, ready for a fight. The wind howled softly in the distance, the setting sun slowly transitioned into night. The energy emitted from this man was the most powerful I have ever felt, but I unsheathed my sword and stood ready.

"Your heart is not pure," the voice said from nowhere in particular. "Vengeance fuels your path, that is why you can never defeat me!"

"Spoken by the coward in hiding," I shot back angrily, "reveal yourself!"

"You are not yet ready to fight me!" the voice said from closer than it was before.

"Is this why you have come here," I said, angrily gripping the hilt, "to speak of my unworthiness to fight?"

"I have come to help you realize your true power. To turn you into the complete fighter you think you already are!"

When I turned, I was staring at a man I knew half a lifetime ago. Although he seemed to have aged immensely in five years, the man looked more powerful than ever before. A sapphire and ruby pendant sat prominently on his broad chest and glistened even within the shroud of darkness. His white silks fluttered softly in the cool breeze along with his long flowing black hair, but the great sword with the ruby engraved in its golden hilt was what drew my attention.

"It has been a long time, my friend!" Brotus said, staring down at me as a god would look upon an insect.

"Why have you come here?" I said, my nostrils flaring. "To take me away to your cave again, to introduce me to a new group of mystical people?"

"Casanova, is that what you thin..."

"Just forget it," I blared, my words were sharp enough to cut through ice, "you will not take me again, my true family is here now!"

"All these years of training and you still think I wanted this!" Brotus shot back angrily. "I never wanted you here with these fuckin' heathens."

"They are not heathens, they are my family!" I roared, intense waves of anger shot through me and it took everything in me to hold back my attack. "And if this was not your intention, then why did you bring me here?"

"No, we are your family!" he returned, his eyes betraying anger. "Did you forget you were almost killed drinking the Solace? Or maybe you've forgotten that the venom in your veins this very moment is the reason you are still alive. You don't even know how much has been sacrificed on your account. You have traveled so far down this path of hate and vengeance that you don't even know that the man you are truly vexed with is yourself."

"You know nothing about me!" I blared, angrily wiping away tears of hatred. I felt the dark serum seeping and oozing through my body, empowering my senses, strengthening my instincts. Power that I did not even know how to fully control was raging through me, but the only thing going through my mind was a bitter vengeance that could only be remedied by a fight.

I leapt forward so fast that everything around me blurred. Bringing my sword down heavily, I almost thought his head would explode on impact, but he side-stepped so quickly that I lost balance and the side of my head crashed hard to the dirt. I leapt to my feet once again and threw away my sword, this fight would require more precision. I reached behind me and unsheathed the two hidden daggers in the small of my back and formed the stance Ghost taught me. I eased forward with the patience of a scorpion, dagger in each hand. Brotus narrowed his stance and held his golden sword at the ready. He attacked first this time, lashing out in a vicious barrage of heavy blows. Iron struck against iron with such intensity that I felt the tremor all the way up my arm from the impact. I countered with a heavy jab and knocked blood from his mouth. He ducked down beneath my blade strike, and when I looked, he lunged up with a heavy knee to the chest, knocking me four steps back and nearly off the edge of the cliff before I steadied myself. I wiped my lip with the back of my hand and spat away blood, but I was only getting started. Lifting my daggers, I breathed in deep and felt my body charging up to an intense peak. There was a dark latent energy within me, Ghost had revealed to me more times than I cared to think of. It was at that moment that I knew I was finally strong enough to perform the Kallehandra, but if I did decide to fight in the tournament I would never be able to recover to my full strength in less than a fortnight.

"Why are you holding back?" Brotus roared, lifting his sword. "You are stronger than this!"

I started to answer, but his sword came down overhead and would have struck skull if I had not rolled out of the way in the last moment. He pushed forward and gave me no time to regroup. The side of my head made contact with his hard shin, or the other way around. I spun around three times before I fell to the dirt so hard that it felt as if my ribs had broken. I pushed myself angrily to my feet, dizzy and confused but still at the ready. In the distance, Brotus was walking off with his golden hilt great sword fixed at his waist.

"You have not yet realized your true strength, Casanova!" he said distantly.

"Wait!" I called out, giving him chase with daggers at the ready, but he was gone, disappearing into the ether. The night had grown dark, I looked at my hands and realized they had been trembling. Ice was running through my veins and every scrape and bruise was now felt exponentially. I had been beaten, for the first time in a very long time, and embarrassed although only the two of us were privy to it. What was it that made him so powerful? And why would he come here now, after all these years, to show me my true power? These thoughts, I pondered on heavily as I slowly made my descent back down the hill.

CHAPTER FIFTEEN
Memorie XV

Caliah Hull
"King Ryelar!"
Catia, Cilan 1875

Warm hands stroked the side of my face, so that now the strands of damp hair were out of my eye. Briefly relieved from the pain, I smiled toward the bearded man staring at me from just strides away. He returned the gesture and reached a broad hand out to me. The warmth of it dulled the pain, and I held onto it like my life depending on it. Years ago, I would have never looked at a man like him twice. He was arrogant, self righteous, outspoken and easily the most obnoxious man on this side of the realm, but he was mine. Not only that, he was strong enough to protect me and all those residing in this village.

The old woman Madalene held a cold compress to my forehead and it cooled my body down, but it was not enough to mask the pangs that soon grew unbearable. I screamed out until my throat grew dry and hoarse, but nevertheless, the pain streaked through my entire body.

"One more push, my child!" the old woman said distantly. Sweat poured down my face and neck. I looked down and nausea waved over me, redness was speckled and spattered everywhere. Clumps of blood rested between my open thighs in a thick pool that soaked into the sheets beneath me. I pushed until my face was beet red, and then instantly the pain was no more. A feeling of bliss showered over me, although I was nearly torn to shreds. The old woman's head disappeared between my legs and reemerged holding a baby boy. He cried and clawed at the smiling lady with little effect as she dabbed his face and chest with a damp cloth.

"He's beautiful!" the old woman said, placing him in my arms.

"The little fucker shall be a king one day!" Raleigh announced to the room, slapping Azla playfully on the shoulder. "Right, Jeth?"

"Right..." Jetha returned smiling, "and I shall lead his army to many victories on the battlefield!"

"Would you not want to be king as well, Jetha? Or maybe even a chief?" I offered, rocking my little king in my arms until the crying calmed.

"I will be neither," Jetha returned innocently. "I want to be the best fighter in the world, just like Papa!" I glanced at the bearded man grinning, he winked back at me.

"The best fighter in the world, huh?" I smiled, looking down at my future warrior, then to Madalene.

"We will call him Ryelar, and he will be yours to cherish and love," the old woman offered, staring at us both for approval.

"That is the perfect name for my child" I said, awaiting Raleigh's approval.

"King Ryelar!" he said to his son, lifting him from my hands gently. "I have much to teach before you can rule the world with your brother Jetha." He rocked him playfully and Ryelar was actually laughing. Such an innocent soul introduced into a world of treachery.

The heavy pounding sent everyone's eyes to the main door of the cabin. Raleigh placed Ryelar back in my hands, motioned to Azla and unsheathed his twin blades, all in quick succession.

"Protect the ladies and watch Ryelar," Raleigh said to Jetha just before he rushed out of the room followed by Azla, who held his bow firmly in hand. "And keep the door closed!" he called out behind him.

"I will, Papa!" Jetha said standing up to his full height, placing a hand on the hilt of his short sword. He was just shy of fifteen years now and he was almost a man's size. Raleigh had been the only father he had since his own was killed, he was never the same after that day. For the passing years he was well trained in the art of the bow and of the sword, but what he was not trained in was how to follow an order.

"Jetha!" I snapped as the boy ran to the door and cracked it open to hear what was going on in the main room. Low voices were heard, murmurs over the sound of the crackling torch fire beside me. I prayed in that moment Ryelar would not cry out and alert them to our presence.

"It must be done before week's end!" an unfamiliar voice said roughly and the murmuring continued. Violent tones were exchanged just before Jetha quickly shut the door and ran back to stand by me. When Raleigh stormed in through the door, there was no sign of the man I knew all these passing years. An angry menacing man came walking back into the room, blades still at the ready. Even Azla held a look of trepidation, his eyes didn't even touch mine when he entered.

"What has happened?" I asked, shielding Ryelar's ears from his abruptness.

"I was summoned by the royal family to make the weapons for the tournament!" he returned angrily. "Jetha, let the wolves out of the stable, it is time to train."

"Yes, Papa!" he replied, running out of the room.

"What is the worry, that is good, Raleigh?" I squinted. "You have to be there for the tournament either way." His eyes touched mine and instantly I knew there was more to the story.

"They say I don't qualify to compete!" He slammed a fist into the wall and cracked wood. Ryelar jumped and cried in my arms from the suddenness.

"I'm sorry, my son!" he said, extending a finger out to the boy.

"Shhh shhh," I whispered softly in Ryelar's ear rubbing his back until he calmed.

"Do not qualify? What more qualification do you need? You saved our people from the Nephilim nearly single handedly." The dawn shown beautifully through the window as he pulled back the silk curtains.

"This is true, but not without drawbacks," he said, holding up a hand with three fingers.

"Only those bearing a grand ruby pendant shall be considered for the tournament!" Madalene replied, shielding her eyes from the glaring sun

"Great!" I quipped. "If I had known you would need a pretty little necklace to show you are the best fighter in the world, I would have stolen one from his mother."

"It is not too late for that!" Azla said baring his teeth. I shot the barbarian a disapproving glance although he had every right to feel the way he did. Raleigh has done nothing but train for this moment, for years, ever since he was separated from that back-stabbing Tiberius. The truth was we all looked to Tiberius for the leadership we believed would guide us to safety. Instead, at the first sign of opportunity he turned his back on us, never to return. For that reason I will never forgive him, even if Raleigh himself chooses to. The man was probably dead by now either way. I shook off the ugly thought and focused on the gift of life in my arms, the future master of sword and bow.

"We have to be smart, my friend," Raleigh offered before turning to me. "Is there anything you need before we train, my love?"

"No, I am fine," I returned kindly. "Go show Jetha a lesson from the best fighter in the world!" I smiled as he approached the side of the bed and kissed his son on the forehead. He lifted his head and kissed my lips with a passion I have not felt in years.

"I love you more than life itself," he said smileless. I returned the sentiment. When he and Azla left the room, I knew somehow in my heart that Raleigh would not let this one go without a fight. Not just any fight, the kind that could only end in one way.

Tiberius Blackwell

"Remove your hand, brother!"
Imperial holdfast, Cilan 1875

"Death!" the masked queen announced emphatically to the vast crowd before us.

She was sitting atop a high throne of velvet and gold. The war arena stood deep in the bowels of the imperial palace, we called it the battle pit. Its entrance was encompassed in flame as the torches lined up to form a daunting archway. The grand steps were flanked by pikemen, each bearing their own torch. Lining the walls on each side were the elder men, black hooded sorcerers whose only reason for existence was to wreak havoc on anyone standing between the queen and the completion of her agenda. Flanking her on each side, Gringus and I stared out across the grand hall as it was quickly filling up with fighters from all levels in the clan of assassins. They were here to become imperials, so far I saw only one that would make it through this day alive. Down in the battle pit, the grinning warrior they called Shinn held a bloodied edge to the neck of his fallen foe and slit his throat.

"How long do I have to wait before I can kill someone?!" Gringus said discreetly.

"Now, now, Gringus," Bambola said calmly, "you will have your fair share of blood before the day is over!"

"I wish to challenge you next!" he said extending his blade toward Gringus. He used a double edged sword that was nearly a man's height and the spiked rope bound by his waist had rough grooves and edges perfect for slashing a group to pieces but not as effective in one on one battle. The warrior had beaten his last three opponents in explosive fashion, deeming him worthy to challenge one of the elite. He was a sleek powerful assassin, with dark features and devastating speed. His style was faster and powerful, fiercer than any I've seen outside of the imperials.

"Challenge accepted!" Gringus said unveiling the double sided war axe that was feared by all. He was a vicious looking man even in the mask and garb. I saw his face one time in all these years, I still cringe at the thought. The queen did indeed have the power to bring life back into one's body, but she failed to mention that the beings she resurrected would never the same as they were previously. They became these hideous, disfigured creatures over a time, all of them. This was truly the reason why mankind should never toy with the dealings of the gods, matters of life and death.

"The next fight," the queen announced as Gringus descended the grand steps, "we will make a little interesting!"

The elder men lining the walls eased forward and formed a circle around the pit. Each of these soulless creatures were empowered by the ruby. A dark mystical force unleashed only when one powerful enough can break its seal. Once the circle was formed the elder men extended their hands out to their sides. The ground began rumbling, shards of rock and gravel fell in dust bits all around the ancient walls of the pit.

"What is happening?" I said, turning to the masked queen. Her eyes were like drops of honey, one would think there was a sweet little flower beneath that veil concealing everything but her eyes, but I would not be fooled in that way.

"A small test!" the queen winked, standing at her full height. "Let the fight begin!" she announced just as the dust cleared. The pit was now surrounded in flame, Gringus and Shinn stood before each other, weapons drawn and at the ready, Gringus attacked first.

"Come, Tiberius!" the queen said easing toward the corridor.

"Yes, my queen!" I nodded, stepping into the dark corridor. We walked side by side in silence until we reached the far end of the hall leading to the indoor garden.

"Thirteen days until the fight you have been waiting for!" she mentioned, casually staring out through the high arched window of the palace. It was midday and the people of Cilan were gathering for second meal. The assassins were gathering to become imperials and I was quickly losing my desire to fight. At first, I was drawn to the power displayed by the masked queen, the power to bring life back into existence, the power to live forever. She was one of the most powerful beings in existence and I wanted that power so bad that I abandoned the people that looked to me for leadership. She resurrected so many people in preparation for the final war that it was alarming, yet she was still waiting.

"The reputation of the clan rests in your ability to win this tournament Tiberius!" she continued.

"I will not fail you, my queen!" I said bowing at the neck.

"This I know, my child," she said, still staring out across the vast expanse of land she held sovereignty over. She pulled a hand out from the inner fold of her black imperial robes and revealed the clear crystal glistening in her palm. She closed her hand over it and stared in my eyes.

"Master is pleased with the progress you have made in returning Cilan back to its original order," she said examining the glowing crystal, "in extinguishing those who stand in the way of the agenda, and for that you will be rewarded."

"There is no need for reward," I said mechanically, "it is my duty!"

"Trust me, General," she said narrowing her eyes, "this is not a gesture you want to refuse. The people of Cilan have come to see you as a terror, but I have come to see you as much more than that. We are much alike, my child, you and I. I have come to see you as much more than the man I met washed up on that shore. I have come to see you as the man that will continue what your grandfather started!"

"You honor me greatly!" I said, placing a hand on my heart and bowing at the neck.

"It is called the crystal arc," she said opening her hand exposing the radiating crystal in her palm. With it you have the power to create your own reality, your own world with which you can rule for an eternity if you choose.

"Yes, my queen!" I took the crystal, completely unaware of the curse I was receiving and tied the pendant around my neck.

"Master would like to meet you," the masked queen said. "He will show himself sooner than you think." I nodded obediently. "Now you may go!" she said before I bowed and spun on the heel of my war boots. "Oh wait!"

When I turned, she was untying a long black piece of cloth from her waist. She handed me the cloth and I stared at the fabric with a wary eye.

"You will need that!" she said, turning back towards her royal apartments, disappearing into the shadowy corridor.

I smelled fire and blood even before I stepped back into the war arena. The crowd of fearless fighters were all murmuring, watching. The flames surrounding the pit were lit to the brightest intensity, and in the middle of it Shinn once again stood victorious.

"What has happened here?" I called out, passing the velvet throne and descending the steps. Silence followed my query and drove me to anger from the lack of an explanation, but then I saw it. Gringus was on the floor rolling back and forth groaning in a pool of blood. I broke through the line of elder men and rushed to his side.

"Gringus?" I said in scarcely a whisper, incredulous. A bloodied hand was covering his right eye and it took everything in him to lift his free eye up to me.

"The fucker got me," Gringus said, moaning in-between breaths, "he got me good!" the bloody dragon hilt dagger lying by his leg was the weapon used; problem is, it was his own dagger.

"Remove your hand, brother!" I ordered, reaching for the black cloth the queen had given me. When he lifted his hand, blood oozed down his mask and dripped slowly to the hard stone floor.

"How did you allow such a low level fighter to best you?" I hissed, wrapping the black cloth around his head and over his eye at an angle, one time, two times, three times until it was tight enough to knot.

"I am no low level fighter, General!" Shinn said. "I trained under the grand master of..."

"Just ready your fucking sword!" I blared, standing up to my height and towering over him. "Today you will become an imperial assassin, or you will watch the tournament from the spiritual realm, see me?"

"I would wish for nothing more!" the man smirked, a smirk of condescension before he drove forward.

Unsheathing my longsword, I met his sarcasm with the edge of my blade. Sparks flew from the impact and I lowered my shoulder to brace for the next blow, but it never came. Shinn was leaned over holding his stomach blood dripped from the unseen wound, I edged forward to examine my work. Before I could blink the man drove the hilt of his sword into my shoulder knocking me back two steps. When I turned, he greeted me with a smile.

"Trust in your mind, and the heart deceives you!" he said grinning stupidly. I gripped the hilt of the dagger concealed at the waist.

Lunging forward, I ducked beneath his blade jab and slammed my hilt up into the bottom of his jaw. His head snapped back and he was falling, but I gave him no time to recover. I slashed for the groin, blade sparked against blade, I kicked for the low shin and connected. The man must have had legs of steel because he didn't even budge. He breathed in deep and as he exhaled, the scars on his face and neck closed up and he was fully restored.

"This is a sword fight," I blared angrily, "not a magick show!"

"Ah, but the magick is all around you, my friend." He grinned. "Behold!"

The assassin extended his hands out to his sides and breathed in deep. His eyes slowly turned into white bulbs of energy. I edged forward to take the open opportunity, but when I got close, he drove a heavy palm into my chest. Everything in the arena went black, even the flames disappeared although I still felt the brush of it against my skin. Moments later, my sight slowly restored and I was on the floor looking at the ceiling. The smell of burning skin brought my eyes down to the smoldering wound on my chest, smoke was issuing from it slowly. I tried to push myself up with my palms, but my chest burned and I fell hard on my back. Looking around at the crowd, hazy apparitions surrounded me each of them standing prominently before the flames. My head was spinning uncontrollably, I felt heavy and uncoordinated.

"What did you do?" I blared incoherently. I reached for my blade, but I was too weak, utterly defenseless in this state. The man approached and leaned in until he was close enough for me to feel the warmth of his breath against my cheek.

"All this potential in you," he whispered, "but you have not once used it to find out that your brother is still alive!" My eyes snapped to attention and the pain in my chest was no longer there. I grabbed the man by the collar and yanked him close.

"Where is he?" I growled. The man grinned stupidly and I could not erase the image of my old friend Raleigh from my mind.

"I'll do you one better, General," Shinn said, "I'll take you right to where he is!"

Filann Gunther
"I did not come here to fight."

Mincia, Cilan 1875

"The gods say this path will only lead to destruction, my lord," the oracle said nervously. She was a young virgin girl of eighteen in appearance, but with a trained eye, you can see the true hideousness of the all-seeing witch. Her eyes spoke of unimaginable terrors, but this was no time for caution, it was time for war.

"And what of the path that leads to victory?" I pressed. "Ask them how victory is possible!"

"The gods cannot be questioned, my lord," she said in a calm, euphoric state. "They give counsel only in time of need."

"This is my time of need!" I shouted to the heavens. "I need you now!"

Cold tears rolled down my cheek as the blade in my hand trembled with emotion. I rocked back and forth trying to hold in the pain, but it kept seeping and spewing out. I was broken inside and it was clear I would have to deal with this wound for the rest of my life.

"I see a man," the oracle said with her eyes in a trance like state, "a man not of this land." I wiped my eyes and edged closer to the woman.

"What is his name?" I asked. "I know not his name, only his rank," she said hypnotically. "He is of mystic blood! In two days he will pass Pavemen's Grove with material for building a sword. You will speak to him and have him build you the sword that will slay the masked knight."

"Paveman's Grove," I squinted. "Where is that?"

"My apologies..." the all seeing witch said mockingly, she was grinning. "The gods are no longer with you, my lord!" Her laugh was shrill and menacing as it echoed through the hollow halls of the castle.

"Leave me!" I commanded. I watched the small girl until she reached the heavy oak door leading to the corridor. The stench of blood from the halls touched my nose once again and disgusted me. Thirteen fully trained and well paid guards could not withstand three imperial assassins. I shook my head as I drained the last flagon of hard ale and tossed it angrily across the chamber. Scrolls and parchment fell to the floor sloppily, and when the flagon landed my eyes drew to a map. I rushed over, grabbed the map and flattened it out on the bureau just before the lantern.

"Paveman's grove," I read aloud, tracing my finger all along the outer edge of the eastern part of the island. It was on the outskirts of a village called Catia. Not only would it be nearly impossible to find a man randomly traveling with materials for a sword without a name or description, but it was at least three days ride horseback. I unsheathed my longsword and admired its rich gleam before shoving a few honeyed biscuits and mead into a satchel and went down to the stable to ready a steed.

The air was angry and spiteful that night as it sliced through doublet straight through to under tunic. It was nearing sunset, but you wouldn't be able to tell by the gather of clouds, it had been dark and dreary for most of the day. My hands were calloused from the long day's ride, but I pressed forward with the determination of a bull. The road before me was long and clearly with no end in sight. Something was not right here, I could smell it in the air. My eyes darted left and right, but there was no one there, it was suspiciously quiet save for the wind whistling and howling in the distance. Cold drops of wetness touched my cheek once, then twice. Looking up at the opening sky, I knew it was only a matter of time before the downpour. I slowed the steed down to a trot, quietly tied the reins to a post and set out on foot.

The wooden post called this village Shintao, it only took one glance to see that the gods had forsaken this village a very long time ago. Not even the red coat patrolmen that policed all the neighboring villages were seen at the entrance of the gate. I unsheathed my side blade, banged the hilt against the gate and waited.

"No outsiders!" a rough voice called out after a moment.

"Please, I have been riding all day," I said in return. "I only need refuge until sunrise." I waited for the response that never came and banged the gate once again, louder this time. "I have coin!"

Chains clanked together roughly and released, a heavy bolt dropped to the dirt and out stepped three men, clad in grey tunic. Two of them were built like tree trunks, all round bulk that would easily be exposed with the dagger at my hip. The one in the middle stood out from the others with his eye patch and long scar trailing down from his forehead to the midpoint of his cheek. Even wearing the patch, the man would strike fear in the heart of any swordsman, but I was no typical swordsman.

"How much coin do you have?" the brute said approaching with menacing eyes. His lip was bleeding and the one to his left had blood pouring down his arm from an unseen wound.

"Enough for shelter for the night!" I said, turning as the three men slowly circled around me. I put a palm on the hilt of my longsword.

"That's a pretty sword you got there, outsider!" the one to the right said reaching out for it. I grabbed his wrist and in one hard twist he was on a knee with his arm twisted behind him.

"I did not come here to fight," I said, holding his limp wrist at an awkward angle before I pushed him to the others creating distance. "I only wish for shelter from the upcoming storm."

"No worries, we have something better than shelter for you, boy!" the brute said baring a set of cracked and rotten teeth, a rapier appeared in his hand before I could see where it came from. Sir patch man stood watch as his fellow brute unveiled nearly a man sized war hammer. These savages came overly prepared to die this evening.

I dodged the first sword thrust and spun low. Blood splattered across the dirt from a deep gash to the side of the knee, the big brute fell to the dirt screaming. A strong wind swooshed past my face, and when I turned the next tree trunk brute with the hammer had luckily missed his strike. I took the small window of opportunity to relieve him of his head. I watched the thing topple and roll off into the darkness.

Before I could react, a surging red beam flashed from just paces away. A sharp pain shot through my side bringing me to a knee. Numbness was spread all over my side, to the point that I didn't even know if my torso was still attached, then the burning started. My vision was blurred, but the gurgling sound of a man being strangled to death could be made out by even the blindest man.

As my eyes slowly adjusted to the darkness again, a shadowy image appeared scurrying off in the distance. The moon was staring down angrily from overhead, the light from it showing the silhouette of a woman. I stood to my full height and strangely felt no pain at all. I raced over to my steed, swung a leg over the top and then I was in hot pursuit of this mysterious woman. She was fast and agile as she dashed through the slalom of trees and wood, luckily I chose the right steed that night.

Wind brushed against my cheeks as I whipped the reins faster and harder until the woman was clear in my sights. I reached behind me for a throwing knife and caught hold of it. She was too far to reach but much too close to quit pursuing. I wiped my eyes with the back of my sleeve, for they were deceiving me. Where there was one woman, suddenly I was chasing three identical figures, then five and then they vanished. In mid chase I slowed the steed to a trot and wiped my eyes once more. It was either this place was haunted with ghosts, which obviously weren't real, or I just witnessed something I was not supposed to see. Either way, I was going to need answers.

The sun rose and set on another day without further incident, yet the image of the past week haunted my thoughts. The northern coast of Cilan was enriched with beauty, but the only thing I could see was the expression of my mother and wife, when I returned to the castle, that gory horror filled expression that one only showed when death called. Even the soil was rich in this part of the world judging by quality of fruits and vegetables displayed in the passing fields, but death was in the forefront of my mind. I struck the reins harder and pushed the thought out of my head.

Slay the knight, huh... I had to laugh at myself. This whole journey was in pursuit of an impossible feat and commissioned by an eighteen-year-old girl that happens to communicate with spirits that proclaim to be gods. Never have I believed the load of horse shit before, but yet here I am.

Paveman's grove was a typical dirt road in the heart of nowhere in particular. Quiet, serene, it was everything I didn't expect it to be. Dry leaves scattered in the wind as the sentinel trees lined up going out to the horizon. It was nearly dusk and I already had eyes on a potential swordsman. He looked young, maybe twenty and five years. I stepped out into the road and approached him.

"Excuse me, friend," I called out, "are you the man with materials to build a sword?"

Strangely the lad halted, dropped his flagon and ran off before I could get within strides. Looking at my hands I realized they were sticky with blood, my face must have made me look murderous. I quickly removed a flask from my satchel and poured water on my hands before the two commoners approached at a distance. After wiping my face and hands, I lifted my hands up in peace before I called out this time. It was a woman and man who drew closer to each other upon seeing me.

"Pardon me," I said, exposing my palms and the lack of a blade within them, "would you possibly be the man with materials to build a sword?"

The woman looked down nervously, the man shook his head as the two of them rushed past in silence. I looked up at the shimmering moon and sighed. I could already see this was going to be a very long night. I gathered the reins of my steed and started my journey down Paveman's grove.

CHAPTER SIXTEEN

Memorie XVI

Brotus Satyre
"Hello, old friend!"
Unknown location, Cilan 1875

"Sister, are you out of your fuckin' mind?" I blared as Isis closed the chamber door behind her. The enflamed walls grew more intense when I was in an angered state, and at the moment it was a blue flamed inferno. The cave served as a safe haven for us all when Dimitrius was in command, but now that he is gone, everything was falling apart.

"I messed up, brother, I know," she said, her eyes a fiery symbol of defiance, "but you know that if I hadn't stepped in then Filann would be dead right now, then all would be lost."

"All would be lost," I shot back angrily, "like all is not lost now? You changed his entire fate, you defied mystic law by helping him, you Isis, the one I need by my side during the battle to come."

"Brotus, I am sorry!" she pressed.

"You're sorry!" I mocked. "Is that you want me to tell the council once they get wind of this? What exactly is the punishment for one that knowingly defied our law, but is now sorry for it?"

"So, what are you gonna do to me, brother?" she taunted. "Put me on punishment like you did Solana? Or maybe continue as if I don't exist like you are doing with Sinistro?"

"Don't ever say that to me again!" I returned viciously, clasping the hilt of a dagger.

"Or you will do what exactly?" she said, releasing the chained blades concealed in her sleeves. The things were vicious looking, as they dangled from her sleeves even to a seasoned fighter, but I would not take defiance lightly. I slowed down reality around me and centered my Qi until I woke up the power deep within me. The chamber grew mad with flames, and lifting a palm in the air, Isis' body levitated with it.

"Put me down brother!" she commanded. "Brotus, what are you doing to me?"

"I'm stripping you of your special ability..." I said, slowly rotating her body in the air.

"Brotus, put me down," she blared, "you are only doing this to seek the favor of the gods. They only accepted you because they do not want to deal with the wrath of Dimitrius, not because of your strength, my darling brother!"

"And I'm demoting you to the fifth degree," I continued emotionless. "You will no longer attend meetings of the council nor participate in the upcoming campaigns."

"Brotus, please, you know you will not win without me!" she said truthfully.

"So be it," I said releasing her, I caught her in my arms before she hit the stone, then put her on her feet. "Then you will watch from afar as all your mystic brothers and sisters are slaughtered because you could not control your actions or your mouth."

When I turned, I knew I went too far this time. But if she was not with us entirely in law and deed, then she would not prevail in the end. I felt her pain within me, felt her sadness. She only meant well, but in her concern, she may have condemned her family to an untimely demise and that could not be taken lightly from any ruler.

I closed the door behind me, she would be weak for a long while. Being stripped of your ability was much more than just not being able to do it anymore. It was a piece of your soul being taken from you, like taking a piece of your lung after you already were full grown and used to breathing. A piece of me was left in that chamber over a century ago, it took a long time for me to forgive Dimitrius for such harshness, but it paid off. I was now a ruler and part of that meant I would be expected to do things people will not like in the moment.

Upon reaching my chamber, I immediately went for the small vial of solace and emptied it. It was only a matter of time before this thing consumed me entirely, but with Casanova, the serum was spreading much too fast within him. It was only a matter of time before the blotches on his skin hardened to scabs, and the scabs hardened to scales. The serum was much too dangerous to be revealed to him at such an early stage, but it was Dimitrius' call, and who would be foolish enough to question the ruler of the physical realm?

Intense streams of energy waved through me as all my wounds vanished, all my senses were heightened, and now my mind was steady and clear for the mission ahead. I felt a presence materialize behind me. I slipped the vial in through the sleeve of my tunic and turned.

"You look like you're surprised to see me!" Celeste said, removing her robe exposing her flawless figure. She pulled on her vambraces and greaves before she went for the body armor. It seemed so odd, having her in warrior garb, but the time she would need to be in battle with us was well overdue.

"I want you to stay close behind me!" I said firmly.

"Don't worry, my love," she said, touching my hand. "I will follow your lead!"

Our lips touched, and I felt the warmth of her tongue against mine. She empowered me, healed me from the inside out with her special ability. Her eyes were glowing, her face, a monument of beauty. I turned to the door before the knock came.

"My lord, it is time!" said Titus, the man I appointed general of the mystic army. He was a very powerful warrior of the fifth degree, only I did not know much of him. He was overlooked all these years from the elite for a reason, yet I had no time to inquire, it was time for battle and he looked fit and able to protect himself. Isis was supposed to be by my side, there was not a better fighter in the clan of mystics, but she went too far this time. My sister is not even aware that her actions may have caused an irreparable wave in the spiritual realm, one that will change the course of all events to follow. We had to find out just how fierce this wave was before it altered the destiny of the one we need to stay alive for the war to come, Casanova.

"Let's go!" I said to my love as our lips touched again, I was fully rejuvenated. I secured my chest plate tight and reached for Golathine. The two handed golden great sword was remarkable to the eye, but it was not effective during close quarter battle in the spirit realm, I had something for that. I unlatched the bolts of the chamber door with my mind, and when it creaked open, there stood a monstrous threat to be honored in both light and dark mysticism.

"Greetings, my lord," he said bowing at the neck. He had two glowing gauntlets in his hands extended out to me. "As you asked!"

"Are you ready to prove your merit, warrior?!" I said slipping on the left gauntlet and then the right. They were dipped in solace for three days, the energy raged through my arms and chest, throughout my entire body.

"Fifty thousand warriors and 500 war chariots awaiting my command," he said confidently. "I was born ready for this, my lord!" "Good, then let us see!" I said, turning down the corridor of ice statues. Passing the war room, the statutes turned from ice to fiery, hard stone skeletons. They each had knight armor but through the open helm the face of death stared back you. When I turned into the crossing chamber, I stopped just before reaching the portal.

"Celeste, are you fully charged?" I said without turning back.

"Yes, lord!" she confirmed.

"Good, save your special ability until it is absolutely necessary. Understand?"

"Yes, lord!" she said.

Stepping through the portal, the sight was much worse than I had presumed. The red tinged earth was swarming with gargoyles and mystics in battle. They must have been ambushed judging by the bad position they were in, getting rushed on both sides.

"Titus, draw them this way and manifest your army!" I commanded.

"Lord!" he said before rushing toward the action. He dashed his flaming spear through the back of a gargoyle and hoisted him in the air. He held the thing up for all to see before slamming him to the red dirt. That caught the attention of nearly twenty gargoyle who came swooping down toward him. I charged my Qi until it reached its ultimate peak.

"Get ready, Celeste!" I warned as Titus came running back this way to ambush them with his army. I looked down at my palms and they weren't glowing. I felt the power release from the gauntlets, but I stood my ground.

"Titus, the army!" I commanded just before the massive creatures came rushing through the line we held. Gargoyles swarmed from left to right slashing viciously at me. A claw ripped through my tunic and cut through flesh. My arm and shoulder exploded with pain, but I pressed forward. I lifted an arm in the air and slammed a fist into the dirt. A circular wave of fire formed around me and scorched six of them, but they kept swarming. I bashed a heavy fist through the crowd and hammered my way out.

"Titus, where the fuck is that army?" I called out to nowhere in particular. I could not turn back to look, I was in defensive stance before an entire army.

"This is the army," I heard Titus say from somewhere close, but as he kept speaking his voice was no longer that of Titus'. "Fifty thousand warriors and the chariots shall be here shortly!" I heard him laugh and in that moment my heart sank in my chest. I turned to see a gargoyle swoop down and grab Celeste. The thing flew off with haste as she dangled from its claws and before I could react I felt my body grow numb. The gargoyles all flew off into the red sky and out from the corner of my eye came the face I swore to kill the next time I saw.

"Hello, old friend," Sinistro said with a grin that sent my blood into a boil. His hair was like white silk and fell down to his waist, although he hadn't aged a day in three hundred years. I lashed out, but I was held back, entangled in binds of magick I knew I could never break. "Did you really think I would not have a gift for you and your beautiful Celeste?"

"You bring her back here!" I roared defiantly, thrashing back and forth uselessly trying to break free.

"And I will," he said, "all you have to do is sit back and marvel at what I have in store!" He lifted his palm and I heard a portal open behind me.

"Until we meet again, brother!" he laughed before I felt his boot cave in my chest and my body flew back into another realm.

Scarlet
"What is the meaning of this?"
Agishi Temple, 1875

"And what exactly are we going to do with this?" I said staring down at the sketch.

"We are going to present it to the council," Albert said excited. "After they hear my proposal, they will have to allow it to be constructed." His speech was much better now after he was introduced to the serum. After that night in the training room with Casanova, it was mandatory that all those in the temple have a daily supply of serum, one vial.

"But Albert, this is just the sketch of a warlock," I said squinting down at the parchment.

"That is no warlock, Scarlet," he said smiling, "it is a suit. A suit constructed with iron and Partrizian alloy, in other words indestructible. I call it the Pecconius suit!"

"How quaint," I smirked, "and when are you going to ever need this Pecconius suit?"

"The final war!" he said confidently, I laughed just before the chamber door swung open roughly. The face that appeared in the corridor was not one of the brother I knew. His red cloak was ripped and frayed already, his face smeared with blood and hatred. He shouldered his way into the room and stopped before us.

"I need more serum!" Casanova said breathlessly. His almond eyes glowed with ferocity. I stared back at him incredulous.

"More serum?" I squinted. "You know we only receive one dose for the day, you already had yours!"

"I need to find out where they keep the supply, Scarlet!" he said turning to Albert. "Your brother knows, doesn't he?"

"Zerolin knows, but you know he cannot just give you more serum, Cas," Albert said truthfully.

"I don't want anyone losing their position here because they helped me," he said fiercely, "but I need to be stronger if I am going to win this tournament, I only have ten days left." His massive arms were trembling with power, his eyes a glaring testament of strength and ability, but the mask of greed embodied him. The muscles beneath his skin were hard and rippling, but the black blotches lining his neck and arms were evidence of too much serum flowing within. He was clearly turning and the fact that he was no longer proceeding with caution scared me. "I know where they keep it!" a voice said from behind, it was Tomin. The big burly blue cloak warrior of the fifth degree stepped into the chamber and closed the door behind him. He was no longer the timid bear of a man as he was before, he was finally speaking my language. "I can show you where it is, but after that you are on your own, brother!"

"That's all I ask, brother!" Cas said, gesturing for him to lead the way.

"Casanova, you must use the serum in moderation," I warned. "Every time you exceed the dose required, you will lose a piece of your humanity, a piece you will lose and never get back."

"Does that mean you are not coming with us?" Casanova said callously. I sighed and turned to Albert.

"When I get back I will go with you to present your sketch to the council!" I said. Albert grinned with excitement.

"Thank you, sister," he said, shuffling parchments. "I will perfect it now!"

I turned back to Cas and gasped at the sight. His cloak was removed and the blotches that started on his neck and chest and belly were now covering nearly the whole of his body. He was scaling and not the ordinary scales that would be removed in the bath, the kind that came from within and spread all over your body until you became a monster. He slipped on an under tunic and the fresh red cloak, concealing all of his weapons and turned to me.

"Casanova, you are turning!" I said, my eyes gaping. The poison tip needles lined the inside of his cloak and down the legs of his britches. Two daggers were criss-crossed and sheathed on his back. The longsword at his waist was rarely used, but ever since he returned from the cliff that day, he was on a warpath.

"Never mind that now," he said turning to the corridor and pulling the brim of his hood down over his eyes. "Time is of the essence!"

It was not until we reached the war chamber that we stopped. The corridor was lined with torches, each one bearing an immortal blue flame that not even the breath of a god could douse. Two sorcerers were guarding the crystal chamber, armed with pikes and blades although those weapons were only for show. The real threat came in the form of powerful hypnotism and torture. They wore the magenta cloak of the guardians, but there could not have been a better two guarding the door that day.

"Malachi!" I called out. When the guardian turned, his stern expression turned into anger.

"Seize them!" he commanded. My heart went cold as I stared at the man approaching with pike and shield. Before I could react three guardians appeared behind him, then more behind us. The three of us stood surrounded in the narrow corridor and the only thing I could do was stare at the man I ate with just yesterday. Spoke of plans for the future with, revealed my secrets to. Betrayal was a dish best served to the weak, I thought as I gathered energy from the immortal flames around me.

"What is the meaning of this?" I said, stepping back into a defensive stance.

"You are being seized, the meaning is captured, taken captive, apprehended." He laughed, turning back to his fellows. "I like that one better, app-reh-ended!"

"Oh, we are in the mood for jokes!" Casanova grinned sadistically. His men shuffled in their cloaks startled by the sudden outburst. "Well I have a funny jest for you. Why don't you call your men down and take a break for the rest of the night, or after this little skirmish you will have a permanent smile on your face, see me!"

That night, he probably should have thought of all the possible outcomes for his outbursts... but he didn't. He wanted a fight, and whether it was six, ten, one hundred guardians, right now he would be just training for what I really knew he was up against. I felt the serum living and breathing within me, another entity infused with my own.

Law one in the book Hymns and Hypnosis, the hypnotist must divert one's mind to the spirit world before taking control of one's physical. I kept that in mind as the flames of immortality intensified within me. When they ignited, a burst of energy surged from within my chest, throughout my arms, my legs.

When I opened my eyes, Casanova moved so fast I barely saw him blur past me dashing two poison darts into the chest of a guardian. His power spiked to such an immense level that his eyes bled. The immortal flame within me was more powerful than any other, I could only hold it but for so long. Tomin grabbed my arm, and when I turned he handed me two gauntlets. I slipped them on just as a bright flash of blue flame exploded from my palm. The three guardians before me melted and dissolved right before my eyes. I looked up to see Tomin dash the head of a guardian into the stone wall. Blood spurted and splattered from his head on impact. When I turned, Casanova was wiping his blade with a cloth and spitting out a spray of blood.

These were the top of the elite in all of mysticism, which was odd, because it only took the three of us a few moments to defeat them. Something about this did not feel exact, but the thought phased away as the door to the crystal chamber was opened and Casanova stepped inside.

The high altar was surrounded by a thousand candles each bearing the symbol of Agishi, a criss-crossed dagger and scepter. Lining the walls and floor was a glistening coat of black crystallized rock, generated from fire and lava and over a thousand years of pressure. The entire temple was built around the materials hidden in this fortress, but the only thing that held my eyes, held all of our attention, was the unlimited supply of serum being produced directly from the soul of the physical realm. The drill before us wedged deep into the heart of the earth and extracted a crystal that once fire is administered, can melt it into the liquid we call the serum or god's blood. There are only two drills in the world, hence the reason that the mystics and the imperial clans are the only two clans that even know of its existence. I could do nothing but marvel at the decadence of the chamber.

As Casanova ascended the steps, I somehow knew this would be a mistake. The very reason the lives of millions will be sacrificed was for the greed of one man, one extremely powerful man. It was a shame he has not yet recognized his own strength, because very soon the entire realm will be introduced to his ability, and by that time it will be too late to stop the darkness living within him.

Raleigh Bines
"All of this for an apology?"
Catia, Cilan 1875

The sky was still dark when Azla and I set out for the journey to the Imperial holdfast, dawn had not yet shown itself. Iron, steel and wood clanked together from the back of the carriage, but we pushed forward, both of us in deep thought. The joy of my son's birth was short-lived and I cursed the very day I got in bed with the enemy, although my life would have been much different had I not. Ryelar was forced into a life of violence and bloodshed before he could even utter his first word, but that would all change once I reached my journey's end. My plan was infallible, Azla served as a perfect marksman and could strike down his target with precision from over one hundred strides. I was only missing two things... a warrior like Tiberius to face the onslaught once the soldiers turned their aggression toward me and a strategist like Nova. The fucker really killed the chief with a crossbow on his first kill, that's more to say for my little poison experiment gone wrong.

    I never could quite forget the two of them, the laughs we had, the near death experiences. Each memory we shared made it harder and harder to push them to the back of my mind, no matter how badly Caliah spoke of them. They were my brothers and the only reason Tiberius would not come back to continue this journey is if he had a bigger plan or...I pushed the dark thought from my mind.

    The thick smell of pollen filled my nose and the soft songs of bluebirds filled my ears as I reminisced on the bittersweet taste of irony. My two old friends were still in the forefront of my mind even after all these years. It seemed like a lifetime ago, when the world still had people I could trust. When the idea of friendship was all that mattered, more than coin, more than power. I stroked the front of my beard and turned to Azla.

"Ease your mind, brother," I said calmly, "we won't be there for another day!"

He was sharpening the dagger I gave him. I told him just aim and push and the blade will do all the work for him, he never put the thing down after that. I was laughing like a hyena watching him do precisely as I instructed, aim, push, aim, push. He put down five warriors that day and I told him to keep the dagger as a reward. Now each of us carried a single twin dagger as a symbol of brotherhood. I would have never thought the two of us would mesh, but here we were, on the mission I thought I would have.

"My mind is back home!" he said distantly, staring out across the passing grove.

"It has only been a night's past since we left, Azla!" I said, squinting.

"No," he returned, "my real home, Candonia!"

I thought of the treacherous jungles I had to pass before I reached the home he spoke of. The mountainous terrain we traversed, the black painted faces of the savage army, Caliah.

She was heartbroken the day her father passed and although we tried, there was no remedy for that pain. No special words that would magically turn things around and reverse the outcome. So I did what I knew best, I fought. I fought hard that day and didn't stop. So much blood was shed, so many bodies were sacrificed to the gods by my blade, it would be no wonder that after my death I would be faced with the darkest corner in the realm of misery, but one thing I do know is... they better have good wine.

The sun was rising above the vast mountainous regions in the east, that was where the tournament was being held in eight days and that was where we were going to pull off the most heinous act I could conjure up in a week's notice. The grove was coming alive, two plump squirrels chased each other up a tree and as the birds sung their wonderful song of harmonious beauty, a man approached.

On a typical morning, the man might have not even been noticed, but this was no typical morning and the man that neared was no typical man. The sigel on his robe was one of status, a very high status judging by the way he carried himself even from such a great distance away.

His robe was dirty and disheveled, yet he moved with a grace that spoke of authority, of dominance.

Keep pushing forward... my mind told me. I struck the reins hard and the wheels of the carriage started thundering down the road, the man did not even look up.

"Man in road!" Azla called out pointing. I was barreling down the grove now, dirt filling the air from the carriage wheels, getting dangerously close to the man who also did not veer to the side. He was testing me and everyone knew how much I loved a challenge.

"I know!" I replied striking the reins once again, staring ahead viciously. The chargers were stampeding down the road, dirt was flying everywhere, the animals scattered in all directions... the man was still approaching. My heart was pounding and punching through my chest, but I pressed forward. It was not until the second before he became food for the scavengers that I turned the reins hard. The carriage tipped and rode on two wheels, but I was able to hold on long enough to... my grip on the reins slipped and the carriage crashed hard over on its side. Wood bits and metal was scattered throughout the dirt. Unpolished greaves and blocks of iron, blade edges and unfinished hilts as well, but when I turned to check Azla, everything looked strange. That was until I realized I was upside down on my neck, my legs dangling in-between the wheel that was still turning on its own and an arm that was not mine. The chargers were nowhere in sight.

"Azla!" I called out, pushing myself upright. He didn't answer right away, in my heart I was already prepared for vengeance. The sweet tangy scent of murder touched my nose and lingered on as I contemplated my next move. Rough, heavy hands suddenly lifted me up and out of the mangled carriage, he did the same for Azla. The three of us sat in the dirt silently for a moment, I did not know which limb of his I would dismantle first. When I finally turned to the man, we locked eyes and the man dropped to his knees.

His face was in his hands and when he pulled them away, his eyes were red, his face wet with tears. He looked as if he had been crying all night. The sadness in his eyes did not match his regal demeanor or the sigel on his chest, but he was not an Imperial and that eased the tension somewhat.

"Wipe your face!" I said roughly, tossing him a cloth from the inner fold of my tunic. He looked at the thing as if it were foreign before he grabbed it out of the air. Azla glared at the teary eyed man with disdain before he pointed a finger at the disaster before us.

"You broke, carriage," he roared angrily. He had a look on his face I had never seen before, yet the anger was warranted. The countless nights we spent constructing this iron and wood contraption was all unraveled in the blink of an eye. The man tossed a small purse at my feet, the coins in it clattered and clanked in the dirt as he stared down at the blocks of iron as if they were worth more than what was in that purse. There was enough coin to turn around and never visit another Imperial holdfast, to never have to eat another one of their hard butter cakes, to have a shrine of myself built if I wanted to.

"My apologies, friends," the man said, bowing at the neck, the customary way of showing respect in this land I guess. I turned to Azla, he was staring down at the purse just as I had been. I don't think he's ever seen this much gold in his life.

"All of this for an apology?" I asked, picking up the purse and examining the glistening contents.

"No," he replied. Azla and I both looked up at the man.

"That is for the materials." He was pointing at the dirt with a sudden sparkle in his eyes. He reached in his robe and removed another identical purse filled with coin and dropped it in the dirt before us. "And that is for you to build me the sword that will kill the masked knight!"

"The masked knight, huh" I said, staring at the man blankly. "You sure you weren't sent by him?" I snatched the familiar sigel off of his robe just as I recognized where it was from. "What's this?" I said holding up the Imperial emblem with one hand, my blade in the other. The man stared at me as if I had not caught him in a lie, as if the Imperials could try to infiltrate my circle without me noticing. I was the master of deception, no one would pull a veil before my eyes.

"I have two more," the man said calmly, "they belong to the Imperials that have fallen by my blade. He sent three assassins to my home in the night, slaughtered my family. Killed my brother right front of me, as well as my mistress." I turned to Azla with deceitful eyes, then back to the man.

"Is that so?" I said, taking my hand off the dagger at my waist. "And you took down three Imperial assassins all by yourself?"

"Yes, I did," he said proudly, my eyes narrowed.

"And I'm guessing you want to get in the tournament and face the masked knight, correct?"

"Yes, I do!" he said. I threw the pouch of coin down in the dirt before him.

"Your coin means nothing to me Filann Gunther," I edged closer, "but we will keep this one as payment for the carriage." He nodded in concurrence, picking up the pouch in the dirt.

"You need ruby!" Azla said. "You have no ruby?"

"My ruby was stolen by the masked knight four days ago," he said forcibly calm. "I just want to go get it back." By the look in his eyes, I knew exactly what he meant by his words. That vicious intent masked with calmness, I knew that feeling all too well. It seems my original plan would have to be altered now, but in the end I will still accomplish what I set out to do.

"Then we are off to go get it back!" I said with the slightest hint of a smirk of my lip.

CHAPTER SEVENTEEN
Memorie XVII

Casanova Volkart

"Agishi!"

Cilan, 1875

"Because you have become a complete and utter disgrace to this temple," Razuhl blared, "that's why!"

"And that has nothing to do with what you put me through to become who I am, right?!" I returned viciously. "If you would just grant me this one req..."

"That is enough," Ghost interjected. "The names of the fighters to appear in the tournament will not be disclosed until the day of the fight, you have nothing to worry about, Casanova!"

"I know my brother is still alive, I can sense him!" I said, realizing the foolishness of my words as I said them aloud. If Tiberius were still roaming the earth he would have found a way to rescue his little brother by now. He wouldn't have stopped unless one of us were dead, I knew him. Every night that passed I still woke up thinking he would be the one knocking on my chamber door in the morning, like he used to.

"If he is any bit of the warrior you claim he is, then you shall see him in the tournament," Ghost said. "Until then suit up, two days until you bring back glory to this temple and redeem yourself!"

"That simple, huh?!" Razuhl roared. "The boy kills six of our guardians, sworn to protect us and the serum and he gets off with a slap on the wrist?" "For now," Ghost replied, "we have already discussed his punishment! But we cannot act as if we have any other opponents for the masked knight but Casanova."

"And I thought I was the one accused of bending the rules for my own benefit," he spat before leaving the chamber. Ghost turned to me and I felt the cold hand of discipline about to be rained down upon me.

"Walk with me!" he said calmly, veering toward the door leading to the courtyard. I squinted nervously, then I followed him through the door.

Stepping out into the blinding rays of sun, the smell of victory filled the air. I never thought that it would come to this, but it appeared we had the Imperials in checkmate. I now had the knowledge of all dark mysteries and arts. I was two days away from showing the world my strength, everything I have trained for will be revealed in this two day display of savagery and there was not a single mortal stronger than I was.

Passing the courtyards and the aisle of sentinel trees leading to the main gate, we walked in silence. Only the man I walked beside knew the ending point of this journey, but once we passed the gates, I would officially be the furthest I have been from the temple in five years. As the sun beat down against my cloak the humid air intensified and sweat filled my under tunic. My chest was broad and powerful, but even the strongest of men needed sustenance to survive; we had none.

The desert grounds is what covered the most land in Cilan, on the outskirts were the villages and holdfasts and everything society would deem civilized. Being secluded from the outside world was what we strived to do here in the temple, unfortunately seclusion had an extreme downside. That was when I remembered Arkon's words from our last game of chess... Seclusion is how you create your own death trap. There was blood in the sand, the poured out souls of our lost brothers. Just like back at home, but Oakwood grove was not filled with nearly as many warriors.

We stopped, the man beside me stared out over the vast expanse of land before us, and I did the same. I cleared my mind, erased all thought of existence, but there was a feeling deep within me that was lingering. It has been nearly a year since I last opened and centered my Qi. The last time, I nearly wiped Cilan off the face of the planet, the first time I obliterated a golinth in the temple. I was afraid that the power I now wielded would open myself to something I could not control.

"Brotus has come to visit you," he finally said. My eyes snapped open. "Has he not?"

"He has!" My lips trembled.

"And after all I have taught you myself, he still bested you?" he sulked.

"Master, he is too fast, too powerful for me in this state," I confessed. "I need to reach the next level!"

"That is what we are here for," he said waving his hand out before the desert land before us, "you will perform the three rituals of death!" he ordered, I turned to the man incredulous. It took me nearly all of five years to even grasp the first two rituals. The last ritual was the Kallehandra, an all powerful smoke spell that will temporarily deem your opponent paralyzed as you remove his soul. It was performed once in the last 300 years and it was by me, only problem was I nearly killed myself. His face was still and placid as he reached behind him and removed the flaming whip. When it cracked against the dirt, the sound was shrill and sharp. No one in the temple has ever seen the whip, nor adhered to the harsh training rituals as I did; I was different. Always have been, for months I was secluded in my chamber, hidden away from the others. Sort of like how we in the temple were secluded from the world. I removed my gauntlets first, then my cloak and under tunic all the way until I was down to britches and war boots.

"Your boots too," he pressed. The blistering sun beat down against my back as I knelt down to remove my boots. "Now begin!"

The hot sand beneath my toes scorched the bottom of my feet nearly to the bone, it was the reason I was moving faster, swifter. My hands waved before me in ritual stance, and for the first time in a year I closed my eyes and visualized Solana. Those beautiful penetrating green eyes, her queen-like elegance, the way it felt when she spoke to me. Something about her was within me and the fact that I couldn't shake it off only meant that Scarlet was right when she said that's what love feels like. My insides roared with energy whenever I thought of her, and it seemed the more time that passed the stronger the feeling got.

"Agishi!" my inner voice said. The voices don't even bother me anymore, in fact I welcome them. I follow the instruction and so far it has kept me out of harm's way. It was like a guardian angel was protecting me at all times, guiding me down the path I was destined to walk upon.

When I opened my eyes, my hands were fluidly moving through the air as I steadied my breathing and calmed my mind. Both feet were planted and it was not until that moment that I felt the scorching. The first ritual was nearly complete when ghost stepped forward and readied himself to perform the second ritual beside me. My feet were burning no matter how much I centered my thoughts, but having my master there beside me was all I needed. Pushing forward, I easily transitioned into the second ritual, I centered my Qi and steadied my breath. When the image of Brotus formed before me, I gasped at the suddenness of his appearance. Had I been with anyone else, I might not have been ready for the fight he was surely here to bring. I turned to Ghost, who stared calmly at the approaching ruler.

"You came back to die?" I called out, reaching for the dagger sheathed on the back of my britches. Ghost lifted a hand so I would not advance. I released the dagger and waited.

The massive man was moving with a sense of uncertainty, his movement was erratic, his face was sliced and cut, he was bleeding in a dozen places. This was not the kind of condition you would ever find the ruler of the physical realm in unless he was faced with something stronger than the physical.

"He took her?" he growled.

"Her?" Ghost said, confused.

"Celeste!" he returned.

Blood dribbled from his mouth as he turned his poisoned eyes toward me. My master turned toward the open land before us and was silent for a moment. I took that moment to reflect on the name, Celeste. She was the woman that saved Raleigh's life, she was also the reason why I was here at this temple. I turned to Brotus, he was destroyed. The look in his eyes was one I would never forget, the pain he felt, I felt as well. No matter what I have learned these past years or who I have met on this journey, I was still of the mystic order and so we were brothers sharing in each other's pain, in each other's sorrow.

"What is it you ask of me, Brotus?" Ghost said.

"The final war is upon us," he said, "it is time we join our armies. The three of us together will be an unstoppable force!"

"You know that is not in my control, brother!" Ghost said. Brotus turned to me.

"I know this," Brotus said, walking toward me, "but it is something an Agishi can command, right?!"

"Yes," Ghost turned to me as well, "only an Agishi!" The two masters stared back at me for the decision that would affect the fate of two worlds. I stared back with a plan of my own.

"We will join forces once you bring me my brother as you promised you would before all of this!" I said sharply. He stepped forward.

"So if I bring you your brother, you will conjoin our armies once you are in command?" he said anxiously, I nodded and extended my arm toward him. As we clasped forearms, the bond of brotherhood was silently forged in the book of history, I only hoped I was making the right decision this time.

Tiberius Blackwell
"You told me he was dead!"
Mincia, Cilan 1875

"Only a short while further," Shinn said, "the temple is just over these hills!" The immense mountainous hills were treacherous looking from afar with its jagged pikes and spiked edges of rock. One slip and you would plummet to a gut splitting, vicious death. The sight would make even the boldest of men cringe, but not me and not for the purpose I was going for. My brother was just across those hills and I would stop at nothing to see if this man were telling the truth. If not, I was going to break him in half.

"You said this temple was less than a day's travel!" I called out breathlessly as my fingers grasped the edge of the rock faced hill.

"That is only when we are traveling without complaint the entire time!" Shinn said grinning as he turned back. He reached his hand down to pull me up. "No worries, we are almost there."

Toppling just over the edge of the cliff, there was an arched entryway to a cave within the vast hill. Stepping inside we were shielded from the harshness sun but exposed to a very different kind of force. I felt the coldness of death brush against my shoulder, and I instantly realized I was gravely mistaking for coming here with this man. Aligning the walls and floors were the skulls and bones of the fallen, coalesced into the very fabric of earth.

There was a male being stepping forward out of the darkness, when I moved for my longsword, I didn't make it in time. He wore a long white silk robe and his hair was white and long flowing, when he lifted his hand I was instantly paralyzed. My eyes shot toward Shinn, who was no longer wearing the grin he had since I met him; his face was vicious and with ill intent.

"Let me kill him now and end it all!" Shinn spat.

"Now what fun would that be?" the white haired man said, his boots clicking at the heel as he approached. "Today you will learn what it means to rule, to do the unexpected, my dearest nephew.

"Wait until the queen hears of this," I said, gritting my teeth, "she will have both of your heads!" The pair turned to me each with their own form of sadistic grins.

"You must be referring to this queen!" the white haired man said stepping to the side. From out of the darkness, the woman I put my sole trust in from the beginning stepped out of the shadows. Bambola stepped forward in-between the pair and the three of them and stood silent, staring.

"The time has come, master!" she said, unsheathing a dagger and walking toward me.

"She gets to kill him and not your blood?" Shinn said. "Nobody is going to kill him, boy!" he spat in return. "You are going to show him your special ability!"

The white haired man turned to Bambola and nodded. When she approached, a burst of flames ignited within my chest and I lunged forward, but I was held back. Confined within some form of magickal bond that was restraining my wrists and ankles. No matter how hard I jerked and yanked at it, the thing would not budge.

"How could you betray me?" I growled. "I trusted you!"

"Your friends, the ones you left behind to join my army trusted you as well, did they not?" she returned, slowly twirling the dagger in hand as she approached. "Casanova trusted you to protect him, you said you would always be there for him. You even went as far as to call him your brother and you turned your back on finding him to fight in a tournament?"

"You told me he was dead" I blared out.

"And you believed me?" she returned viciously. "You disgust me, warrior, you are not half the man your grandfather was. After this is done, you are going to wish for the honorable death I gave him."

She removed my mask, slowly lifted the dagger up to my chest and stripped my armor. My heart thundered in my chest, never have I felt as vulnerable as I did in that moment. Is that really what Raleigh and Caliah and all the rest of them think of me? I called myself sacrificing my own life for their safety, when truthfully if they were overcome by any danger it was because I wasn't there for them as a true leader should be. My brother, still alive and breathing after all these years, and the only image I remember of him was the one she presented me. The knife in a monster's hand, his body butchered and beat to a pulp. I closed my eyes and prepared for the worst, even hoped for it in that moment, but the pain didn't touch me. When I opened my eyes my heart turned to ice as I stared at the image of myself before me.

"How could you betray me?" Shinn said in my likeness just as he put on the iron face plate. "I trusted you!"

His voice was that of mine, even the way he walked, down to the small limp from the leg wound no one else knew of. Bambola was handing him my armor, the white haired man was staring at me like a wounded animal. His face was hard and stern, dark villainous grey eyes stared back at me. When I turned my eyes to Shinn he was fully clad in armor, even I would've been fooled by the guise.

"Just ready your fuckin' sword!" he growled. With or without face plate, the man was likely to wreak all kinds of havoc in the name of the masked knight. I only hoped I could unravel a plan before it was too late.

Scarlet
"Do not call me sister!"
Agishi torunament 1875

"Five more minutes and he will be disqualified!" Rahsorz said stepping into the warrior's pit. "Where the hell is he?"

The sky was an eerie grey on the day we would claim our new Agishi. Tens of thousands gathered in the grand arena just outside to bear witness to the most brutal contest in the history of combat. Fourteen masked warriors were in the pit around me each trained, disciplined and ready to claim their glory or die trying, I was number 4. Looking around I tried to spot the man who could possibly be

Casanova's brother, but I saw no resemblance, six of them were masked and the others were too old to be his brother; father maybe.

    We were in the underground holding chamber we called the pit. Torch lit but still dark, the dreary feel of it all was muted by the fact that I was here. Over a dozen of the best fighters in the world stood before me and I made it. Although I have never exceeded the fourth degree, my power only grew more intense with each passing day.

    "You know he doesn't tell me much of his doings, Rahs!" I said calmly, glancing around the room for the nearest torch. "He will surely be here before that five minutes is up!"

    I snapped my fingers and a flame rose from my palm, the warrior across from me stared silently. He was a bearded brute with a keg for a body. His weapon of choice was a double headed axe, his armor was none and he bore no banner identifying what clan he represented. Only one of the warriors seated across the pit posed a real threat, although it was only his reputation that preceded him.

    The legendary masked knight, the murdering savage that claimed the lives of countless Cilanians, I couldn't wait to get my hands on him. He was seated alone in the far corner of the pit. His weapon of choice, the notorious black longsword. He was said to have wreaked terror upon nearly every clan in Cilan, but never the mystics. Dark mysticism was shrouded and occulted for more than six centuries. Neither of the clans dared to attack an enemy they could not see or even know still existed. This tournament is the only opportunity they would have to expose us.

"Look!" Zerolin said with gaping eyes. He was staring at the approaching man in red cloak as if he saw his entire life flashing before his eyes. Casanova was stalking toward us with the fury of a vicious warrior, but that was not even what made me nervous. The scales spread over the entire right side of his face until he was scarcely recognizable save for the red cloak he wore. I warned him of the power of the serum, how easily it could consume you, how dangerous it was ingesting the liquid more than we were advised. Now, he was clearly venturing to the dark side and once it consumed him there would be no more of the mystic brother we once knew and loved. There would be none of the innocent lad that came here to the temple in search for his brother, he would become something different entirely, a monster.

The man was on a mission and whatever that mission was, it did not include the safety of those he called friends. I no longer think he even knew the true meaning of friendship, nor even a true sense of brotherhood after what he did the other night. We could have been killed, and worst of all, we had to kill. Then again, when a man has his mind fixed on immortality it was hard to tell how many people he would sacrifice to make sure he stays alive to find it. I ousted the flame in my palm and pulled the brim of my hood down over my eyes.

"Warriors line up and remove all cloak or armor," the gatekeeper said stepping into the pit. "When your number is called you will step forward and remove your weapon. You will be provided with your weapon of choice and shield. Have your grand rubies ready, they will be collected at the second gate when you enter the arena. Any form of magick or energy infused relics are prohibited in this tournament regardless of degree or power." Casanova shouldered his way through the middle of three warriors and stood between us. He leaned toward

Rahsorz and whispered in his ear. Then he turned to me and leaned toward my ear.

"I'm sorry my sister!" His eyes had a dark gloss in them, they were almost entirely black as they gazed back at me. A drop of blood formed in the corner of his eye and I watched as the redness streaked down his cheek. I felt the serum raging through him, felt its power emanating through his very pores and was disgusted at his lack of self control.

"Number 13 and number 6," the gatekeeper called out. I looked to my brothers and they didn't move.

"Do not call me sister!" I returned sharply, my words were fierce and direct as they echoed throughout the dreary pit. Rahsorz cut his eyes to me, but I didn't cringe as I usually do. Anger was flowing through my veins and judging by the look everyone was giving me, I knew my eyes must have been flaming.

"She has every right to be mad, brother," Casanova said, staring ahead as the two warriors made their way toward the gatekeeper. "But an urgent matter is at hand and I need both of you alive after this is all done, see me?" Only Zero nodded.

Number 13 and number 6 stepped forward, removed their cloak and weapons and proceeded to the iron gate leading to the arena. They were massive men as most of these brutes were, although I knew that would be a disadvantage for them in this kind of fight. Speed and constant aggression was needed to win this. I doubt they would last more than a few seconds against either of us. As the gate creaked open a streak of light filled the small pit and the applause of tens of thousands filled my ears. The time was nearing, my heart was beating and pounding against my chest, but I held my composure.

"Number 3 and number 9," the gatekeeper announced. Rahsorz turned.

"Glory to the mystics!" Casanova said staring at Rahsorz's opponent as he swayed past. Casanova was strangely distant, deep in thought. His eyes darted back and forth between each fighter and I didn't know if it was his form of intimidation or his form of nervousness, but something was happening.

"Glory to the mystics!" he repeated before he turned to me and winked. "Remember what I showed you!"

"Always, brother!" I said nodding. Rahsorz slowly made his way to the gates when Casanova turned to me.

"I know you are upset, Scarlet, but what I did was to solidify the glory of our clan, believe my words or not. There are many things you need to know about why I have been..."

"Number 4 and number 16."

"Glory to the mystics!" Casanova said eying my opponent cautiously. I turned to see the masked knight standing to his full height, my heart pounded in my chest as I saw him for the first time, the legends were true. Cold sweat ran down my under tunic and cloak as he turned toward me. Our eyes touched and held, instantly I felt as if I knew him although I was sure we never crossed paths before; it was a strangely familiar gaze. "Aim the assault for his right leg, he is wounded!"

"Glory to the mystics!" I said nodding. I locked eyes with my mystic brother for what would possibly be the last time.

"Until we meet again, Casanova!"

Stepping out into the sands of the arena was something I have dreamed for since I was sent here to this temple. A small naive girl transformed into a sorceress, a witch, a killer. The pace of my life was drastically altered when Casanova arrived, for he pushed me to depths I never knew I could reach. Although he had crossed far pass the line of insanity, he still had an important matter after the tournament, still had a mission he had to accomplish, he was still pushing. He was always reaching to greater depths within himself trying to reach his ultimate potential and although I shunned him for his lack of self control I admired his persistence. He never gave anyone the chance to say he couldn't do something; he would prove it time and time again.

When the sun finally touched my face, it wasn't nearly as glamorous a sight as I had imagined it would be. The steaming sand was tinged red with the blood of the fallen, weathered bones and scattered limbs turned the glorious arena that I've envisioned for years into the ultimate death trap, one way in, no way out.

Sixteen of us walked into the arena, all of our heads held high. By the way things were looking, only one would walk out of it with the glory, the others missing a limb or even worse, missing their life. The cheers sounded all around us, common folk who viewed us all as savages that killed each other just for their sadistic pleasure. Fighting was our life and I was determined to prove that today. There was a man in the middle of the arena, a sorcerer I had never seen. His hair was long and white, his white robe sparkled against the sunlight, making him seem godlike. He waved his hand toward where we were to wait. We each lined up and stood in position, waiting to be called.

"Behold, the best fighters in the world stand before you ready to compete for the glory of Cilan, for the glory of the Agishi. These warriors have fought and bled and earned their way into the arena today and we commend them for their bravery!" The cheering was ear splitting, but my focus was on the masked knight... go for the right leg, Scarlet, right leg.

"First fighters, step forward!" the white haired man called out, the tension in the air was so thick, you could taste it.

Raleigh Bines
"Let's get to work, fellas!"

Agishi torunament 1875

"Quick this way!" I called out as two imperial guards appeared at the far end of the corridor.

"I thought all the guards were in the arena when we delivered the weapons?" Filann said leaning back into the shadowy corner of the doorway.

"I thought so too!" I said breathlessly, I turned to Azla and signaled for him to ready his bow.

Peering around the corner, the guards were halfway down the corridor heading our way. A couple more steps they would discover the bodies, and then they would alarm the others, then we would be trapped. I reached down my leg for the throwing knife and jerked it from its sheath. The strides of heavy war boots neared as I lifted three fingers toward Azla, then two, then one. At once we both sprang out in the open startling the guards before they could react. I flung my knife swift and hard aiming for the face; it caught his throat, just as an arrow slammed through the head of his fellow guardsman.

Dragging their bodies out of sight, we pressed down the corridor in search of the crystal chamber. Every holdfast held a crystal chamber with all of its most powerful elixirs and weapons, even spells. I charged down the vast hallway nimbly and with a dark intent all the way until we reached the tall arching doorway leading to the chamber. Two torches of blue flame sentineled the chamber door like twin pillars of energy.

Inside, there were a thousand lit candles. Rows and rows of books and symbols, pentacles and relics from a time before any known spells were conjured. There was a glowing magic circle in the middle of the chamber just before a massive high throne covered in a black glossy crystal like coating.

"Why are we here and not in the arena?" Filann said staring in awe at an underworld he never knew existed.

"First you destroy the source of their power and once they are weakened and distracted, we strike," I said, searching the book of conjuration. "Azla, give me a hand!"

The barbarian leaned forward and cupped his hands down before him. I stepped up onto his hands and leapt to the highest ledge of books. The tips of my fingers caught hold of it, but the ledge was flimsy and I came crashing back down, only to have Azla break my fall. Wood and books came toppling down on top of us, Filann attempted to pull us out of harm's, way but in the chaos he just stepped in and shielded us. When the rain of books cleared I looked up to my new ally.

"Thank you my friend!" I said, as a flicker of light caught my eye. In the ceiling, just above the ledge I brought down was a beam of light shining through, it was sunlight. The sound of screams and applause filled the chamber, thousands of different voices and the sound of weapons clashing spilled into the dark chamber.

A piece of the wall was broken and through it the stands of the arena could be seen from whatever underground chamber we had stumbled upon, we just had to find a way to get up there. I brushed the dust off my tunic and extended my hand to Azla.

"You okay, brother?" I said. He nodded. When I turned, Filann was blowing dust off a thick yellow paged book. He held it up before me, and when I read the title, I felt my face transforming into a sadistic grin.

"Let's get to work, fellas!" I said. My plan was soon to be in full effect.

Brotus Satyre

"Who the hell are you?"

Mincia, Cilan 1875

This is impossible... I thought staring into the crystal arc. No matter which path he chooses, he will die!

The crystal arc has been a relic in the mystic order from the genesis of our existence. The source of our foresight lay within this small crystal bulb before me allowing us to witness many events within space and time. The clause is although we have the power to alter these events, it is against mystic law to change anything, that was the mistake of both my sisters. We cannot take matters of space or time into our own hands, we are not gods.

"Brotus!" the voice from behind broke my focus on the energy bulb, but when I turned I was alone in the chamber. Chills ran through my body and I was weak, sweat formed on my nose. I lifted a trembling hand into the inner fold of my tunic and reached for the small vial. I knew it was only a matter of time before I started turning, before I embarked on my truest potential as a mystic. Casanova no longer had the burden of time, he was already at a level only a god could measure up to. One day I will tell him that if it were not for Golathine, he would have beaten on the hill that day.

"Brotus, the cave." The whispers in my head were constant, the same voices that were surely plaguing Casanova as well. I lifted the vial to my lips and drained it, my body jerked upright from the intensity. Memories of past and future events swirled before me in a medley of thoughts and images. An image of Scarlet, the last daughter of King Sedachy appeared before me. She was bred from a long list of sorcerers and warlocks and she has not even tapped into her truest potential as a fighter yet. She was to fight next against Casanova's brother Tiberius.

As the thought of Tiberius crossed my mind, the masked knight did not form in the bulb before me. Instead, there was hill and a cave. The hills of Aragon, I remember them from when I was a child. Sinistro and I would see who could climb the hill the fastest; he always won. He was better in everything, everything but being a mystic.

Why these hills? And why when the thought of Tiberius crossed... The image of Tiberius formed before me, he was confined within the cave, shackled and bound in dark magick. The same darkness I was held in when he took the last thing I held dearest to me. Sinistro was behind this, he was behind it all. I now knew what I had to do for my family.

Stepping into the cave, memories of my past plagued my mind. I was never good enough... that thought would often linger in my head whenever Sinistro was around. He was always faster, always smarter. I knew that when Dimitrius would finally reveal me as his successor, Sinistro would lose all respect for the order and he did. Yet, that did not explain his hatred for me as a person, he was my brother. I loved him as if he were more than just my mystic family, I loved him as if we shared the same blood, I would've died for him.

I warned him of his intentions, that if he continued down this narrow path of greed it would consume him, he wouldn't listen. He always had a plan, a strategic attack aimed right for the heart of the problem and then he would eliminate it. Dimitrius took the option of a plan away from him in one swift decision. Now that Dimitrius is out of commission, this is his time to strike.

The low hanging spiked edges of rock hung down lower than I remembered them, but I pressed forward. A shuffling noise drew my attention toward the shadowy part of the cave. Seeing him for the first time in the physical, I did not realize how massive the man really was. His head lifted, his eyes narrowed cautiously as I approached.

"Who the hell are you?" he growled, his voice was rough and gravelly as he thrashed helplessly within his confinement.

"I am a friend," I said lifting my hands in peace. "I'm going to get you out of here!"

"Do you take me for a fool?" he returned savagely. "My next guess is you want to reunite me with my brother, right?"

"That is right!" I said calmly. The man eyed me carefully as I unsheathed Golathine and stepped toward him. In one heavy slash I broke the bond holding his wrists and then his ankles. Only with the power of the ruby fueling

Golathine was it strong enough to break the powerful bonds of magick confining him. I looked at the man in his eyes and the results of a savage past stared back at me. He looked down at his hands as if he were surprised that I stood so close to a wild beast that had just been freed. "We have to move fast, the tournament already began and somehow you're already in it."

"I thought we were going to get my brother?!" he said sharply. I turned to him and saw that the man really did not know that his brother may have been the most powerful being on the planet. Five years of separation really made a world of difference when you see how far he has advanced.

"It seems we have much to talk about, young warrior!" I said, as we stepped out into the beaming sun.

Filann Gunther
"What is this?"
Agishi torunament, 1875

"What is it looking like up there, Azla?" Raleigh said from beside me. Azla was wedged in-between the ceiling and the hole that was formed in the wall, front row to the mayhem going on out in the arena.

"Girl fight with mask knight next!" Azla said.

"We have to hurry!" Raleigh said, glancing at me. He flipped endlessly through this book of conjuration as he called it, for some spell that was said bring forth some kind of magical being, I wanted nothing to do with this plan. The man I needed to kill was in striking range and this fool wanted to stay down here and hide from the mayhem. I checked my sheath and the dagger Raleigh forged for me, it was not much to talk about. Maybe the oracle was wrong, or maybe I had chosen the wrong man. Either way, the rage flowing through me at the sound of the masked knight drove strange ideas into my head. "Ah, I found it!"

"What is this?" I said looking down at the weathered book in his hand.

"You will see!" he said ripping the parchment from the book. He charged over to the magic circle and stood within it. Reciting words from the parchment the magic circle slowly began glowing rotating. I lurched back at the sight, I had never seen such devil's play. The man was chanted in an unknown tongue and there were shadows leaping back and forth within the circle.

"Something happening," Azla called down with gaping eyes, "girl fell to dirt! Mask knight corner her!" Raleigh read the last words of the chant and stopped. His eyes touched mine, and just as they met sand poured into the crystal chamber bringing Azla down hard from his hiding spot. It seemed as if the entire chamber was collapsing within itself. When I looked, it was filling the room fast that in a few moments we would be consumed.

"Azla, grab my hand," I heard, but the ceiling nearly collapsed on top of me before I got out into the corridor. Stone and wood came crashing down over head as I charged down the corridor, the whole place was coming down. Could this have been the spell Raleigh was reciting? To destroy the entire holdfast, with us still in it?

It took all my strength to leap out of harm's way into the entrance leading to the pit. Sunlight formed at the end of the long tunnel and it was a thought if I had already passed into the spirit realm without fulfilling my goal. Stepping out into the glaring sun, the chaos only continued. The arena was in an uproar, screams of terror sounded from a well off distance, swords clashing and striking one another in an all out battle. This was nothing of what the tournament should have been. Regardless, I was on a mission and determined to meet its conclusion.

    I darted around the courtyard all the way until I reached the side entrance of the arena. There were no guards outside the gates, so walking in was not the problem. The problem was what I saw when I stepped inside. Over a dozen imperial assassins were fighting in the middle of the arena, although I could not tell who was who within the storm of sand, the masked knight was not hard to find. I unsheathed my dagger and charged forward.

Casanova Volkart
"I am not your brother!"
Agishi torunament, 1875

Leaping out the way of a pike, I charged forward and slammed two darts into the Imperial's neck. Blood and poison shot out on impact, I didn't even wait for the body to drop before I moved to the next target. Scarlet was cornered by two assassins in the far corner holding her own, but every time I killed one another two sprang out from nowhere.

"Scarlet, I'm coming!" I called out as I rolled between two fighters and drove both my hidden daggers into each of their chests. Someone forged our weapons so they would easily break as Rahsorz came to see. The brother lost an arm and he would never see out of his right eye again. That someone was going to pay for that when this was all said and done.

I reached Scarlet just as a chained blade swung and caught the side of her face, leaving a memorable gash in her cheek. I tossed three darts out at the culprit, all three got caught in his throat. Scarlet was on a knee holding her face, but there was no time to heal wounds; we were in battle. Just as the thought touched my head a pain exploded through my shoulder. I looked down at the tip of a longsword gaping out the front of my chest with disdain.

"How does that feel, brother?" I turned to see a massive man with dreads and an iron face plate. His voice sounded familiar, it was as if I knew him. As if he were actually my brother, Tiberius. I shook off the insanity.

"I am. Not. Your brother!" I said choking in-between breaths. Blood slid down the side of my mouth and everything around me was hazy and slow. I turned and reached for my dagger, but in the motion I fell to my knees. In the midst of chaotic battle, the man stood over me staring. As if he knew who I was, or even what I was. "Would you just kill me already, get it over with!"

The massive man knelt down over me and reached a hand behind his neck and removed the iron face plate. My heart lurched in my chest as I stared back at the man I would easily die for in an instant.

"Tiberius?" I said in scarcely a whisper. "But why?" He leaned down until his lips were just beside my ear.

"Because you deserve it, brother!" he said just before he jabbed a dagger into my stomach. The burning started in the pit of my stomach and then spread throughout my body. The shock of impact jerked my body upright before I fell hard on my side. There I was, alone, just as I have always been when the time truly called for it. My own brother, the one I have had on my mind since the day we were separated, was the one who defeated me. Irony is bliss? At least that's what the gods say. From that point, everything was a fog.

Amidst the chaos, a golden sword slashed down, lopping the head off my brother. Brotus was calling out to me, but I was fading, in between the realm of spirit and the physical. Ghost was beside him, followed by Scarlet and Tib... my brother burst through the crowd and grabbed my hand.

"My brother!" I heard him say in my ear. "It's me, brother, hold on!" His eyes touched mine, but the world around me was spinning. The sound of battle faded, the sound of my heart beating was the only thing I was aware of and even that was dim.

"Tiberius, look out!" were the last words I recall hearing before Raleigh leapt in front of the dagger intended for Tiberius. His life was lost before he landed because he fell just beside me, and I was staring death right in the face. We fought the good fight, I wanted to say, or rest easy, my brother. I wanted to say something a true warrior would tell one he viewed as a brother before he passed to the spirit realm, but everything was fading. My thoughts, my vision, my life, were all fading into the shadows as the entire world around me was slowly consumed in darkness...

To be continued

<<<<>>>>